THE
LIFE AND
LIFE OF
DAVID
PANGLOSS

To Carolyne
Hope you enjoy
the read
love & best wishes
Leo

18/2/2022

THE
LIFE AND
LIFE OF
DAVID
PANGLOSS

LEO SAMUEL GOATLEY

The Book Guild Ltd

First published in Great Britain in 2022 by
The Book Guild Ltd
Unit E2 Airfield Business Park,
Harrison Road, Market Harborough,
Leicestershire. LE16 7UL
Freephone: 0800 999 2982
www.bookguild.co.uk
Email: info@bookguild.co.uk
Twitter: @bookguild

Typeset in 11pt Minion Pro

Printed and bound by CPI Group (UK) Ltd, Croydon, CR0 4YY

ISBN 978 1914471 230

British Library Cataloguing in Publication Data.
A catalogue record for this book is available from the British Library.

MIX
Paper from
responsible sources
FSC
www.fsc.org   FSC® C013604

Contents

Works of fiction invariably draw on life events. In this novel the part played by George Beurling during the siege of Malta is historically accurate, but is interwoven with the fiction of this novel; likewise, the account of military psychiatric establishments during the second world war. In the remainder of the novel the stories and descriptions of people populating the pages are entirely fictional and any appearance of similarity arising from occupation, position, event or circumstance is incidental and in no way intended to portray, parody, caricature or represent any living or deceased individual, who may otherwise be assumed as identifiable or proximate in any way to any chapter or episode in the novel.

The author's time working in insurance was with colleagues who were generous and accommodating and the atmosphere within the corporate group was one of commercial propriety, decency and with emphasis on sound HR and support for employees.

The author acknowledges the ongoing love and support of his wife, Katherine, and is grateful for her proof reading of the draft and also the valuable and insightful comments of his son-in-law Matthew Davey.

1

Return to Nature: The Walk Begins

Silver-washed fritillaries and purple hairstreak butterflies danced around a great oak. Abigail walked up through the woods following the southerly path. The high canopy of the trees offered a pleasing shelter from the warmth of the early autumn afternoon. The sun beamed through the foliage, scattering shards of light, illuminating a divinely clad woodland carpet and offered a dappled brightness across the lush surrounding vegetation. First, a shaded cool breeze, then fleeting immersion in a warm corridor of light; nature's improvised, gentle, therapeutic massage to those blessed to wander through this retreat.

The wood had been meticulously tended and planted with a large variety of trees from around the world. Abigail ambled along through the enclosure of Japanese maples, past Chinese lily trees, then thriving bamboo intermingled with Scots pines and Herefordshire silver birches. One tall birch, whose upper leaves had changed colour from the ambient immersive green of the arboretum to a magnificent translucent salmon pink, appeared to glow as a beckoning focal point.

The only sound was a melodic birdsong: willow, garden and wood warblers, chiffchaffs and blackcaps, spotted and green woodpeckers, unsullied by any distant echo of cars. A gentle breeze wafted in from the lower fields beyond the wood. This sublime tranquillity was both soporific and seductive, as nature irresistibly imbued the senses, a hypnotic harbinger of otherness and beauty, of arriving at some special moment, in the now, something perfect, a moment where the soul would long to remain. Abigail was alone. This could only ever be a solitary journey except for contents of the two neatly fitting urns in her back-pack.

Her attention turned to the fresh rustic scent of newly planed wood comprised in the fine bench hewn from oak felled only a stone's throw away. She had commissioned the engraved bench as a just and fitting commemoration of her parents.

Even with her admirable credentials, it had not been straightforward to get a memorial bench approved for this most perfect of places. In a modern secular society there was competition; many others wished for such a tribute for their departed loved ones. There was an application form and questions to answer from the trustees and a not-inconsiderable fee to pay. And then there was the matter of scattering of the ashes; a most delicate subject requiring utmost discretion and ultimately sanctioned in a rather tacit, qualified manner, based upon ambiguous rules and unregulated assumptions.

And more questions:

What sort of cask was provided by the undertaker? Please confirm that the body was cremated with all metallic or man-made composite materials such as knees or artificial hips collected from the furnace? Please confirm that the coffin was wholly biodegradable and if so whether it was made of wicker- or basket-type construction?

But Abigail understood the idiom; she understood the reserve of these cautious elders and custodians of ecological purity: the nuanced religiosity of their quest, the conflicted liberalism of a cabal of anally retentive vegans who populated the committee. She was so familiar with their workings. And she well knew that while some things are unspoken, it is nevertheless possible to decipher the difference between a silence that means 'yes' and a silence that means 'no'.

2

Early Years

Before turning into the street a vibrant cacophony of children's voices could be heard echoing from the terraced brickwork, playing, singing, laughing, jumping and yelling; a greeting of spirit that surely defied adversity. Any visiting stranger would behold the teeming vista of unperturbed young urchins chasing footballs, playing British Bulldog, leaping on squares of hop, skip and jump, dancing ring a ring of roses, mischievous climbers up alley walls and dissenting, precocious young devils tapping their toes as they sneaked a pinched cigarette, posing as they leant on a lamppost. This was to behold a dance of unchoreographed complexity.

On closer observation it could be discerned that improvisation extended beyond the innovative play, as grubby little legs rushed by in unmatched scuffed shoes, some without laces, some without heels, some without stitching in the uppers. Trousers were held up with string, some shorts too long, some too short, socks full of holes and shirts with grubby worn collars and buttons missing, jerseys and coats discoloured and ripped at the seams. Then, a brief pause in the play might offer a glimpse of a pale, little face, bright eyes, gleeful and not at all self-conscious, yet underweight and small for his years, who by some marvel of nature seemed to conjure energy from the Mersey air.

It did not matter what your dad did or was supposed to do; there was little difference between a docker, a brickie, a carpenter or an accounts clerk if they were all unemployed. All the kids in the neighbourhood played together with a strong sense of community. There could be factions and bullies, but the sheer number of kids soon smoothed out any oppressive imposition of bragging rights by some big bruiser. As no one had anything, what use were bragging rights anyway? The church had played a valuable role; with so many families 'on the parish' the pastoral role of priests was often pivotal, not only in keeping families together but sometimes out of desperation making alternative arrangements, which usually meant youngsters being placed in care.

The year was 1940. There was a grim irony as men whose lives and those of their families had been blighted by years of industrial inertia were now finding work because the world had become enveloped in a war.

Many will argue that it is unnecessary to contextualise this setting by elaborating on the social and cultural melange of Liverpool. Many will argue that it is a place that needs no introduction. But it is from and in the remote foreboding shadow of its mighty facades, of the so-called three graces, the Royal Liver, Cunard and Port of Liverpool Building, of St George's Hall, of the Victoria Gallery, Albert Dock and India House, that a social historian should cast an eye. They must look beyond these temples of the industrial and global trading supremacy of the British Empire and beyond the exquisite mansions and elegant rows bestowed on confident capitalists for whom the profits of joint stock companies flowed from the triangular trade in sugar, spices, tobacco and slaves. Then in the dark, narrow, cobbled grime of teeming labyrinthine streets and dwellings the real story of the people of Liverpool is to be found.

It is in its deficits, consequent on exploitation of labour, amidst poor housing and endemic disease. It is in the extraneous grey, dusty wasteland, broken cobblestone, rusting pipework, where leaking effluence spontaneously generates unwelcome ecosystems of wet green slime; that an unvanquished spirit will jest back at you. It is in the lack and grime, slung tumbling sodden brickwork that housed the migrant multitude, that invention and ingenuity was spawned. While the collateral damage in disease and death and loss of opportunity was never far away, it was this same maelstrom that effected change and had its own spirit, energy and genius. Ask The Beatles, or maybe, if you could, Dixie Dean, Beryl Bainbridge, William Gladstone, Bessie Braddock, Ken Dodd or Henry Tate.

Necessity is the mother of invention. Anthropologists have suggested that because prehistoric humans were weak and vulnerable and got the last pickings after the lions and hyenas at a kill, they would find nutrition by scraping the marrow from inside bones and in this way found the high-fat, high-calorific content to enable their brains to grow and attain the capacity to imagine, to create art, to make tools, to invent myth and language. In modern industrial social anthropology, is it not so unreasonable to postulate an analogous leap?

Within the spontaneity of this bustling, imaginative domain, what law informed these undernourished children, that in spite of their dire material conditions, together, en masse, in their play, they had the world at their fingertips, a right to discover an unbridled freedom to be what they wanted to be, to dream, to go where they wanted to go, to have what they wanted to have?

This awareness was not present in all kids and there were leaders who dreamt up ideas, invented games, organised teams and made things happen. Foremost of these was little Cecil

Pangloss. Although he could never be about brute force or the use of malevolence to organise his mates to intimidate others, which he well could have; rather, he had an instinctual sense of the art of persuasion, a talent admittedly gifted to him by his parents. Akin to this, among his many talents he was a natural-born diplomat. You may ask is it really plausible to attribute these higher qualities of human nature to a skinny little proletarian street urchin? Surely, such sentiments and refinements of character are the preserve of princes and aristocrats, of nobility and bishops, men of high birth, those creatures of entitlement, purpose and destiny?

Well, by the general consensus these plaudits were no flight of fancy; this was no glowing theory plucked out of the air, no hyped-up local legend, just because he happened to be popular so that everyone was well disposed to him. No, on more than one occasion Cecil had risen to the occasion and earned his reputation.

This was a time when Liverpool was assimilating an exotic diaspora of immigrants; while most were from Ireland, they arrived from all over the world. This often stirred negative jingoistic sentiments that viewed foreign nationals as inferior, as unwelcome imposters, who could only make worse the numbers who had been unemployed through the 1920s and 1930s.

There was particular racial prejudice in relation to the Kru people who arrived on ships from Sierra Leone, Liberia and the Gold Coast. These strong and resourceful Africans proved to be good sailors and for generations had shown their worth on the trading ships. By tradition they would ink a blue tattoo on the centre of their foreheads which then became a line down the bridge of their noses. This had developed in the time of slavery to show the Kru were free men who were employed sailors on the ships. Many of the ships from West Africa docked in Toxteth, south Liverpool, where the Kru would stay in sailors' hostels, leading a transient existence before signing on to another ship bound for West Africa or the Americas. Some of the Kru would, on arrival, jump ship and become permanent residents finding work in other occupations. In any event there were advantages to settling in Liverpool, including the higher wages paid to sailors if they set sail from a British port rather than from West Africa, greater employment opportunities outside of shipping, relatively better standards of living and, for some, relationships with local Liverpool women.

Sadly, nefarious race riots occurred as small-minded resentment boiled over into violence. After a few pints in the pub it was not difficult to stir poverty-stricken unemployed men to find some ill-conceived reason for their predicament.

The Kru were routinely patronised by many white folk and were spoken to as though they were children, usually referred to as 'boy'. Cecil had witnessed this on several occasions and his empathic nature made him feel the affront to their dignity. He was impressed with the way these resilient, proud men did not react and simply smiled at each other. Although his mates thought he was stupid and was risking a beating or even worse, perhaps having a spell cast upon himself, as there were rumours that the dark men from Africa were sorcerers. Cecil nevertheless cheekily decided to spark up a conversation with a group of Kru, who had just been verbally abused in a corner shop.

They had just bought some tobacco and had guitars with them and wandered back to their friends who were stood in the street outside their hostel. They were shouting back from a distance at some abuse they had received: 'It licks the one that licks it, it kicks the one that kicks it. The buttocks rubbing together do not lack sweat. It licks the one that licks it, it kicks the one that kicks it.'

They all burst into laughter and carried on down the street. They walked as sailors walk, with a discernible tilt, but were also light on their feet; stealthy and co-ordinated, they moved as one. Their eyes were alert and characterful; there was a humour, but they had no wish or need to share their fun with anyone else.

As the autumn air was mild, they had brought out of their hostel a little table covered in green felt with some chairs to sit and play a card game.

As Britain was now at war and the Battle of Britain was in full rage further south, a sombre mood pervaded most of the country; even the laid-back Scousers were less jovial. But these guys appeared not to have a care in the world and were amused by the young Scouse kid's inquisitiveness.

Cecil: 'My mum plays the accordion and my uncle plays the piano.'

Kru: '*Nu fue wah?*' (How are you doing?)

Kru: 'Says his mama has a squeeze box, well, that is sometin'.'

Another Kru: 'Ma baby mama ain't no time for a squeeze box, ma baby mama care for ma baby?'

All the crew burst into laughter, displaying cavernous dark mouths with an array of dentition ranging from sparkling white teeth to gaping voids, and yellow, tobacco-stained, sugar-eroded specimens.

'It's de man has the squeeze box.'

The first Kru contradicted the second: 'Baby mamas sing, some baby mama has a squeeze box, yeah, man, in Freetown they does, baby mama always they sing, man.'

One of the men with a guitar started strumming, a fusion of calypso and African rhythms that they called Highlife and Palm-wine. Soon the whole cohort, whether sitting or standing, was merged in a rhythmical movement, swaying arms, legs, shoulders and heads.

They then broke into the swaying chorus of 'Swing Low Sweet Chariot', an anthem that they had learnt on the American eastern seaboard.

This was followed by 'Nobody's business, nobody's business, nobody's business but my own', a palm-wine favourite from Sierra Leone.

As they did so one of their number reached into his jacket pocket and produced three shiny wooden balls, about the size of billiard balls, and started juggling them, tossing all three in the air and catching them in rapid succession as one ball was always airborne. He then lifted a leg and carried on juggling the balls from under his raised leg and then doing the same with the other leg.

They stopped to roll some tobacco before slouching back through the door of their hostel. 'Na pah pah yo.'

Cecil was impressed and his mates had to admit that they enjoyed the entertainment and were not intimidated by these foreign men. Any preconceived notions conjured by ignorance that these were savage with wild, unpredictable temperaments were soon allayed.

For Cecil this was cultural progress, breaking down a barrier, of learning something and enjoying the process. He determined to watch out for the group of West African sailors to see what other songs and tricks they might perform.

The next occasion Cecil saw the Kru sitting at their street table playing cards he went up to them to say hello. At first they ignored him as they were concentrating on the card game.

'No, kid, we're busy, go on kid go and help your mama.'

Even though at that stage nothing had been arranged, but in the hope of his words having impact Cecil announced, 'I need your help. We're going to have a concert in our parish hall. Can you and your friends come and play your guitars and sing and do some juggling?'

One of the group, who was peering over the table watching the game with his hands in his pockets, turned and finally greeted Cecil. '*Enujay, enujay, nu fue wah.*' (Good, good, how are you?) Then he pointed to himself and nodded. 'Nemaiju, call me Nemaiju.'

Cecil: 'Hi, Nemaiju, I'm Cecil. We are going to have a musical evening at our parish hall and we would like you gentlemen to perform with your singing and guitars and juggling.'

Kru: 'Cecieell. *Ha enujay,* how much money is it for us to play?'

Cecil: 'Well, it's for charity, to raise money for the homeless and sick children.'

Kru: 'Oh, Cecieell, ha, ha, you say no money, *tabataju, tabataju.*' (Bad.)

Cecil: 'But it's for a very worthy cause, it will help young children.'

The group then turned away from Cecil and continued playing cards, but they were talking earnestly, some making moaning sounds, others talking quickly in Bassa Vah, the Kru language and another swinging on a chair speaking animatedly to the sky.

Then the man Cecil had spoken to looked at him and said, 'OK, the guys are on board. When do we do this thing? Where is your church, Cecieell, *naje?*'

Cecil: 'Cor, that's great. I will come back on Thursday and give you all the details.'

Nemaiju: '*Ne peh peh yo.*' (Take it easy.)

Cecil had got ahead of himself, which was a predisposition of a young man prone to venturing such speculative bonhomie. He needed to call in some favours, of which, to be fair, he was owed a few. That morning he knocked on the presbytery door to speak to Mrs Kelly, the priest's housekeeper, for whom he had on a number of occasions done errands to the shop. He had also fed her cat when she visited her sister in Ormskirk the previous autumn.

By cooking his favourite meal, Mrs Kelly was able to soft soap Father Ignatius O'Reardon into agreeing that a concert at the parish hall for such a good cause would be a great idea, even if an initial reticence could be discerned as he murmured some reservation about how it might impact on the already desultory Sunday collection. There had been a tendency, in order not to lose face, for parishioners to toss metal washers when the collection came round. They made a loud, convincing, clanking sound that drew approval and admiration but, as the priest observed in one particularly draconian sermon, it was the one sin the culprit or culprits had never confessed to in his confessional.

Within the month the concert had been announced both from the pulpit as well as in the bulletin for the parish of Our Lady of Mount Carmel and St Patrick.

Cecil's mum and dad and cousin Eamon did a set with accordion and piano. The Kru men slouched in late, smelling of alcohol but in good spirits. They jumped onto the stage, pausing for a long minute to stare at the sea of white faces who were staring back at them with expressions ranging variously between curiosity, animosity, humour and expectation. The impasse was broken when Nemaiju gave a big toothy grin to his group and started tapping his foot on the stage; the others followed suit, some then bending low to slap their large open palms on their thighs, then the guitarists started strumming energetically and the melodic harmonies of the Highlife and calypso commenced. The animated performance kept everyone dancing for the next hour. The evening raised the not-inconsiderable sum of three pounds eight shillings and sixpence, which was handed to Father Ignatius less five shillings, which was made available to buy a few crates of beer for Nemaiju and his friends.

'*Ne peh peh yo.*' (Take it easy.)

'*Ne peh peh yo.*'

'Swing low sweet chariot, coming for to take me home...'

The Kru sang in unison as they laughed and sloped off, bouncing and tilting and rolling their shoulders as they disappeared into the night.

II

Cecil was close to his cousin Mark, who was a year older and by all accounts had 'a lot of bottle' and never backed away from any of Cecil's riskier adventures. Riskier meant scaling walls, climbing on rooftops, firing at pigeons to bring home the pigeon pie, climbing down drainpipes, standing ground against boys bigger than themselves. Cecil would never entertain an escapade that he believed would break the law; although it is possible that his idea of law and sense of justice may have been unwittingly at odds with the strict letter of the legislature. There was no doubt that Father Ignatius, who had been with the missions, instructed that moral law, as understood from the gospels, was the strict moral compass upon which we should be focused when we direct our actions. This included some interesting and rather flexible concepts about rights in a loaf of bread, where need and hunger were genuine issues. Such arguments, which had on occasion been speculatively advanced in defence by more creative lawyers before the newly established juvenile courts, received short, sharp shrift from the worthy bench. But Mark was more direct, less cautious in his choices, at times positively delighting in delinquency. He got into trouble often.

Then, there was the stand-off over conkers long recalled by the kids of Monro Street. In the autumn of 1939, 'the last autumn of innocence', as the mates would later fondly say. There had been a 'situation' as Cecil and his pals roamed into Sefton Park, where there was an abundance of horse chestnut trees. This was a territorial issue, a kind of turf war, as there was no comparable stash in their neighbourhood. While there were plenty of trees in Princes Park, catering for a wide diversity of flora, quality conker trees were hard to come by.

And so Cecil and his mates had been venturing to Sefton Park with large boxes mounted on two soap-box carts they had made from old pram wheels and wooden boxes donated by the local greengrocer. The design and refinement of these wagons was a marvel of engineering. They had well-balanced wheels with suitably oiled bearings and proper steering and brakes. Once in motion there was hardly a hint of friction in the moving parts and so, with established momentum, they would just keep going even with the minimal of slope to enable gravity to do its job. The drivers were smaller younger boys who had sufficient nous and nerve to properly steer the machines.

Cecil had a younger brother called David, a bright little chappie, as wiry as his elder sibling, who always liked to know what the time was and how much time it would take to do something or get from one place to another. This impressed Cecil; it appealed to his sense of organisation. It told him that David was a younger brother upon whom he could rely. For David's part, he doted on his big brother, who was always at the centre of the adventures happening in the street. In an unassuming manner he was swept up in the kudos, seeing kids listen for every word Cecil uttered and then watching dozens of his mates follow his big brother down the street.

And so it was with great sense pride when David, at the tender of age of seven, was selected as one of these intrepid pilots. His uncle had given him some motorcycle goggles, which he had adapted by tightening the straps to fit around his little head. His face brimmed with joy and laughter at the sheer exhilaration of racing along on the roads with the breeze on his face and the excitement of the boys running along at the side, occasionally needing to give a good push if there was a bump or stone or having to slow for a bicycle at a junction. Occasionally, they would see a delivery van, a car or a tram bus, but for the most part he felt he was the master of speed. Could there ever in the whole world be anything as much fun to be part of?

With discernible frequency the group of children raced the two soap box carts through the streets and across the main road into the park to plunder the newly fallen chestnuts, ripping the conkers from their spiky cases to check for 'gooduns'. On some days these sorties would be repeated two or three times from early morning through to teatime.

Eventually, the Sefton Park kids who, after all, had ruled supreme in conker contests through generations, realised they were being left with duff husks and grotty conkers that would fall apart when skewered and laced with string, even after baking. The Sefton boys had some justification therefore for their ire, and this soon manifested itself into a vigilante watch on the park entrances that extended to hiding in the bushes either side of the gates with rope extended and ready to pull tight to block and wrap the boys as they arrived with their soap-box carts.

Cecil had realised that these sorties might invoke annoyance, but he was also mindful of the fact that no one had an exclusive claim on the windfall and the overriding principle was 'finders keepers'.

This risked making enemies and confrontation, of scrapping off their patch and of probable casualties. Some of the bigger lads were up for it – for some it was even the raison d'être – but others were worried, ill at ease. This was the way the diminutive David felt. And yet the whole gang wanted their share of conkers.

In the evening over tea David asked Cecil if he thought he should do the raids and whether he was worried.

Cecil replied, 'I have to – when you have people believing in you, you can't let them down.'

David: 'What, you mean you do things just because people believe in you?'

Cecil: 'Yeah, of course. And I think it's right as well. I wouldn't want people to believe in me to do things that are wrong.'

David: 'But how do you know that it will be alright?'

Cecil: 'If it is the right thing to do, then it doesn't matter; it will be alright in my book.'

But the risk of ambush was something that could not be ruled out and Cecil had been preparing, looking for suitable scenarios in his *Boys' Own* comic and read that when you take the same route twice on the trot then you expose your men to surprise attack.

The problem was it was miles to circumnavigate around to the other side of the park and with the soap-box carts they could not just jump over the metal fence, the posts of which were a deterrent in themselves. So, they were left with an option of two entrance points, both of which could feasibly be covered by the local boys.

Cecil, in consultation with his fellow movers and shakers, decided to stagger the approach, first sending in a small detachment of tougher boys with the second soap box, which had had its good wheels and wooden box replaced by older kit. An attack predictably occurred and while the advance detachment was initially encircled, outnumbered, bound several times in a length of rope and immobilised, Cecil and the follow-on detachment, who had been observing from the corner of a street on the other side of the road, quickly advanced to arrive in good time. The balance of power instantly shifted to the Toxteth kids, and while at first some of the bigger bruisers were up for some fisticuffs, presenting white knuckles and started raising their tatty shirtsleeves to expose skinny arms, with fixed uncompromising glares, Cecil was ready to talk.

He identified the boy who was in charge of operations for the Sefton crew and asked him to undo the rope. He just needed to point out with a sweep of his hand the strength in numbers he had, saying that there was no need to fight. The other boy reminded him angrily that they were fed up with all their conkers being nicked.

Cecil at first replied by stating that they no more owned the horse chestnut trees than his lot did. But before the discussion descended into an acrimonious shouting match, Cecil conceded that he and his mates had done well with collecting recent windfalls and then pointed to a box full of large shiny conkers on the back of the main soap-box car, the Rolls-Royce of their soap-box carts, driven by David.

Cecil then said that as long as the Sefton boys were agreeable to him and his mates turning up for a collection every other day while the conkers were still available, then as a peace offering he would give the box of conkers to him and his mates. This seemed very reasonable and as Cecil was negotiating from strength, as there was on that day no equality of arms, his opposite number was happy to agree and they shook hands on it. All was resolved. As a closing observation, it should be pointed out that Cecil was aware that the conker season had by now all but run its course and there would be very few conkers now to harvest, as autumn had served up the season's horse chestnuts for the year.

'Carp diem,' Cecil uttered as the group retreated back to Toxteth.

'Eh?' replied his mates.

'Never mind – just another saying from a *Modern Boy* and *Modern Wonder* comic,' replied Cecil.

III

Monro Street was a mean, grotty row of poorly built houses down a long stretch of even older properties. This was for no other purpose but to make money and give little in return. This was the street in all its squalor. The rooms were small, with low ceilings and the houses often subdivided with two or more families in each, all severely overcrowded. There were no bathrooms, but there was an outside lavatory shared by several families. Of course, there were no refrigerators then and no proper place to store food. At most, there might have been a meat safe with perforated zinc sides to protect food from the flies nailed to an outside wall and reached through a window; otherwise, it was inside the room. A family living in one or two rooms would have had to buy food every day, as nothing could be kept. To add to this, there were mice, bugs and fleas. Such was the condition of the working class the length and breadth of Great Britain in the years before World War Two. It was a great irony that housing was then under the Ministry of Health.

Yet to the two young Pangloss boys, Cecil and David, it did not feel drab; it was home. And there were hundreds of thousands of kids like them.

Their mother, Deirdre, as a devout Catholic, would always talk of being thankful for small mercies. She felt lucky that she had retained a part-time job at the fish stall in the market three days a week. The five shillings a week she earned was a valuable input to the finances and meant that the family was not entirely dependent on the parish, but more importantly, it meant that that on Saturdays she was given leftovers for fish stew and occasionally some nice kippers which were a cherished treat for tea or breakfast. Nevertheless, there was often an uncertainty about what food would be available for a meal and usually required a certain amount of improvisation.

Harry, their father, had grown to be a nervous man, gripped by an innate sense of vulnerability and a realisation of how much further it was possible that the family fortunes could fall. He well knew the tsunami of misery unleashed by the 1930s slump, which still wrought havoc in the lives of ordinary working people. He had become a Marxist although paradoxically had no real stomach for revolution. It was not that he did not believe in the inevitability of the overthrow of capitalism; it was just not in his nature to be a street-fighting man. He was, rather, a man who believed that theoretical discussion should be enough to make the capitalists realise where their avaricious ways were heading.

Millions had been out of work and yet nothing seemed to be happening to improve matters. Everything had been at a standstill, multitudes living in appalling housing conditions. So, all in all, the Pangloss residence, with its two up, two down, backyard, and its own washroom and toilet in the brick shed extension, was relative luxury to be coveted by so many less fortunate than themselves.

But as was typical, their space was shared with another family: paying lodgers Betty and Phil Smith and their daughter Agnes. Betty and Phil's presence was slightly dubious, on account of them paying rent to Deirdre and Harry, who were themselves renters, and the agreement did not permit subletting, but as the actual numbers in houses often fluctuated, as babies were born and then died in infancy, or when a couple decided they had had enough of the misery and split up or a father went to sea, or children were taken into care, or when a family 'on the parish' simply could not make ends meet and starving, disease and lack of clothing in the winter really did condemn them to a death sentence. Whatever, to be safe, when talking to the neighbours, Harry and Deirdre always referred to Betty and Phil as cousins. Even so, Harry found himself awake at night, wrestling with his conscience as to whether or not the arrangement made him a capitalist in his own garret.

Agnes was a few years older than Cecil and David, and the boys noticed that she had grown taller and looked physically mature. She had a screen that divided off part of one of the downstairs rooms. The room was only small and the divided-off part barely had room for her bed and little table and chair, with her clothes hanging from a hook on the peeling yellowy wall. It was her space and was strictly out of bounds for the boys. Deirdre had made that clear.

For young boys there is a natural magnetism about an area that is off-limits. It attains a gravitational sway that teases their curiosity, and the longer this persists the more agonisingly preoccupied and obsessive the mind becomes. While Cecil was more respectful of boundaries and had more to occupy himself with, spending a great deal of his time making plans and organising adventures out on the street, David, being that little bit younger, spent more time in the house. It is true David may have been more sensitive, more susceptible to his nascent emotions than Cecil; some might call it a matter of strength of character, but then Cecil did set the bar at a very high level.

Beyond that there might have been a good argument to give David the benefit of the doubt, as the house was so small and it was inevitable that living in such a close space that more intimate personal moments may not be as private as they would otherwise be. A couple of facts need to be pleaded in support of this contention. Firstly, the screen was an adapted simple cotton bedsheet, which had been variously darned and patched to cover the holes and worn areas. It had a lining around the edges, so that it could be firmly secured to a flimsy, moveable metal clothes rail that had been discarded by a haberdasher's shop. This was fine when the light in the room was sombre, on bleak days or at night, but when the sun shone brightly the rays would beam into the south-facing room and, after highlighting the particles in the dusty air and dancing over the cluttered bric-a-brac and essentials of day-to-day living, would land on the centre of the screen in a way that was undeniably transparent, so that bodily movement in the space behind was hidden with only the slightest opaqueness.

In addition, there was an unwritten rota within the house for use of the tin bathing tub. The Smiths' days were Monday and Saturday. Agnes was given the Saturday-morning slot. She would move the table and chair into the main part of the room and then take the tub to her space behind the screen. A large pan was filled with water and then heated on the coal-fired stove in the adjoining room. Several pans of hot water would be needed to make bathing tolerable and by the time the final panful was added the initial water would be lukewarm. Nevertheless, Agnes would have a good soapy scrub with her own bar of Wrights coal-tar soap and then shampoo her hair. Compared with how long other members of the household took, she spent an age at her ablutions. And this timeframe not only tended to become more drawn out; there were occasions when she would move the goal posts, so to speak, and partake in this almost ritualistic routine on an early Sunday morning or even a Friday afternoon.

So, there is also the possibility that Agnes herself was aware of her own emerging voluptuousness and the effect her nubile young body had on the lingering eyes of boys when she was at school or out and about. She may even have sensed that little moments of forgetfulness, in betraying her modesty, somehow made her the centre of attention. But was it possible she knew of the transparency of her screen?

Ultimately, upon an objective view and even allowing for David's tender years, it would not be possible to entirely exonerate his conduct. While it may have initially been purely accidental, just being in the wrong place at the wrong time, he did thereafter loiter with intent on the scheduled Saturday bath days. But it was not always sunny and so, unless Agnes happened to put the lamp on in her corner, the view was indeed opaque. He could hear the splash of water and see her shape emerge from the tub, her arm reach for a towel and shake her hair and wipe herself down. Sometimes she would hum a little tune and he could see her just standing behind the screen.

One Saturday David was standing near the door to the room and as Agnes got out of the tub she leaned on the side of the frame holding the screen, which caused that side of the frame to slide a good two feet across the room until it jarred with the little table and chair. David and Agnes's eyes met. She was holding the towel up to dry her face and ears, so her arms covered her breasts. David immediately blushed with embarrassment, while Agnes seemed to just stand there. As David's eyes dropped he became transfixed on a luxuriant bush of red pubic hair freshly rinsed and radiant in the sunlight. He could see Agnes's milky white body, her shapely legs and curvy hips. In a moment of mishap, tease, torment or jest or just plain exhibitionism, David still does not know, Agnes suddenly dropped the towel and lifted her arms to gather her hair in a bun. David wanted to run but felt anchored to the spot. As Agnes gave him a naughty smile, the mortified young boy turned on his heels and flew up the stairs to his own corner, where he sat on his bed in near-paralysis for the best part of an hour.

Agnes was a woman for sure; she just seemed like a girl to talk to when she was dressed. For the young David this novel adventure was the most intoxicating thing in his life. Yet it came with a price.

Interspersed with these delightful mischievous happenings his weekends were busy with an imposed schedule of religiosity as he was under instruction preparing for the sacraments of confession and Holy Communion. It meant staying behind after church on Sundays to attend catechism lessons with Miss Lonsdale, the Sunday-school teacher.

She was a spinster of sorts with a devout faith and no sense of humour. She had been a nun but left when in her thirties and married an estate agent, who turned out to be gay. The marriage was never consummated and so was eventually annulled following a petition for a papal decree. Most people felt that she might as well have just stayed within the convent sisterhood. In her teaching she was traditional, doctrinaire and a disciplinarian. She had the full support of Father Ignatius, who would always make a point of poking his head around the door, with a jolly grin, as though he was Father Christmas. There was a particular odour about him: a mixture of church candlewax, incense and a strong vapour of altar wine, as well as an old man off-smell of sweat and tobacco in his clothes. He would usually ask some unsuspecting child a question from the catechism, which the child did not know. He would look at Miss Lonsdale and say, 'I think this one needs a bit of work.'

David was obliged to learn by rote the catechism:

Q. Who made you?
A. God made me.
Q. Why did God make you?
A. For His own glory and in His image and likeness.
Q. Who is Jesus Christ?
A. He is the son of God.
Q. Are His enemies powerful?

A. They have come to nothing.

Q. What happens at the resurrection?

A. Christ judges all men's deeds.

Q. What of those He deems righteous?

A. They dwell with Him forever.

Q. What of those He condemns?

A. They perish forever.

Q. What is the penalty for sin?

A. Death.

As can be imagined, this was all stuff the young David really did not want to be hearing after his clandestine erotic sorties to feast on the visual magnificence of Agnes in the bathtub. How could those magical Saturday illicit little interludes be called sins of the flesh?

Then came the day of first confession. What was supposed to absolve David and lift a great weight from the boy's troubled conscience had the opposite effect. It was more troubling because Cecil said it always made him feel better and his dear mother had faith in the healing quality of the sacrament. What could be more wonderful than forgiveness by God?

If he could have felt not just reassurance but actually trust in the muttering man of the cloth on the other side of the screen, the humiliation and trauma may not have endured through his life.

Why was it that the old priest was so interested and at the same time so aggressively condemning?

'In the name of the Father, the Son and the Holy Spirit. Bless me, Father, for I have sinned and this is my first confession and these are my sins. I have sworn and disobeyed my parents when they gave me chores to do. I helped Mark nick some penny gobstoppers.'

The priest just said, 'Bless you, my son'. And then David said there was another thing he should mention and the priest said, 'Go on, my son.'

After a nervous pause David said quietly, 'I watch Agnes in the bathtub, and when she gets up to dry herself I see her titties and hairy minge, Father.'

The priest was silent and breathed heavily. And then he said, 'And how many times have you done this, my son?'

And David said, 'At least a dozen Saturdays this year.'

And the priest was silent and breathed heavily again; he then said, 'Is Agnes your sister?'

And David said, 'Certainly not, Father – her family lodges with us.'

And the priest was silent for a long while. David thought that he may have been pausing for a drink of tea, although there was a smell of altar wine on his breath wafting through the confessional curtain. It sounded as though he was sighing and then he said, 'And this Agnes, is she a well-developed young lady?'

'Oh, very much, Father, she has big titties and lovely red hair on her minge.'

And the priest was silent and was breathing very heavily. David became anxious. Perhaps this was stuff God did not really want to hear about?

Then David could hear a prayer muttered in Latin behind the curtain. The priest then said that for deceiving his mother, theft and swearing, as an act of contrition he should say one Hail Mary.

With regard to the prying on the intimate moments of a young woman, the priest said, 'You know that has to stop. Sins of the flesh are dangerous; they are wicked and impure. They go beyond the doing, the action – they infect the mind as well with lustful thoughts. It is indeed the devil's work that you should have those feelings at your tender age. Do you know there is a place called Hell for serious sinners? And you, my son, are dicing with eternal damnation. You will ask the Lord for forgiveness and say three Hail Marys and four Our Fathers, and I want you say a decade of the Rosary each day until Sunday; is that understood, my son? Now go in peace, my son, and sin no more.'

IV

Deirdre had two sisters: Moira, who was eight years older, and Mary, who was three years older. Moira was married to Harry's older brother, Patrick Pangloss. She also had two brothers in Ireland. When Moira married Pat, a car mechanic, they moved to Wigan, where they had a relatively good quality of life.

For Mary, though, life was hard. The exhausting drudgery of her daily life made Moira's lot look easy. She had been a good dancer; her lightness of touch made Moira and Deirdre look like cart horses, but as there was nothing to keep her in Ireland she followed Moira in getting the boat to Liverpool. The spark and joy of the days when she innocently walked down Lime Street wondering if she would find love had long since passed. Her remaining hope was that her kids get a decent education and maybe one day they would have an inside toilet and hot water.

Mary had five kids and lived in a one-bedroom flat, three floors up on Mill Street in a Dingle tenement. At ten years old Mark was the eldest: a little devil, great with a catapult and he often brought a slain pigeon home for dinner and had been known to pull apart a park bench for the little corner-piece fireplace, so that in the long cold damp winters his younger siblings would feel the smoky glow from the hearth.

Four families had to share an old toilet with a defective flush which was situated on the landing. There was usually a queue as a couple of dozen people used that stinking latrine. There was no sink and nowhere to wash your hands. While hygiene was a challenge for everyone, some made more effort than others. While an effort was made to keep the toilet clean, some occupants, in desperation, would defecate on the floor.

With a teething baby, Mary would alternate between watching the potatoes boil, keeping an eye on the sausages and making sure her baby did not drown in the sink as she washed him one-handed while holding back a toddler from the oven. Once the kids were fed she would boil water for the dishes as there was no hot running water, no washing machine, only a small one-ring cooker with an oven. Sometimes she might heat up the kettle on the coal fire.

Her old man had found some work in the docks and returned home, demanding the dishes out of the sink and the hot water for a wash. She would then serve him his tea. Mary taught the kids to sing songs in the landing as they waited for the loo to get empty so that the children could relieve themselves. Her chap would then go to the pub, eventually to return home drunk and fall asleep. Exhausted, Mary would finally get to bed as she had to get up at 6am.

There were singular, isolated days of relief, days when just for a while the drudgery of place and the wretched, hand-numbing, elbow-aching routine could be forgotten. Family is, after all, family and within the fondness of those ties Deirdre would go to great lengths to make possible a summer excursion to New Brighton. One year they actually made it all the way to Crosby but found the sand a little too quick and the tides a little too rough, so avoided in later trips.

David recalled the family all agreeing what they would pack for a picnic. They would use the bedspread off Cecil and David's bed as a cover to sit on at the beach. Moira, Deirdre and Mary would write to each other as early as April and then arrange an evening get-together at a local pub to sort out the details. One year, Pat did three runs in his car to first pick Mary and the kids up and then Harry and Deirdre and the two boys. But most times they caught the ferry and or the bus, which Cecil and David loved, because the whole family could sit together and the chatter from kids and adults alike could be heard at every stop from the Dingle to the centre of Liverpool and then all change on the bus through the newly constructed Mersey tunnel through Birkenhead and Wallasey, eventually arriving at New Brighton.

Mary's old man did not participate. He preferred to be in the pub with his mates if there was no work on; otherwise he would claim that he was on shift and needed to put food on the table. It did not seem to matter to Mary. Deirdre and Moira gave her welcome help with looking after the kids.

The boys were free to roam and beachcomb all day: running and splashing in the surf, romping and hiding in the dunes, fishing for sticklebacks off the concrete sea defences. The family would visit the Perch Rock Fort and view the lighthouse beyond. It felt like the seaside; it was the seaside. The air was so different, that of a fresh salty spray always breezing in on the waves. The time would fly in their inexhaustible enthusiasm from the time they arrived in the mid-morning July sun until the evening sun started to set when they had to pack up and catch the last bus home.

Pat had a Brownie box camera. It was a novelty that he more than anyone enjoyed. He marvelled that mass production brought such technological innovation to the common man. Like motor vehicles, to him it was more than just a convenient artefact of modern life. He prided himself in understanding the workings and specification. Before taking a picture of impatient sitters, he would become geeky about the marvellous piece of kit in his hands:

'The Kodak Brownie Number 2 is a box camera manufactured by the Eastman Kodak Company from 1901 to 1935. There are five models, A through F, and it is the first camera to use 120 film. The model I have also comes with a viewfinder and a handle.'

Any other time Pat might have captured Cecil, David and Mark's attention, but there was too much else to be doing. Instead, Eamon, who came along to help out because he enjoyed the company of his younger cousins, gave his dad a smile and a wink and slow, sarcastic clap as the kids rapidly dispersed before the words of Pat's impromptu little lecture had time to issue from his lips.

Pat took very good photographs – even the standard little square black and white images had a timeless charm – and as he was a member of a local photography club, he was able to obtain larger prints from the negatives. There were group pictures of the extended family and close-ups of the young boys grinning into the camera, showing the state of dentition as second sets of teeth erupted through gums. They waved their agile, skinny arms at Pat, as Eamon stood behind them trying in vain to rein them all in. And there were pictures of Deirdre and Harry sitting on the sandy blanket with their arms embracing the shoulders of Cecil and David. These pictures and the memories they held were priceless; they endured and were treasured for a lifetime and beyond.

Later that summer of 1940 Mark got arrested again for pinching. He had already been warned by the constable and Cecil had on a number of occasions reminded him to curb his excesses. But it was too late now. A summons was served for him to attend the juvenile court but found its way to the wrong garret within the labyrinthine Dingle tenement.

As a result, Mark was detained for court. He characteristically braved it out and pleaded 'not guilty'. He had no legal representation. The chairman of the magistrates' bench frowned at him, as though a headmaster about to administer the cane. The prosecuting police sergeant wiped his moustache, cleared his throat and rose to his feet to read in a perfunctory, sanctimonious way the facts upon which the prosecution relied to explain how the boy stole and then ignored a summons and had to be detained to ensure his attendance at court.

Mark commenced his own defence: 'I never done it, Mister.' Mark was found guilty and in sentencing him to twelve months in a borstal training establishment, the chairman of the justices told Mark that he found his lies disgusting and deceitful, and reminded him that he was a thief and if he had his way he would bring back the birch for reprobates such as he.

Thankfully, by this time there had been important developments in the youth justice system. The Children and Young Persons Act (1933) required courts to have regard to a child's welfare, raised the age of criminal responsibility to eight years old and abolished the death penalty for under-eighteens. Home Office-approved schools were also created, replacing the old reformatories and industrial schools.

Even if the chairman of the magistrates viewed the spirited urchins that came before them with a Victorian harshness, at least a line between children and adult offenders had been finally drawn and the system curtailed the handing-down of mean, destructive and inappropriate sanctions to the young and impoverished.

For Mark a succession of offences in his youthful years marked him for life. Despite the times when, as a man, he made genuine efforts to get his life together, he spent his late teens and early twenties in and out of prison. There was some attempt at rehabilitation in one institution where he discovered a talent for art, which, when he was released, he followed up by learning the tattooist's craft, which, with the many sailors in out of Liverpool went well, for a while. Alas, he spent his hard-earned profit on drink, so his wife left him and he sank into alcoholism before dying an ignominious and premature death.

Let us, just for a moment, digress from trawling the trials and tribulations of British working-class social history.

3

Some Family History
and Philosophy

I

Before Cecil and David came along Deirdre had lost two girls in infancy, so they were now a nuclear family of four: Deirdre, Harry, Cecil and David.

Harry's father, Troy, was from the second generation of Greek immigrants. They claimed to trace their ancestry from a time when they were well-to-do scholars and owned land with vineyards and olive groves. There had been different spellings of 'Pangloss' on different birth certificates. Between cousins and second cousins and even, in one case, between siblings the precise spelling appeared to morph as new variations appeared, particularly with those family members who had moved to England and began to lose their native tongue, even more so with the second generation.

There was 'Pangloss' and 'Panagos' and 'Pangalos' and 'Panakos', and there was 'Panagopoulous' and 'Panagiotidis', then

'Panagiotopoulos' (which actually means son of Panagiotidis), so all this served to further confuse the unquestionably elaborate myth-making surrounding the origins of the family name. The generally accepted version, which had in some overarching way imprinted itself on the psyche of successive generations, was that to be a Pangloss meant that you were by nature an optimist, that things would be for the best and this in turn meant family members were supposed to laugh out loud in the face of adversity: to turn the other cheek, to be sanguine and stoical no matter what the misery. All of this was, of course, absurd and yet in some bizarre, counter-intuitive way it kind of worked. They got through against all the odds – well, at least quite a few, but not all by any means.

In the family folklore passed down through the generations there were tales of the learning of remote forefathers who came from Minas in Southern Greece and who had studied the classical texts. There was talk of Lycurgus, the philosopher of ancient Sparta, who acted in accordance with the Oracle of Apollo at Delphi and who lived in circa 850 BC. He is credited with the three Spartan virtues of equality, military fitness and austerity, and was referenced by Plato and more particularly written of by Plutarch. Many great things were written about Lycurgus. It was he who introduced the Olympic Games in 776 BC. It is said that he may even have known Homer and studied the laws of Minos after travelling to Crete. And it is also acknowledged that Lycurgus may never have actually existed at all and was just another great legend.

But all of this just seemed to beg further questions. What on earth did all this have to do with being an optimist, of living life as though everything was for the best in the best of all possible worlds, even seemingly in the squalor of dilapidated back-street housing?

Well, the remote learned forefathers were not put off by this apparent lacuna. They found an explanation in the writings of

Aristotle and how he dealt with the legend of Pandora, the first mortal woman of Greek mythology, whom the gods created with many charms and great beauty but even greater guile and a virulent toxicity in the form of 'plagues and evils to men who eat bread'. All this was, according to the legend, packed neatly in an ornate jar, presented as her dowry to her hapless betrothed, Epimetheus. But one day, out of curiosity and not malice, Pandora lifted the lid of the jar, thus instantaneously releasing all evils and diseases into the world. Shocked by what had happened, she quickly tried to put the lid back, managing to merely trap Hope inside it. 'Only hope was left within her unbreakable house; she remained under the lip of the jar, and did not fly away...'

So, since then and through the subsequent evolution of the whole human race, hope is the last thing that dies in a man and a woman. It is the only consolation humans have for all the troubles Pandora let loose on the world.

Now the personification of the spirit of hope is Elpis. Aristotle distinguished between Elpis as expectation for the future and Euelpis, expectation for a good future. In order to have Euelpis, one must move through fear in the direction of courage in order to continue to have hope that there will be a good outcome. Furthermore, for there to be hope there has to be the ever-lurking possibility of failure. All this did sound quite Spartan. And so by this circuitous survey of Greek mythology the Pangloss elders felt justified in reconciling Lycurgus with their admittedly ever-diminishing, lukewarm claim to be optimists, as though, so to speak, by some kind of inborn genetic propensity.

In recent centuries this tradition of scholars versed in the philosophical discourse of ancient Greece had manifested itself in more mundane occupations, such as the proprietors of Tavernas, wine waiters and chefs, well respected for their Tzatziki and Moussaka. And in hard times family members would migrate to pastures new, although the industrial revolution offered little in the way of scholarly rural idylls, where erudite family members could while away their days in shaded glades engaged in philosophical discourse.

As the family diaspora progressed, another mythical tentacle emerged, on account of a cousin who had migrated from Kalamata to Athens and whose preoccupation was specifically with vegetarian cuisine based on Mediterranean salads with olives, tomatoes, peppers, garlic, rocket lettuce, feta cheese and halloumi, omelettes, mushrooms. This led to the assertion or rediscovery of an ancient philosopher whose wisdom derived from a mystical deity that gave rise to the cult of the herbivore. It was claimed that the myth was most closely associated the writings of the much-acclaimed and celebrated poet Hesiod. The claim was then more precisely associated with Herbigloss, none of whose writings survive, and who, if he ever did exist, was ignored by Socrates, Plato and Aristotle, probably for good reason. Eventually, it is told, because of the nature of man, the philosopher and his disciples were eviscerated and wiped from the face of the earth.

The gist of the Herbiglossian thought was that it was an oversight by Zeus that resulted in the evolution of carnivores, highly efficient breeders, who, through the generations, morphed into a multiplicity of burgeoning species and in so doing propagated a fundamental defect, namely, that this meat-devouring, aberrant mutation instilled in a large component of nature's rich and bountiful diversity a wish to annihilate each other. In other words, but for carnivores there would have been no war; there would have been peace on earth, just love and justice and reconciliation between fellow creatures.

If one discounts the Judeo-Christian Old Testament account that the fall of man was due to an apple and pride, then the contention holds good. All this was so unnecessary, a terrible mistake; carnivores in the kingdom animalia should have been hardwired on Mount Olympus as taboo. And even then, just to confuse, but in no way detracting from the logic of the argument, carnivores occurred also in the kingdom plantae in the form of the exotic pitcher plants of tropical Borneo. The supernatural unboundaried excesses and grotesque consumption of the gods should have had no place in the mortal world. To merely explain it as some physical nutritional balance sheet, as the inevitable efficiency of a line of least resistance that the gods could not prevent, is really not acceptable.

If horses and hippos and rhinos and elephants, as well as beef cattle and giraffes and zebras can get by by eating plants, trees and grass, surely the gods slipped up in this fundamental design fault?

If reliance is placed on an analysis of the fossil record of the nearest cousins of homo sapiens, then some have argued that the herbivorous specialisation of diet by the big-jawed and big-toothed paranthropus robustus led to their extinction when climate changed, whereas homo erectus, with a palette amenable also to the consumption of other animals, enabled its survival. But the jury is still out. And it does not explain the extinction of the Denisovans and Neanderthals, who not only walked the planet with early homo sapiens but also had sex and interbred, where all were meat eaters but only homo sapiens survived. Does this not exemplify the implicit brutality of feasting on blood and gore?

Well irrespective of the evidence in support, not only was this myth discounted as a ridiculous invention, it was also ridiculed as a myth that could never have existed as a myth since classical times. When is a myth a myth and if not a myth is it not then the truth? This is itself a question even Socrates in his dialectical method did not address, as noble lies and pious fiction were of more pressing enquiry.

And anyway, classical Greece could never have countenanced such a speculation. How could there ever be greatness without courage, strength, conflict, guile and cunning, challenge, fear, loathing, jealousy, blood, war and conquering?

Furthermore, if there had been an ounce of credence in such an idea then the Panglossian default position of things being for the best in the best of possible worlds would have to be completely refuted. By implication it would have to be rendered demonstrably false by the Herbiglossian speculation of some more perfect arrangement.

So the old ideas persisted even though they were constantly questioned by many family members. The ancient scholars had their ideas updated, revamped and bolstered in modern times by such philosophical luminaries as Leibnitz, when he postulated the prospect of a multiverse in the mind of God and stated, as it just happened, that the universe that God chose for humankind made in his own image and likeness, according to Christian teaching, must surely be the best of all possible worlds.

Yet a multitude through the generations of the Pangloss lineage wondered how the many branches of the family could have such stark, often diametrical experiences of this best of all possible worlds?

How could such divergent fates and fortunes ever be reconcilable with this instilled philosophy? How was it that from such lofty heights, within sight of Mount Olympus itself, through history, family members could fall so low?

Should they have been concerned? In Christian teaching, high or low is neither here nor there. Christ the king was born in a manger and rode into Jerusalem on a donkey. And just to confuse us all, if the fall of man was the apple, his redemption is in the transubstantiation, when the herbivorous wheat and grape are miraculously turned into the very carnivorous flesh and blood? How so? Is there a nettle in scripture that humanity has yet to grasp?

And this overlooks another Panglossian blood descendant, who was born in London and became – well, yes, you guessed it – the 'Protein Man'.

'Less Lust by Less Protein: Meat, Fish, Birds, Eggs, Cheese, Peas, Beans, Nuts and Sitting: Protein Wisdom'. Stanley Green, with his legendary, much-filmed signboard, was a constant feature for several post-World War Two decades at London's Hyde Park Speaker's Corner. He was said to be the most famous unknown person in the country. Many a scholar would argue that this accolade is also shared by a number of precursor classical luminaries, not least Hereclitus and Lycurgus.

Protein Man extended this unpopular branch of philosophy to embrace passion and libido, which made him at odds with both Panglossian meat-eating traditionalists and the ridiculed pacifist herbivores, who naturally wanted their fair share of unbridled passion.

In a reluctant acknowledgement to Protein Man, it has to be conceded that herbivores, even though not engaged in the horrendous brutality of the carnivorous food chain, are nevertheless not without their own demonstrations of extreme aggression, particularly in competitive mating habits. And let there be no mistake, the potency of testosterone in an elephant, a hippo or rhino is every bit as lethal as that of apex predators, whether lions, tigers or big grizzly bears.

Can it be that there really is some awful fundamental rule of nature to the effect that we cannot propagate without also possessing an innate propensity for killing each other?

II

But let us get back to the misery that had befallen the Liverpool Panglosses in the inter-war years. There was a rub in the tale of Troy. When Harry was twenty years old in 1922 and was making arrangements for his own marriage to Deirdre, Harry's mother received an official letter from the foreign office notifying her of the death of Troy Pangloss in a penal colony in the Andaman Islands. The letter further stated that in his documents, in addition to confirming that he had died penniless – well, actually with a number of fines outstanding – he had named Harry Pangloss as his next of kin.

No doubt, Troy had continued to offend and somehow found himself in India, probably by conning his way onto a ship from Liverpool and was then transported to the remote Indian ocean island. Harry was deeply moved by the irony of having a father, who, though he had never met him, had never made the slightest effort to contact him, write to him, visit him, send him a present, let alone support him; really as though for each other they'd never really existed. Yet while rotting in some stinking-hot hell-hole of penal servitude just as he drew his last croaking breath from his parched mouth he should declare Harry as his next of kin. Harry mulled over this thought endlessly.

What sense? What meaning was he to glean from this? Eventually, he realised that whatever motive Troy had had, it was not about some residual charge of affection that had endured, some latent endearment to the son he had chosen to become estranged from. No, it was more about a man who had reached the end, a man who had a fear of being completely forgotten, of facing the impossible terror in confronting the dark abyss, the lostness that lurks deep in all our souls. It was then that he could console himself with the most tenuous claim to some possession, to some attachment, something that would adorn him as having some history within the human race. All Harry was, was the incidental collateral of his father's last self-serving solace, his father's last act of fraud.

In contrast, Harry's grandfather had worked as a steward on a ship, and while docked in Liverpool, he met a young woman from Irish farming stock. It was from this side of the family that he inherited his thickset navvy's frame, while the balding dark hirsute face was clearly from the Greek side. It was his grandfather who had taught him to play the Bouzouki, to which Deirdre would, on special occasions, accompany him on the accordion, blushing at the bawdy sea shanties but joining in on the ballads. The boys loved these relaxing moments and Deirdre taught Cecil to sing. She kept the shining instrument, with its inlaid patterns and complex buttons, in a box on top of the wardrobe in their bedroom.

When Moira and then her sisters decided to get the boat across the water their family always had misgivings. Each year there was a steady stream of conscientious young people taking a chance for a better life abroad only to flounder through no fault of their own, unless, that is, you regard a certain gullibility consequent on growing up in a close-knit and trusting Gaelic backwater. Some did make it. Of the others, the lucky ones would return, but many became immersed in the slog and impoverished misery and disease of life in the tenements. At least in the Irish countryside, even though there were solid stone, albeit primitive cottages, admittedly without proper sanitation, the mountain stream water was pure, the air was clean and there was an inexhaustible supply of peat available to cut and load on the family horse-driven cart and bring back for the kitchen stove and fireplace.

Harry had been a docker and though only still in his thirties was no longer capable of any kind of heavy physical work. He was no shirker. At a time when it was luck whether a man might get a day's work as a stevedore Harry stood out as a man worth his weight. Even so, being a grafter and lugging more than a man should was no guarantee of a wage and there were days when he would scuff his boots on the pavement and wander the short distance home, hands in pockets, dejected and frustrated with a profound sense of injustice at the way the economy worked.

This, though, did not translate into him becoming an agitator; that was not his nature and his apparent stoicism often annoyed his mates at the working man's club, but far from being blind to the inequality that pervaded, Harry believed reason and sound argument would change the world. Neither he nor Deirdre had any stomach for militancy.

In Deirdre's case all the answers were in prayer and faith. She went to mass twice a week and volunteered as a church cleaner. Harry, in moments of mild inebriation, would mock her hours of kneeling. 'Been chewing on your beads again, lass?' And he would jest with the boys. 'You know your mother is a one of a breed of professional mourners, ooh aye, if there's a funeral she'll be there singing the dirges and weeping with the best of them. It doesn't matter whether she knew the person in the coffin. She'll be there even when members of their own families are not in attendance or just remain unmoved by the passing of their kith and kin.'

If Deirdre was annoyed, she did not let it get her down. Her reaction in response to disrespectful comments might be to smirk and throw a tea towel at him, but she knew Harry was neither resentful nor malicious, just understandably a man frustrated at his circumstances and whose faith was conflicted. She reasoned that he must have had some belief in the almighty in order to question why he allowed so many injustices.

Harry now needed a walking stick, old before his time. His back was arched and he walked leaning to one side. Propped with a cushion, he was fine sitting down. From a distance it made him look much older than his years. He would not usually want to talk about his industrial accident, other than to comment positively that at least as head of the house he had been entitled to medical treatment, without which it all might otherwise have been much worse.

There were occasions, Christmas or a birthday, after a couple of pints of stout when he would tell his story to family and friends gathered. He spoke with an acceptance of his lot; a philosophical insight made listening evoke not pity, which was the last thing Harry wanted, but a sense of privilege at being a party to his account and the insights that flowed from it. The story always began with an account of an early morning discussion he had with Deirdre about his options and prospects for that day's work at the docks.

He had had a long run of luck, better than most during the grim, drab inertia of the thirties, but even so work was not always guaranteed. He had been working in Stanley docks in 1936. It might have had something to do with his good fortune in being a Southport supporter, who, while very much in the minority, had a keen ally in the gaffer chargehand, Billy Baker. He was a big confident bloke, usually cheerful but could be intimidating, who also happened to support them and had actually played in goal for them a few years earlier when they got to the quarter-finals of the FA Cup, only to be stuffed 9-1 by Everton. Evertonians, perhaps understandably, always felt at a disadvantage.

Even when Billy Baker did take them on he would find opportunities for a wind-up in the lunch break making comments about their appearance, that they had big teeth or pronounced foreheads, and then laugh out loud.

As a fit and agile man, respected for his strength and ability to carry more than his share of cargo weight, Harry had suffered a serious injury while unloading crates of rum. On the fateful morning Harry had attended the holding-pen area of hopefuls. He was early and got the nod from Billy. With his usual enthusiasm to please and demonstrate his worth he tried to support an unstable load that fell on top of him, resulting in his breaking his back.

Over a game of cards or dominoes in the local, Harry was impervious to the banter and valued the camaraderie of his working-class mates. Harry's daily exercise comprised shuffling himself to the Dingle pub, the Dick Jennings, named after its then accommodating landlord, Richard. It was on the corner of Mill Street and Hill Street, a stone's throw from the docks where he spent his earlier years grafting.

Pub mate: 'All right for some?'

Harry: 'I'll tell you what, I'd swap my bad back for one of your windswept night-shifts any day of the week.'

Pub mate: 'Ay, wasn't a good one, was it? Tommy was on that job – they reckon those hoists were dodgy, had been for years. And Tommy's a goner now.'

Harry: 'Yeah, I remember his funeral. Doc said they couldn't find anything wrong with him, just died of old age when he was forty. Your move, by the way.'

Pub mate: 'Do it give you much gyp then?'

Harry: 'Hah, as long as I stay bent over and twisted to one side I'm fine, except at night it can be painful unless I get into the right sleeping position. I always put a plank of wood under my left shoulder – I find that helps.'

Pub mate: 'Sounds romantic.'

Harry: 'Let's not go there, mate, Deirdre is a very understanding wife. I'm lucky to have her. What pains me more when I think about it, which I often do, is that it was rum and sugar in those crates. Not exactly essential items for the life of the nation, for the good of ordinary folk.'

Pub mate (jokingly): 'Ooh, don't know about that?'

Harry: 'I mean, these days the lads are busier than ever with cargo from the USA – been like that for a few years, mind, machinery and the like. From what I hear it does not always arrive across the Atlantic, what with German subs and the like.'

Pub mate: 'Aye, true.'

Harry: 'Should have carried on as a longshoreman portering – the holdsman and shiphatch labouring work was never bloody properly regulated or supervised.'

Other pub mate: 'Should have been in a union, they'd have looked after you more.'

Pub mate: 'Would they heck. There speaks Garston's favourite shop steward. Tin-pot fuckin' dictators paid to sit on their arses and do management's bidding.'

Harry: 'I was in TGWU for a while, but it was like he said in those days. I looked to the Labour Party in Parliament to press for reform to protect workers' rights.'

Other pub mate: 'So much for the workers rising up and overthrowing the capitalist system then – what happened to your Trotskyism?'

Harry: 'No, I was never a Trotskyite, but aye, I was – still am, for that matter – sympathetic to Marxist-Leninism, if you don't mind.'

Other pub mate: 'Obviously a pro-Stalinist Bolshevik?'

Pub mate: 'How can you talk of Parliament when say you believe in revolution? It's one thing or the other, mate.'

Harry: 'Maybe that's why I'm better at cards and dominoes than you. Look, I believe that for all to be best for everyone in the best of possible worlds there must be equal distribution of wealth, that the value of something equates with the labour that went into its realisation as a product. That is socialism; that is the end goal.'

Pub mate: 'But what about the revolution? You've got to have the revolution, that's the way it works – "workers of the world unite", mate?'

Harry: 'You think lazy union officials claiming to be Marxist-Leninists and taking back-handers from the bosses and then being opposed by unofficial walk-outs by Trotskyist-inspired stevedores' and longshoremen is going to change the world for the better? Will it fuck. All I'm saying is revolution can be democratic. The workers can unite and vote for their own Parliamentary representatives. There's a lot more of us than them.'

Pub mate: 'Really don't sound like revolution to me. I put it to you, good sir, that you are not really a communist?'

Harry: 'That's the problem with all the theory and talk. Yes, it appeals to an angry crowd striking for more pay because they can't feed their families or they have just been laid off, but that's just the rhetoric making the heart rule the head. Reason will win through. You don't need to shed blood to have a revolution; you can be a communist, a true socialist, without using violence to achieve your aims. Thesis, antithesis, synthesis, dialectical materialism; it's a process, it doesn't imply violence. Can't you see, the raison d'être is the end, not some hair-brained adventure along the way.'

The landlord rang a bell. 'Last have has been called, sup up, come on.'

Other pub mate: 'I say fuck 'em... fuck 'em all, the long and the short and the tall, fuck the bosses, fuck the unions, fuck the politicians, fuck the bishops, the rabbis and fuck George Formby. You have food on your table because your missus has a job down at the fish market.'

Pub landlord: 'Time, please, gentlemen, that's enough for one day.'

Harry: 'Thus spoke Zarathustra. OK, mate, I'm gone. Can you help me out of this chair? Cheers, mate. Cheers, Dickie, old man, see you tomorrow.'

With that someone struck up on the piano, tinkling the ivories, and the late-night well-oiled inebriate cohort burst into:

Fuck 'em all, fuck 'em all, the long and the short and the tall
Fuck all the sergeants and WO1s,
Fuck all the corporals and their blinkin' sons,
'Cos we're saying goodbye to them all, as back to their
*   billets they crawl*
You'll get no promotion this side of the ocean, so cheer up,
*   my lads, fuck 'em all*
They say if you work hard you'll get better pay
We've heard all that before
Clean up your buttons and polish your boots
Scrub out the barrack...

4

Disease and the Blitz

Operation Pied Piper was a dilemma for the Pangloss family. As early as 1938 the government had been making recommendations that children, mothers with infants and the infirm should be evacuated from inner cities and sent out of harm's way to safer rural areas that were unlikely to be bombed. There had been, even before war commenced, reports in the newspapers of the new horror of warfare in which the simple citizens of Guernica had been obliterated by modern airborne killing machines from Germany.

The strange thing is that written accounts, perhaps presented with a photograph of peasants sitting on the rubble of their homes, remain a proxy, a second-hand version in which the vital sense of doom and immediate danger is lost. Nevertheless, even at a distance the new terror of aerial bombardment had struck a sickening unease in the nation's psyche. The Blitz was the new instrument of war ready to annihilate the already subjugated multitudes.

For the Pangloss family it was a subject of endless debate. Maybe Liverpool would not be bombed. Cecil and David were no longer babies. If they were to be evacuated to the countryside Deirdre knew she would not be able to go with them. And the advice was that Harry with his disability should also be relocated. Did that mean that Deirdre was supposed to remain at Monro Street on her own?

There was no way that was going to happen. Harry had said that whatever happened, the family should stay together. And besides, the scheme was voluntary; they could not be compelled to leave their home. Yet it was clear that the Mersey had been flagged up as a likely target. And Monro Street was literally a stone's throw – no more than two streets from the quayside of the docks.

Then the war came and the theorising ended and minds became concentrated with the intensity and vigilance of survival mode. It was after the Battle of Britain that things started to happen. Between September 1940 and May 1941 there were sporadic raids, while London and a few other centres took the brunt of bombardment. Then Liverpool was increasingly pounded, lest any Atlantic shipping should succeed in outmanoeuvring the German U-boat wolf packs. It was in January 1941 that Deirdre had a change of heart. Despite her own anguish and the boys becoming uncharacteristically unsettled at night, Deirdre had been determined that the family should remain together under the same roof.

Her attitude changed when, on successive nights, the menacing drone of aircraft engines came ever and ever nearer until, even at twenty thousand feet, they made a terrible din and it was never possible to know exactly where they were. It felt as though the whole formation was right overhead the entire time of a raid. And then there were those horrendous explosions, sometimes distant, then sounding as though Monro Street was the epicentre.

At first the boys thought, in some strange way, that it was exciting, the confidence of youth making it impossible to envisage the reality of instant annihilation. But the raids were persistent, and the noise and chaos in the north of the city started to play on the minds of even the most resilient and adventurous child.

A terrible isolated incident occurred as a result of a stray bomb, as the raids appeared predominantly to be centred on Bootle.

The bomb exploded on the corner of Monro Street. It demolished a house and blew out a large corner-shop window. A little girl, who was in bed in a downstairs front room just up the street, was blown by the shockwave through the rickety window and decapitated by a shard of glass. The impact of the explosion sent her little head rolling furiously down Monro Street. The decapitation sprayed a pattern of blood on the cobbled stones and pavement before finally stopping outside the Pangloss front door. The grim scene confronted Deirdre when she opened the door early the next morning to sweep the step. It is believed that the boys did not witness this and were spared such a truly horrific sight. If they did see something, then it must be hoped their senses shut down to prevent their young minds contemplating the terror of such a spectre. But Deirdre witnessed it, fully assimilated the terror and was deeply distraught, gripped with a panic unlike any anxiety she had ever felt. Her faith was her refuge, and she knelt and prayed the rest of the day.

In the evening she went to mass and talked with the priest after confession. Upon returning home she told Harry and the boys that she had been selfish wanting to keep the boys at Munro Street at risk of bombing. And besides, if they were near to the countryside they would get plenty of fresh air and exercise, living healthily and sleeping in their own warm bed each night; really, it would be good for the pair of them. And Cecil, though he would never admit it, had not been well. He was invariably wheezy and would often cough all through the night. He looked pale and had hardly grown an inch in the last two years; if anything he had lost weight. But his bright eyes, cheerful disposition, engaging wit and conversation made him seem in better shape than many of his peers.

David had always been small in stature, perhaps a little meek, yet sensible and sociable. He loved listening to Cecil's ideas and enjoyed joining in conversation, offering his own ideas, which actually were often those he had heard from Cecil. David idolised his 'big' brother. The thing was Cecil did not need muscle to dominate the other boys. He was a leader through sheer wit and intelligence. He could win over any argument with some comical and reconciliatory story, even when it looked like trouble might be looming.

The truth was that the Christmas of 1940 was the last festivity, the last precious quality time that the Pangloss family would have together; indeed, the last occasion this little branch of the Panglosses as a nuclear family existed.

One early evening in January 1941 Deirdre made the boys bread and marmalade sandwiches with the last of the fruit preserve left over from Christmas. She asked them both how they would feel about going to stay with someone who lived away from the bombing, away from Liverpool.

David: 'Will you and Dad come too?'

Deirdre: 'No, dear, this would just be you and Cecil.'

Cecil coughed and asked where his mother had in mind, to which Deirdre replied, 'I've not made the enquiries yet, but I hope it would not be too far away. I am working on it. I don't want to be apart from my little darlings, you know.' She gave them both a warm embrace.

David: 'How do we know it will be safe?'

Deirdre: 'Oh, don't worry, it will be safer than if you stay here.'

David: 'That is what I mean, Mum – how can we know that you and Dad will be safe?'

The Life and Life of David Pangloss

Deirdre: 'Well, my darling, we are grown-ups so you don't need to worry about us.'

David: 'I do worry about what might happen. What can we do to make sure everything will be safe?'

Deirdre: 'Where is your faith, little man? You have just made your first confession and Holy Communion, haven't you? You know that the Lord Jesus is looking down on us and will look after our family. Think of Mary, Joseph and the baby Jesus in the manager?'

David look coy and embarrassed, as though his mother's comment had triggered an uncomfortable feeling, and he half muttered in a semi-audible way, 'But the priest... he is just a man, he's not Jesus.'

To which Deirdre said, 'Yes, Jesus was just a man, but he was also the son of God.'

Cecil joined in as though concerned that the conversation was leading off track and going somewhere that might not be helpful to constructive dialogue. 'It must be for the best, David. If we have Jesus and Mary looking down on us and we say our prayers, then everything that happens will be for the best in the best of possible worlds.'

David: 'I wish I could feel like that.'

The following day Deirdre contacted the local delegates organising the Anderson scheme for relocating children and asked that her boys be placed somewhere safe but pleaded that they not be sent too far away. She got her wish when she was able to negotiate that they be housed with her sister Moira and her husband Patrick in the nearby Lancashire town of Wigan. This arrangement alleviated fears of impossible distances, culture shock and estrangement. The boys were less than twenty miles away. They were safe, or relatively so, and the seven shillings payable under the scheme went to Deirdre's sister. Nevertheless, the trek to the bus stop was emotional. It was about half a mile's walk from Monro Street. Harry accompanied Deirdre and the boys, with a walking stick supporting him in one hand and a suitcase of David's luggage in the other. David carried a shoulder bag and Cecil insisted on carrying both his suitcase and his shoulder bag.

For their part, Betty and Phil Smith arranged for Agnes to be evacuated. Her train journey took on her many miles away to stay with a family in Glastonbury, Somerset.

Financially, Moira and Patrick were better placed with Patrick's work as a garage foreman. Their son Eamon was a sensitive, intelligent lad, already in his late teens. His real love was playing the piano, but it was unrealistic for a working-class lad to dream of going to music college, so like his mates he left school and commenced an apprenticeship as a mechanic before joining the RAF. They rented a suburban, three-bedroom, Edwardian semi which had a galley kitchen and small garden with a rear wall backing onto an alleyway. Moira worked part-time with the WVS and, like her sister, devoutly invested much time in the local parish church. Patrick had a vegetable patch in the small garden area, which he cultivated with great efficiency to provide onions, potatoes, carrots, as well as tomatoes and lettuce in the summer. He also found space for his pigeons.

Despite his brave face, Cecil did not seem to settle well. He missed the strange comfort and familiarity of that improvised quality of life carved out of the squalid material reality that was Toxteth. As a cheerful ten-year-old who not wishing to add to the family's woes had remained quiet about just how ill he really felt. And besides, it was no foregone conclusion that a doctor would be prepared to examine him anyway. There was no spare sixpence in the house to cover the expense. His condition had not improved, his pale skin had developed alarming blotchy areas and for several days he was coughing up brownish gooey phlegm. The congestion was affecting his breathing. It was evident that he really was not well. As it turned out, when Moira contacted her doctor he agreed to call in to examine the young lad. After listening to his chest with a stethoscope and tapping his back in various places, the doctor wanted to get Cecil to hospital.

He had reached a diagnosis of diphtheria, an illness that plagued so many people, living in cramped, unsanitary deprived conditions. It was a condition caused by bacterium, which was very treatable once screening, vaccines and medication became widely available on the National Health Service a few years later. Left untreated it would often ravage the body, overcome the immune system, cause raging fever, a rash, sore throat, and congestion. And there might be other complications, including myocarditis, inflammation of nerves, kidney problems and bleeding due to low levels of platelets. Myocarditis might then cause an abnormal heart rate, while inflammation of the nerves may result in paralysis.

Pat had always paid his national insurance stamp as he had remained in continuous employment at the garage, servicing the few motor cars of the well-to-do, including their doctor. On the advice of his employer he had also paid an extra sixpence a week into a private health insurance scheme. The upshot was that he could get medical treatment when needed, both for himself and Moira and, for that matter, other members of his household.

The general rule at the time was that only the breadwinner in most working-class households was entitled to medical cover. In that respect the move to Wigan was timely. It was no foregone conclusion that a doctor in Liverpool would have examined young Cecil without payment. What with Harry's disability, the Pangloss household would have needed to appeal for medical treatment under a scheme that did not automatically entitle members of the family who were not breadwinners to receive any treatment at all. In effect they were at the mercy of charity, or, as some would say, 'on the parish'.

And so within the first week of arriving at his place of safety Cecil, on that cold, rainy afternoon of 11th February 1941, wrapped in a warm blanket by Pat and Moira, was packed onto the back seat of their car with young David sitting next to him and driven to the Royal Albert Edward Infirmary at Wigan Lane, Greater Manchester. He was admitted to the children's ward and first placed in isolation before being moved to the main ward. His bed was at the far end of the left-hand row as you entered the ward from the entrance door.

Nurses in neatly starched uniforms were making beds, changing bedpans, drawing and opening curtain screens around beds. The matron was busy giving instructions to her staff and in the background little intermittent coughs and cries and meek and weary chatter and murmuring could be heard.

The following day a little girl, Winnie Taylor, was brought onto the ward. She too had been in an isolation room for two days and then moved to the general ward to be kept as comfortable as possible. She was aged eleven years old, but her size and weight were more like that of a child of eight or nine years old. She was placed in the vacant bed next to Cecil. She was pale and languid; actually, her little white face possessed a cadaverous shadow lurking not far beneath the cherubic innocence of her natural prettiness. Because the build-up of phlegm caused a thick grey-white web coating across the back of her little throat, she was finding it difficult to breathe, so upon arrival, to keep her alive, the doctors had carried out an emergency tracheotomy, which required cutting open her throat and inserting a pipe to ventilate her airways. She also had a fever.

Cecil heard the doctor telling her distraught parents that he would do his best and make her as comfortable as possible and would do what he could, but he was concerned that the disease had already caused too much organ damage and that they should be prepared for the worst. The diphtheria had by now sapped not only her physical strength but also her spirit. She was hanging on to life by a thread. The doctor, who was well informed and clearly had some knowledge of epidemiology, explained to the girl's parents that the wretched disease was the third-largest cause of childhood fatality, even though immunisation was known and in principle available from the 1920s, but antibiotics just were not widely available.

To lift her spirits, Cecil mustered all the energy he could to get out of bed to talk to her.

Cecil: 'What's your name then?'

Winnie, with a painful whispery croak, said, 'Winnie from Liverpool. I am staying here to be safe.'

Cecil: 'Same with me and my brother. I sing, you know. I sing at the church, like a chorister, and I serve on the altar, but that doesn't stop me getting up to things.' He then gave a toothy, cheeky smile and coughed a hacking cough before regaining his composure. He held on to the side of his bed as though his fragile frame had difficulty standing and then, conjuring energy out of thin air, he spontaneously commenced a little dance routine. Then, with the clearest and most lyrical cherubic voice, he sang to the ailing little girl:

'There is not in the wide world a valley so sweet
As that vale in whose bosom the bright waters meet;
Oh! the last rays of feeling and life must depart,
Ere the bloom of that valley shall fade from my heart'

Winnie was so pleased and beamed at Cecil with sparkling eyes. She found that she could manage a laugh and told Cecil that he had made her happy even though she felt so ill.

When he was finished Cecil gave Winnie the most sympathetic and concerned look and briefly held the little girl's hand.

Cecil: 'Don't worry, you'll be fine, everything works out for the best in the end. Good night, Winnie. Hope the bugs won't bite.'

When Winnie awoke in the morning, nurses were on the ward doing their rounds, opening curtains, checking temperatures, and she was smiling. She remembered sweet dreams, and while she felt her chest was weak and congested, the fever that had sapped her strength and made her feel so ill and miserable had subsided, and better still, she could breathe without feeling she was suffocating. She felt she was in some new place, with revived hope.

She remembered the boy in the bed next to her singing so beautifully to her and doing that funny little dance routine with that cheeky smile on his face. She turned to look at his bed, so looking forward to spending the hours on the ward with Cecil.

There was silence. Cecil had not stirred. Winnie noticed that he looked so pale and still.

A nurse came in and then a doctor and then they pulled a screen around Cecil's bed. Winnie heard the medical people talking. They opened the screen and there brave little Cecil Pangloss lay with a sheet pulled over his face. He had passed away during the night.

Winnie was crying. A nurse went over to her and comforted her and arranged for her to move to another ward. She was told her family were visiting in the afternoon and could stay as long as they wanted. It was a consolation. Winnie eventually recovered and went on to live a long life, even though the illness had left her with a frailty and deafness in one ear. She never forgot about little Cecil singing to make her feel better and would tell her children and grandchildren the story.

David was only seven years old at the time but looked up to Cecil as his anchor, his strength; nothing could go wrong in the world with a brother like Cecil. He was profoundly affected in a life-changing way by his older brother's death. He had not been allowed to visit the hospital and so the abruptness of his being in the house and then being gone, never to return, made the sense of loss even more intense. It was something he felt was impossible to grasp: that such a force, such an embodiment of goodness and strength could just be gone in the passing breeze of the night. David vowed to try and follow his brother's example; even though he knew he could never emulate the strength of his character and charisma, he felt he could make a difference by the small kindnesses and thoughtfulness that that his brother dispensed in spades every day.

When life conjures such cruel emotional trauma in those tender years of childhood they form a shadow in the psyche; they do not go away, they affect a person's actions in seemingly unrelated ways for the rest of their lives. The unconscious mind is where it is, always, time independent, the unchanging self that lurks in the shadows only to pop up and affect your actions in those moments when you later might ask, 'Why was it that I did that?'

Cecil's parents had agreed to his little body being retained for 'as brief a period as possible' for organ samples to be examined, with bacterial cultures to be prepared and studied together with analysis of organ damage caused by the diphtheria. His mother insisted that all his organs be returned to his body for Christian burial according to the rites of the Church of Rome. The hospital was grateful for the family's generosity, forbearance and largesse of spirit. At such times it is not easy for most people to understand how such gestures can benefit the community. Harry and Deirdre knew that that was what young Cecil would have wanted. And the hospital was sensitive to Deirdre's wishes and ensured that the various investigations were concluded within the agreed period of three months.

Deirdre had been to mass every day and knelt at the rosary each evening. She prepared a eulogy befitting such a brilliant and noble young son. Harry and David had prepared their own anecdotal recollections that were uplifting and happy and heart-wrenching at the same time. Sympathy and a nod of quid pro quo by way of some nice cuts from the fishmongers ensured extra flowers from the florist stall at the market could now adorn the church for the solemn day.

It is hard to imagine the cruel twist of fate in that interminable mocking flow that destiny so often serves up. And so it was to be that Deirdre's devout and lovingly time-tabled minutiae to mark the passing of her son should prove to be the order of ceremony, not just for Cecil but for his dear parents also. While wicked despots might try to invade and conquer foreign lands and so shift the course of history, the true human measure of monumental events is not in the dates or the size of armies or the amount of TNT, but only ever exclusively in the tragedy, pain, pathos, resilience and heroic fortitude of individuals, who otherwise remain largely unknown as they navigate with honest toil their decent, anonymous lives.

The former Mill Road Hospital, in Everton, was another struck by a parachute mine on 3rd May 1941. According to Merseyside Fire and Rescue records, blocks C and E were demolished, including half the maternity unit. Tragically, eighty-five people died, including many mums and new-born babies. At the time, the *Echo* reported, 'The assistant matron, assistant medical officer and a number of patients, nurses, students and surgeons were fatally injured.'

On the night of 4th May 1941 Hitler's Luftwaffe, in accordance with Goering's blitzkrieg policy, sent a large formation comprising many squadrons of Heinkel and Junkers 88 bomber aircraft over Liverpool docks and surrounding hinterland. There had been many similar air raids in the preceding months, but now there was a callous stepping-up of the show of terror: one last campaign to disrupt shipping supplies and distribution. One last campaign of terror for the people of Liverpool, before Hitler shifted his attention and military resources to Russia and the Eastern front. Most of the casualties that night had been in Bootle in the north of the city. Overall, Bootle suffered most during the campaign, with the majority of the four thousand Liverpool dead being in that area. Nevertheless, if your house took a direct hit, it did not matter where you lived and amongst the hits in Toxteth that night was 43 Monro Street, with the resulting total obliteration of the crumbling old fabric along with the hapless inhabitants, Harry, Deirdre, Phil and Betty.

The parish church of Our Lady of Mount Carmel was located in the Dingle an area, close by to Toxteth. It was a fine red-brick Victorian building completed at a time when local diocesan wealth ensured that it was well constructed and beautifully adorned with altar pieces and frescoes.

Father O'Reardon had received a copy of the eulogy from Deirdre, when she attended to discuss the hymns for the requiem mass as she wanted him to read it as her personal testimony about her dear departed son. The priest now had the distressing task of adding an addendum to cover her and Harry as well as Phil and Betty. Father O'Reardon was a man of about fifty years of age from Galway. He spoke as though he had only left the Emerald Isle yesterday, but actually his ministry as a parish priest had brought him to Liverpool twenty years earlier and prior to that he had worked as a missionary in Africa. He fully admitted that he had once been a drinker but now claimed to be, by and large, a teetotaller. His parishioners had grown fond of him over the years; even if he was not proper Scouser, the working-class neighbourhood knew he was on their side in matters of social alienation and the impossibility of managing material depravation. They were nevertheless still amused when he would commence mass 'in the name of the farter' and he would talk of the 'mutter' for mother and 'childa' for children.

Pat and Moira set off early with young David sitting in the back. The journey from Wigan to the church was less than an hour. It was an overcast day for May; to say the mood was sombre would not do the melancholy and grief justice. David had repeatedly asked to visit his home. He could not grasp that the damp, decaying terrace to which he referred was now a heap of smouldering rubble. Moirra thought that the route should at all costs avoid the streets near to his home. But Pat felt that David needed to see what was left now to help him understand. As it turned out, because of rubble in the road it was not possible to drive within one hundred yards of what had been his home. In that dense network of cramped housing one hundred yards was quite a long way. They drove on to the church.

David was trying to connect and process too much. His young mind was in overdrive; he was numb trying to work it all out. He was missing his mum and dad but particularly his mum. He had yet to fully comprehend the death of his dear big brother and had cried every night, the grief of loss so manifest, physical and raw. Then, impossibly, the loss of his mother and father; how on earth can a child begin to process that?

All he had was a deep pain in his heart and in his mind. Other than tears he could not communicate it. The loss of what he called home. That was a reality that could be confronted, at least; however grim, there would be a lasting image in his memory of seeing where his house had been. Perhaps from there he would be able to start to process what had befallen his family.

From that time on David's expressions possessed a haunting, lugubrious air, present even when he smiled, even when he was in love, even, dare it be suggested, when he was happy. Perhaps it was not so much his expression, his facial muscles, after all, were as pliable to jollity as anyone else; perhaps it was just a glimpse present in his eyes providing a lingering pathway to the innermost unshakeable sadness evident in the gaze of an honest but tragic man.

On that spring morning in May 1941, Cecil's little white coffin was situated on a table at the top of the aisle and just in front of the altar rail. The diminutive size of the cask seemed not to do justice to the huge character who lay within, yet it reminded all those gathered that their dear Cecil had suffered the physical frailties of depravation during his life.

Undertakers then brought in two coffins holding what remains of Harry and Deirdre as could be retrieved from the crater that had once been their home. These larger brown casks were really artefacts of illusion, substantially to represent the physical presences that had once been, a sensitive gesture to calm the fear and anxiety that gripped even the most faithful in the parish. Father O'Reardon addressed the packed church:

'Welcome to the good people of the parish, welcome all our friends and especially welcome young David and Moira and Patrick to this gathering of pain and sadness in the church of Christ.

'What do people really mean when they say that only the good die young?

'It is true with time there is more opportunity for temptation, more opportunity to sin and it may be that unavoidably the ways of the world temper and dull the innocence with which we are born then to receive the cleansing in the sacrament of baptism. But are we not all children of Christ? And is not anyway our church a church for sinners?

'The vigil for young Cecil preceded his parents by one day, his devoted family suffering the pain of losing the inspirational life force that was the eldest son. And now they are gone too, an impossible double tragedy for their dear surviving young son. But no fear, David, we are your family; all those gathered today share in your loss and grief. Let us not forget that when Christ had finished his work on this earth and was crucified on the cross, he too went before his worldly mother, Mary.

'Dear brethren, it was only a few days ago that I sat with Harry and Deirdre in the presbytery discussing the arrangements and eulogy for dear young Cecil, and now I find myself officiating at a requiem mass for the three of them. How can this happen, you may ask? Is this not what our faith is for?

'Let me remind you, dear brethren, of Ecclesiastes 3:1–11.

'"There is an appointed time for everything, and a time for everything under the heavens. A time to be born, and a time to die; a time to plant, and a time to uproot the plant. A time to kill, and a time to heal; a time to tear down, and a time to build."

'And, my dear brethren: "Hope does not disappoint us, because God's love has been poured into our hearts through the Holy Spirit that has been given to us." Paul 5:5–11.'

The further readings proclaimed to the assembly the Paschal mystery, remembrance of the dead, conveyed the hope of being gathered together again in God's kingdom and encouraged the witness of Christian life. Above all, the message was of God's design for a world in which suffering and death will relinquish their hold on all whom God has called his own; it was the promise of the best of all possible worlds.

David had sat and wept through the ceremony as he had wept in the car on the way to the church, as he had wept all through the preceding days. Day in day out he wept; it was impossible to distract him from his utter desolation. Eventually, an idea formed in his mind. There were only so many tears that it was physically possible for a person to shed in a lifetime and he had shed all the tears his body could ever make. And so, when he did finally stop crying, so far as it is known, David Pangloss never wept a single tear for the rest of his long and eventful life.

As the church had been painstakingly prepared for the funeral, with the choir rehearsed and the altar and aisles dressed with floral bouquets and the air light with the scent of lilies and lavender and incense from the thurible, the diocesan authorities agreed that the Our Lady of Mount Carmel should be the venue for a number of other funerals in the ensuing few days, commencing with Betty and Phil on the following morning and then a number of the casualties from Bootle to ease the burden of the parishes in that district.

The onslaught of May 1941 proved to be a concluding crescendo to the Blitz on Liverpool, and soon after, apart from occasional aberrant strikes, the bombing of Liverpool ceased and life went on; people were busy making a contribution to the war effort.

David, understandably, became beset by anxiety. He came to assume that such crushing upheavals are somehow the norm, that such emotional wrenches are to be expected; that it is just the way life is, that it is what it is, a kind of normality of everyday experience. This disturbing impact on David's nascent psyche would influence the trajectory of his character formation. He would carry the psychological shadow of such devastation until his dying day.

For now he had to adjust to life in Wigan. There were a number of blips that need to be explored, but first the story diverts to the air war of cousin Eamon.

5

The Air War of
Eamon Pangloss

I

If the events of 1941 had been incoherent to David, swept as he was in a maelstrom of tears and heart-rending grief, perhaps unable at the tender age of eight to fully process the enormity of the tragedy, Eamon was a different kind of casualty.

As a young man, he had been allowed, without interruption of war, to enjoy his childhood and grow up in the love and warmth of his family, with stability and consistency, and then had at least some experience of the world as a young man.

His processing and awareness of what had first happened to his dear little cousin Cecil, and then that tragedy so cruelly and violently compounded in the deaths of his aunt and uncle, created in him an anger, a rage that cried out in the depths of his soul. How could such acts be forgiven?

Only revenge could vanquish this outrage perpetrated so personally on his close family members.

He was an able and sensitive young man. Moira had taught him to play the piano by ear. It may be said that he shared his mother's 'facility' for music. Then at school his teacher had taken him under his wing and taught him to read music. He could play Bach and Chopin, but he was also aware of free forms of improvisation imported from America. He loved to play in the evolving jazz idiom in all its variety.

He was good at school but ultimately decided as a working-class lad to learn a trade and start earning. He followed his dad and started an apprenticeship at the garage. By the age of fourteen he had a sound and practical ability with the internal combustion engine. It was no surprise when the war broke out that he applied to the RAF for an apprenticeship at Halton working on Rolls-Royce Merlin engines for the Spitfire fighter aircraft. On that fateful night in May 1941, when the bombs rained down on Liverpool, eviscerating his aunt and uncle, Eamon was on the night shift in a hangar on the base, assiduously following instructions in the fitting and testing of an engine.

The RAF had a tradition that had been established by Lord Trenchard way back in the days of the Royal Flying Corps, whereby all recruits, whatever their rank or background, if they wished, should have the opportunity to fly. It was well known that natural aptitude to fly a plane, to manipulate controls, read instruments, use the radio and effectively operate the cannons, could not be determined by the school a recruit attended or the level or sophistication of education.

Eighteen-year-old Eamon had, within months of joining up, seized the opportunity to fly. By 1941 he was a competent Tiger Moth pilot. Then, applying for operational pilot training, he was accepted and, after a further period of instruction on Hurricanes and Spitfires, was awarded his wings as a sergeant pilot. In April 1942 he was posted to 249 Squadron. By May 1942 the commanding officer briefed the squadron that they had orders for embarkation aboard HMS *Eagle*. It was only when the carrier arrived at Gibraltar in June 1942 that orders were given that the squadron would be flying into RAF Ta Kali where it would be based to play its part in the defence of Malta.

Ta Kali had only recently been established as a RAF base; it was a flat grassy/earth strip built on the flat base of a dried-up lake. It was not a good runway, with a tendency for hard, cracked and parched ground in the summer and patchy grass and mud in the winter. The ancient citadel of Medina was nearby and what had been the airfield is today the location of the national football stadium.

The main RAF base was at Luqa. When the war came bulky rocks and other obstacles were placed around the perimeter of Ta Kali. It was heavily bombed throughout the war.

Despite the best efforts for the RAF to keep the terrain as functionally Spartan in its dour camouflage colours and scorched-earth perimeter, local flora of spider orchid, red dragonfly, purple Mediterranean thyme, spurge, toad-flax and blue medicinal borage thrived in the dusty borders around the base. In May 1942 Wing Commander Warfield took over as station commander. Days later 249 Squadron landed their Spitfires after flying the short hop from the carrier located a few miles out in the Mediterranean.

A Bellman hangar and offices were situated at the south-eastern corner of the airfield and four double aircraft shelters were cut in the hillside on the northern boundary. Predictably the billets, mess, sleeping quarters and ops room were pre-fab standard twenty-four or thirty feet wide Nissen huts, with typical rounded structures covered with corrugated iron and painted in a yellow ochre Maltese sandstone colour with interior décor ranging from ghastly green to duck-egg blue. There were also pre-existing square stone functional structures with hardly a window. These rudimentary huts and stone blocks are still evident as an austere reminder of those dark days of existential threat.

On an aesthetic level, with an innate appreciation of good engineering, Eamon had loved working on Spitfires. Its workings and specification were second nature to him, and he was acutely aware of each of its many modifications and improvements. Prior to its deployment to Malta 249 Squadron had consisted of Hurricanes. They were commanded by Squadron Leader 'Laddie' Lucas DSO, DFC.

After the Liverpool blitz Eamon's personality had changed. While he was quiet and determined by nature, there was now an edge, a grim determination, some might say a sullen look in his face, perhaps betraying a controlled simmering rage. To his commanding officer and superiors his austere focus was seen as a positive, as a sign of maturing, the necessary loss of innocence and naivety. Perhaps it was of use, seen as part of the constructive, destructive military mashing, where young men become sufficiently beasted and bruised into effective killing machines. Eamon was acutely aware of the killer instinct welling up inside himself. While disinclined to mess-room high jinks and jollies, banter and demonstrable esprit de corps, Eamon's talent on the piano always meant that he would fit in and be welcome at a party.

Soon after arriving in Malta, Eamon wrote home:

18th June 1942

Dear Mum and Dad,

I hope you are both well and that David continues to settle in. I am missing home but busy enough to not let it bother me, although I do dream of Lancashire hot pot and roast beef with Yorkshire pudding, but the way things are, what with rations, I expect you do as well?

At least you have a ready supply of vegetables from the garden allotment. On a good day we might get some rabbit stew and I fear other meat might also end up in the pan. There is no fresh milk and the powdered stuff ruins a good cup of tea, and I definitely need my supply of water sterilisation tablets as 'funny tummy' is a big problem.

Perhaps I should be grateful for small mercies? At least the Hun have left off with the Blitz on Liverpool for the time being. I will write to David separately as I know he will appreciate it.

I cannot say too much about what is happening over here, but it is a good squadron with some excellent pilots. It is hot with no rain since we arrived, probably not the best time of the year to try and acclimatise. Even so, if it was not for the war, the rations and dodgy water, the sparkling Mediterranean would be rather beautiful. I am billeted with a Canadian bloke, who knows his stuff, is very religious and a bit of an odd chap in some ways. He is always saying 'screwball', so that is what everybody calls him. He does not always get on with some of the superior officers, but he is always kind and supportive to me, so I regard him as a good mate. In addition to us two there are another couple of sergeant pilots in the squadron…

There is an old piano, which amazingly is in tune, although the C on the lowest octave does not work. Nevertheless, it is good for some boogie-woogie jazz on an evening off. The lads generally enjoy it.

I do hope this reaches you.

Love,
Eamon

George 'Screwball' Beurling was flying with the RAF rather than, as would be expected, with the RCAF. This lanky maverick fighter ace, whose career was characterised by lethal effectiveness in action, a penchant for insubordination, non-conformity, a disdain of team playing and strangely sanctimonious Bible bashing. He proved himself one of the greatest fighter aces of World War Two, before being firstly rested from active service then, at the tender age of twenty-three years, politely retired from the RAF well before the war was over.

He was killed in 1948 serving with the newly formed Israeli Air Force while taking off from Rome Airport in an old bomber. There was a suggestion of sabotage, as many of Beurling's kills over Malta were Italian, including a celebrated aristocratic colonel. If there had been foul play, the name put forward was of a British Army sergeant by the name of Leavington, who was shortly thereafter killed by the Israeli secret service.

Beurling's body was unrecognisable, not least because his head had exploded from the intensity of the heat due to the full fuel tank. His immolated remains were placed in cold storage in Rome for two years waiting for someone to claim them. They were eventually interred in Haifa. It had been Beurling's wish to buried on Malta.

When Eamon and Screwball first met both were sergeant pilots, although Beurling's courage, initiative and ability in the air, and the rapidity with which he accumulated confirmed kills necessitated his being granted a commission as a pilot officer. By the end of 1942 he had been promoted to Flight Lieutenant, had been awarded the DSO and the DFC and bar, and had accumulated an astonishing thirty-one and a half confirmed kills.

He was an odd sort of bloke who had dropped out of high school at the age of fifteen and learnt to fly before the war, earning a commercial pilot's licence flying for a Canadian freight company at the age of seventeen years. It was all he had ever wanted to do, but his application to the Royal Canadian Air Force was declined, ostensibly for lack of qualifications. This did not dampen his crusading desire to find the action, and there is evidence that he tried to get to China to join the Flying Tigers, before he travelled to the UK with the sole purpose of enlisting in the RAF.

In 1940 things were desperate and so Beurling's capability as a pilot got him in. He honed his skills as tail end Charlie for Ginger Lacy before being assigned initially to 41 Squadron, which consisted mainly of Canadian expats. He thereby saw action over France and on coastal patrols. While his adeptness as a pilot was praised, his maverick attitude and cavalier manner in relation to orders were a continual issue and he was unpopular.

As Eamon wanted to learn from Screwball, on rest days he would follow him onto the airfield and roll a Spitfire out onto the dusty scorched verge and set up an old target so that Eamon could see how most effectively to line up the cannons mounted on the wings with the target. On flying days he was shown how to approach the enemy on a curved trajectory, preferably from above and out of the sun, then flying in as near as possible before firing. Screwball stressed that 250 yards was the best distance to fire the cannons. Eamon realised how perilously close this really was when flying at 360 miles an hour, equating to less than a second to avoid collision. It was a margin that Eamon achieved only once as his cognitive response time obliged him to fire and pull out at no nearer than 350 yards, which was still pretty close.

The other aspect of Screwball's flying technique that Eamon preferred to avoid at all costs was the highly reckless and unorthodox stall spin dive, the so-called ' bullet dive'. As any pilot will tell you, stalling an aircraft is regarded as a loss of control, with all trainee pilots taught how to avoid stalling in the first place. They then undergo careful training on how to pull out of one, which, incidentally, in some aircraft, including the Spitfire, may be impossible. To go into a stall and not pull out will be catastrophic. So, for Eamon to learn that Screwball had incorporated the stall dive into his flying repertoire was, quite frankly, astounding.

Beurling explained that he had perfected the technique for a very definite purpose, as instantly shutting down the effective aerodynamic capability of the aircraft was the surest and quickest way to fall out of the sky and disappear after a millisecond of intense, up close and personal attack on an enemy aircraft. After a vertical spin descent of a few thousand feet Beurling would, by second nature and honed instinct, use the controls to counter the spin and then throttle up and fly away to fight another day.

Quite frequently the squadron would suffer from a bout of Malta stomach, actually waterborne dysentery, that at first might affect one or two people before rapidly affecting others, who spent much of their time together, either doubling up in mess billets or sitting around in the hot seat ops room waiting for the next scramble. The enemy did not adjourn the siege or cancel raids to alleviate the gut-wrecking havoc visited upon the pilots of 249 Squadron. Upon the scramble buzzer, shits or no shits, pilots had to rush across the rough tarmac to their aircraft, even if they had diarrhoea running down their legs. This, of course, only became worse as they had to focus on getting their aircraft in the air as soon as possible and then be consummate in the intensity of air battle.

Strapped in the glass canopy of the cockpit in the Mediterranean heat, amidst the constant din of the engine, the steaming shit would create an unholy stench that would mix with the smell of oil and fuel and the rubbery taste of the oxygen mask. Thankfully, the pilots would become immune to this as their nostrils became accustomed, as their minds were so completely engaged in the game of survival and death. While the time in the air might often be less than an hour and actual enemy engagement could never be more than minutes, not least because the fire power capacity of the 12mm double-barrelled browning cannons mounted on each wing was fifteen seconds maximum. Beurling told Eamon that he always reckoned on no more than a one- or two-second burst to effect a kill.

In a period of downtime Eamon asked Screwball what he felt like when he got a kill; later he thought this a strange conversation. What Eamon might superficially have had in mind was some idea of an objective measure for what a pilot should be trying to achieve; after all, that was what they were trained to do. He assumed the feeling would always be the same; there would be some constancy for doing well, of succeeding on the mission. But feelings are not static and what one man feels will not necessarily be what another man feels, and even the same man, dependent on his mood and circumstances, may react with different feelings on successive occasions. While there could be nothing pyrrhic in a victory over fascism, on an individual level the consequent deficits from such an engagement may never be healed.

And so Eamon would listen to Screwball waxing lyrically about the three-dimensional mechanical dance of death, the dogfight in the sky. At the time, each crunching detail seemed to sooth Eamon's inner hurt, to offer justice for the abomination that had befallen members of his family, to validate his own desire for revenge. Beurling described with an animated intensity, shaping his arms as though they were handling a joystick and throttle, then positioning his head at an angle of attack, as though turning into the kill.

A shared pleasure and triumph pervaded the intimate conversation, as though some esoteric truth about the nature of life was being revealed, a truth that could only ever become known to a few chosen by extreme experience. And with it Eamon's inner anger was quelled as it made him feel some kind of resolution.

Screwball would thumb through the dog-eared pages of his much-worn Bible and show the written word as he would quote in justification of the horror, passages from the Bible, Leviticus 24: 19–20: 'And if a man cause a blemish in his neighbour; as he hath done, so shall it be done to him; breach for breach, eye for eye, tooth for tooth: as he hath caused a blemish in a man, so shall it be done to him again.'

At the time, both men conveniently chose to overlook the Sermon on the Mount (Matthew 5:38–39) and talk of turning the other cheek.

Beurling would then close the good book and draw closer to Eamon, his hands resuming on the imaginary joystick, his eyes lit up with a wide manic grin expressing delight from ear to ear. He gesticulated in graphic slow motion, as though capturing and processing every millisecond of the awful moment. He was gushing in his explanation of how great it felt to see at close and ever closer range, sometimes in the post-fire flash at less than one hundred metres, the enemy canopy shattering and then looking into the terrified eyes of the pilot as his head burst into an exploding shower of blood and brain, instantly splattering on the remaining canopy. Then, on pulling out of the attack he would turn to witness the enemy aircraft, in flames, rudderless and out of control, tumbling out of the sky to destruction and oblivion.

Eamon listened with a strained glee. He forced himself to smile with approbation, while disguising a sick sinking feeling in the pit of his stomach. Yet part of him longed for his own opportunity to savour such a moment. With so much that is governed by emotions this tormented and resolute man with an unavoidably sensitive and empathic nature should have been more careful in what he wished for.

While in his spare time Screwball might have taken pot shots at ducks in the local village pond just to see how many he could kill for fun, Eamon would rather play the piano or tinker with an internal combustion engine. Eamon was a romantic at heart, who enjoyed refined touches, courtly gestures and treating women with respect. He also wanted to be a team player, who did not see himself as a solo act.

Whatever his great talents as a fighter pilot Screwball was not a team player. Also, his connection with women was for some reason arrested. He wanted them, desired them but did not relate in a mature way that might foster an enduring meaningful relationship. His exploits created plenty of interest and he was briefly married. In reality his heart and mind were focused on soaring to another kill in the skies. It is perhaps no surprise that he became known as the 'Falcon of Malta', after he had ratcheted up so many kills.

This may be a harsh judgement as he was still in his early twenties and the distraction of the fairer sex at such a point in history could have been fatal. His closest friendship was with a member of the squadron called Paradiso, a French Canadian, who, for whatever reason, also found himself flying with the RAF.

The truth was probably much darker. The Bible-bashing, individualistic 'Screwball' may have had psychopathic tendencies, although his lack of empathy tended to be selective and seemed to equate to a dismissive attitude to authority and his superior officers. Yet he was also a reliable friend and mentor to those he was close to. There was no doubting his religiosity, his abstinence from alcohol and tobacco, and his equally passionate hatred of the Nazis.

It is also true that he possessed a supremely narcissistic belief in his own abilities. He was the perfect beast to send into air war against the Nazis. His superiors respected him, feared him and resented him. As it turned out he was shot down several times and was lucky to escape death on more than one occasion. He spent most of August and September of 1942 in bed, laid up with dysentery and illness as a result of the starvation diet that the RAF shared with the besieged people of Malta. He was eventually flown back to a hospital in the UK at RAF Halton to heal a gammy foot. The Canadians then advised they now wanted him in their Air Force and so he returned across the Atlantic and for a while found himself giving talks and promoting war bonds.

A Montreal paper carried a story dated 8th May 1944 with the headline: 'The Germans are beaten, no fun anymore, says Beurling'... He continued, 'They don't show up anymore... I sure would like to go to the Pacific where there's still plenty of action. The inactivity over there is getting me down. We never hunt the Huns anymore. They've lost all their spirit. As soon as we spot one during regular sweeps… he dives away and stays away. You can't shoot down Huns if they never turn up.'

Mess food at Ta Kali did little for squadron morale. While falling short of causing outright malnutrition, the rations were, to say the least, challenging. What the food lacked in calories was not compensated for in flavour.

There were many civilians on the island who were starving. The preferred Maltese dish of rabbit was now hard to come by and the meat finding its way into the pot may well have been cat or dog or even rat.

Matters reached a head one evening just as the padre had finished saying grace. A senior aircraftsman fitter, who happened to be sitting next to Eamon, asked the waiter as he wheeled in a tray of lumps floating in a brown fluid.

Fitter: 'What the fuck is that?'

'*Rissoles a la casserole*. Here, pass the *a la casserole*,' the waiter said as he spooned some of the gunge onto a plate.

The padre, who was in the process of making a retreat to the officers' mess, interjected with a nasally high-pitched laugh, to say, 'Surely you mean to say simply "rissoles". Dear God, please just "rissoles".'

As the waiter stood looking puzzled the padre had time to explain that '*passer a la casserole*' meant either kicking the bucket or coercing a young woman to have sex, neither of which translations he was sure was intended.

Then someone else groaned loudly, 'Not fucking arseholes again. Arseholes for breakfast, arseholes for tea, Jesus.'

With that the cook poked his head out of the kitchen, to which someone shouted at him loudly, 'Cunt.'

Things were getting out of hand. The senior warrant officer stood angrily and ordered silence, and then, in his loud parade-ground voice, he demanded to know, 'Who called the cook a cunt?'

From the hungry heads huddled over tables, after an initial silence, someone replied at an equal volume, 'Who called the cunt a cook?'

The mess erupted into laughter as the warrant officer grimaced and sat down.

While the decision whether to drink water or the local Cisk beer was never a dilemma for most members of the squadron, it was a problem for Eamon. Unlike Screwball, who was perversely a complete teetotaller, Eamon was not, but he was nevertheless sufficiently focused and seriously minded to agonise over the choice posed. It is true that all airman were supplied with regulation water purification tablets as part of their kit. These were contained in a neat little tin suitably labelled and containing two bottles each with fifty tablets. The idea was that you stirred a tablet into your water, preferably boiled as well, and this would kill any amoebic dysentery or any other bacteria or virus that might play havoc with the digestive system or even kill the consumer. Military personnel reported that the water took on a slightly chlorinated taste.

The problem was people still got serious diarrhoea so the simple solution widely adopted was to drink Cisk beer, a tried and tested method for killing waterborne bugs. But, in sufficient quantities, as a diuretic, the alcohol would dehydrate as well as inebriate and cause lingering drowsiness and hangovers. Once in the cockpit a blast of oxygen could counter this, perking up a hazy mind, but in so doing would often cause a mild euphoria that could result in reckless decision-making. On balance, Eamon chose to risk the discomfort of a bout of the shits and be sure of a sober mind.

This mess-room calculus did not go unnoticed by top brass. There was a quest to optimise the battle effectiveness of all members of the armed forces, particularly after the debacle resulting in the retreat at Dunkirk. Much consideration had been given to how chemical intervention might positively enhance concentration and aggression. It was known that the Germans were giving their airmen amphetamines for this very purpose. And so the station doctor would ensure 249 Squadron got other essential medication, in addition to the water purification tablets and Cisk beer.

Eamon was able to get another letter home:

30th July 1942

Dear Mum and Dad,

I hope you are both keeping safe and that you have sufficient rations for mind and body.

Let me know how David is getting on. How does he enjoy learning about motor engines from Dad?

I feel well established in the squadron now and have learned much of the skill and craft of air war from Screwball. He seems to have worked out stuff that they do not include in the manuals and at times it is quite a hoot when he upstages his superiors, although they then warn him about insubordination, which happens frequently, but he does not worry because he is so good at his job.

We have all had dysentery, which is bloody unpleasant when you have to scramble. You cannot ask the Hun to wait while you wipe your bum!

In addition, for the most part the grub is still pretty grim. We realise now that as the chief of staff is based at HQ RAF Luqa, they post all the decent chefs there. Each evening we get served a meat dish that the chef describes as rissoles. Some of the chaps have a less flattering name for them.

Someone got pretty fed up with the platter the other day. The language got out of hand and the mess warrant officer stepped in. But you have to laugh. Nothing happened about it.

The squadron leader is a fair-minded bloke. Some afternoons he likes to smack golf balls around the place. I suppose it helps him take his mind off things. I think he usually eats the same gruel as the rest of us, although some evenings a staff car picks him up, I guess to get some decent posh nosh up in the mess at Luqa.

Anyway, I remain in reasonable shape and morale is good. We have our fair share of success with few losses, although the Hun are more of a challenge than the Ities.

Will write again soon.

Love,

Eamon

19th September 1942

It was not long before an opportunity arose for Eamon to test himself and determine whether his inner anger could unleash that untapped ruthlessness needed for the cold, calm annihilation of another human being.

The Maltese weather in the summer months from June through to September required far less analysis. Every day was pretty well guaranteed to be hot and dry with wide open, cloudless blue skies. This blank canvas not only offered a playing field where chance would play less of a part and the quality of the aircraft and relative skill of the dogfighting pilots would always determine the outcome.

As there were fewer weather variables there was less agonising over operational planning by the commanders than there would have been with adverse weather conditions. Dense cloud cover provides a place to hide, a place to disappear and evade the ruthless efficiency of air aces like Screwball. There would also need to be a revised assessment of how or whether the enemy might reschedule sorties. Dense cloud cover requires instrument flying and would be counter-productive if there was an increased risk of friendly fire. The cut and thrust of intuitive, up close and personal visual flying air combat is then no longer possible. Malta was under siege; the war was being brought to the island. The fighter role was to react and intercept, disrupt and prevent. Even so, Malta became the most bombed place on the planet.

On the morning of 20th September a formation of Junkers 88 bombers escorted by twelve Messerschmitt 109s took off from Luftwaffe 2 airbase at Comiso in southern Sicily. Because of the proximity to the coast and Malta being less than a hundred miles away it would take them no more than half an hour to approach the north of the besieged island and the five ports of Valletta, where there was a daily battle for the allies to land supplies from cargo ships in the Mediterranean. If the raiders took off from the Sicilian base at Catania, this gave the RAF a few extra minutes to scramble and gain air positions with tactical advantage.

Eamon was acting as wingman for the flight commander having moved from tail end Charlie following the arrival of new pilots from Gibraltar. The squadron had lost a few members. Some, like Screwball, were laid up in bed, while others had been killed in action. This included Screwball's best friend Paradiso. In the weeks that had passed Eamon had been practising his own version of deflection shooting, which so far had not pulled off any results and remained a speculative exercise, mainly because of the nerve required not to pull out but rather get close enough to the enemy to have a real crack at a kill.

The squadron was scrambled at 10.20 in the morning. The sun was bright and warm and the sky predictably a clear azure blue. Upon scrambling an aircraftsman assisted with securing Eamon's parachute, as he then climbed on to the port-side wing, unlatched the cockpit to climb in and adjust his seat, buckle up, attach his helmet, mask, secure the oxygen attachment and immediately start take-off checks.

The drill was now instinctual: check fuel gauge, undercarriage indicator light, flaps, elevator and rudder trim, directional indicator, magneto switches, check outside cockpit with ground crew for all clear and chocks away. He then pressed the starter button, released the break, throttled up, carbo heat check, check instrumentation panel: airspeed indicator, tachometer (revs per minute), altimeter, attitude indicator, vertical speed indicator, turn coordinator, heading indicator, magnetic compass. Then there was a full burst of throttle as he followed the leader down the runway, and after about 230 yards with a speed of eighty-five miles per hour, he pulled back on the stick and alighted, climbing to fifteen thousand feet at about 180 miles an hour.

Within five minutes the aircraft was fifteen miles from base and within ten minutes cruising over the ocean at twenty thousand feet in sight of the enemy and ready to engage.

In combat the Spitfire mark 45Vc had an effective range of three hundred miles. Enemy interception was a brief and brutal matter requiring acutely honed reflexes and excellent eyesight. A tiny speck way off in the distance on a clear day might within a second close on you and end your existence on this planet. As the majority of enemy sorties were against the harbours of Valletta, the enemy formations would fly due south from the Sicilian Comiso base. Given that every minute was crucial, Ta Kali was not ideally suited for morning intercepts, as the sun was still in an easterly position and so as the squadron formation climbed it would sweep eastwards to obtain an essential altitude advantage with the sun behind them. For intercepts later in the day, the squadron would tend to sweep westerly. British radar had been developed and applied with great effect during the Battle of Britain and was equally crucial during the siege of Malta.

It is said that no battle plan survives the first day of battle. When it came to dogfights all there ever could be were rehearsed tactics, airborne radio orders from the squadron leader, so as to preserve some semblance of command and control, and beyond that there were the split-second instinctual reactions of the pilots drawing on every ounce of their skill, training and experience in a raw mechanical dance of death. This repeated scenario over the skies of Malta would rapidly morph into a high-speed chaotic hell in which the most skilful could nevertheless make their own luck.

As Eamon was flying as wingman on the left of his flight, he was the last to swoop and join the fray. By the time he arrived several Messerschmitt 109s had peeled off and were climbing, trying to circle and get behind the now-broken formation of Spitfires. It was evident that a number of aircraft were already engaged in dogfights. Eamon found himself above a Juncker 88. He nosed down and fired, and as he swept past he could see the Luftwaffe aircraft's engine on fire.

Eamon then rapidly turned and gained altitude again. Then, as he swooped back with the sun now higher in the sky, he found himself above and to the left of a Messerschmitt 109 that had apparently just made a similar manoeuvre. He was about four hundred yards away, which was usually close enough for comfort and where Eamon would normally fire the cannons, but now he was already in the turn. He felt a kind of graceful inevitability about continuing, as though trapped in a choreographed moment of harmony with the enemy aircraft, as their parabolic trajectories seemed destined to intersect and with their airspeeds similarly intertwined.

Eamon felt a surge of adrenalin, but also a cold resolve welled up within; he knew this was the moment he had longed for, the moment he had practised in his dreams and in his training and re-enacting the insights Screwball had passed to him.

The instant was a gift to him, some greater force saying, 'Here you are, this is the situation you wanted so badly, so get on with it.'

The weird thing was when Eamon later recalled this moment, even though he knew without a shadow of doubt that all those thoughts had gone through his mind, he realised there could never have been the time to process the whole encyclopaedia of ideas and emotions that were captured.

And he remembered peering at the enemy canopy as though it was taking an age, watching the solitary pilot, sensing that he was isolated, vulnerable, within his grasp, somehow fixed in suspended animation, dead before the kill.

At two hundred yards turning adjacent he could see the German pilot clearly grimacing with awareness of Eamon's dangerous tactical advantage, as he was perched above his shoulder. Eamon pressed the cannon button with two short bursts a shade in front of Messerschmitt 109's propeller blade. In a flash the Spitfire was swooping across the beleaguered enemy aircraft. As it exploded, Eamon saw the cockpit first turn red with blood and gore and then turn to an inferno as the fuel tank ruptured.

How can a split-second glance at the moment of annihilation of another be so intense in its horror?

Two rapid time frames from a cognitively alert airman: firstly, seeing his adversary desperately adjusting his controls to get out of imminent danger and then in the next frame his enemy's exploding face, brains, blood and eyeballs eviscerated in the charnel cockpit. How is it possible to process that sequence in a millisecond travelling at a speed of 350 miles an hour?

15th October 1942, RAF Ta Kali

Dear Mum and Dad,

It has been hard going, but I have received good report from the squadron commander and they have granted me a commission to pilot officer. To tell you the truth it does not particularly raise my spirits. I look forward to being out of here. I hope against hope for peace and would more than anything like to become a musician, maybe even train as a teacher. I am in a low mood and realistically do not see an end to all of this.

We may be 'Panglosses' but I am less inclined to the myth than ever. I never felt that we had some pre-ordained propensity to view the world we inhabit as the best of possible places, and the wretchedness of this place and the horrors of the Blitz have given full justification to my view. I would not say this to David for fear of disavowing any false sense he may have, as faith in such a myth may even be a source of strength, maybe that is how it works?

I will write again soon.

Love,
Eamon

Two days later Eamon was again in action when there was an intercept of another squadron of Messerschmitt 109s. Just before the formation broke to swoop. Eamon felt a paralysis. His mind was telling him this was not for him. He aimlessly threw his aircraft around the sky without being aware of either his comrades or the enemy; he pressed the cannons for a full fifteen seconds, exhausting his armaments; the altimeter needle moved round to the right as he flew higher and higher, reaching twenty-five thousand feet; and then, recklessly, he did that which he had always avoided and deliberately stalled the aircraft into a bullet drop, instantaneously causing a rapid loss of altitude in an uncontrollable spin.

More through luck than skill Eamon somehow, by about five thousand feet, had cut the throttle right back, used his rudders to counter the spin and then, once straightened, had throttled up and flown out of his predicament. While his mind was in torment, practice and intuition or survival instinct had somehow kicked in and saved him.

The sun-drenched clear blue sky offered a panoramic vista of the island of Malta as he approached across the sparkling Mediterranean. By the time he had straightened up and regained control he was flying at two thousand feet. He could see the sheer face of the Dingli cliffs looming up just a couple of miles away. Within seconds the cliff face had become large. He was now flying just a whisper above the sea, waving his wings as though in some kind of victory roll.

This time there was intent: full throttle to 350 miles an hour, now at less than a hundred feet and a second from the now-huge solid limestone wall. He closed his eyes – at last, annihilation, the peace and serenity of oblivion. There could have been no way out. By the laws of physics, by his velocity, by the relative masses of the aircraft and the cliff face, by the strength and toughness of the aircraft's superstructure and the soft plasticity of his anatomy, all that could be left would be a flattened, mangled wreck at the base of the cliff and mortal remains reduced to meat that had been through a butcher's mincer wrapped in a ragged, blood-soaked flying suit.

Peace and serenity there was, but not oblivion. A light breeze bristled across the field. The sun warmed the plane's canopy. The Spitfire had come to rest amongst grapevines, the juice of which oozed out across the wings, which were flat on the ground. This was not intuitive survival. Some force or fate had countered Eamon's deliberate action. It is a matter of choice whether the event could be attributed to divine intervention or simply that the weather conditions momentarily included a freak thermal uplift as a result of localised climate. On approaching the hot land, sea air may be driven upwards like an escalator lift. The aircraft was light after flying aimlessly for an hour and thereby had an empty fuel tank. Because of this and the fact that he had discharged all his armaments, there could be no inferno on crash landing. So he remained alive, seemingly unable to escape the demons that plagued him.

He was soon rescued by Air Force emergency services and was required to file a full report of his flying time on that sortie. He did not try to disguise what had happened, even if his fellow squadron members might have preferred he had treated just as a blip.

The CO immediately referred Eamon to the doctor and this felt like a reprieve, as though someone was understanding his inner torment. In the doctor's office the extent of Eamon's emotional meltdown became evident in a desperate, tearful, emotional rant as he held on to the doctor's coat while demanding an explanation for the barbarity of the enterprise they were engaged in.

'This world is such a fucking cruel place. To survive we beast ourselves, we are trained to numb our sensibilities to kill or be killed. What does that say about our nature? What does it say about our civilisation to resort to the same barbarism as our enemies? How does that preserve those finer human attributes that we rightly hold so dear?'

And so Eamon was signed off by the doctor as suffering from combat stress. He was grounded and placed on an aircraft to Gibraltar. From there he was flown to RAF Halton. This was not regarded as leave; as a serving airman, his orders were to proceed as notified. While he longed to return to his parents in Wigan, he directed to attend the Hollymore Military Hospital at Northfield in Birmingham, under the psychiatric supervision of Lieutenant Colonel JD Pearce. After a few months he was moved to Guy's Hospital, where the psychiatrist Air Commodore Gillespie specialised in the particular combat neuroses of air crew.

6

Eamon's Psychiatric Treatment and Beyond

I

The regime felt neither medical nor military, although all the patients without exception were military. New ideas of psychotherapy and psychoanalysis were practised with an emphasis on restoring confidence and initiative through communal therapy sessions, a club-like association with informal games aimed at empowerment through involvement of the patients in the organisation of events.

Strict hierarchies were not evident. If there was chain of command it was subtle. In particular, a great effort was made to remove the power dynamic that inevitably exists between doctor and patient. The idea was that in this environment patients felt more inclined to revisit traumatic events that had paralysed their minds. The aim was to tackle neurotic disability as a communal problem, with a view to instilling self-respect and personal responsibility; as the psychiatrist liked to explain, 'abreaction' was the process of discharge of emotion attached to repressed experience.

Eamon found himself in daily sessions of 'talking therapy'. The only perversity in this eminently sensible regime was the overriding objective to restore men to battle-readiness so that they could be sent back to their squadrons and so revisit the terrors that had tormented their minds in the first place. This lacuna in official reasoning was, for Eamon, irreconcilably conflicted.

'They can convince you that you are battle fit, you can convince them that you are battle fit, but battle fit means reversion to the beasting and bastardisation of parade-ground drills and assault courses, of barracks, bull and sergeant majors, of hot and cold, of building you up and knocking you down, of feeding you and then exhausting you, of dropping you in ice-cold water and depriving you of food: all the stuff that made you fit, tough and resilient; all the stuff that made you battle-ready. That was the measure of the man. That was where the talking therapy should take you back to.'

All this meant switching off the mechanisms that made the idea of killing other human beings utterly repellent. Even after that, battle-ready meant pepping up as ordered on amphetamines and then taking downers to grab some sleep, the chemically controlled super battle-fit mind; battle-ready meant the oxymoron of a fiercely focused, functional, dysfunctional, messed-up mind. Who in their right mind would wish to succeed in a talking therapy designed to take them to such a place?

For the first couple of months he remained angry and withdrawn, suspicious of those around him; particular neuroses were a recurring nightmare of being enmeshed in the same burning blood and gore cockpit with the exploding German's head enveloping him, as though they were merged as one person. In killing the other pilot, he inevitably killed himself. Secondly, there was an all-pervading paranoia that the object of the exercise was a test of his loyalty and patriotism, that he was viewed with suspicion, as a coward and traitor on account of claiming to be ill.

Eventually, he found some comfort in participating in group sessions relating to shared experiences. His trust grew; angst and terror incrementally unravelled. He played piano for the group at the hospital club, interludes pivotal to recuperation.

One day he was asked directly about his experiences and whether he was willing to share them. He had felt humbled and privileged to hear the inner torments that had visited fellow patients through warfare. He felt ready to talk, to describe how he had come to try and kill himself.

He described the Liverpool Blitz and the burning anger and resentment of the Nazis that this had sparked, feelings that the mere fact of war had not hitherto stirred in him. This had been all the stimulus and encouragement he had needed to become a killer in air war. He described how his aggressive feelings were encouraged as part of his training and very much viewed by his superiors as a good attitude, 'the proper adjustment for a military man'.

He described how he was billeted with Screwball, who mentored him in air war, dogfights and gunnery. He discussed how Screwball expressed an intense hatred of the enemy, which he felt had a greater vitriol than his own, and he wondered how and why this should be, as the Germans had never bombed Vancouver, so there could be no deep, personal reason to hate them.

He wondered whether it was all really a game of acute skill and nerve to Screwball? Did killing the enemy have no effect on him? Did he really lack empathy of other human beings, whether they were German, Italian or whatever? Was that what a true psychopath was?

The doctor stated that Screwball was not his patient and suggested he was a man of great resilience; yet Eamon knew that

Screwball had become irritable and had been shipped out for insubordination. Did that conduct count for anything? Did it betray any underlying battle stress in the air ace?

There was then a discussion about the difference between a psychopath and Screwball.

He discussed the family connection with the spurious Panglossian philosophy and then puzzled aloud how the hell and thunder of air war during the siege of Malta was for Screwball as good as it could ever be. Screwball had told Eamon that he would give ten years of his life to relive the fortnight in July 1942, when he shot down so many enemy aircraft in the skies over Malta, an island obliterated by bombing and starvation. How on earth could that be for him the best of all possible worlds?

Eamon went into his home life, about his cousin David and talked fondly of his young cousin Cecil who had died of diphtheria, simply because of the damp, inadequate housing of the working class in Liverpool. He talked of how Cecil had at a tender age thrived and was loved for his wit, charm and vitality amidst the slums and dilapidation of Toxteth.

And then Eamon mused on Cecil's ultimate gesture of courage, that notwithstanding the ferocity of his fever as foul bacteria devoured his spirited little body, he had made himself get out of bed and dance and sing for the little girl so ill in the next bed, and how that was Cecil's last performance on this earth. Maybe that too, for Cecil, that selfless sacrifice, was the best of all possible worlds?

Lieutenant Colonel Tom Main, another psychiatrist at Guys, widened the scope of the experiment to include everyone in the hospital, coining the term 'therapeutic community'. He later wrote: 'The treatment of the neurotic patient, who suffers from a disturbance of social relationships, cannot therefore be regarded as satisfactory unless it is undertaken within a framework of social reality which can provide him with opportunities for attaining fuller social insight and for expressing and modifying his emotional drives according to the demands of real life… An attempt is then made to reinforce the ego by strong suggestion, and to "come to terms with reality"… [The soldier] is told that he has come through the incident safely, that he must try and extricate himself from the past, that as he succeeds in doing this, so the tension causing the impediment [movement and speech disorders] will go.'

The York Clinic at Guy's Hospital had been set up by Air Commodore Robert Gillespie, who had written a paper entitled 'Psychological effects of war on citizen and soldier'. He had been recruited into the Air Force on the outbreak of war and first posted to the RAF Officers' Hospital, Torquay, to investigate the nature of breakdown among air crew.

The experience of treating men with no history of mental illness and who did not fall into the traditional asylum diagnoses led Gillespie to consider social and cultural factors in the causation and treatment of psychoneuroses. His programme was designed to treat 'psychological illnesses of all kinds, from the mildest condition commonly called "nerves" to the more severe illnesses involving mental alienation'. The York Clinic ostensibly only accepted voluntary patients.

Gillespie committed suicide at the end of the war.

Eamon remained at the York Clinic far longer than he had anticipated and much longer than most other patients. Many of his cohort were transferred to other hospitals for 'alternative medical treatments', which he understood to include electroconvulsive therapy or psychotropic drugs designed to induce seizures. A number did return to their fighting units, while a few were assigned alternative duties away from front-line engagement. Others were simply discharged from the services on medical grounds.

Eamon was not entirely sure where he stood in all this. On the one hand he remained nominally a patient for nearly two years and yet for half of that period his modus operandi was as a kind of social mentor or agony aunt offering tea and sympathy. This was made more conducive by the organising of an afternoon 'happy hour' with piano concerts. No one was trying to disavow him of his now-entrenched anti-war views nor of his fundamental reasoning on the lunacy of the raison d'être of the establishment. He was also given a rail pass to visit his family. He was still a serving officer in the RAF and respected the obligations that imposed on him. He always returned after a few days away. In a way he felt useful, that to some extent he was making a difference to the lives of mentally disintegrated air crew that he met on the ward. And he was still being paid his salary.

In early 1945 Eamon was finally discharged from York Clinic. He was given a rail pass to return to RAF Halton. The war was now moving towards defeat of the Nazis. With the Normandy landings a few months earlier the Allies were now sweeping throughout Europe, progressively liberating large tracks of the continent.

If he had imagined that an honourable discharge into civilian life would follow within days, he was mistaken. Instead, he was advised of a formal posting as a training officer instructing new recruits in basic flight training on Tiger Moth biplanes, the type of aircraft he had learnt to fly in years earlier. He was surprised that the authorities would again trust him in the air, let alone with a student in tow. Apart from anything else, he had developed a slight nervous twitch. This was not a facial twitch, like a squint of the eye or an involuntary movement of the mouth, as he had noted was the case with one or two of his contemporaries. Rather, with Eamon the movement was bodily and discrete, but nevertheless over time would become quite evident. It was actually more of a flinch than a twitch and would cause his right shoulder to drop ever so slightly. It was perhaps the rapidity rather than the extent of the movement that made it discernible.

What was remarkable and reassuring once back in the cockpit with the engine turning and chocs away, was that the twitch, or flinch, as it more precisely was, disappeared, only to recommence once he was safely back on terra firma.

And by this time he had discovered that a few of the other former fighter pilots tasked with similar duties had issues that made his own mental frailty pale to a mere trifle. Whenever one of his colleagues walked into a room he invariably brought with him an unmistakeable waft of alcohol, a scent that also made its way into the cockpit. If that was bad enough, a couple of pilots actually had hands that trembled.

It is one of those forgotten statistics that of all the tragic loss of air crew during the war, a considerable percentage died during training rather than when engaged in enemy combat.

It was bad form to make too much of his battle stress, of his mental breakdown. His station commander felt that emphasis on psychiatric issues would only hinder his opportunities to find employment in civvy street. He had done his bit and the war was fast coming to a close as the Allies pushed the Germans back to their bombed-out bunkers in Berlin. Over the coming months there would be multitudes of broken men trying to pick up the pieces and quietly reintegrate into civil society. Their collective silence meant that the horrors they witnessed revisited them in nightmares that remained inaccessible to others. What was it about these morose and withdrawn men, alarmingly mercurial as their irrational laughter would in a flash turn to anger and despair and they would take offence at an innocuous comment in polite society?

Eamon always felt that it was his piano-playing that kept him in the RAF once hostilities had ceased. After VE Day, it was not his flying that his commanding officer was interested in but rather his contribution to the celebration. His honourable discharge finally arrived without any great ceremony. Eamon resigned his commission, bought a two-piece suit and trilby, and returned to civvy street. It was Christmas of 1945.

He had been given a cheque for his back pay, plus flying

pay that had yet to be credited to his account. Before arriving in Wigan the train stopped at Liverpool Lime Street. After his time in Malta, the few broken, bombed-out buildings looked mild compared with what he had become used to during his brief, seemingly eternal stay on that island in the Med.

II

Back home, the grimy familiarity of the streets and roads and parks, the smells of the bakers and the butchers and the waterway beckoned with a curious beauty. It was a moment of joy; there was a strange, long-lost elation welling up as he walked from the station to his home. The liberating goodness and peace he could feel translated within him into a physical sensation that slowly enveloped his being, manifesting as an intense pain in his temples, and from this followed a stream of involuntary tears cascading down the returning airman's face. This cathartic moment, hitherto inaccessible, even in the prolonged therapy of a psychiatric hospital, moved Eamon's spirit as though a new dawn where all he had been through seemed to make sense and he knew there could be hope for a future, dare one say, a place where he might be happy again?

His arrival surprised his mum and they had to await David's return from school and his dad's finishing at the garage. But that evening was special. Moira conjured an excellent meal from the vegetables from the garden and the scrags of meat available for purchase at the butchers.

Eamon was in no hurry to move on. For a year he was pleased just to help out at the garage and rekindle old friendships and meet up with family, although he had decided music was what he wanted to do with his life. It transported his mind, made him forget, made him content, and it made other people happy and he was good at it. In post-war Liverpool there was no shortage of singers having an impromptu sing-song around a pub piano.

Folk had been gathering around the piano to raise their spirits for decades, and even though radio had made the upright not quite the essential item of furniture in the living room that it had once been, it very much remained so in the local pubs. This for any aspiring piano player was usually as good as it got. As for paid professional pianists, it was neither the time nor the place. The big bands could swing with their four sections of percussion, rhythm, saxophone and trumpet without a pianist. A rare example was Count Basie, whom Eamon particularly admired.

Eamon nevertheless had sufficient mastery of the ivories; he could read music and with great facility also to play by ear. As a result, he eventually secured a season in the cocktail lounge at the Adelphi Hotel on Ranelagh Street, in the centre of Liverpool, playing to all the transient rich folk as they prepared to embark for New York. He found the selection of requests rather pedestrian and would have much rather stepped up the gear with some jazz improvisation. While there, he wrote a tune called 'Turtle Soup' based on the Adelphi's fame for traditionally making the dish.

Eamon, perhaps for purposes of self-promotion, or maybe he just could not get it out of his head, kept playing the tune, to the palpable chagrin of a number of the guests, who wanted 'A Nightingale Sang in Berkeley Square', or 'Danny Boy', or 'Chattanooga Choo Choo'. Anyway, despite his obvious competence, Eamon's contract was not renewed. He played a few local gigs with Lita Roza, but her star was looking up and she joined the Harry Roy Orchestra, going on to greater things, finding fame with 'How Much Is That Doggie in the Window', ultimately a song that embarrassed her so much that she eventually refused to perform it.

He then found himself doing a couple of rehearsals with Hank Walters, but it was all country-style guitars and a piano player really did not fit in. It seemed that a lot of grassroots, bombed-out venues in Liverpool were getting people through the door to listen to young men playing guitars. Eamon thought it was laughable and realised that it was obviously just a fad that would not last, but he was not prepared to hang around while it did.

One evening on his way to catch the train back to Wigan, he was taken with the versatility and breadth of emotion he could hear in someone in a street nearby, really putting the vibes through the gears. He turned the corner; under a streetlight outside a pub, he saw an African man in the distance, playing the alto sax. He was spellbound by the sound and stood and listened, then put a shilling in his case. When the tune had finished Eamon told the saxophonist how moved he was by the playing and explained he too was a musician, inviting the busker for a pint. The man's name was Earl King and he was an Afro-American from Chicago, Illinois. He had been demobbed and had decided to travel to India, where he heard there was a 'good jazz scene and folks didn't have no prejudice with black men'. He was heading to meet up with Chic Chocolate and Rudy Jackson and tour, playing some in gigs in Bombay, Goa and Calcutta.

He planned to travel cheap on his demob money and any cash he could earn busking. Cunard-White Star line had ships travelling to the Near and Far East. Even by 1948 troops, ex-POWs and displaced British citizens were being repatriated and so it was possible to get a cheap outward journey, as long as you were not planning to return anytime soon. In that pub, on that rainy evening, Earl King, the busker, gave Eamon an impromptu audition as Eamon played some freestyle jazz improvisation on the piano and Earl accompanied on his sax. Earl said he was hired, it was a deal, but Eamon would have to chip in the rest of Earl's fare. Eamon was heading to India.

For a couple of years Eamon and Earl toured before doing a season at the Fairlawn Hotel, in Calcutta, where it was regally declared that during the 1940s, 'there was no unpleasant music, only jazz'. Jazz ruled the social scene, and stalwarts like Duke Ellington and Dizzy Gillespie played in venues packed to the rafters. These were good times. What mattered was the music, the style; for a brief while no one seem to care about caste, race or religion. That was how it appeared to Earl, who had known his share of racist bigotry back home in Chicago. He felt welcome; he liked being a foreigner in India. It was a time when foreign was good, and things that happened abroad were great. One well-respected Indian hotel manager would say, 'Calcutta was like Las Vegas or New Orleans!'

In a few short years the same hotel manager would say ruefully that for a while anyway it was a part of the country's culture that had been lost in transition rather than translation.

In the midst of the bloodbath and anarchy that reigned during the terrifying events of Partition Eamon decided to fly to Bombay and then travel on to Goa. As a European and a jazz man, he felt an immunity, a disconnection from the misery and slaughter that befell the sub-continent in that tumultuous swell of the late 1940s. After all, it was not his war. He had already had his fair share and, while feeling embarrassment for British incompetence in blindly orchestrating the mayhem and then making a speedy exit, he remained politically and emotionally detached. Actually, his detachment went further. Something in his mind shut down to prevent him even comprehending the terror evident along the roads as he travelled from his hotel to the airport. Yes, he did drive past rotting corpses, mutilated bodies, hordes of starving, dispossessed and displaced people. These things were visible to his eyes yet blanked to his mind.

Besides, India was always a frantic place of dense human interaction. The spectre of animal carcasses and human cadavers, charred, incomplete cremations from multi-various funeral pyres along the Ganges, was a familiar sight, as was the thinly disguised stench of death that would rise and waft with the rising heat of the day. The corpses he saw only became comprehensible to him as dead cattle, not people; the dispossessed he only saw as commuters and traders going about their daily business. To see and not see, to be a witness and turn a blind eye may have made Eamon susceptible to accusations of callous acquiescence or even cowardice. But this was not the case, as he really did not mentally assimilate and process the horrors paraded before his senses on that journey.

He had friends in Goa. The atmosphere there was a friendly, heady mix of Indian and European. The music was good there too and he liked the food; he believed he would be more settled in the Portuguese-Indian Catholic community, with whose culture the region was imbued.

7

David's Schooling

Wigan is a town in the gravitational sway of Manchester but is its own place. At first David found it fairly nondescript in comparison to Liverpool's sprawling maelstrom of greatness, misery and social contradictions. By comparison the street where Pat and Moira lived could be described as sedate. And yet, it was Wigan, not Manchester, Leeds or Liverpool where George Orwell chose to write his biopic on the conditions of the working class in England in the 1940s.

Life in Pat and Moira's household was very different to Monro Street. While there was an unspoken sadness, David also felt that his aunt and uncle made a great effort to try and compensate for his loss and he appreciated this. It was, of course, not their fault and besides, Eamon, their only son, had been so changed by war, and it distressed them greatly to watch him battle his demons. When he decided to live abroad it felt like a bereavement to his parents, but there was also tranquillity and moments of understated fun and amusement.

When he was twelve years old the war had finally ended. Victory in Europe remained a special day that David would always celebrate. For him it had the redemptive impact of any feast day, even Christmas. It was a day of hope; it happened to be springtime, and he would associate it with new foliage appearing on the trees and seasonal blossoms, with their fragrances filling the air with newness, rebirth, rejuvenation. Yes, there was a future and the dark clouds of war could be lifted. It was one of those happy, significant moments; something that went some way to quell the enormity of the emotional deficit that had torn him apart those few years earlier.

It was also the time when he was offered a place at the local grammar school. He had sat the competitive test without actually fully appreciating what it was about and had done well enough to be offered a place. David tended to spend many hours in his room doing puzzles and, just for the sake of it, working through a book of arithmetical problems. Moira and Pat were proud of him and went out of their way to build his self-esteem by telling him what a great achievement it was. They both felt that his numerical facility and logical mind had made the difference and would stand him in good stead.

As a gift on his twelfth birthday, Pat and Moira bought him his very own Swiss watch. That was a rare and precious possession in the austerity of post-war Britain. David cherished the timepiece and wore it every day, an ideal artefact for a boy who liked to know the time. If he was playing football at school, he would always hand it to the teacher for safekeeping.

One might attribute his interest in time as indication of a neurotic hyper-vigilance resulting from living through air raids prior to evacuation and the subsequent trauma of losing his parents, but it will be recalled even in the happy days of play and soap-box carting David was always Cecil's timekeeper.

It is doubtful much can be gained in presenting a detailed narrative of those intervening post-war school days, of old red-brick school buildings with high ceilings, duck-egg blue painted walls and huge Victorian radiators that often did not work. It serves little purpose to recall the monotony of double Latin on a Tuesday afternoon, or science classes with exploding jars and failed experiments with dodgy Bunsen burners or the smell of sweaty feet as uncoordinated, gangly, acne-ridden boys attempted elaborate gymnastics in the gym. And while it is often said that all pupils remember one teacher whose encouragement had a positive formative effect, so influencing a career choice, this is probably an exaggeration and in a lot of cases does not apply at all, as was David's experience.

Yet his school days cannot just be skipped over. They were a time of learning and revelation, not just for David in his discovery of the world around him but also about David for those educators and carers charged with his welfare.

The time that David spent in his room occupied with his own thoughts was not entirely beneficial to his emotional development. He could be forgiven for periods of distraction and remoteness, although it was a concern where maudlin moments might take him.

The first indication that all was not as it should be was when he started his new school, looking as fine, smart and alert as any other boy with his new, neatly pressed uniform and starched white collar and school tie.

At morning register the teacher always called surnames only, unless you were named Smith or Jones or otherwise happened to have a name shared by another member of the class, in which case first names were also called. This, of course, did not apply to David Pangloss.

At lunch break, while casually kicking a ball in the playground, the new cohort started getting to know each other.

Other boy: 'Hi, mate, what's your first name, Pangloss? Put your blazer down here for a goalpost.'

As David obliged the other boy said, 'What sort of name is Pangloss?'

David felt like being flippant. 'It is a classical name of hope and optimism, the name of a tribe that believes everything will be for the best in the best of possible worlds.'

Other boy: 'Oh, I say, you sound grand. Can't say that about my name, nothing very classical about Greenhill.'

David: 'Only joking, but really you can call me Cecil, that's my first name. I'm Cecil Pangloss.'

Greenhill: 'Nice to meet you, Cecil Pangloss.'

David: 'Nice to meet you, Greenhill.'

So to his schoolmates David became Cecil, a friendly, engaging, slightly humorous, affectionate name, within which the holder's young and ambivalent persona would make itself known in various guises to his schoolmates. On one level you have to ask, does it really matter?

After all, it often goes with the territory of juvenile development for children to try on different images of themselves; different personalities emerge and subside. On another level, that simple declaration by David was a symptom of some complex aberration within.

There had been limited research into the phenomenon of the 'necronym', the naming of someone after a dead relative, an occurrence that attracts a particular poignancy when the deceased is an elder sibling. And in David's case this curious artifice was entirely auto-referential.

There was another pattern of behaviour that caused concern. Some mornings David would set off to school with, in addition to his satchel of books, a fully packed suitcase, as though he was travelling somewhere or even moving house. Moira, who had witnessed him do something similar soon after he moved to Wigan, had stopped him on a couple of occasions, but there were times when he surreptitiously managed to arrive at school with all his luggage. The other boys in the class thought he was being a joker, just doing it to wind the form master up.

It was inevitable that this and the 'naming issue' would eventually be the subject of comment, and so following a parents' evening the schoolmaster quietly took Pat and Moira aside. Shocked and perturbed, but also defensive of their young charge, they enquired as to why he was doing these strange things. They said David did not pretend to be Cecil when at home. As a result a referral was made to the local education authority's school medical officer, who then wrote to the educational psychology child psychiatric services. Post-war child psychology in health and education was soon recognised as a necessary area for development; David was far from being the only child coping with trauma as a result of war-time family loss and breakdown.

The psychologist, Dr Baker, said he found it an interesting case.

He viewed taking a suitcase to school as fairly predictable. The crushing upheavals had for David somehow become the norm; in his mind emotional wrenches are to be expected. That is just the way life is, that is what it is; extremes assume a kind of normality, experiences someone with such tender years might just have to accept. The starting at a new school may have triggered anxiety that made those feelings more intense and resulted in him so acting. It was a behaviour that would and did rectify itself.

The use of Cecil's name, the doctor concluded, was essentially an identity problem, complicated by grief and sad gratitude.

He embarked on talking therapy with David. He responded to the probing questions in a full and articulate way. This in itself was a positive first step.

David: 'I used to stand in my room in front of the mirror and say out loud, "I am Cecil. There is no loss. I do not cry."'

Dr Baker said that this was described by an oxymoron, as an absent presence.

David: 'I don't feel like a substitute for Cecil. I chose to be Cecil. I was wearing his name in place of him. It was kind of comforting, as though he was with me, alive in me, sort of like what the priest would say about Jesus at mass. Then when we visited the cemetery and saw the headstones, I could look at my mum and dad's and could feel the pain of loss that had lasted for so long, but it was as though Cecil's name was not there. I did not want to take it in. It did not seem right. Cecil was fine. I was Cecil.

'I didn't want to do things differently, but I knew there were things that I liked that Cecil did not do. I knew I had sinful feelings about Agnes that Cecil told me he didn't. I know that really he was a better person than me.

'It wasn't just for me. It was for my mum and dad, my mum in particular. I felt it was what they would have wanted, for Cecil to carry on and fulfil whatever it was that he was going to do. I know they loved us both, but I have this idea that when they passed away they were following Cecil because of their love for him and because of how we all believed in him as a force of nature.'

In his report the educational psychologist stated, 'Since David, of choice, adopted the necronym of his deceased older brother Cecil, this evoked the annihilation of the referent, namely Cecil, as caused by his death and the annihilation of the reference, namely, David, as caused by his choice to rename himself. The task for a young man to build his own identity is greatly complicated by his determined investment in adopting the perceived idealised image of his deceased sibling, who has in any event been transformed into a ghost of incomparable, enviable beauty and goodness, merged in an inevitably imperfect way in his own being. Ultimately, in David's taking of the necronym, he is choosing the emptiness left by death, which in logical terms as nothingness is a deeply negative concept. This results in an implosion of meaning and assuming this absence of dimension as part of one's identity, which inevitably will cause confusion and disorientation.

'There is, of course, a fault line in this, namely, David's own natural sexual impulses, that while it must make David feel at a profound level unsettled, dissatisfied and unhappy, it is also perhaps the reality check that stops a complete alienation of self, resulting in oblivion, leading to psychosis and eventual insanity.

'It cannot be ascertained with sufficient certainty, given any other psychological trauma in his life, that either the persona or ghostly alter ego of his deceased brother Cecil will not re-emerge in some shape or form or that David's suppressed self will not manifest itself in some extreme or unexpected way in the future.'

So, the wonderful vision of Agnes in the bathtub, half hidden behind a screen, was the very mischief that reminded David that he was fundamentally not the same person as his deceased, idealised, saintly sibling, and this had thereby saved him from insanity. But his little proclivity cannot just be left there and be allowed to conveniently disappear. We are obliged to follow the innocuous drama of this sexual charade further.

II

As a start it can be agreed that David's precocious interest in Agnes was much more than a mere anodyne fondness. His fascination encompassed a nascent sexual awakening, where an early juvenile inquisitiveness for what was different, what was hidden, what was in some way taboo, what was concealed behind a screen, was subsumed into his emerging sense of the erotic. This created a powerful obsession that became magnified by its very secrecy and the thoughts he could not share; indeed, the one occasion when the conflicted boy told a priest in the confessional of his 'sin', the grave nature of the aberration was spelt out and writ large in terms of eternal damnation. Yet it was the subversive quality and constraints thereby demanded that became essential to the repertoire, that dictated the rules of the game.

Agnes was five years older than David. Her earliest affections were directed towards Eamon, who was five years older than she was. Eamon seemed sophisticated and grown up; he was well dressed, not boastful but kind and friendly to Cecil and David. He liked to hear their news and what they were up to, and he would sit down at the piano and fill the room with wonderful music.

Agnes, often out and about at weekends, would conveniently happen to be waiting on the doorstep when Eamon was expected, or if he was sitting in the front parlour, she would have to brush past him to collect something she had forgotten. He would glance up and momentarily smile at her before continuing his dialogue with Cecil and David or Deirdre or Harry. For Eamon the eye contact and smile was without subtext or consequence, whereas Agnes made a vivid mental note, as though the moment was a significant milestone towards some future dalliance.

If there had ever been a fledgling spark, it was soon lost in those tragic childhood years. After her evacuation, which thankfully also saved her from the fateful bombing, Agnes never returned to Liverpool. She lost all touch with David and with Eamon. She married a doctor and developed a love of horses and was often to be found riding across the open fields. In the meantime, David remained living with Pat and Moira.

The forties and fifties were a time of ration cards and austerity, yet the majority of working-class families had for generations lived on the poverty line anyway. But it was a time of peace, a new beginning, a time of hope, the advent of the National Health Service, an effective welfare system, of building new homes, a time for recognition of workers' rights within the industrial process.

Occasionally, on Saturdays if Pat was not doing overtime and United were playing at home, he would drive David up to Old Trafford to watch a game. Pat and Moira always made sure there was a holiday at the seaside each year. Blackpool was a fun place to go. They tended to check in to the same guest house each year, on the front and with a car parking space.

The go-carts were a favourite and David would while away hours in the amusements arcade. He rarely bothered with the gambling machines but spent much of his pocket money on the section 'What the Butler Saw', as he would idle away an afternoon with his eyes glued to a mutoscope, watching a saucy movie created by winding a handle which flicked a bundle of cards in quick succession.

There was no proscription on who used these machines, although the content was adult, with antique images of ladies caught in various stages of undress or more recent glossy-coloured images from America of women with big hair, rouge red lipstick and high heels doing explicit strip shows. David would then have his fortune told by a dummy in a kiosk called 'Zelda'. The automaton would move its hand over cards which then reveal what the future held.

Later, when David's life had moved on he looked back with amusement at those happy juvenile interludes.

8

Starting Out:
Work and Marriage

I

David, from the moment he set out on his own into the world, was guided by a desire for security and stability, both in personal relationships and material wellbeing. Unlike many young men of his age, he was never visited by that intoxicating exuberance for freedom and adventure at the expense of planning for the future. His modus operandi was to avoid risk, so living in the moment was rarely an option, which was a pity because, after all, that is where living is done. But then, if your primal expectation presents you with complete uncertainty, where there should be no expectation that your home and familial connections will be preserved from teatime to breakfast, is that not reason enough to be psychologically invested in the future at the expense of the present?

At the age of sixteen David left Wigan Grammar School with decent passes in his school certificate examinations.

While he could have stayed on to study some specialist subjects in more detail with a view to going to university, such a trajectory had never been on his radar, as was the case for most of his cohort. The anticipated aspirational path was either to get an apprenticeship in an established trade, which often meant toiling in blue overalls in a factory accumulating oil and grime under fingernails, or alternatively work in an office and get trained in some administrative job and earn good money.

It is true he had been tempted by Pat to become a car mechanic. He had developed an interest in cars and engines and appreciated the skill and ingenuity of understanding the engineering precision and beauty of the internal combustion engine. Even though his choice was to aim for a white-collar job, doing up and maintaining old motor vehicles as a hobby remained a life-long passion for him. This greatly pleased Pat. It reaffirmed the genuine practical impact in the nurturing of the orphaned young man.

He was offered a job with Prudential Insurance as a trainee broker. While for the first couple of years he was a glorified tea boy, then a post boy running errands, it was an opportunity to listen to the conversations and see what paperwork was generated. David, a bright lad and good at figures, soaked it all up.

What appealed to David was that there was a man-made arrangement that could guarantee the future; there was paperwork, which meant if your plans did not work out, if anything happened to people, to loved ones, to houses, cars, property, then it could all be sorted out. There were contingencies in place. You could get financial recompense. Of course, you cannot replace people – money cannot do that – but maybe, if it was appreciated in advance that if people were so valuable then perhaps they would look after themselves better and other people and nations would treat them with more respect?

The Life and Life of David Pangloss

Even so, none of this prevented disease and illness and earthquakes... all the terrible things beyond reach that were listed in the exclusion causes, the 'acts of God'.

As he had never been able to rationalise either the abrupt death of Cecil or of his parents, he pinched himself to realise it was naïve to indulge in a kind of escapism and think that such a loss could somehow be equated with money. There was, though, a residual comfort in such amelioration. For him the insurance industry was the way out and he was prepared to burn the midnight oil to pass his associate exams of the Chartered Institute of Insurers, which he completed in 1957.

Pat had given David a wreck of a 1947 Riley CMC convertible, which David held on to, restored to its former glory and kept for the rest of his life. It was a magnificent specimen; while of course not aspiring to be anything as grand as a Bugatti, it had a British charm and authenticity that made a statement of the style of a bygone era. All of the chrome work re-coated, a respray in deep scarlet, a new white canvas hood and a reupholstered white leather interior. The engine had been taken apart and reconditioned, with new pistons and a re-bore of the engine block, the timing calibrated, new gaskets, new wheels, and the dashboard and instrument panel polished. The car ran as though new from the factory.

The years passed. David became the young man about town, pretty much a down-to-earth Lancashire lad, who was outwardly straightforward, if anything perhaps too disarming in the transparency of his petty foibles. That was how he lost a couple of girlfriends. On such occasions it was always more a matter of heady disinhibition, of reckless posturing, a temporary abandonment of perspective, rather than any lack of moral compass or understanding of social cues.

For a start, inviting young ladies that he met to share the thrill of the sleazy seaside mutoscope at Blackpool did nothing for his social standing. It did not occur to him that his girlfriends were not interested in what the butler saw. One young woman nicknamed him 'Perv'.

But even if he was prone to occasional mood swings and phases of maudlin introspection, he was otherwise by nature polite, intelligent, presentable, with good job prospects and a well-maintained open-topped Riley. He enjoyed car rallies and touring. During the football season he would often go with Pat to watch Everton or Manchester United play.

As it was, he found himself in his late twenties unattached, which really did not bother him that much. When in 1959 his company offered him a job at their office in Berkshire he was ready to move on.

II

Then there was Edwina, the goddess who waltzed into David's life after he was persuaded to attend a CND meeting in1960. In David's mind the use of the term 'goddess' was not such an exaggeration given the impossibly idealised pedestal that he initially placed her upon. If she had stayed there, if he had not been able to shift from that paralysing vision of perfection, then their relationship could never have happened. This can be said because David knew the tragedy of earlier lost opportunities, of being gripped by a paralysis at the crucial point when a man needs to seize the moment and effectively communicate his interest.

It was a time when David was encouraged to join the Campaign for Nuclear Disarmament by Eamon, who in his Christmas and birthday cards and letters home usually included some cautionary post-script about how fragile peace was and the menace of the emerging Cold War. Eamon described the 'Pacific Proving Grounds', the name given by the United States government to a number of sites in the Marshall Islands and a few other places in the Pacific Ocean where it conducted nuclear testing between 1946 and 1962.

David did not need much convincing. For an insurance man invested in preserving stability the television adverts telling people what to do in the event of a nuclear war, as well as news footage of British soldiers being exposed to hydrogen bomb test explosions in the Marshall Islands, was all the impetus neeed for him to join the pacifists on their protest marches.

The first meeting he attended was in Trafalgar Square. He was for a while taken with the passion, sincerity and rhetoric of the keynote speakers, Peggy Duff and Sidney Hinkes, who introduced Bertrand Russell to give a brief, insightful address. There were then some folk songs, 'That Bomb Has Got to Go' by Peggy Seeger and Ewan McCol, and, of course, Seeger's de rigueur protest anthem 'We Shall Overcome'.

For a man of controlled passions, David found himself quite fired up by the event. He had driven in from Slough and parked at Kew before getting the District Line, changing at Embankment then to Charing Cross, emerging into the Easter afternoon sun and heaving crowds swelling around Nelson's Column.

He hardly remembered his journey back to Kew, so full was his head of Armageddon and we shall overcome. But when he found himself back at his car he became aware of the quiet, just an occasional vehicle in the distance, then some intermittent birdsong. For no real reason, other than that he was a young man with time on his hands, free to do as he wished, he decided to spend the rest of the late afternoon wandering around the gardens.

In the Palm House the air was warm and humid, as though he had wandered into a tropical rainforest. Little robins and wrens had taken refuge and were merrily chirping and then the incongruous sight of a sprightly little Japanese water dragon proudly strutting by the water lily en route to the papaya. Tropical fruit were everywhere in abundance; it was so tempting to tug at an inviting banana just waiting to be picked. Then there were huge palm trees and bamboo sprouting way up to the ceiling. As David ventured further into the equatorial vista he brushed past an array of vast pitcher plants, with their vegetable gullets wet and hungry for the meat caught within, slowly dissolving a carnivorous platter ranging from flies and bugs to small rodents.

There was a young woman, tall, who even in a working uniform, comprising a light vest and khaki skirt, looked smart and fashionable. She was clearly enjoying her work, standing on a ladder with some small pruning shears. The pieces she removed from the plants she placed in paper bags that she then labelled.

David moved nearer to her. Close up he could see that she hadn't shaved her armpits and had hairs that were wet with perspiration from working in the close, humid environment. Other visitors ushered past and politely manoeuvred with a hand on David's shoulder in order to navigate a path to the next specimen. This gently shoved David even closer to the young woman on the steps pruning the palms, standing so near to her he could smell the fresh wetness of her perspiration. In her elevated position he could see her legs exposed to the knee. She was not wearing stockings and when she shifted he, despite his best efforts, got a view of her pink knickers. The woman on the steps then slightly lost a footing on a step and in momentarily stabilising herself she grabbed the nearest thing, which happened to be David's shoulder. With uncharacteristic confidence he reached out with his arm to further protect the lady on the steps from falling, but as she was a foot or two above him, instead of holding her around the upper torso, his arm wrapped around the warm, giving firmness of her nubile, shapely buttocks that felt so unavoidably close and present under her light Palm Room dress. She composed herself and turned to David, who immediately let go, actually recoiling in fright at the sudden intimacy of their situation.

Through beads of sweat and with biggest bluest eyes and the most ruby-red lips and pearly sparkling teeth she said, 'Oh, thank you. Glad you were there to save me, didn't fancy landing in the bamboo.'

David was in awe, gobsmacked, a man entranced. There before him he beheld the very image of a goddess, and as she'd nearly tumbled from her pedestal he'd been the hero coming to her aid; she so perfect and vital, sensual, warm, so at home amidst the exotic environment of this tropical rainforest.

'Well, er… the pleasure's mine, really, pleased to be of use…'

There was an uneasy pause between the two of them as she gave him an endearing and welcoming glance, which in response, amazingly, David found the wit and presence of mind to persist and not let a magical moment just evaporate, which it could so easily have done. What if she had turned her head away or if he had taken one step to the side of the banana bush? That is the beauty, the tragedy, the comedy, the fleeting flux, fluency, danger and fragility of those intimate perfect romantic nanoseconds that so often dissipate into passing pangs of regret. But just occasionally, when the gods smile kindly and the souls linger for a while, long enough for kindred spirits to acknowledge and get to know each other.

This is the subtle dance of Eros that then gets forgotten in the banter and practical arrangements people indulge in during the subsequent courtly performance. When children ask their parents how they met, that intoxicating first moment is never explained. It is like the first second of universe, so brief yet packed with so much history.

David: 'You look as though you are ready for a break. Would you like a cuppa and something to eat?'

The woman walked off the steps and stacked her things neatly then turned to face David in a welcoming way. 'Well, I finish in half and hour and then need to clean up and get out of my work togs, but if you have the time to wait then yeah, thank you. Oh, by the way, what's your name? Mine is Edwina.'

David: 'Lovely to meet you, Edwina. I'm David. Shall I wait for you over in the Pavilion? I'll get the drinks in. I expect you might prefer something cool?'

Edwina: 'Well, as you're asking I wouldn't mind a gin and tonic.'

At that moment CND seemed a distant memory. He was alive with anticipation and excitement. 'My God, I think I might have a chance with the most beautiful lady in the world.'

And so the romance began, from the gallant in the Palm House to first nervous exchanges, to sips of gin and scampi and French fries with halloumi salad with tzatziki, then a walk to his fancy open-top car, to her acceptance of the offer of a lift home to her parents on that mild late spring evening, to the exchange of telephone numbers and an arrangement to see each other again.

Edwina lived in Chiswick. She was thirty-two years old, which made her five years older than David and living at home with her parents. She had been engaged but for some unspecified reason it had fallen through. David understandably assumed it was because the fiancé was not up to her expectations. Indeed at that point he feared the same about himself. By any estimation she was a striking-looking lady with wavy red hair and a fine, curvaceous body. Edwina's family was well-to-do. She even had a bit of a plum in her voice, but she was far from being a snob. She was quite an intellectual and, like many women, was more astute than the slightly innocent posturing which made her feel more comfortable socially.

She had wanted to be an actress but had studied horticulture at UCL and while a student, to earn a few extra pounds, had worked as a waitress at some restaurant in London called the Windmill. She was obviously very much into her horticulture but had a curious mix of conservatism and a slightly wilder, understated libertarian side.

Edwina probably viewed David as a rather serious, dour young man. She later admitted that she was attracted to the distant, lost look in his eyes. She also realised that he was young, well groomed, thoughtful with good prospects and obviously besotted with her. She also loved his Scouse accent, which gave her hours of amusement even though David had been making a concerted effort to flatten his vowels and consonants to southern tones, which actually made Edwina laugh all the more.

That summer of 1960 David and Edwina were inseparable. He would finish at the office in Slough and drive into Kew. In their leisure time he would learn about horticulture and she would go with him on weekend car rallies to Devon and Cornwall and the Welsh mountains. She was also persuaded by the arguments of CND and they both became members attending meetings and, on one occasion, going on a march, although the car was parked at a strategic point so that in the early evening they could drive to a quaint pub in the Berkshire countryside for a supper and drink.

The proposal and wedding were both unspectacular. They both knew they wanted to be married to each other and did not need the distraction of nuptial razzmatazz. The good taste and ambience of the garden party at the Kew Pavilion should, however, not be underestimated. What David and Edwina arranged with sensible economy would have been a dream for many couples. The fact that Edwina was on the staff meant they were offered a sizeable concession. And with the Riley, they did not need to hire a limousine; the stylish coach work, sweeping side panels, leather seats, wooden dash and retractable hood gave all the finesse the bride and groom could desire. David did make it a strict condition that no tin cans would be attached and spray paint was not to get anywhere near the vehicle. His only concession were a few coloured balloons and a little placard saying 'just married'.

It is not necessary to dwell too long on the honeymoon night. After all they had, as Edwina put it, 'already done the business'. This observation had prompted profuse protestations of love from David, assuring her of his sincerity and how he wanted to spend the rest of his life with her. His neediness and passion amused Edwina, but she loved him and was touched by his sensitivity and reassured him that his feelings were reciprocated.

The first time was at the grand mock Tudor Caer Beris Hotel built in the meander of the River Irfon just a few miles north of the Brecon Beacons. They were touring. The Riley Club had parked for the night. David had booked a large bedroom with a four-poster bed and en suite bathroom with a large bay window overlooking the car park and main entrance door to the hotel. Edwina disappeared into the luxury free-standing bathtub to soap and soak for the best part of an hour. Meanwhile David sat on the bed watching the television, wondering at one point whether a less ostentatious room to the rear of the hotel might have been better because of the rumpus outside, what with merry new arrivals whistling and jovially talking to each other.

But when Edwina later emerged clad in the scantiest night gown and lounged next to him on the four-poster he knew Christmas had arrived. They loved each other, so the intimacy had a warmth and feeling that elevated the physical interaction; while there was never any doubting the reciprocated desire, the passion remained, restrained by a socially mediated expectations of decorum and politeness that acted to quell the potential for wild, unbridled libido.

This was something they would soon overcome in their sexually charged repertoire. It should also be admitted that the four-poster bed had a very noisy spring that created a resonance first in the mattress, then the room and then, so it seemed, during the middle of night to resound through the timbers of the Tudor-style building. What initially amused the conjugating couple eventually, admittedly after hours of fun, manifested itself respectively in temporary frigidity and drooping embarrassment.

David made good progress and by the late 1960s he was running the Slough office of the insurance brokerage. He was conscientious, hard-working and he believed in the financial products he sold to his clients. Bright and knowledgeable, he acted with a refreshing professional transparency in his dealings with people. It gave him an added gravitas to be able to give his own opinion on the best current options for investment having regard to present market trends, rather than spouting spoon-fed market information handed down from the head office managers. And it turned out his prudent instincts were usually right. It might be argued that David had such an acute sense of how terrible the future can be that he left no stone unturned in charting what he believed was the most efficacious route through it. His staff used to fondly call his monthly written product briefings 'the best of all possible worlds'.

David: 'You need to care about the people you meet. Insurance is a people business. You have to like being with people, talking to people, being interested in what they do. It is the weave of an ornate blanket, networking life's rich tapestry. You do it because you like doing it, otherwise you find something else to do. And you do not just want to network with people only like yourself; you want to meet people who are not like you, who do things and have skills that are different to your own. That way you have reciprocity, you can help them, they can help you. That's the way it works. And trust me, it's not just about the money, well, not really, though there is a thing called opportunity cost. So you meet some people in a pub and none of them rich or money-minded; they just have a few bob to socialise. And finally, remember this:

'I calculate there have been one hundred generations of humans on the planet since the birth of Christ. That does not seem that much, does it? Actually a very containable, very tangible number. At a stretch, I could probably trace ten generations on either side of my family and multiply that ten times takes you back two thousand years. So then you start to believe in the notion that we all only ever, at most, six people removed from someone we are related to. And that is all you need to know to sell insurance, my dear friends.'

This narrative was typical of the impromptu pep talks David would give his team of brokers, which were always viewed as inspirational. They rang true because it was the rant of a man thinking aloud, as much to remind himself of how he was motivated to go about his business and then to be reassured that it was an attitude that worked because he had arrived at where he was.

David would explain, 'When I was starting out I got to know a few footballers, great sportsmen, but in those amateur days, even if you played centre forward for Everton it didn't mean you had loads of money. But ten years on they were managing professional teams and, of course, I was there to advise on investments and insurance. My first policy sales were to second-hand car dealers. In the fifties and sixties there was always plenty of cash to be made there. And then there was the music scene. Through my cousin I set up a number of savings and pensions contracts for people here and in India. Through that I got to know a couple of movers and shakers in the music scene in Manchester, then in London. I wanted to do something for musicians, but most of them got ripped off by promoters and record companies, but a lot of money was swishing around by the sixties. What do you do when you meet a guy who has a hit that everyone has heard on the radio and he combines his creativity with being hell-bent on self-destruction?

'It happens all the time. And I'm trying to sell a pension to protect his future and he just is not interested, just wants to trip out of his mind. How do you help someone like that? Where's the business in that? You telephone the hospital to see how he is and then get on with your business.

'But there are various ways to be loyal to people. Not everyone values keeping a neat book full of names and figures – it's just the way I am, always have been. Always needed to know how many conkers in a sack.'

While David was never much of a tough guy, neither could he be described as a nervous type. He was risk averse and never set out to stress himself. He was not interested in testing the limits of his endurance; maybe he felt life had done that for him already. More recently, his emotional apparatus got all the testing it needed by his beloved Edwina. So David much preferred operating from within a comfort zone.

Edwina wanted to carry on with her work at Kew, so there were no immediate plans to start a family; in fact the planning was that there would be no children for several years to enable them to be financially 'set up' and also to enjoy their time together with excursions, rallies and holidays. As couples go they were pretty well wrapped up in themselves, their love was exclusive for each other. The intrusion of the pitter-patter of tiny feet in those early years would have been unthinkable.

They had bought a three-bedroom detached Wimpey home with a garage and an en suite to the master bedroom. It had a good size garden on account of being a corner plot on an estate just outside Maidenhead. One of the additional bedrooms Edwina used as her workshop for her books of dried flowers. She had salvaged seeds and cuttings over the years. Pride of place was her pitcher plant which she kept in a greenhouse just outside the backdoor with the temperature and humidity carefully regulated.

David was mindful of the marketability, equity growth potential and tax-exempt capital gain on a principal private residence that would provide a good launchpad to move upmarket, as indeed they did on several occasions in the ensuing decade. This was facilitated by the concessionary interest rates that he was able to secure through working in financial services.

So life was good. There was work, there was routine, there was comfort and leisure, they had their health. They had never had it so good.

9

More About Intimacy
and Progress at Work

I

Life happens either side of the front door of a home, and inside
the home it happens in the rest of the house and then in the
bedroom, between the sheets, and then it happens in the minds of
the occupants, it happens in the restless consciousness sculpted
by the vagaries of individual biographies and the consequent
luggage that those individuals carry with them.

In exploring the story of a family, to avoid the risk of
accusations of mere prurience, there should be good reason
for enquiring into the more intimate aspects of relationships.
It is a well-established legal principle that there is no public
interest in the private lives of private individuals, even though
some jurisdictions regard public figures as not having the same
entitlement. And of course, although a successful insurance
man, David never sought to run for public office or become a
celebrity – that would have been anathema to his nature – and

so he had every right to feel their private life was in no way for a wider audience. After all, what a couple do in the intimacy of the marital bed should remain a matter between them only and not subject to prying scrutiny by others.

Yet it is with reluctance and at risk of an accusation of salacious intrusion, that in hindsight and fairly, in order to give the reader a more informed view of this family saga, some elaboration of the marital history must be disclosed.

The fact that David was five years younger than Edwina was never disguised, as indeed it often has been in many families, where the wife is older than her husband. They preferred to laugh about it and Edwina would tell people that David was her toy-boy. It would be easy to attribute their age difference to mere innocent and unsuspecting coincidence when they first met in those fond, far-off idealistic days, in the steamy environs of Kew Gardens. But is it possible that their reciprocal chemistry, those neurotransmitter signals dove-tailing their pheromones may even have factored in age difference as an ingredient in the beauty and energy of that first chance encounter?

Even in a house of sobriety and moral propriety, cramped living conditions can conspire at situations where a young, impressionable boy may be susceptible to experiences of a delicate nature, as David well knew in his watching Agnes. And thereafter David was aroused by the prospect of an older woman.

II

The years rolled on. The couple upsized, moving to a succession of grander houses, with David proving adept in his timing of the slump boom of the property market. So as the surroundings and adornments changed, David's love and neediness for Edwina seemed to grow stronger. There is always a risk in circumstances of over-emphasised emotional dependency that the other party may feel a certain inner stress. If Edwina did so, then she had the grace to suffer in silence as she rarely betrayed any sense of frustration or dissatisfaction.

III

Edwina was in the bedroom. It was a large bright room but curiously compartmentalised to accord with the owner's taste. The colours were bright, the pile of the carpet luxuriant, the space was broken with ornate Indian linen chests and a mini statue of Rodin's 'Three Graces' nestled on a table at the foot of a large double bed. There were two fine large indoor plants, a monstera delicosa by the door and a tall kentia palm in the centre of the room. In the corner furthest from the bed was a statue of the weeping Madonna perched on a stone plinth, rather like the kind of artefact that can be purchased from architectural reclamation yards, where such ornate pieces end up after the decommission of an old church building. The over-ornamented space felt cluttered. Maybe David needed space to feel cluttered?

And then there was an oriental bi-folding screen, the panels of which were lined with fine embroidered silk with central areas comprising a large patterned transparent grid. Behind the screen there was an expensive free-standing copper bathtub with gold-plated taps, which for all intents and purposes appeared superfluous, as there was an en suite bathroom and a walk-in wardrobe with silk curtains across the opening.

It was Saturday morning. David had returned from the local shop. He arrived at the bedroom door but did not enter, just seeming to loiter, when of course it should be perfectly appropriate for a married man to freely enter the bedroom he shares with his wife.

In the moment before, as David could be heard coming up the stairs, Edwina, who had got out of bed and dressed earlier, and so it may therefore be assumed she was already washed, made her way not to the en suite but rather to the copper bathtub behind the screen. In a choreographed way she continued, ignoring David's presence, although it would be highly unlikely that she did not realise he was inanely tarrying at the door to his own bedroom as though his presence there was subversive or taboo. It must be concluded that the illogical posturing of Edwina suggested that she was complicit in this intimate, complex, innocent little shenanigan.

David look gaunt and intense. He leaned against the door and sloped down as though shrinking, while behind the flimsy screen Edwina started to undress, until she was down to her bra and knickers; she clumsily nudged the screen so that even with its transparency there was a gaping opening on the side to the bedroom door. She then climbed onto a step by the tub which seemed to make her two feet taller, particularly as she was still wearing high-heeled shoes.

With the theatricality of a burlesque performer she unstrapped her bra, which she slung over the screen and then, briskly wriggling her milk-white bottom, removed her knickers and turned towards the door but with her head and eyes firmly fixed on some remote point outside the bedroom window. She held that pose, when you would have expected her immediately to be stepping into the inviting tub of hot water, but she just stayed where was, shaking her hips and wriggling her shoulders so that her breasts wobbled in a display of unabashed sexual bravado.

In the brightness of the room, while David's cowering frame wilted in the shadow of the doorway, Edwina appeared taller, so elegant and confident, looking innocently preoccupied, her pubic bush fully luxuriant and untrimmed, red and bristling, so explicit. There, present yet frustrating unattainable, her bright worldly eyes betraying the pretence of being alone, as precisely prescribed by the garbled rules of this curious charade.

David remained transfixed; his paralysed expression made it impossible to know whether he was shocked, surprised, offended, delighted or actually highly aroused. Edwina, for her part, given the awkwardness and artificiality of her situation, looked perfectly innocent and unperturbed.

But for whose satisfaction was this: his or hers or both?

What was the true narrative that created the highly charged electricity of this ritualistic enactment, this sexually potent, subtly fetishistic melodrama?

As to where the control lay, who would doubt the ascendency of the goddess?

Yet was she not just fulfilling so admirably the role of a burlesque performer and would it not be true to say the real designer of this sexual melodrama was David?

Perhaps that underestimates Edwina's own sophistication, dare it be said her own lack of innocence. Was there not something in her background that required David to demean himself to play the meek and mild voyeur?

It can rightly be contended that beyond needless prurient interest it really does not matter and is of no concern to anyone else; likewise the intensely passionate but equally brief and exhausting love-making that followed. As a couple they were blessed and should be admired that this liberal, intimate compatibility would ensure the longevity of their union in a sustained marital bliss that is rare to find.

But as with so many things in life and nature, it was the unity that also spawned the seed of division. The exclusivity of this exotic little sexual psychodrama was so ornate and so perfectly reciprocated that inevitably it came with its own price. What if Edwina, with her demonstrable propensity for exhibitionism, enjoyed her role too much?

This tendency was so essential to the performance yet must only ever be disclosable to David, her husband, and no one else. What if, human frailty being what it is, that Edwina, if given the opportunity, bestowed her charms on some other? What if she had already done so?

Sometimes when David was at work or driving or when he was at home and Edwina was shopping, these covetous and jealous thoughts gnawed at his mind.

He did not discuss these inner negative feelings with Edwina. To tell her of his insecurities would somehow spoil the conjugal melodrama, yet his distraction at the very notion of Edwina displaying her charms to others resulted in him visiting a psychotherapist, a jolly Welshman, Dr Aaron Goronwy Jenkins.

In his spare time, when not earning large sums of money with his thriving private practice, he was an amateur thespian, treading the boards in honour of the bard. He was fond of quoting Shakespeare, which, whilst erudite, did not, as far as David was concerned, do anything for his counselling 'bedside' manner.

Dr Jenkins: 'Oh, the green-eyed monster, been around a long time. Oh, curse of marriage, that we can call these delicate creatures ours, and not their appetites! I had rather be a toad, and live upon the vapours of a dungeon, than keep a corner of the thing I love for others' uses.'

David: 'Well, I guess it is that sort of thing, but I am not sure if that helps me, Doc.'

Dr Jenkins: 'Trifles light as air are to the jealous confirmations strong as proofs of holy writ. '

David: 'Please, Doc, help me out of my torment. Try explaining something to me that doesn't sound like a Shakespearean riddle.'

Dr Jenkins: 'Profound words of the bard. Iago to Othello, so much of human nature is in those words, Mr Pangloss.'

After many sessions and hundreds of pounds spent on Dr Jenkins' talking therapy, they seemed to be making progress. He had got David to talk through his early traumas, later proclivities and his inescapable anxieties about the exclusivity of his relationship with Edwina.

Dr Jenkins: 'I can help you understand why you feel the way you do and hopefully that will give you some peace, some means to rationalise your thoughts, but I cannot promise that these thoughts will go away.

'And I do hope that we have dispelled the myth that jealousy is a sign of love, because I tell you it is not; if it's not, then what really motivates these jealous responses?

'As we have already discussed, I do not believe that you generally display low self-esteem, but because you lost your brother and parents you naturally have deep-rooted feelings of insecurity and possessiveness. It may well lead to a chronic orientation towards romantic relationships that involves, even requires, fear that your partner will leave you or won't love you enough. The fact that your wife is five years older than you may in itself, from an early time in your relationship, cause feelings of inadequacy. You know, you should discuss that with Edwina, as it is possible as she gets older the age difference may actually cause her to feel inadequate.

'Also, I do not think you overtly display neurotic tendencies; you are not emotionally unstable, yet you describe a strong emotional dependence on your partner. I think it is this that necessitates the voyeuristic scenarios in your marital sexual repertoire and it is this very enactment that carries with it negative connotations for you. Implicit in the performance is the possibility of other hypothetical scenarios, where while Edwina remains the actor, instead of you being the agent, someone else is. As to who that someone is I do not think we should speculate, but it is this that of course makes you feel jealous.

'Generally, though, David, you need to take on board that all of these factors that relate to jealousy are about the insecurities of the jealous people, not about the love they have for their partner. Yes, I advise you to talk it through with Edwina, but you need to understand those home truths in yourself.'

David accepted that the problem was with his own insecurities and with his confidence restored and his mind at ease the happiness in his home life proceeded without the nagging shadow of doubt. That said, it would have been unimaginable for the pair of them to abandon the staged adventure of the bedroom burlesque.

IV

Throughout his life David's joy, particularly in the good summer weather, would be to take a leisurely trip into the countryside in his Riley with Edwina by his side. There was a freewheeling, timeless contentment in tearing along with the bracing, wild breeze pressing on his face, passing walkers and cyclists, then other cars, houses, gateposts, shop fronts, colourful signboards, all the usual urban paraphernalia. And then cruising into the countryside with green fields and narrow country roads, cosy hedgerows closely hugging the open car, and with it David found himself transported to a memory of a remote, unassailable bliss, so precious yet so evasive to recapture, a resonant joy of being on his soap-box cart with Cecil running by his side.

David was now a senior manager of the brokerage division with a major player in the insurance industry. He presided over his managerial domain from a swish office away from the hurly burly of the open-plan area where his team mingled. He had meetings with directors from direct sales and with underwriters and the company secretary. He often had lunch with two of the vice presidents and had also dined with the chairman, with whom he was now on first-name terms. He had his own video screen to see what the FTSE100 was doing each day. His own copy of the *Financial Times* was delivered to his room by the delivery boy from the post room. He could check the equities, gilts and property funds in which the company's unit-linked products were invested.

It was not in David's nature to be loud and brash. In his work he led by example with hard work and thoroughness. He also had the ability to make people feel valued. Unlike many managers, who followed training manuals that stipulated that senior managers should keep their distance from junior staff and rely on delegation and briefing through memos, he was engaging and approachable. It was endearing and impressive that he knew the names of all the people in his office and recognised and acknowledged them if they passed him in the corridor.

Like all good salesmen, because fundamentally that is what he was, he bestowed the product he sold, not only with a compelling backstory, but also with a philosophy that made his work sound more like a mission, a service for all mankind. His insurance work became elevated akin to a religious faith and the occupation of the broker and salesman a quasi-priestly duty. The tidy profits that could be earned were similarly reconstructed as more than just material gain, more than mere pursuit of self-interest in the accumulation of wealth. No, the payments were more like those made to a mediaeval monk for indulgences, and while what was on offer did not quite extend to eternal redemption, by the time David had done his magic it would feel not too dissimilar and the payment a mere trifle by comparison to the benefits conferred by the policy.

The commissions were even described as adding to the value of the product by demonstrating its worth. All this assumed utmost integrity, so that there could never be a possibility of mis-selling and an innate understanding of the suitability of the product having regard to the circumstances of the customer.

Sharing this infectious fervour with the junior members of his team was like seeding the essential mindset to be competitive in the marketplace.

The company had a fleet of beige Mercedes, which were allocated to the directors and a few very senior managers. They were the only cars entitled to park in the designated car-parking spaces outside the insurance building. David had heard it suggested that if his figures remained as good as they were, there was a possibility that he too might allocated his own Mercedes. This fuelled his ambition. In the meantime it was a pure coincidence that he had purchased himself a beige Mercedes, admittedly second-hand and a few years old and not quite of the specification of the fleet, but not bad. He always arrived early for work and would park his car in the street adjacent to where the fleet was parked. He rightly felt he was going places when his designation in the internal company telephone directory changed from 'Broker Manager' to 'Group Broker Manager' and also noted that a specific secretary had been designated in the directory as secretary to him. His name was now also in someone else's job title.

David was not in any way glib or superficial, but even the most well-grounded, common-sense people harbour innocent eccentricities that may take the form of mildly affected pretensions to the accessories of status and success. It is like a little idea nestled in their minds from early days, a fetishised accoutrement, a detail of how they would be when they became what they were, when they first formed the notion of their self-fulfilling prophecy. In David's case he could have avoided the expense of his forgivable affectation because the chairman had already ordered a Mercedes for him. He was now a fully-fledged company man, one of the faces upon which the brand depended; a human custodian of the corporate myth.

10

Abigail's Progress

Abigail Pandora Pangloss was born in Maidenhead in 1970. Like her mother she was an only child. David was thirty-seven years old when she was born and her mother, Edwina, was forty-two. They had waited to have children until David felt financially secure. Then when they did try, they found it was not so easy. Edwina did not just get pregnant when they deemed the time as right and sadly, two earlier occasions of conception ultimately resulted in miscarriages, one at about ten weeks and the other at twelve weeks. Edwina, being that much older, started to worry that time was running out for her.

She had always cared about her appearance, even in her quasi-hippy alternative lifestyle days, when she dallied between conventionality and Bohemia. She was fresh-faced and fecund; it required no effort for her to look good, whether in improvised shabby chic or dowdy dungarees. Now for the first time in her life she made a conscious effort to be fit and healthy: jogging, breakfasting on fruit juice and smoothies, a routine of early nights, cutting down on the wine and gin, no more cigarettes.

It was not entirely clear where the reproductive hiatus lay. It could have just been age-related, but it may have been poor-quality sperm or low sperm count on David's part, as much as any issue with Edwina's follicles or uterus.

Whatever, while it is said that a workout in the gym with free weights can increase a man's testosterone levels, there is also a view that male hubris and a sense of corporate power works in a similar way. Power in any form is a potent psychological intoxicant, tweaking the necessary neurotransmitters, stimulating the hypothalamus and rousing endocrinal secretions.

Though such biological observations may be contrary to modern social constructs in the realm of sexual politics, women, or maybe just some women, do get excited over men with power. Power is power in any shape or form. How often has some hunched, wispy-haired, chinless wonder of a politician managed to bed some voluptuous young woman?

So what is simultaneously happening in the woman's hypothalamus?

Does the answer rest in the theory of the evolutionary role of the female as potential mother and nest builder, who will look for the best socially adapted male to provide security for her baby to facilitate nurturing of the offspring?

Or is it nothing to do with biology at all and more a matter of some women opting for chances they think will be advantageous in their careers?

Or is the whole scenario just a male delusion, where predatory behaviour always results in women being sexually abused by men?

Edwina always expressed the view that women were well capable of making their own decisions on matters such as career and were never as reliant on men as was often imagined.

Anyway, David's performance between the sheets tended to fluctuate with stock prices, at least that was what he reasoned, although Edwina sometimes wondered whether the 'antipasto' was just a little too emotionally draining for her sensitive husband?

It did not seem to matter to her; when it was good, she thought it was very good, and besides, he knew how to bring home the corn. No doubt, like most husbands, he would have been furious had he been aware of the idle banter over a cup of coffee, when Edwina got together with her lady friends, those little personal slips about nuptial blips exposed in the sharing tittle-tattle of girlie talk. Those indiscretions are beyond the domain of men. What could David do anyway if Edwina was reading articles about G spots and the female orgasm in *Cosmopolitan* or advice on the best dildos on the market?

It might be suspected that Edwina approached these matters with a certain amused scepticism. As an intelligent woman secure in her relationship, she was not easily swayed by feminine sexual politics, which were at that time in their infancy. Like most women, what really turned her on was a husband who was loving to her and treated her with respect and consideration. She was well aware of the playful little demon that lurked within her soul and she was not about to share that with her pals.

Nevertheless, share prices had not been performing well for some months and so Edwina was delighted when David returned home one evening brimming with energy and exuberance, primed for a night of unbridled passion. This, they believe, was the night that Abigail was conceived. It is strange to contemplate the causality between the price of bauxite, Brent crude or Brazilian coffee beans, or even a man's designation in the company telephone directory and the consequent coming into being of a beautiful baby girl.

It was not an easy pregnancy, with the months punctuated by angst and morning sickness.

On a sunny morning in the early summer their baby girl was delivered after Caesarean section, both mother and baby were healthy and doing well. Abigail's arrival was a joy: a healthy bouncing baby girl with a birth weight of seven pounds fourteen ounces and a shock of black hair.

The parents' love for their child was never in doubt, and while both doted upon her, each felt a curious selfish sadness as their universe of two had ended. This subliminal chord created a barely detectable unease. Such is the flux of life; this unwitting deficit which, if David and Edwina were not oblivious to, they never admitted to either themselves or to each other. Yet to the bright young Abigail it was obvious. It must be a reasonable speculation that this grit in the oyster helped shape the young girl's personality.

Baby naming had been a lively topic of conversation throughout the pregnancy and, if the truth be known, even before the child was a twinkle in her mother's eye. David had explained another curious tradition in the Pangloss family, and that was to give all daughters the name Pandora, but always as a second or sometimes as a third name. In modern times this tradition had fallen out of fashion. 'Pandora' meant 'all gifts', surely a great compliment anticipating the future promise of a new-born child?

David had researched the provenance of the tradition with an old uncle of a second cousin, who had told him Hesiod's story of the legend of Pandora.

II

In 1976 the family moved to Cheltenham. David had been head-hunted to the senior role he occupied at a large insurance company in Gloucester.

On reaching the age of eleven years Abigail went to Cheltenham Ladies' College. Edwina's parents had both passed away, leaving a sizeable inheritance. It was decided they would invest some of it in their daughter's education. They had been prudent and their mortgage, at a concessionary rate, had been paid off early. The family expenses extended to weekly living, with a foreign holiday and meals out. David's hobby with motor cars meant that often he avoided garage bills and he had the expertise of his friends in the vintage motor car club to maintain and buy spares for his soft-top Riley, which had pride of place on the family's suburban driveway.

Much the ancillary family socialisation seemed to revolve around the school; with concerts, plays, sports events, charity balls and exhibitions, the Pangloss social calendar soon filled up.

The investment in school uniform – shoes, ties, scarves, gym kit, fundraisers, piano lessons, school trips, etc. – on top of the basic fees per term proved a not-inconsiderable draw on the family finances. But so much came with it, so much that gave the family an unspoken kudos. Abigail was a day girl. Edwina would normally collect her in David's Riley, although as she got older, she preferred to catch the bus. She was the only girl on their road, which had many fine houses, to leave in the morning and return in the late afternoon wearing that distinctive heavy woolly, combat green skirt and blazer. There could be no argument. The family Pangloss had arrived or rather returned to their mythical heritage. The future would surely be populated with philosophers and landed custodians of erudition and good taste.

Life proceeded in a mechanical and predictable way that gave David peace of mind. His self-deluding desire for a deterministic world was, of course, the legacy of his tragic early years; yet he well knew that the only certainty in life was uncertainty, that change was the only constant. It was his stock in trade, packaging and marketing of such harsh realities that built a successful career. Yet there was something unwittingly smug, perhaps even unavoidably supercilious in this neatly pruned middle-class Shangri-La.

It was not problematical to talk of 'moving in one's own circle', which, if the expression is analysed, it must be hoped that the said circle did not tend to decrease to the point of disappearing into its own orifical extremity.

In her teen years, Abigail's best friend was Charlotte, born worldly-wise with a keen sense of adventure. Her mother, Deborah, was certainly someone who talked about 'moving in one's circle' and worried about Charlotte's apparent lack of restraint, particularly agonising over the suitability of her boyfriend Rodney. She eventually decided he was acceptable, even if his father was a mere partner in a local firm of solicitors and spoke with a detectable London accent. Deborah liked to think she was broad-minded and just sighed over a cup of afternoon tea with Edwina 'Oh, I suppose these things are sent to try us, ha. We shouldn't judge, should we?'

Edwina smiled back, feeling assured that David's Scouse accent was now beyond detection, but credit must be given for how he developed an intuition for avoiding syllables that might betray his lilt.

Quite apart from appearances and the fact that one' s child was rubbing shoulders with the children of the nation's elite, not to mention the progeny of some of the most corrupt politicians and money-laundering spivs from around the world, the school had so much to commend it.

But that is no fault of the school. Children are innocent and deserve an education irrespective of what their parents get up to. The ethos and sentiments could only be praised: enthusiasm and kindness (wherever possible), responsibility and compassion towards needs of others, girls equally valued and respected and their individuality embraced. Even the most churlish critic could not dispute the altruism and worth of emphasising and instilling these virtues into the young women passing through the school.

Unlike some of the college boys who moved in their circle, Rodney did not have a chauffeur or minders, and chunky gold rings and neck chains were absent from his attire. The romance happened when he had got drunk with Charlotte at a friend's summer garden party. Someone had come up with a game called thirty-nine steps, vaguely modelled on the Hitchcock film from 1935. Anyway, they ended up losing their virginity to each other after someone produced handcuffs and locked the pair of them together. They spent an uncomfortable night in the sprawling garden and after Charlotte had puked all over Rodney, as much to make it up to him, but also to alleviate the boredom, they ended up embroiled in a fumbling contorted coitus. When romance happens you have to grab it with both hands, cuffs or no cuffs.

Abigail, by her late teens, had grown into an intelligent, quick-witted, perceptive young woman, not afraid to express her feelings. She had a milky-white complexion, rosy cheeks, brown eyes, fresh expressive lips and lustrous raven hair which, if not cut, would soon grow into swirling long locks. She followed Edwina's advice to wear it in a gathered bunch on top of her head so that it did not bother her when she went about her many activities. She was shapely and, compared to many of her school friends, quite tall at about five feet eight inches.

Her opinions on so many subjects were at odds with her parents. While through the generations different perspectives and philosophies had been adopted by the Pangloss family, myths Abigail was well versed in from an early age, she sensibly treated it all with great circumspection. For her part, she was bemused at how her father, of all people, could assert that there ever was such a tradition or if there was then that there could ever be a shred of truth in such wacky, blinkered misapprehension. Her speculations were never idle nor her arguments vague and uninformed. At university she would later choose options along with her science subjects so as to delve into these myths and mysterious beliefs.

Her time at the ladies' college was not wasted. She had made good progress and taken full advantage of those educational opportunities. Before entering sixth form she had achieved excellent GCSEs, done her Duke of Edinburgh Gold Award, been skiing in the French Alps, got her school colours for lacrosse and spent a summer vacation with two friends, one of whom was a princess, at the palace of the Sultan of Terengganu.

And she did not consciously decide to rebel. There was no cataclysmic moment. It was never a case of her becoming irrevocably outraged and defiant at some argument or sanction applied to her. Her parents' house was her house, welcoming for any friends she wished to bring home. David and Edwina would have done anything for her, did do anything for her. They were not by nature overly assertive; on the contrary, they listened with interest, even if they were often shocked and bemused at ideas she expressed. In many ways much of what she had to say was founded in altruistic principles immanent in the ethos of her privileged education. It was simply that she was headstrong and knew her own mind; she felt that if she believed in something she should say so, even if it lacked sensitivity so to do, even if it might hurt others' feelings, even if those feelings belonged to her parents.

Abigail's appearance and dress sense, untypically for a teenager, never seemed a great concern. Her style was practical, but she knew how to look good, how to be sexy and attract boys, but that was never a preoccupation; if anything it was a role she would play out of curiosity to understand the power wielded by this allure. She was never going to be swept away or taken in by the attention of boys. This game, whatever it was, was always on her terms. While other weaker, more prim, proper and prudish or less confident girls might fret at the need to balance popularity against preserving their honour, self-respect, even weighing their parents' old-fashioned ideas about future value in the marketplace, Abigail cared not a jot.

In a way this is all quite understandable, but it was her other early-life choices that left those close to her bemused.

Perhaps it was experimentation. Perhaps it was a peculiar need to feel grounded with the underclass, a means to empathise, grow strong by embracing that which is awful, through negative as well as positive experiences reach a wholeness of understanding of who she was as a person. She would have been mindful of her father's own background and how that was the raison d'être for all his aspirations, in particular the promotion of the life chances of his darling daughter.

So was it that Abigail wondered what would it be like to rub shoulders with the great unwashed, to bathe in the primordial slime?

Was it a spiritual desire to descend into hell?

Was there some kind of nascent sexual motivation to be ravaged by ignominious hoodlums?

Was it some wild adventure to shock her cosseted school friends like some valiantly unchaste badge of honour?

Or was there actually some perverse romantic notion?

III

Abigail's adventure started when she was invited by Charlotte to 'Phillip's Fondue', a new restaurant that had opened on the upper high street in Cheltenham. Phillip was an ageing hippie, very seventies in his style. Abigail's best bet was that he was in his fifties, but he could have been younger and just looked older because he liked to hang out with younger people, or it was possible he was even older and just looked young for his age. He had very long, straggly grey, brown hair, with a most discernible receding hairline and matching bald patch on top. His complexion was that pale unhealthy hue of creatures of the night who, apart from dancing when they are high, take no exercise. He was tall and slim except for a pronounced pot belly and chubby face with a double chin. He wore loons, a 1970s variant on bellbottoms, except more casual and made usually from cheap fabric, tight-fitting until below the knee when they flapped baggily when he moved. He also had a penchant for embroidered round-necked long-sleeved cotton shirts, which went well with his Afghan coat. He wore sandals and always doused himself with a liberal splash of petunia, the hippie oil that scented the air wherever he went. Many thought it was a useful means of disguising the underlying pervading smell of cannabis.

The doubtless carefully manufactured Phillip persona, whatever it precisely was intended to be, was completed with a woman on his arm, where his taste seemed to be very sixties. She was always a slim, peroxide-blonde woman, with stylish short hair and an even shorter mini-skirt, showing off her athletic figure. She wore heavy black makeup around her eyes, perhaps a well-nourished version of heroin chic, an exotic creature and an essential accessory for this purveyor of the zeitgeist.

Phillip owned, or perhaps it was that he just managed the Promenade Club, which was a trendy snug basement disco club in Cheltenham. It was a busy place where it was necessary to queue outside for a long time, until a guest left and then it was possible to enter; unless, of course, you were 'someone' or knew 'someone', and then you could just jump the queue and be ushered in by the doormen. Inside it was a hot, airless, smoky, steamy den with a cramped bar and loud disco music blasting.

This created what some people called 'atmosphere', while other more sober observers would call it a health and safety hazard. It presented what for the polite was a problem, while for others an opportunity, where everyone was so crammed together that even reaching into a trouser pockets to get cash for a drink or manoeuvring to put a cigarette in your mouth was likely to result in a sexual assault on any unsuspecting woman standing next to you.

It was rumoured that Phillip also owned a club in St Tropez, where he would disappear to for a few months each year; although during one of his absences someone on the scene had been visiting an aunt in Padstow and had seen Phillip on a little inauspicious sailing 'yacht', moored at the end of the quay.

As a self-appointed style guru, he drove around in an old Mercedes. There was something astute about Phillip, but then old-timers hanging around kids can appear wiser than they really are. He tried hard not to be a pseud. He was all about a trendy, upmarket, contemporary bohemian lifestyle. He once arrived in the Promenade 'Beer Gardens' with a Formula One racing car unloaded from a truck. The livery was very impressive, but it is doubtful that there was an engine. There was then an ostentatious photo shoot with his blonde girlfriend stripping down to a bikini and straddling the bonnet in a manner suggestive of simulated sex with the vehicle while Phillip squeezed himself into the driver's seat.

Whatever else this flamboyant spectacle was about, the performance enthralled the spaced-out drop-outs munching on magic mushrooms and blowing on their spliffs on the lawn nearby.

So his latest venture was this fondue restaurant on the upper high street. 'Fondue vigneronne', 'fondue bacchus' or 'fondue bourguignonne' cooked with wine or oil. Red wine fondue consisted of red wine boiled, and seasoned with salt, pepper, garlic, onions and herbs; the white wine version was spiced with cinnamon, chillies, coriander, white pepper and enriched with chicken broth. The guests would then dip meat, fish or vegetables in the caquelon and top them with bearnaise sauce, tartar sauce or simply French mustard.

Fondue was eaten by spearing a piece of meat on a fork, swirling it in the pot and putting it into the mouth, and if you lost a piece of bread in the caquelon this, as was the tradition, was penalised by buying a round of drinks, singing a song or running around in the snow naked.

This enhanced sociability of fondue meant that Phillip's restaurant had no tables as such but just a big rug where everyone sat round in a circle, talking, drinking and periodically pitching their little wooden spear into the pot of nosh in the middle. All very intimate, as indeed it was designed to be. While it was the ideal precursor to an orgy, hygienic it was not, as diners would slurp and pool and puddle their respective saliva in the slushy sloshy communal pot of stew.

And it was to this place that Abigail went with Charlotte and Rodney to dine out one Saturday evening. Her invitation was assured by the farcical premise demanded by Charlotte's mother that Abigail should attend as a chaperon for Charlotte. It mattered not that it had been Charlotte who hitherto instructed Abigail in the ways of the world and more specifically about boys.

Phillip believed in having an eclectic mix of people. He had no problem fraternising with drifters, pimps and drug dealers, as well as schoolgirls, dissolute aristocrats, artists, musicians and a retinue of pseuds, social climbers and hangers-on. What mattered was that they were, on some rudimentary level, 'cool', 'on the scene' or 'far out'. Often a permutation of this ungainly cohort would be seen driving around Cheltenham in Phillip's rather dated Mercedes car, either in the process of doing a deal or looking for some good-quality Red Leb, Moroccan or Afghan Brown or a bag of weed. In the days before mobile phones this complex ritual would sometimes take half the day. If some shadowy 'Clive' or 'Trotters' had moved on from their usual haunts it could all get quite desperate. Proceedings were also delayed by a pervading paranoia when a member of the familiar undercover drug squad was recognised or someone feared they were being followed by an unmarked police car. Word would quickly pass in a whisper around the Dirty Duck or Cotswold: 'Look out, it's "Scabies, Price and Doris".'

Nervous freaks would go to the toilet to hide their stash where the sun does not shine. Happy days. Some nights it was just a matter of biting the bullet and tripping out on dodgy acid.

It was a moment of memorable triumph for Phillip when that veritable Marco Polo of philosophy, Howard Marks, turned up in Cheltenham one rainy Sunday afternoon with some gear and dined at Phillip's Fondue; another signed celebrity photograph for the restaurant wall?

But even before trading standards and environmental health paid a visit, the onset of the mysterious AIDS epidemic in the early 1980s had made customers think twice about such gratuitous body fluid-sharing cuisine.

Abigail found herself sitting, or rather squatting cross-legged, next to a rather oily and uncouth individual wearing a grubby jacket proudly displaying 'Hells Angels' on the back. He ignored her at first. Most of the gathering were sitting cross-legged with their eating accoutrements neatly placed in front of them, but he was lazily slouched over to one side resting on one arm with his back, emblazoned with his grubby motor-club insignia, partially blocking Abigail's view.

His large lanky frame was sprawled in an ungainly fashion across the floor; there seemed nowhere in the room to fit his large feet encased in even larger motorcycle boots, which constantly kicked, imposed on and interrupted the space of other diners. His thick, long, dirty fair hair swiped the air each time he moved, his odour a none-too-subtle mix of engine oil and unwashed body odour. For most young women it would actually have been quite intimidating, but the feisty Abigail had the resilience not to be ignored and intimidated. She tugged at the shoulder of his frayed denim jacket.

'Hey, you, you're blocking my view.'

The fellow diner obviously believed not only his demeanour but the local notoriety of his reputation would preclude the audacity and disrespect of touching his person and challenging him in a such a way.

Keck was in his early twenties, lanky, at about six foot four inches tall. He always seemed unsteady on his feet, some said because he had extra leather on the bottom of his boots to look even taller than he was because he felt he was not big enough. While he did not naturally have an unpleasant face, it seemed as though he went out of his way to look as angry and ugly as possible. Apart from being a master of eyeballing anyone who dared look at him, he surely had spent many hours practising the art of gurning.

He was taken aback by Abigail's forthright manner. At first he shrugged and muttered, 'Fuck orrrf.'

But Abigail persisted, so he turned round and faced her and soon realised that the eyeballing was having absolutely no effect, so, angry but disarmed, he said, 'What?' And then, without waiting for a reply, he moved himself out of Abigail's space, muttering something to the effect of, 'You want to be careful, bitch.'

There was no doubting Keck's lack of charm. Something in his life had obviously made him disaffected and antisocial, but despite his lack of social grace, he was with a glamorous young woman. Tall, blonde, well presented, with carefully manicured nails and with the greatest attention paid to her makeup, she glanced around with large seductive eyelashes, smiling with glossy bright lipstick; very much a femme fatale. She had a sweet, slightly squeaky voice and yet her conversation appeared to be not at all innocent or, for that matter, lady-like. Abigail did not feel comfortable with her. While she was friendly and silly, there was a fussiness about what drink she should have and how she held her glass, which she did with long slender fingers affectedly dressed in fingerless gloves, so that the elegance of her painted nails could be seen.

She smoked a Black Russian Sobranie using a garish, kitsch cigarette holder. If anyone had set out to construct a femme fatale masquerading as a Marlene Deitrich pastiche, then this babe had it all.

'Oh my God, what shall I have, darling? A gin and tonic, heaven forbid a half of lager and a dash of lime. No, no, rather a pink gin with strawberries, of course, maybe… or maybe rather a pina colada or a pear martini. Oh, darling, what shall I do? No, no, I feel like a margarita.'

Definitely something of a poseur, more than slightly affected, dare we say false? These were thoughts passing through the minds of those gathered. At some prodding from what appeared to be his girlfriend, Keck eventually said, 'I'm Keck and this is Bubbles.'

Bubbles was then all giggly and lifted her glass in the air and said, 'Hi, everyone. Oh, baby, such a gas, ha, ha.'

Rodney fancied her. He thought she was sophisticated, the complete woman; there was nothing juvenile or innocent about her. His wandering eye annoyed Charlotte and he then shifted his cross-legged position on the large Indian floor rug to be in a better position to communicate with this exotic creature. He tried some trite, saccharin clichés, which, for the sake of preserving a semblance of subtlety of prose, will not be repeated here.

Rodney then asked her how she knew Phillip.

Bubbles: 'Oh, Phillip knows everybody, darling, what about you?'

Meanwhile Keck looked on, curious, not apparently angered; if anything his expression betrayed amusement.

Rodney, with some social bluff: 'Oh, me, I get about, you know.'

Bubbles' expression became more fixed and her girlie giggle subsided. It seemed that her squeaky tone needed effort and at one point might even have dropped an octave. She then said, 'Hound dog.'

To which Keck laughed and Rodney said, 'Eh?' Bubbles then changed the subject to discuss the Elvis song.

Bubbles: 'The bit I like is about being high class but that it was just a lie' at which she burst into a weird, squeaky, staccato, cackling laughter. When she had finished she turned to Rodney and said quietly, 'Hound dog.' She then winked her big curly false eyelashes and said, ' You're no friend of mine you know.'

As she started cackling again, Rodney turned his attention back to Charlotte, looking for much-needed relief and reassurance.

Abigail was fascinated by this odd encounter, though rather than attempt to talk herself, she just looked on with a bemused expression.

After that evening Charlotte chucked Rodney. A few weeks later when she was shopping on the promenade with Abigail, a couple of Hells Angels roared up onto the pavement, parked their bikes and wandered into a newsagents to get some Rizla papers. Abigail recognised one as Keck and decided, for whatever godforsaken reason, to waylay him as his oily ungainly frame swaggered back to his bike.

Abigail: 'Hi, you.'

This prompted a less than friendly response from Keck: 'Eh, you what, hey, bitch, what are you, jail-bait or somethin'?'

But the Hells Angel he was with put his hand on his arm as if to say, 'Wait a second, slow down.'

Keck then said, 'This is my mate, Cat Weasel.'

With that, the tall, slouching, sallow individual standing next to Keck glanced sideways coyly at Abigail. He had what were actually delicate facial features, gypsy-like, with long dark greasy hair and what looked like large sideburns but what closer inspection would reveal to be ingrained engine oil. If Abigail had not known better she might have thought that this local warrior was embarrassed in some way.

She noticed he had tattoos spelling 'love' on the knuckles of one hand and 'hate' on the knuckles of the other. Cat Weasel was a complex individual. The weirdest, most alarming aspect of Cat Weasel's demeanour was whether you caught the glare of his right eye or left eye. If you caught the gaze of the left eye you felt as though you were being embraced by a warm, sociable, tranquil soul at peace with himself and the world. If you caught the glare of the right eye, though, then you sensed a wild fury, an uncompromising rage, engagement with a presence ready to kill, almost wishing for a fight to the death, someone really offensive and nasty.

And on more than one occasion people had said that this unprovoked wildness from within was no imagining and would usually result in Cat Weasel doing a little Red Indian war dance combined with a rather unmanly screech, as he put his hand down the back of his neck and produced a lethal-looking flick knife that he would point in the direction of any unfortunate person in his sights. This was not someone to be messed with.

What was not always appreciated was that, without fail, in these unpleasant encounters, Keck would be in attendance, standing nearby, at his side or behind him, supporting Cat Weasel's mental energy, helping to generate the toxic vibe.

But Abigail's interest went beyond intrigue. Something in this low-life weirdo had captivated her. She was smitten. What initially repelled her came to attract her. She was sixteen years old, a virgin, but possessed of that intelligent and sophisticated preoccupation with things sexual that many young women who are schooled cooped in elite female domains, strictly segregated from the danger of lascivious male overtures, seem to be so susceptible.

Teenage hormones, rebellion and girlie fantasies besides, something in Abigail's predisposition and the quirk of circumstance had brought her into close proximity with this grubby reprobate. Whatever it was, for a brief time she became a Hells Angel chick and all that that entailed.

The day Cat Weasel first gave Abigail a lift home on his Triumph 650 Edwina recoiled in horror, and despite protestations that her biker boyfriend was courageous, kind and chivalrous, her parents remained aghast and despondent.

Three facts should be remembered about Abigail's relationship with Cat Weasel, if the truth and the schoolgirl's reputation is to be salvaged from the myths and rumours that persisted.

Firstly, she was not gang-banged by all or any of the Angels, even if they were the first in line to encourage the belief amongst the weak-willed, stoned and inebriate miscreants who wasted their lives in the town's less salubrious hostelries. There really had not been the alleged frenzied and thoroughly sordid penetration of all her orifices. The supposed chick initiation ceremony remained a theoretical idea that Cat Weasel and Abigail discussed over a beer.

Cat Weasel spoke with a local West Country accent in which he tried hard to make his vocal cords sound lower than they really were. This resulted in syllables formed from primitive prolonged vowels and hurried consonants, which, apart from making difficult to understand, added to his savage-like demeanour. But Abigail seemed to get it; she could interpret what he was saying and his ideas were intelligent; remarkably, she was on his wavelength.

Secondly, the physical side of the relationship between the two of them involved what might be better described as frottage, rather than kissing and cuddling or anything more intimate. Actually, whenever they had tried kissing Cat Weasel would burst into an embarrassed, screeching laughter. He would have one eye on Keck, who was always close at hand anyway with a puzzled look on his face; so intimacy in the full sense of the word was never an option. For most girls that would have been the end.

Thirdly, unlike a proper Hells Angel chick, while she did hang out with them quite a bit, she never moved into their squalid communal garret. This was a residence in a squat at the top of Montpellier, a sprawling apartment of decayed elegance, with peeling paint, broken sparse furniture, a leaky roof and miles of groaning lead pipe and their de rigueur Triumph 650 machines hauled up the stairs and parked, spewing oil, in the lounge.

Triumph had been adopted as sufficiently authentic for a British motorcycle gang. Much time and conversation was spent talking about their machines, replacing telescopic front forks to make choppers, sorting out brake drums, boasting about the size of the valves on the alloy cylinder head or the high compression ratio in the pistons on the camshaft and how they got on with the customised drop bar handles. Harley Davidsons were expensive to import, scarce and beyond the means of unemployed layabouts relying on some impecunious 'old lady', usually meaning their mother, to finance their wheels.

They all had emblazoned on the back of their dirty, fading, blue denim jackets 'Hells Angels Cotswold Chapter'.

But there was more to Cat Weasel than most realised and Abigail's friendship was based upon her becoming aware of certain facts. When he was not wearing his colours, Cat Weasel simply loved to dress up in ladies' clothes and turn up at the Stable Bar and the Pavilion Club, the very same pubs and clubs that as an Angel he would terrorise, yet as a lady he would be charming and friendly, although perhaps a little bit giggly and silly, but very much a fashionable young 'chick'.

She was, no less, 'Bubbles', the exotic party girl Abigail had met at Phillip's Fondue, in her finely groomed long blonde wig and neatly varnished nails, being so fussy about what drinks she would let young men buy for her. This was the chick who liked to listen to early rock and roll numbers to the point of making her young male admirers monopolise the juke box with Bill Haley, Jerry Lee Lewis, Little Richard and, of course, Elvis, 'Hound Dog'.

To the unsuspecting this song provided the cryptic subtext to the nasty dangerous aberration that lurked under the face cream, wig and mascara.

The soundtrack was dependent upon on which persona turned up; if it was as a 'she' then you would find her dancing to Bowie's 'Rebel, Rebel', which played repeatedly during the evening. On other evenings, when ensconced on a platform with the fellow gang members, the favourite was a live act called the Rebounds, who were a bunch of ageing country hicks from Gloucester with greasy 'duck's arse' hairstyles with long sideboards, suede shoes and felt collars on their blue Crombie coats. They used to play cretinous, cack-handed covers of early rock and roll, particularly 'Rock Around the Clock' and 'Blue Suede Shoes'. The band practised three nights a week at the Plough Inn at Quedgeley, and while that was a noisy disturbance for the locals, they still sounded awful on a Saturday night.

When they played at the Pavilion Club, most of the teenage boppers would become disgruntled, hoping for some Roxy Music, Bowie, maybe some Beatles or at least the Rolling Stones, Cream, Led Zeppelin, Pink Floyd, Black Sabbath or Genesis; it was just no one was going tell the Angels what music was going to be played.

It is difficult to overstate how weird, dysfunctional, alarming, unstable and really quite dangerous the Cat Weasel was. He/she was the archetypal, love-hate merchant, the devil's own child.

It is appropriate to introduce Abigail's new-found social circle – just a potted biography to give a flavour of the people in the milieu of her privileged young life for a brief while.

In addition to Keck and Cat Weasel there was Fez, Frenchie, Grinner, Mohawk and Norman.

Now it is easy to dismiss gang members as people with a herd mentality, uninspiring losers with personality deficits which they make up for by acting within the larger group. Often on their own they may have deep anxieties, but in the group they are fearless and strong; they can feed off each other's mental energy, where one person's humour is their humour too, where another members anger is their anger too. A number of these guys had been to grammar school. They had become interested first in motorbikes and then the cult that evolved around the machine. They had all seen *Rebel Without a Cause* at the cinema. They had dropped out of school. They had become street-fighting men, sunshine soldiers, local heroes with a penchant for self-destruction.

A freakish facet was the unexpected individuality of members, which ranged from variations in the way they wore their denims and colours, preferences for different drugs of choice, even different methods of being unpleasant and violent. Some liked fists, others threatened with knives, some laughed, some were angry, but they all had Triumph 650s and they all had the same motif on their backs and in one way or another they all needed each other to feel secure.

Fez by this stage was past thinking about winning the hearts of young maidens. He had always maintained a certain individuality and chose to wear his colours on the back of a lady's fur coat (probably pinched from his mother), sloping about town, hands in pockets, with denim jeans and canvas shoes rather than biker's boots. He was notably hirsute with long dark hair and a large bushy beard that covered most of his face. His skin was sallow with dark sunken eyes that stared out with a lostness, not vacant, rather soulful and lugubrious. He was a heroin addict. Most of the time he did not even own a bike. He had sold it to buy some gear. It was true he had a couple of chicks who used to follow him around, but he was more interested in cadging a joint to take the edge off his clucking between hits.

And his proclivities may have rested in some more aberrant place as many years earlier he had appeared before the juvenile court allegedly for interfering with a young boy in the park. Despite being hooked on smack Fez had retained a certain discernment and care about the world, as was evident in him buying *The Guardian* each day, and if he did not like the way a joint had been rolled he would say, 'Hey, man, too much bandaging.' He would explain that he didn't need a woman because he was wed to the white lady, by which he clearly meant smack. It was difficult to know how his two young chicks felt. There was no sex in it. Maybe they just helped him jack up.

Grinner was a charmless man, a local heavy, a bully by nature, who did not mind mixing it in a fight and thrived on a punch-up, whether in a pub with anyone he did not like or generally as orchestrated street-fighting, as a sunshine soldier on summer days. He was a local yokel who had cut his teeth on mopeds around the nearby village of Bishop's Cleeve, but he was such a dirty, ugly, hairy bastard with a face covered in patchy stubble complemented by a toothless grin, that he believed himself cut out for greater things, or maybe that was what the villagers told him in the hope that he would fuck off somewhere else.

Whatever, Grinner moved all of five miles into downtown Cheltenham, where he soon passed his initiation to the Angels by biting the head off a hapless pigeon on a Thursday afternoon outside the post office on the promenade. He was drunk on cider at the, time and he and the other gang members present had a bloody good laugh. The improvised verbal citation recognising his admission to the fold noted in particular how his actions had deeply upset an old lady who was feeding the birds at the time.

It did not go well for Grinner. Firstly, his mental health started to deteriorate after he was given some acid with his scrumpy one evening, which sent him tripping for a couple of days and did some serious stuff to his celebrated stupid head. As he slowly regained a grip on reality, some skinhead, who had been bopping to the anthem 'Skinhead Moonstomp' all evening at the YMCA and had run out of speed and was starting to feel too knackered to walk home, came across a motorbike primed and ready to go. Grinner had just nipped into the fish and chip shop at the time. On the skinhead hopped and he was off. Before he got home the skinhead realised it would not be wise to park the machine outside his house, so at the railway bridge he alighted, took the plates off and chucked the bike over the bridge onto a passing goods train, which had open wagons taking coal from South Wales to London. Grinner never saw his bike again. He felt unable to report the bike missing as it had been cobbled together with stolen parts. He did, however, put the word around the pubs giving a graphic description of what he was going to do when he found the motherfucker who had nicked his bike. This appeared to involve various forms of torture and bodily evisceration, including shoving the culprit's teeth so far down his throat that to clean them he would need to put a toothbrush up his arse. The anatomical feasibility of this proposed redress must remain in doubt.

Frenchie was a married man. He had a couple of kids and went out in the morning after his missus had made breakfast, and he came back at night, when his wife would have dinner on the table. Well, most of the time anyway. Sometimes he had gainful employment, sometimes he did not. When he was with the wife and kids he liked to dress as a teddy boy. He was of that era, a bit older than some of the other members. He was physically of diminutive stature but did not fear anyone and was known to hold his own in a fight, which might explain why he had so many teeth missing. He was another local bloke who preferred to stay within his tribe but did actually have a sociable side; it is even possible to go as far as to say he had a sense of humour, which made his demeanour less intimidating than that of some of the more dysfunctional, messed-up members of the cohort.

The leader was, by all accounts, Mohawk, mainly because he had been around the longest, knew a lot about bikes and had a genuine penchant for violence. He was bona fide from the wrong side of the tracks; there was never any need for him to cultivate his antisocial, disaffected nastiness. The guy was a natural. And that was why he did tend to spend rather a lot of time in prison. He had the reputation; he might be turning up with the pack or he might not. Whatever, it made people worry. And yes, he had a Mohican haircut.

Then there was Norman, a cheerful bloke always ready for a laugh, who had no fear of any situation and spent a lot of time doing pub party tricks like swallowing knives and eating wine glasses. He came from a skinhead family with a fearsome reputation, yet chose to become a Hells Angel, because he said he preferred hairy music and LSD to speed and northern soul. Such are the choices a young man must make.

Some of these reprobates had been on the scene for a long while. Back in 1969 the Angels had joined the cortege during the funeral for Brian Jones, as it moved slowly up Cheltenham promenade. They also turned up as self-styled security at the Hyde Park concert given in his memory. Generally they spent their days fixing their bikes, cruising around and boozing with their smelly boots up on the table in the beer gardens or the Cotswold pub. They often had guest chapters turn up in the town.

IV

It is another contradiction that those grand houses that had become so out of fashion that they could be abandoned to the grease, grime, abuse, neglect and iniquity of the Hells Angels are now again restored to their former glory. Today property speculators assiduously renovate and refurbish such properties, creating niche neighbourhoods lovingly marketed in the finest glossy brochures, and these properties are now worth a fortune, fetching prices akin to high-spec residences in London.

These grand old Cheltenham houses were originally constructed in the Georgian period, but then greatly and elegantly expanded in the Regency period with rows of Palladian mansions adorned with Doric columns surrounding spacious porches, huge rectangular windows with intricately styled metalwork balconies enabling the luxurious interiors to bask in a flood of dappled light that would then dance around the interior walls and flicker on the hypnotic scrolls of the cornice and coving.

The funding for these grand residences was derived either directly or indirectly from the wealth of the East India Company. Much of the building work was commissioned to provide genteel residences for employees returning from India to sedate retirement amidst the decorum of Cheltenham Spa. Cheltenham was a veritable Anglo-Indian paradise, known at the time as Calcutta in the Cotswolds. Many old colonels and their wives settled down to see out their days taking the waters in the Pump Rooms, strolling on the promenade, enjoying afternoon tea and cakes in a café, boating on the lake in Pittville Park and a gentle game of bowls or tennis at their club.

Much of this history is lost, as is the way where over time fluctuating, arbitrary decisions are made by individuals, households and institutions about what random piecemeal material should be saved and catalogued and what should be ignored and consigned to oblivion. What might be regarded as important today may have been viewed as insignificant in earlier epochs, so nuanced little idiosyncrasies of detail and minutiae often disappear.

Of particular susceptibility to this vanishing are those papers and artefacts that betray some scandal or indiscretion, obviously to avoid the embarrassment of secret family histories, rather than because those events objectively had no intrinsic historical value. Why, for example, would an old colonel choose to offer to posterity the sword he used at the charge of the light brigade or the blood-stained tunic he wore at the siege of Malakand rather than the history that included that of his second family in the Punjab and details of the Indian restaurant he funded for his bastard son in the High Street in Cheltenham?

No doubt festering in some dusty vault can still be found documents now growing whiskers that evidence Cheltenham's social life of the eighteenth and nineteenth centuries. Much is, of course, known of visits by George III, Princess Victoria and foreign royalty, by the Duke of Wellington, Lord Byron and Jane Austen, but just how colourful and ostentatious was this lively retreat from the empire?

There is a strange disorientation in contemplating the trace of a place through time, to look at a space, a pavement, a road and imagine all the events that had occurred. It is said that physically you cannot do this in the Arctic because the exact position of the North Pole changes over time; a disturbing prospect to be drifting rather than to be anchored in space-time.

After a few glasses of wine at one of Cheltenham's wine bars on one of those warm breezy late summer afternoons, it is a playful thought experiment to embrace the tree-lined vista, as though a palimpsest. And then to imagine the layers that have been papered over, re-turfed, new soil and slabs on old, the lines of absent buildings, peeled floral William Morris wallpaper discarded under floorboards, buried in the ground, brick over plaster, plaster over brick, replaced facades, modern retro-designs over faded post-war town-planning eyesores. If you focus meditatively there is point where you can journey through the cladding and catch the layers of time that imbue a building or a street, that give it its vibe, the ghosts of time that look back at us from their time-worn dusty secretions. But all those events imprinted in this transcendent anthropological record really did happen, all those spicy mishaps, faux pas and aberrant misadventures, particularly while at leisure, which is, after all, why most people came to the town.

To catch time; well, it feels like a disservice to treat it merely as a physical variable dependent upon the speed of light. Time is so much more. It is the theatre of nature, the backdrop to human drama, the matrix for pathos, of tragicomedy. And time is only vital in the now, only ever the summation of the present and all the present moments that have passed. The future is not time at all. It does not exist, except as a probability, an idea best suited to optimists. For the philosopher Berkeley even the present did not exist unless he could empirically prove it with his senses.

While the military returnees from India would strut with their retinues on the promenade, in colourful uniforms and shiny buttons, or be carried in horse-drawn carriages to the spa; nevertheless, while undoubtedly snooty, they had discipline and decorum.

Prior to 1857 the East India Company had its own private army, several times larger than the British Army, so these strutting moustachioed colonels with their noses in the air had never actually served King and country. Even so, the real extravagance and exhibitionism must be reserved for the glorious company of bean counters, who amassed huge fortunes and became self-appointed nabobs, with all the ludicrous, quirky paraphernalia they attached to their retinues. Although the word kitsch had yet to be invented these accountants aggrandised themselves with fashions and combinations that took bad taste to a new level.

The first thing you would notice about the nabob bookkeeper from Manchester who had decided to settle in Cheltenham was that his attire was that of a maharajah, with fine silk ornate gowns, jodhpuri pants and turban. He wore a necklace and his fingers were bedecked with diamonds as fine as those of the Nizam of Hyderabad. What's not to like, you may ask, even if he was carried in a sedan chair decked out in the skin of a Bengal tiger with its scowling majestic head and gaping fangs protruding at the front of the carriage?

Well, perhaps it was one-upmanship for the decorative old colonels and the fine lace and bonnets of their wives, as they passed on the promenade, but was it not going too far to insist on servants that followed carrying monkeys and parakeets on their shoulders? And the monkeys wore the shiny buttons of colourful uniforms of the old colonels. Of course, in those days if you were a senior company man returning to England with a fortune there was no custom officer that would dare challenge you about the diverse and weird personal effects stored in crates on your ship.

And that brings me to the forgotten piece de resistance of showiness on the Cheltenham Promenade. Yes, you guessed it, our Lancastrian nabob had brought his own elephants, three of them, back with him, which he paraded through the town centre from his luxury villa in Montpellier all the way to Pittville Pump Rooms. A Punjabi driver with a turban and loincloths was seated on an elaborate ovular rug on top of the elephant's head, and behind, over a huge magnificently embroidered carpet that was draped over the animal's back, was strapped a brightly coloured carved wooden cabin in which the accountant and his wife sat. There were a dozen Anglo-Indian servants in attendance, who, for some unfathomable reason, held large colourful fans to sweep the air to ensure a cooling breeze. As Gloucestershire in springtime has a most moderate climate this affectation was, of course, absurd, although having the servants following on behind with exotic wide-brimmed shovels to collect all the dung deposited as the retinue passed by was a thoughtful gesture.

While such historical bravado could never be upstaged, the irritation caused by legions of revving motorbikes on the promenade made the good citizens of Cheltenham puzzled as to why it took so long for the police to clamp down on these hoodlums.

V

Cat Weasel: 'Here, mate, move your car, I've come to see my girlfriend.'

David: 'Do you mind? This is my driveway. Please remove yourself as you are clearly at the wrong address.'

Cat Weasel: 'I want to see Abbi.'

Keck: 'Yeah, come on, mate, move out of the way, no one fucks with us.'

David: 'No Abbi here. Go away or I'll call the police.'

Cat Weasel: 'Abigail lives here. I've been before, mate, while you were at work.'

Shocked and perturbed, David enquired, 'Abigail? You want to see Abigail? Why? What do you want? I expect Abigail is busy.'

Cat Weasel and Keck looked at each other as though they were the ones who had a right to be offended. Cat Weasel started scratching the back of his neck, to which Keck said, 'No, don't, mate, I'll sort out the old cunt.'

With that Keck strolled right up to David, grabbed him by his shirt and shoved him hard so that David went flying across a neatly pruned low privet hedge and tumbled onto the lawn.

The Pangloss family lived in a regency property. David and Edwina had developed a taste for these elegant old buildings that in the 1970s could still be purchased cheaply, if you had the imagination and resources to appreciate their potential. Moving from the home counties, they had been mortgage-free and able to buy a fine Palladian example, which they restored to its former glory. Apart from being a stone's throw from Abigail's school, it was, as Edwina intimated at coffee mornings, wonderful for entertainment and had the space and style expected, what with David's career progression to the more senior positions in the insurance industry.

But right now all that finery, all that distance from his humble origins seemed sullied by these greasy yobs loitering and being abusive on his driveway. He found abhorrent these self-indulgent, disaffected, lazy young men who chose to wreck their health with alcohol and drugs and then risk their lives on motorbikes.

And all the while they lived communally a few blocks away in a building condemned by their own handiwork. It was something they chose to do to quell their inferiority complexes and then present their aberrant useless endeavours as some kind of rite of passage.

David, as he always reminded close colleagues in more sombre moments, had known no safety net; he had witnessed close at hand an existential battle against sickness and disease, where the desire for cleanliness was challenged every day, where there was no hot water for a bath, lavatories were communal, there was no choice about crowded, damp living conditions; illness and disease were unavoidable. It seemed to him that for these guys, being scruffy and unwashed was a perverse fashion accessory.

VI

The charge sheets read out by the clerk to the justices at Cheltenham Magistrates' Court seemed to tame the dishevelled crew, some of whom were squeezed into the dock and the others told to stand in a line in front of the dock. It was the formality, the use of their actual names rather than street names, it was the giving of dates of birth that reminded the court that these individuals were born to mothers, had families, rather, as they would have you believe, primitive wild creatures who had been around on their motorbikes since the mists of time.

It was in the stating of the offences which were in the general scheme of things, pretty tame, that made an observer wonder why this motley crew of reprobates had not actually done something much worse. To tell the truth, for those sitting in the gallery, it was slightly disappointing, like wanting to tear your ticket up and ask for your money back.

To start with there were the motoring offences: driving otherwise than in accordance with a licence (the fact that they had licences in the first place let the side down), driving without due care and attention, failing to stop at a red light, carrying a passenger while holding a provisional licence (bloody hell!) and being in charge of a motor vehicle while unfit through drink and drugs.

Then there were the other matters: Section 5 Public Order Act, Section 4 Public Order Act and Affray (Section 3 Public Order Act, 1986).

Then there was theft of petrol which was amended to making off without paying and then changed following a discussion with the clerk to obtaining a pecuniary advantage by deception. Then there was theft of a wheel, carburettor, brake cable and crankshaft from a breaker's yard. This was followed incoherently by theft of ladies' knickers and assorted lingerie from Marks and Spencer on the high street. And, of course, the common assault on David.

The group were all wearing their colours. They had taken the trouble to be particularly smelly, hairy and greasy. What was weird to behold was how, en masse, their mood could sway from an unexpected snivelling deference, where they timidly answered the charges, 'Yes, sir, yes, sir,' without any prompting and with their heads bowed low and almost clinging to each other, as though gripped by fear and anxiety. It did appear that Cat Weasel wet his pants. But then, one of the number made a strange, at first a quiet, groaning sound, and the next thing the room was filled with a raucous laughter as all of them, in unison, became uncontrollably hysterical with incomprehensible merriment. This went on for a good minute with the clerk to the justices repeatedly demanding silence. Eventually the bench warned the gang that if they did not stop they would be sent to the cells for contempt of court.

The laughter subsided and there was a silence as the prosecutor attempted to open his case. But again the proceedings were interrupted and his efforts proved to be short-lived, as now occurred what at first was a barely discernible howl, but as with the previous outburst, this rapidly grew into a deafening crescendo of discordant howling like a sick pack of wolves.

Three Justices of the Peace were sitting. The chairman was

councillor Vince Pye dressed in his regulation dowdy unpressed grey suit. This charmless, wizen old man was a journalist, doyen of the *Gloucestershire Echo*, champion of boring parochial news: births, deaths and marriages, court cases, parish council meetings, church fetes, the annual Bluebell Ball. This was the stuff of interest, the crowded copy that sold papers. There was no end to the litany of parochial, uninspired, mediocre tittle-tattle that Pye felt inspired to peddle to the good citizens of Cheltenham. He was deeply conservative, vehemently opposed to change, a stalwart of traditional values, a man with an ice-cold, uncompromising and unforgiving glare. What had anyone ever done to him to make him thus?

Well, there was another side to this highly respected hack, who in his own way appeared to wear his crumpled dowdiness as a badge of incorruptible honour. This other side was rather more colourful than he would ever wish to be commonly known. Indeed, at night the diminutive toad would turn into the sparkling Queen of the Promenade, shining so brightly in a sequined frock and high heels with a gorgeous coiffured blonde wig with delicate tints of purple. Rouge blushed her cheeks just enough while those eyelashes would have put Ginger Rogers to shame, and her array of perfumes from Cavendish House were carefully selected: Chanel, Dior, Yves St. Laurent.

Pye was joined on the bench by Reginald Gibson MBE JP, an officious man who liked to present himself as salt-of-the-earth, a veritable fount of wisdom, who would attempt the occasional witty comment to lighten the solemnity of the occasion, but he would soon snarl and resort to a mean spirit if those gathered did not respond with at least a whimsical smirk. Gibson was chief of the local boy scouts. He liked the boys to call him 'Gold Eagle'. To emphasise the persona he made a point of dying his grey hair a bright peroxide yellow. It was presumably in this capacity that he chose to wear his boy scouts uniform when officiating on the bench.

The final constituent of the bench that day was Miss Gertrude Blick, a likeable lady of strict morals and a strong social conscience. She had had a career at GCHQ.

The bench had a question for the clerk and the chairman was seen to tap him on the shoulder and whisper down to his desk beneath and in his ear. The chairman enquired as to whether the prosecution intended to proceed with the ladies' knickers. The prosecutor, bemused at this interjection, replied he did and why would he do otherwise?

It was possible that the chairman was concerned that such a detail might distract from the gravitas of the case if reported in the evening headlines; or he may have had other concerns?

The gang had all refused legal representation. When asked if anyone wished to address the court in mitigation, Keck stated that they did not believe in law and order so the proceedings didn't have any meaning for the gang. The clerk explained that if they refused to enter a plea then the silence would be treated as a 'not guilty' and the charges would proceed to trial. The gang dropped their heads again while slyly looking at each other. They remained silent except for a brief, barely coherent muttering from Cat Weasel, who looked at the chairman of the bench and told him that he didn't like him.

The clerk told Cat Weasel to be quiet. The prosecutor then asked the clerk to remind the defendants about costs, which he explained would be considerably increased in the event of a trial in which numerous witnesses would need to be called and there would have to be an adjournment to allocate a trial date. In the event of findings of guilt considerable costs would be added to any fines imposed, non-payment of which would result in court enforcement proceedings and ultimately committal warrants to custody.

Cat Weasel responded, 'Well, we ain't got no money?'

Chairman of the bench: 'You all have motorbikes that the court bailiffs could, in such an eventuality, seize.'

There followed a repeat of the collective wolf-wailing and a further strong unequivocal warning from the bench. There was then some murmuring amongst the gang. Someone was heard to say, 'Anyway, it looks better if we get done, don't it?'

Another said, 'Yeah, it's creepy pleading innocence. We don't want to be innocent, do we?'

Another said, 'And they ain't going to do nothing, are they? I mean, I ain't having my bike nicked by some fucking bailiff.'

The magistrates briefly whispered to each before the chairman asked the gang if they required a brief adjournment, perhaps ten minutes to consider their position.

Keck looked up and said, 'Nah, we're going guilty.'

Thereafter the specific charges were each put to each individual and grudgingly guilty pleas were entered.

With their street credibility shot the riotous crew soon, by default, disbanded as the miscreants went their own separate, insalubrious ways. No longer would this cohort be seen interrupting the genteel spring and summer flow of families taking a beverage or light lunch at the cafe in the municipal gardens. No longer would they be seen slumped with their feet on the tables, bikes parked across the paths and the air filled with foul profanity.

Grinner had a bad trip and became a down and out. Frenchie had a wife and kids to support and traded his bike for a milk float.

Fez died. The coroner's report stated that he had choked on his own vomit while in a comatose state after an overdose of high-purity heroin. It was said, though it may just be folklore in the rougher town hostelries of the time, that he bequeathed his flea-ridden fur coat to the Battersea Dog's home.

Keck went to prison for glassing a bar manager. Some said he needed to prove that he was more sinister than just common assault and points for driving otherwise than in accordance with his licence. Mohawk was already in prison anyway. Shortly thereafter Norman returned to the skinhead fold. And it was rumoured that, much to the chagrin of Councillor Pye, Cat Weasel, aka 'Bubbles', went with Phillip to live in St Tropez.

VII

When Abigail eventually extracted herself from her early experiments in alternative living, in riding pillion on the wrong side of the road, she spent her final summer before going to university in a rekindled relationship with Rodney. Charlotte had moved on to another boyfriend, who was rich and had promised to get her into fashion modelling and help her become an actress. So she felt no resentment when Abigail and Rodney became close; if anything she felt sorry for Abigail.

Most of the summer was spent socialising in Cheltenham – nothing spectacular: cosy picnics and boating in Pittville Park, a summer ball at the Pump Rooms, a lunch party here and a naughty little spliff there. The set was largely an extension of the cohort who arranged extra-curricular activities with the boys from the gents' college during sixth form. Some of the more sophisticated girls found the whole deal rather parochial and twee and were keen to move on to pastures new.

It was often suspected that the genteel air of these jolly jaunts was purely cosmetic and more orgiastic liaisons were politely negotiated and would take place well out of earshot at some rich pile as they had done during term time or in the holidays in some sunny retreat or on a luxury yacht moored on a rocky crag in Ibiza.

'But that was money and that was discrete, so let us not go there. One should always turn a blind eye.'

As Charlotte's mother had so magnanimously put it when her daughter had met her rich suitor, adding, 'He who is without sin can cast the first stone.'

Alas, the relationship did not survive Abigail's first term at university. Once she had discovered abseiling and scuba diving

Rodney became history. He had decided to stay in Cheltenham and accept articles of clerkship to become a solicitor in the same firm as his father. He was given the incentive that when he passed his Law Society exams he would be given his own car and once he qualified he would be in line for a partnership after three years. This was a time when conveyancing was booming and Rodney had always shown a keen interest in the varieties of land charges and intricacies of land registration as well as planning applications. He also covered probate and wills. He was no one-trick pony. Life was good.

Edwina: 'Abigail could have done Oxbridge, you know. Balls and gowns and boaters, strawberries and cream and picnics in punts on the Cam and all that stuff was really not what she was about anyway.'

Edwina was quick to point this out at a coffee morning in the November of the first term following A-level results. Rita and Marg did not doubt it. They just nodded as they held their cups over the saucers, talking between sips.

Marg: 'The social side of things does matter, you know, Edwina; making connections could be very useful to her, might meet a suitable man. I mean, none of us like it, but if you can't beat them, join them, as they say. You should know – I mean, you sent her at great expense to the Ladies' College.'

Edwina well knew Abigail was a clever girl and did not care where she had gone to study. There is always a superfluity about 'should have, could have, would have'-type conversation. Simply, Abigail preferred the course in environmental science at Bristol, but this was the banter of competitive parents who have invested so much of themselves in their academically gifted children. It did not make her any more or less clever, where she went to study and whatever lessons Abigail had learnt at school, they were not about social climbing. Her studies included many field trips. She was more anorak and wellies than little black party dresses by Versace and Dolce and Gabbana; though, when she chose to make the effort she looked stunning. 'Scrubs up well,' was her only articulated concession to herself.

Her thick wavy raven hair and brown eyes were from the Greek side of the family; the milky-white skin was from Edwina and the Scottish side of her father's lineage.

Her preference for dressing down had a sensible practical side, but the dungarees, baseball caps and muddy boots did make her butch. While that in itself was not proof of anything at all, it did prompt comment from her mum and dad, who were from an age where aspirations for an only daughter included some vague notion of presentation to good society.

As a matter of fact, when Abigail was eighteen years old Edwina bought her a fine gown for the Bluebell Ball at Cheltenham Town Hall. She only went because some friends were also going. She got drunk on Babycham and was sick all over her frock. The chivalrous little Lord Fauntleroy who had been following her around during the evening had already become greatly underwhelmed when this virginal debutante, upon whom he doubtless had designs, announced with an inebriated slur that she had been gang-banged by the local Hells Angels. This, incidentally, as we know, was a gross exaggeration. Whatever, the putative suitor disappeared quickly and Edwina came to pick her up early.

It turned out the baggy trousers, roll your own fag, cheers, mate, mine's a pint attitude was the impression Abigail wanted to communicate. Later she would admit that she did not yearn for that persona and with hindsight recognised it as a naïve and unnecessary performative gesture, a prop she chose to adopt to parade those artefacts as a means to, so she thought, reveal something about her sexuality.

Anyway, she spent three blissful and fulfilling years in Bristol, during which they kept close contact, usually returning home during the holidays. For their part her parents continued to fully support her financially and would never regard the sums paid on her behalf as anything other than a gift. Abigail had set her compass points. She was ready for the world. She knew her direction of travel. She had studied environmental science, became an earlier adopter of sustainability, was effusive on the risk of the carbon economy; she was passionate that we are just trustees of the world's delicate bounteous resources for later generations. As an adjunct she decried as cavalier and irresponsible the way humans continued to reproduce. She would quote statistics on population that would deprive flora and fauna of their habitats, as rainforests were destroyed to make way for new cities and agriculture. Even then she feared famine, war and misery that would blight the future. Her particular bug bear was the destruction of tropical rainforests, 'the lungs of the planet', to cultivate palm oil.

11

Passage to India

It was a twelve-hour flight on British Airways from Heathrow to Mumbai. On Eamon's advice they spent two nights at the Taj Mahal Hotel. Quite apart from the luxurious décor and service, Mickey Correa was still resident for evening jazz sessions in the grand ballroom.

Even in the late twentieth century, with its technological sophistication as an international hub, Mumbai was a culture shock for newly arrived pale-faced Europeans. Beyond the modern architecture, slick highways, swish decor, living rooms with lush piled carpet, there is always an otherworldly irrepressible ambience. Carried in the air, even as you exit the aircraft, everywhere there is contrast, whether this is dusty, bumpy tracks next to new roads, multitudes of auto-rickshaws amidst sleek modern cars, spices and incense mingling with petrol fumes, designer perfumes, heaps of burning rubbish and the pong from unregulated effluent streams next to state-of-the-art sewerage systems. And the tropical vegetation, thankfully unremittingly alive, irresolute, spreading its seed, comfortable in the luxuriant eco-system, yet to be defeated by greenhouse gases, ready to encroach and recover swathes of urbanised land.

Amidst the ornate grand palaces and temples and the proud structures of the colonial era, amidst the glass and concrete of high-tech modern obelisks, the city is adorned with coconut palms, mango trees, tamarind and banyan trees.

Salsette Island was once the haunt of wild animals, tigers, leopards, jackals and deer, but those are no longer found there; now there are only cows, oxen, sheep, goats and other domestic species, as well as monkeys, although vultures, pigeons, peacocks, cranes and ducks remain the ever-present birdlife.

From Mumbai, Goa is about an hour's flight south. Eamon's place was on the beach of a village called Ozran, heading north from Vasco de Gama, where he had originally lived after moving to the area. The quaint, unpretentious beach Palapas was full of charm and personal touches. Inside was a large living room, which had the air of a jazz lounge with a baby grand piano next to a personalised bar, behind which there was a large picture of a Mersey ferry as it passed in front of the Liver Building. On the wall there was a framed picture of Eamon playing at the Taj Mahal's ballroom with Earl King, Chic Chocolate and Mickey Correa, dated 1954. Next to that was a photograph of 249 Squadron RAF Ta Kali, signed by members of the squadron and dated October 1942. There was a model of a Spitfire on the piano. The ornate bi-folding doors led out to balustraded decking, with a colourful awning neatly slung from the thatched roof and framed by lush sweeping palm trees offering shade and comfort in the extended space for outside living. And always in the background was the soporific lapping of gentle waves breaking on the shore as the warm tide ebbed and flowed. Ozran was surrounded by green hills and rock formations.

The year 1998 was good for the Pangloss family, variously a time of peace, progress, relaxation, travel and unity. David had at last retired. Abigail had completed a postgraduate degree and continued her research in the Amazon.

David and Edwina had sketched in a travel plan and Abigail's acceptance of an invitation to accompany them was an affirmation that the nuclear family was alive and well; fears of alienating their outspoken daughter were ill-founded after all. For her the pretext for travelling was the opportunity to visit a relative she had heard so much about but had never met.

When they arrived they were greeted with a warm embrace by Eamon. He appreciated their visit. Despite best intentions how often do family dispersed across the world simply pass away without ever meeting again? And circumstances were such that Eamon felt a special need to express his love and pleasure at their company.

Now long settled in Goa, he looked slim and tanned and healthy for his seventy-four years. Recognition and reconnecting after so many years can be disconcerting. There is a mixture of nervous excitement and curiosity, a reticence about how to rekindle a familial commonality. People are never quite as you remember them, as time moulds and withers our physical presence, and yet there in an expression, in the depth of the eyes, in a verbal intonation, something that makes immediate the past closeness, a spiritual connection that resonates across the intervening years.

Eamon's wife Natalie was also on hand to greet the guests with a welcoming smile and embrace. They had married in the late 1950s. Natalie was a Goan artist and the sister of a fellow musician from Calcutta. As a Portuguese-Indian woman she had serene beauty, with silky dark olive skin, a soft voice and a natural capacity for empathy. She moved with a svelte grace. A refreshing floral aroma always followed her. When she moved her hands and arms, they breezed through the air with a gentle motion.

David could not do otherwise than admit to being enchanted, watching as she appeared float in her light shimmering silk sari. Even though a Catholic by birth she was not someone who needed to rush to mass each week; actually a refreshingly independent thinker, something that impressed Eamon and added to her allure. And of course, a Hindu tilaka painted on her forehead was merely a fashion accessory rather than for any remotely religious reason.

David had first met her when he visited Eamon while on a solo business trip to India in the mid-1970s, shortly before he moved to Cheltenham. The company had some established clients through a brokerage on the sub-continent and it was proposed to assign that business to a new undertaking in Mumbai.

In some ways that had been an unfortunate meeting, an occasion when bonhomie and expectation of rekindled familial spirits turned sour. David, perhaps overly focused on his business, perhaps not anticipating the strength of the fortified local wine, maybe weary and unguarded after his travels, for whatever the reason, uncharacteristically made what sounded like a brash and impolite comment. This was interpreted by his host as an insulting personal condemnation. In consequence the usual flow of correspondence between the two cousins cooled for a couple of years before eventually ebbing back to a kind of normality. Even so, there remained a feeling of unresolved business.

Eamon had been recounting how he came to be in Goa. He mentioned how he switched off to the mayhem of the Partition when travelling from Calcutta. He had said that it was not his war, not something he needed to get involved in, that he just wanted to remain politically and emotionally detached, and get away from all the slaughter and misery.

David had then responded with a number of sanctimonious comments about Eamon turning a blind eye, not facing up to reality, not doing his bit as a compassionate soul, even going as far as to suggest moral cowardice. Eamon was furious.

He dealt with the matter by aggressively hammering a twelve-bar blues scale on the keyboard while mockingly repeating every ill-considered word that issued from David's mouth. This prompted what sounded like the appropriate gesture of making an apology, though David's modulation was inescapably more performative, politic and polite than with any air of sincerity.

The conversation ended when Eamon slammed the piano cover shut and muttered in an abrupt and depressed manner that his bloody mind had shut down to it anyway and that they should park the matter and get something to eat. After the twenty years that had passed it was surely now water under the bridge?

Eamon had many friends in Goa. The atmosphere was a friendly, heady mix of Indian and European. He enjoyed a healthy diet of fresh seafood with a plentiful supply of locally sourced vegetables. The fusion jazz music was good and he been assured work with a resident band. And though he had adopted alternative forms of meditation he settled well in the Portuguese-Catholic community. For him, even after the spiritual relevance had vanished, the feast days, ceremonies and hymns offered a temporal primal comfort, resonant in some way of the fervent religiosity his mother bestowed on his childhood in Wigan.

But there were still dark days when he would withdraw to fight his demons. Natalie would anticipate the onset of morose bouts, which initially manifested as uncharacteristic irritability. He would express his torment by sitting at the piano for hours on end playing sounds that would range from discordance to light, ethereal melodies.

David carried two divergent impressions of his older cousin. There was the man Pat and Moira told him about as a young boy: the war hero, all the daring-do minutiae of a military man of action, of an exciting, dangerous life of adventure, of his involvement in air combat. And then there was the man who was one day sitting at the kitchen table on

David's return from school. This man was quiet, insecure, lacking confidence, at odds with the world, even meek, yet wanting to hear all about David's progress. He recalled how the conversation had a staccato feel, as though there was shame, as though Eamon had done something terribly wrong and owed a debt to society, the demeanour of someone who had nothing interesting to say. His only spark was when the conversation turned to music.

Later the correspondence between the two men provided an ongoing therapy. David respected, even revered his cousin. Eamon had influenced the way David had determined to treat people during his working life. If someone appeared brusque and difficult he would think twice and make allowances. This understated style of discretion and leadership had seen David soar to great heights in the insurance industry. The positive overriding influence that the older man had on the younger therefore only served to compound those intemperate comments of the earlier visit and made them doubly perplexing and irritating.

Now a calm elderly sage, pretty well at peace with himself and the world, so different from restless earlier years, Eamon nevertheless enjoyed the company of friends, good food and the occasional imbibing of a glass of wine made in the local vineyards.

Eamon: 'Music saved me… as well as Natalie, of course. I can lose myself for hours. I've had bad nights; the bloody devils persisted for years. No psychotherapists around here, mind, not that it would have made any difference; besides I've been through that process, the "talking cure". It didn't make the demons go away.

'I took up meditation after being in India a few years. Natalie suggested it, but it demands a routine, discipline, has to be part of daily life. I found a teacher, the whole eastern mysticism thing. I have not looked back. It really helped me.'

David: 'Yes, like me, you turned your back on Rome. I didn't realise Auntie Moira was as religious as Mum, maybe she just went easy on me. I mean, as a kid I really believed it all, as kids do in an innocent unquestioning way: catechism, mass, prayer, confession, communion, benediction, holy days and feast days. It did my head in after a while. Cecil served as an altar boy, you know, but was never angelic about it, just seemed a contented little bugger. God, I didn't like confession. "Him", the mighty Him, up there, knowing my grubby thoughts, and the priest was his mate, the man you tell it all to. If it was supposed to sanctify, make you lead to a better life, then I think even then I knew it would not work for me.

'Just for Cecil it was all so harmonious. After he died I imagined that he was really just like Jesus as a boy. I idealised his memory. I suppose I still do, but I know he was not perfect, it just seemed that way. Whenever I tried to pray I found myself thinking of Cecil, praying to Cecil and thinking that if Cecil had had the chance to grow into a man he would have had greatness, like Jesus, and performed amazing deeds. Then I worried that thoughts like that were also sins, you know, worshipping false idols. I had a lot of confusion about Cecil.

'Then I suffered from that stupid guilt trip... seems so ridiculous now. I could have only been seven or eight years old waiting to watch Agnes, wait until she filled the old tin bath. I would use any excuse, make myself busy with things that I didn't need to be busy with, then watch at the door when she was behind the curtain. I could see her outline and listen to her sweetly singing in the tub. I knew that I was prying, invading her space. Now I know it was the awakening of a sexual inquisitiveness. Then she would show me as though it was OK. But it made me feel guilty, like I was doing something wrong. I told the priest in my first confession and the old fucker threatened me with eternal damnation.'

Eamon smiled. 'Good old-fashioned hell, fire and brimstone, best way to keep the flock in their pen. I often wonder whether the imagined prospect of damnation is really worse than the real experience.'

David: 'Well, no, thankfully I realised early on that I was not going to go through life with some old priest messing with my head, so I went off the whole bloody shebang. If there had been anything to salvage it was lost when Mum, Dad and Cecil died. When they were taken from me – well, I knew if there was a merciful God he would never have done that.'

Eamon: 'Yes, but that doesn't prevent the hell, fire and brimstone of psychological torment, of witnessing and living with the memories of terror. You should know as well as I that that stuff haunts us.'

David: 'Well maybe, but I chose a career in insurance. I don't claim to have been an action man. I didn't do all that "stuff".'

Eamon: '"Do all that stuff". Do? Hmm… I am talking about what is in the mind. You don't choose to do what is in the mind, do you?' I didn't want to bring it up, but for some reason your drift reminds me of those comments you made years ago, last time you visited.'

David: 'Comments? Oh, about Partition. Yes, you did take those comments rather to heart, didn't you? I said I was sorry. Actually, I was surprised that you should have reacted in that way. It did concern me when you stopped writing for a year or two. I was quite hurt by your reaction.'

Eamon: 'I think maybe there still is a bone we need to chew. Hasn't gone away, has it?'

David: 'Bone to chew?'

Eamon: 'Pot calling the kettle black?'

David: 'Pot calling the kettle black?'

Eamon: 'Chose a career in insurance. Don't do all that stuff? We don't always have a choice whether that "stuff" comes knocking on our door, wrecks our peace of mind, tries to destroy our lives. Have you forgotten or are you claiming some sort of immunity, David?

'You accused me of copping out, turning a blind eye, of moral cowardice, when really what I was saying to you was that the terrible sights of slaughter during Partition prompted my cognitive responses to shut down, albeit temporarily. It was a coping mechanism. I had been through enough in Malta. I had talked it all through with shrinks. It might not have made me feel better but at least I understood what was happening to me. I think I had a right to say that it was not my war. Why do you think I continue to meditate every day? And I joined up to do my bit for King and country against a wicked Nazi creed. Well, I did all that stuff because I also felt a duty. True, as a young man I had an inner rage, but if you had been older how do you know you would not have made similar choices?

'And you chided me. The reality is you continue to block out that awful cloud from your childhood. I don't blame you. It's just you need to know that bloody luggage lurks within you. It seems you've chosen to forget about it, pretend it doesn't exist. It won't just go away, you know.

'Years ago, that moment of spectator's indignation, you as some kind of objective bystander, untainted, entitled to be judgemental, incensed me at first. But I thought about it and realised it is you in denial, not me. I know my demons, but I worry that you have buried yours deep in your psyche. They are there and may one day emerge with a vengeance.'

David: 'I think you're being alarmist. I mean, for heaven's sake, I've retired. I have a loving family, a good pension. I chose insurance not air combat. What's not to like? Maybe I do have some "luggage", as you say, but doesn't everybody?'

Eamon: 'I worry, David, sometimes innocence can be a convenient hiding place for the unchallenged monster within. Are you saying you have never been racked by troubling thoughts or disturbing dreams?'

David: 'Funny you should that. You know I've always had a dream that never came true. Well, I say dream, it was a dream that constantly morphed into something else. As my life moved on then the dream would change, even if it always felt like the same dream. What remained constant was a feeling that it had a meaning I yearned for but could never find, and because the dream kept changing it could never come true. But that really didn't matter, it was the dream that propelled me on, fired my endorphins, gave me purpose, a reason to get up in the morning. Yes, it did stress me up, but what's wrong with a bit of stress?

'The ever-changing dream was my personal myth, a subtext to my existence, a neat little delusion within the grand narrative of God or Mammon or whatever.

'I mean, of course, I always knew Cecil was at peace. His life was the best of all possible worlds. He never visits me in dreams, yet strangely my dad does. It's weird, it's like double vision. He walks in as a parallel presence, a three-dimensional shadow, without his own shadow. His presence is never alarming, actually familiar and friendly. I become aware of his presence as I stir in the night to have a piss.

'In the dream I'm maybe driving a car, and I pull up and find a fence bordering a park so that I can relieve myself. I realise that as I arrive at a pissing post, one hundred yards further along the fence Harry is also pissing in synchronisation. And then I realise that a further shadowy figure walks into line to piss upon a post a further one hundred yards along the line and that this is Troy and I realise that Harry does see his own shadow but does not see a shadow fall from the physical presence of Troy. And then likewise, like a kaleidoscopic proliferation of images, through the generations, the fathers of fathers line up to piss, each seeing their own shadow but not that of their father. And then I wake up and go and have my piss.'

Eamon: 'Right. Well, I can't help you with any of that, David. I think we're getting off track. Don't you ever wake up with cold sweats, overwhelmed by the most debilitating uneasiness, tormented by hideous images?'

David: 'No, I can't say that I do.'

Eamon: 'Well, maybe it turns out you've been lucky, blessed with good karma? Can I top your glass up?'

David: 'No, I'm OK. Anyway, on days when that dream has faded I would buy a lottery ticket, but you know, the last thing I wanted to know was what the winning numbers were; rather I felt I was getting value for money by holding on for several days to the outrageous possibility that the numbers on the piece of paper in my pocket might be the winning combination. That was something to savour, to contemplate, time to question what I would do with the money, how much of it I would give away, start to worry about the problem of investing or spending such vast sums, eventually convince myself that I really did not want to win the jackpot at all because of the headaches it would cause, but be happy, just enough to live comfortably.'

Eamon: 'So you find solace in out-reasoning chance? Not even blighted by idle hope? Does sound like good karma.'

David: 'Maybe I don't have the need to lose myself quite in the same way you do? I do hear what you say. I realise you confronted your own personal hell in Malta. I appreciate it must have been terrible.'

Eamon: 'It's all a long time ago. Like I said, I've spent a lifetime trying to deal with it, but I well know from years of therapy and meditation, just trying to bury a bad memory is not an answer. There inevitably has to be some cathartic process which can be excruciating, but in confronting the demon eventually you contain it.'

David: 'Does it still cause you pain to revisit those few months in 1942?'

Eamon: 'Not now. Look, I have these photographs. There was a lot to be proud of. Those guys on the squadron were all pretty selfless in putting their lives on the line. I mean, the people of Malta were heroic too, crawling out of bomb-shattered caves every day to carry on as normal. They were people with incredible faith.'

David: 'What about Buzz Beurling? You used to mention him in your letters home.'

Eamon: 'Screwball and air war? That sums it up. That's all there was. How to be lethally efficient, how to kill. But if you mean about life? About leadership? About people? About love? What do you expect me to say?

'You would learn nothing of the finer sensibilities. And why should you? Not his style, and he was dead at twenty-seven. The man was a psychopathic cyborg, a symbiosis of man and machine, perfectly honed to his Spitfire; but let's not forget, undoubtedly courageous and consummately single-minded.

'What else was there? Maybe he had the same doubts and frailties as the rest of us, though I doubt it. He quoted the Bible enough, but only because it gave a moral narrative, a premise for action that he would never want to explore too closely.'

David: 'I thought he had a wife.'

Eamon: 'Ha. A trophy wife; when they shipped him back to Canada to sell war bonds. He was a fish out of water. Hated the whole celebrity razzmatazz. Can't criticise him for that. His wife was a lady from a good family. I'd heard she'd been married before, so not exactly a spring chicken, but genuine; though settling down was not what Screwball was about. His love was air war, not women. We used to joke in the mess that when it came to women he had no idea which buttons to push and laugh that the girls were not so keen on his deflection shooting in the bedroom, but let's not go there. Anyway, him and his wife ended living separate and apart after a few months; but by all accounts she was a good woman, stayed loyal to him.

'Enough of war, let's talk of peace, love, music and that gorgeous Sula wine that Natalie brought back from the market. Here, fill your glass up. Where's the Sula, dear?'

David: 'Can't argue with that. Talking of trophy wives, you have to be congratulated.'

Eamon: 'My soulmate, you mean? Not sure if Natalie would like me calling her a trophy. But I know. It's been good. So lucky.'

David: 'What happened to the guy you travelled out here with?'

Eamon: 'Earl was a great musician and a good man, and I tell you, he had some beautiful women. Maybe that meant people accused him of being fickle in love, maybe they were jealous at his success in bedding them, but you know, he just couldn't hold on to them. I think he had an addictive personality, addictive to whatever was going. Like Satchmo, he never played without first rolling a joint and dosing up on laxative. The one chilled him out and made him feel good before going on stage; the other made sure he didn't shit himself blowing too hard in the higher register. Ha ha.

'He never settled down, a true rolling stone, but despite all the bigotry and racism, I think he missed his home in Morgan Park, Chicago. He used to say, "It wasn't nothing, but it was home, good beer and great music."'

At that point Abigail returned to the villa from a night out.

The evening was warm; an aromatic breeze wafted in, mixing sea-salt scents with surangi and jasmine. Through the darkness the surf could be heard melodically lapping on the sandy beach a short distance away. On the veranda little gnats darted around the lights. Just beyond the balcony a swarm of fireflies would suddenly illuminate the darkness and then fade from view.

Abigail appeared. She was on her own, merry in her familiar adversarial way, ready to prod and poke in jest. She was suitably attired for the warm night in a light floaty dress over her bikini, with a light silk shawl wrapped around her shoulders and was carrying her sandals in one hand. Her long hair had become knotted and the ends sun-bleached, her skin tanned, and she wore leather-coloured bangles around her wrists that she had purchased from one of the many beachside traders.

She had a bottle of Kingfisher beer with her.

It had not gone unnoticed that Abigail had met a group of people on the beach and was spending an increasing amount of time away from Eamon's place: swimming, surfing, having beach barbecues and partying. After the years of hard work at university and commitment she had made to her post-doctoral research, it was good to know she was relaxing enjoying the idyllic setting.

Abigail: 'God, I'm knackered. The beach party last night went on to the early hours.'

David: 'Well, you're looking rather exotic, full of eastern promise ha, ha.'

Eamon chipped in: 'Wandering around like that I bet a lot of the boys are eyeing you up. And I say that only with complimentary intent.'

Natalie: 'You look wonderful, my dear. Here, come and sit next to me.'

Edwina: 'Be careful, Eamon, she's sensitive about those sorts of observations.'

Too late.

Abigail: 'Oh, not you as well, another dirty old man. You disappoint me, Eamon.'

Edwina: 'Be polite, darling. No need to be offended by our lovely host.'

Abigail: 'But it's the same old tripe, Mum, same old assumptions. Men need to learn.'

David said, quietly and politely: 'Shuut up. Lass, you're too sensitive. Eamon's just telling it the way it is. I mean, it wouldn't do to wear those dowdy things you have at home?'

Abigail: 'Dowdy clothes?'

David: 'You know, the dungarees, baggy jumpers and wellies that you like to slouch around in?'

Abigail: 'Oh for God's sake – no, Mum, I won't be quiet. Christ, what do expect me to wear on muddy field trips?

Anyway, it wasn't just about that. You know, that elephant in the room, the male gaze.'

David: 'The male gaze?'

Abigail: 'Yes, the male gaze. Dirty old men, and not just old men either, pervy chauvinists of any age, ogling at women's bodies with depraved intent, objectifying women, seeing women as mere sex objects.'

David: 'Eh, now wait a minute, young lady… you mean men appreciating the beautiful female form, what's wrong with that?'

Abigail: 'No, I mean lust, erotic desire, lecherous intent, the heterosexual male's primordial desire for pleasurable sexual looking, what the textbooks call scopophilia.'

David: 'Oh, really, is that so… excuse me, if you'll pardon me for saying, but scopo my derriere?'

Edwina: 'I think your father knows exactly what you mean, dear. I should know.' Edwina took a large sip from her glass of wine.

David: 'Whose side are you on? I never noticed you objecting to some tender affection and attention.'

Edwina: 'Tender affection and attention, mmm.'

David: 'You know what you like, Edwina. These things cut both ways, you know, between a man and a woman. I've never heard any complaints about our compatibility. It takes two to tango, you know.'

Abigail: 'Have I missed something, Mum?'

Edwina then said, thinking twice through her obvious inebriation: 'Well, no, never mind, dear, perhaps we should park that one.'

Natalie: 'Hey. Come on, you guys, peace and love. You are here to enjoy yourselves.'

Abigail: 'Park what where?'

David: 'No, now wait a minute. If I look at a woman it is because I appreciate her, what's wrong with that? I mean, no one would challenge you for admiring a beautiful flower, so why not a beautiful woman? And I tell you, the only woman I have ever looked at is your mother? So why are you not pleased that I found your mother sexy and beautiful?'

Abigail: 'That's precisely it. I'm talking about men who don't actually see women as people, as thinking, feeling individuals but just as objects that turn them on, make them leer with lascivious intent, with lustful desires. The unwritten narrative is entirely about what the man can take, what he can get to satisfy him and nothing about what can be given. It is purely about taking, not giving. That is an assault on dignity that has no respect for another person's individual integrity and feelings.'

David: 'No, no. It's flattering for the woman. They like it. That's true, isn't it, Edwina?'

Edwina took another sip of her wine and looked wide-eyed at the ceiling.

Natalie: 'Well, is it not that the gaze is inscribed in nature. Is it not the female peacock who admires the plumage of the male? I doubt that the male feels objectified by being admired. And what about the beauty in the colours and fragrance of lotus, hibiscus, jasmine or sunflowers? You attract the bees, darling, and they spread your pollen for fertilisation.'

Eamon: 'I think you should take note of Natalie's wise words. There's no need to fight about such a subject.'

David continued: 'I mean, if men didn't fancy women they would never marry them. Where would the fairer sex be then, eh?'

Abigail: 'Probably a lot better off.'

David: 'Any road, what about queer ones? Don't queer folk look at each other in that way too? What do you call their gaze or doesn't that count?'

Abigail: 'Grrr, for God's sake, you're making my blood boil.'

And with that Abigail impetuously threw a good half-pint of Kingfisher lager into her father's face, soaking his new, colourfully printed holiday shirt.

David: 'Why? What's the matter? What did I say, lass? Look, I love your mother and bloody fancy her, always have, is that so awful? What sort of morality is this anyway? I don't know what problem it is that young women have these days.' David shrugged his shoulders at Eamon as he wiped himself in a towel.

Abigail: 'What a bunch of fucking backward-looking, pissed-up, ageing hippy freaks.'

David: 'Hey, hey, now come on, that's quite enough of that.'

Thankfully, with a friendly interjection from Natalie, steering the conversation to places of interest that the guests might visit, the inebriated minds were soon distracted to a less volatile subject matter. Abigail was drowsy and went to her room to sleep.

Breakfast the next morning was late as it had progressively become as the holiday incrementally morphed the guests into nocturnal people. David and Edwina just wanted peace and hoped that the dust had settled.

David: 'About last night, let's just let sleeping dogs lie, eh? Things get said after a few drinks that can be misinterpreted.'

Abigail: 'Hmm.' She changed the subject. 'Oh, by the way, I'm going to stay near Dudhsagar Waterfalls for a few days. I am going with my new friend, Sappho de Souza. I should tell you that we are in a relationship.'

Edwina: 'That sounds wonderful, dear.'

David: 'What sort of work does he do?'

Eamon: 'I thought Sappho is a girl's name?'

Abigail: 'Yes... a girl.'

Natalie: 'I know Sappho. She's a sculptor. She has a studio next to mine. Attractive, stylish young lady. We exhibited together once in a group show. Very talented. I think she may even have visited here once.'

Eamon: 'I didn't know that. Well fancy.'

Abigail: 'That's right. She said she knew you.'

David, still hungover from the night before, was confused and stared blankly at Edwina as he sipped his coffee.

Edwina offered Abigail a drink and then put an arm around her, almost leaning on her shoulder, as though breaking the ice with a pretentious gesture of girlie solidarity. She understood something that David had really not cottoned on to.

Eventually David responded: 'In a relationship, you say?'

Abigail: 'Yes, Dad, in relationship.'

David: 'You know, your mother and I – on certain issues, that is – hold traditional values. Now I'm not being judgemental when I say that.'

Abigail: 'What values are they, Dad?'

Somewhat uncharacteristically, Edwina broke ranks, and, with defiance infused with a certain glee, she interjected: 'Speak for yourself, David.'

David: 'Well, I am.' David then, with a curious, dislocated logic, said, 'Does this mean that we will never have grandchildren, that our Pangloss line will end?'

'Oh, go piss, Dad, for God's sake,' said Abigail. 'Get a life. This isn't about the fucking bloodline and all that bunkum that I thought you more than anyone had dispatched to the dustbin of history a long time ago. No, this is about me and my life and my happiness – yes, call it the best of all possible worlds if you like. It is for me anyway.'

David: 'Well, no, I don't call it that at all. I must admit, I am surprised. I mean, you're both attractive young women, and this Sappho wears stylish things as Natalie says; you both go to parties and no doubt wear bikinis to go swimming. I mean, I thought, what with lesbians and that, that one of you would have short hair and wear baggy trousers and look masculine, you know, like women with hairy legs and a bit of fluffy growth on their upper lip. Well, that's not my Abigail and it does not sound like this young Sappho.'

Abigail: 'Can't believe my own father could be such a moron. Just idiotic stereotyping; doesn't mean a fucking thing. If you must know we met at that beach party I went to on the second day we were here. We hit it off. There was a spark. Then it just happened, we became more than just good friends.'

David: 'A "spark", so does that mean you'll move in together?'

Abigail: 'I didn't say that.'

David: 'Well, alright, go away together, as a couple, I mean. Not much difference, is there, these days? Aren't you being impetuous? You've only known each other five minutes. You know, your mother and I had a spark for years before things progressed. I had proposed before we went away together. We didn't move in together until we were married.'

Abigail: 'From what Mum has told me that sounds like a rather sanitised version of events. Anyway, it does not feel impetuous to us.'

David: 'I'm just saying what I think is an appropriate and acceptable way of carrying on and what isn't.'

Abigail: 'Oh, so is this one of those never darken our doorway again moments?'

Edwina: 'No, of course not, your father didn't mean that. It's just he's upset.'

Abigail: 'Upset, about what, for Christ's sake? He spends enough time on his hobby horse about the hypocrisy of the church. Who is he to pontificate on what is and isn't moral? Look, Dad, I wouldn't dream of judging you so please do not judge me. I am old enough to make my life choices and I know myself well enough after all these years to know what is right for me. If you don't like it then fine, we can go our own separate ways.'

David: 'Don't judge me, you don't judge me; well, I think you do nothing but… I don't know why you say these things. People can have differences, you know. Of course it doesn't mean that they stop speaking. Sometimes I worry that I haven't brought you up to appreciate those values in human relations that mattered in my humble childhood.'

Abigail: 'Oh, the same old hobby horse.'

Natalie: 'Woah, wait. Peace, love, harmony, and please do not accuse me of using those words glibly, Eamon will tell you I am no pseud. They are not uttered as some naïve, juvenile, poetic notion of hearts and flowers.

'You know, when I explain my art to people I always say that life should reflect art as art should reflect life. There will always be bad things going on, there will always be a lot of everything going on, but it becomes tolerable and doesn't matter so long as there is balance. Good karma.

'Life should be colourful as art should be colourful, but that does not mean that I indiscriminately plaster my canvas with everything in my paint box. To create incoherence and chaos is not art, just as a life of chaos and incoherence is not a life that anyone would want to live.

'And just as in human relationships where opposites attract, so in art contrasts cohere: black and white, black and yellow, yellow and blue, blue and red, red and green. That sounds very heterosexual, I hear you say. Well, equally coherent and satisfying are the complimentary hues and tints that sit right next to each other on the colour wheel. Yes, shades of sameness also aesthetically attract.

'But just as importantly, you always have to exercise moderation. If a bank prints an unlimited amount of money it soon becomes valueless; if you party the whole time the celebration wanes and joy turns to misery. Well, it's the same with the canvas, where a little dash of colour amidst a subdued backdrop becomes bright and glowing with a magical intensity, while colours liberally splashed in indiscriminate and unchecked gaudiness lose their value. It leads to a ghastly sensory overload devoid of aesthetic beauty.

'I say in art as in life. Karma is in the balance, firmness and moderation in what we like. Why can't we all respect that in each of us?

Edwina: 'Well, I think that restores a certain civility to breakfast time. Why we should squabble in this idyll in the first place God only knows.'

Eamon, to Natalie: 'Well, I think that might have reassured us all, darling.'

David and Abigail looked at each other, silenced, disarmed, each almost disappointed as the other that the gentle intervening words somehow prevented them from continuing into their full verbal adversarial mode.

Edwina: 'Just take a deep breath, you two. Overcoming pride to accept wisdom can be painful.'

Abigail: 'No problem for me, Mum. Really, I think it is a beautiful comparison.'

For Eamon there was an added pleasure in seeing David momentarily humbled with his horns trimmed, as though the present humiliation and defeat served also as a poetic chastisement for the enduring rancour of that earlier distant pomposity.

12

Abigail's Career

I

On returning from Goa Abigail did a post-doctorate fellowship at the Swedish University of Agriculture and was co-opted to the Intergovernmental Panel on Forests. This enabled her to attend the eighth session of United Nations Commission on Sustainable Development in New York in May of 2000, as she had contributed to a paper that was presented. This led to a bursary to research and review sustainability papers for the OECD (Organisation for Economic Cooperation and Development) and was what brought her to France in July of 2000. After a week in Paris she had a few free days before attending a symposium in Brussels. She had hired a car for a leisurely journey to Belgium, taking in some of the war graves monuments of Thiepval and Ypres as well as a stop-off in the Champagne region.

On returning to Paris on the 25th her scheduled flight back to Heathrow was not until the following morning and she would need to return the car to the vehicle hire centre at the airport. A sizeable deposit had been taken as a condition of use, so Abigail was cautious to avoid any scuff marks or coffee spills on the upholstery.

As it would be an early start on the 26th she decided to look for an inexpensive hotel conveniently located. It was the height of the summer tourist season, so while there were plenty of little hotels and hostelries dotted around the vicinity of such a major airport the task was not so straightforward. Eventually, she found and checked into the Hotelissimo, a functional modern flat-pack economy establishment in the commune of Gonesse in the north-eastern suburbs, located thirty minutes from the centre of Paris. The commune lies immediately north of Le Bourget Airport and is six kilometres south-west of Charles de Gaulle International and fairly and squarely on its flight path.

The staff were friendly and the woman on the desk had explained that they were booked up with two coach-loads, one scheduled to arrive soon and a Polish group who had arrived earlier in the week but were presently on an excursion and would be back later that night. They were all accommodated in double rooms, but as the walls were thin, the indication was that it could be a noisy evening. The woman stated that she had one room left to the rear of the building and at the far end of the ground-floor corridor, if Abigail was still interested. As needs must, Abigail had opted to take the room.

The 25th July was a warm, dry summer day with open blue skies. A few moments before 16.44hrs a charter flight of an Aérospatiale-BAC Concorde arranged by a German company had been cleared for take-off by air traffic control. The wind at the airport was light and variable that day and was reported to the cockpit crew as an eight-knot tailwind as they lined up on runway 26R. The destination was New York to join a cruise to Ecuador.

The pilot, Captain Christian Marty, had completed final checks after taxiing onto the main runway and had moved the controls to full throttle. The sleek beast was now thundering down the runway to gain the requisite two hundred knots to enable the supersonic aircraft to become airborne.

At some point one of the undercarriage wheels went over a thin sliver of metal, not much more than a piece of foil. It pierced the tyre and violently tossed red-hot shredded rubber on to the underside of the aircraft's delta wings. Upon impact the rubber ruptured the aerodynamic ultra-thin superstructure cladding the fuel tank. The result was catastrophic. A full load of high-octane aviation fuel started spewing out and because of the heat of the rubber and the oxygen from the slipstream, this immediately ignited as the aircraft approached take-off velocity.

The consequent raging inferno behind the engines on the massive delta wings was highly visible at the control tower. The air traffic controller immediately radioed to the captain to abort take-off. The flight control voice recorder recovered showed that the timespan from freak damage on the underside of wing to catastrophic crash was one minute and seventeen seconds.

The supersonic beast alighted from the ground as a raging inferno. Captain Christian Marty, who had flown Concorde for twenty-five years, believed the best bet was to get airborne for a matter of seconds and then make an emergency landing at Le Bourget. It proved impossible to either control the aircraft or gain sufficient height, and following a sudden complete shutdown of propulsion from the flaming Rolls-Royce engines, in a flash, the Concorde flew into the front of the Hotelissimo and exploded into a fireball, instantly killing the ninety-six passengers and thirteen crew members on board.

It was a miracle that anyone in the hotel could have survived. Several died, but almost impossibly twelve people managed to walk away from the burning charred ground that was all that was left.

Abigail was one of them. She had heard the sudden immense, angry screeching sound of the doomed aircraft and was then blown across her room as the walls caved in and the place became engulfed in flames. Her ground-floor window was wide open as she always insisted on the circulation of fresh air, rather than breathing the stale, cooped-up recycled air of a budget hotel.

She later recalled somehow effortlessly jumping through the window and running across a field to get as far away as possible. As she ran it felt as though the hot, thick, acrid smoke was following her, no matter how fast she tried to run and however breathless she became. She could not shake off either the heat or the smell of the gaseous fog and fumes that seemed to envelope the land in every direction.

She recalled crossing a main road and finding herself in a wilderness wasteland of landfill. In front of her were yellow and black hazard signs warning of dangerous chemicals, benzene and methane. She noticed vent pipes to allow escape of gases from the sprawling tip. When she turned around, the horizon from which she had run was heavier than ever with smoke and flames and in front of her a sprawling dystopia. With her acute sense of negative environmental impacts this was, for her, an image of hell.

Eventually, she found herself in a field about a mile away from the Hotelissimo. There were horses grazing on sparse scraggy tufts nearby. She lay down and rolled into a foetal position, burying her head in her hands. She was spitting out sinewy black phlegm that tasted of charred metallic rubber. She was coughing and spluttering from the hot, stultifying gas that had consumed the air.

Much later Abigail felt a personal victory that aided her healing, upon hearing that the mayor of Gonesse, Jean-Pierre Blazy, had closed this landfill wasteland into which she had escaped. A report claimed that the pollution of aquifers was significant. During the following years vegetation gradually covered the garbage as wilding replenished the local eco-system.

As was reported in an environmental report: 'A spontaneous biodiversity has developed on this no man's land after redevelopment of the waste domes. The size of the site and its one hundred per cent natural character are an excellent means of raising the awareness of the local population on questions of respect for the environment and local biodiversity.'

Slowly, perhaps after half an hour, it might have been less, it might have been more, Abigail stirred and checked herself. She was in one piece even though trembling uncontrollably and still coughing and spitting the now less discoloured phlegm. As she put one foot in front of the other and walked slowly back she could see a charred and smoking horizon with dispersed pockets of flames and hundreds of fire engines, ambulances and airport officials. Cars had stopped all the way along the road and there was a silhouette of a mass of people crowding a line to observe the terrible aftermath on that warm, lazy, tragic late afternoon in July.

She was disorientated, as though in retracing her steps, she was treading an entirely different path. The earth was scorched black; a field of long grass had vanished, between the flashing blue lights, sirens, vehicle engines and the gush of flame smothering foam, there were intermittent moments of silence that dove-tailed with blackened spaces in between the littered debris of broken fuselage, shattered jet turbines, passenger seats and grim, barely recognisable, charred lumps that were human remains.

The hotel Abigail had been relaxing in an hour earlier had disappeared completely from the landscape. By the time she got back within a couple of hundred yards of the accident site the emergency authorities had cordoned off the area with metal stakes and yellow tape. This thankfully saved Abigail from wandering through the field strewn with burnt body parts.

When she told an official manning the cordon that she had been in the hotel, he looked at her with disbelief and then said 'Non, non, ce n'est possible, allez, allez vite, c'est tres dangereuse.'

She realised that she still had her mobile telephone in her pocket and her credit card.

She wandered through the encroaching throng of people, walking against the tide, having to squeeze past the weighty mass of shocked human observers, moving as though bound in a collective trance, their eyes fixed and their minds locked in the ghastly horror of the moment. Abigail felt anger as she shoved her way through, as though she was invisible, ignored, anonymous, yet she felt more invested, more entitled to be seen, to be heard, to be acknowledged for the involuntary proximity she had endured to this catastrophe.

Eventually, as she seemed to double back on herself, she was again wandering in a strange wilderness; the crowds thinned out and she walked dazed into the little suburb of Gonesse, where she found a café. She ordered a coffee and as she sipped could feel for the first time a slight discomfort on the back of her right arm. When she inspected more closely she discovered a scorched graze up the side above her elbow.

She started to order her thoughts. She telephoned for a taxi to take her the short distance to Charles de Gaulle Airport; strangely, foremost on her mind was a need to notify the car hire company that the little Citroen she had been driving around for the last week was now an incinerated wreck, melted to the scorched ground that was, until that afternoon, the car park of the now-vanished Hotelissimo. It was two hours before the taxi arrived, and because of the traffic blocks and detours it took another hour to take a circuitous route back to Charles de Gaulle.

At the airport there was a tense atmosphere. There were stunned expressions as uniformed men and women tried to remain smart and business-like, though they were shaken to the core by the dreadful tragedy that was instantly known yet impossible to fully process.

Already on the multiple television screens at the checking-in and transit areas news bulletins had film obtained from a motorist.

Abigail had her flight ticket in her pocket along with her debit and cheque card and passport.

The first time anyone actually listened to what had happened to her was when she made her way to the Hertz car hire desk to report the loss. She made a detailed statement, which was met with great compassion. She was given a cup of coffee and sat in an easy chair. She explained that her suitcase and her travel things had been destroyed in the hotel. The Hertz car employee contacted airport medics. Thankfully, someone was available, even though most had been driven up to the crash site. On checking her over and reminding her that she was walking, talking and in one piece, they advised that on reaching her destination she should get a check-up with a doctor. They gave her some paracetamol.

Many flights had been cancelled. It was too early to know if Abigail's scheduled flight would go ahead. Air traffic control were in crisis management mode trying to reschedule incoming and outgoing aircraft on other runways, with many redirected to nearby airports.

Abigail decided she did not wish to go anywhere but rather wait at the airport to obtain information about her flight, which was not due anyway for another fourteen hours. She had some vague notion of finding a comfortable space to get some sleep. Hertz said she was welcome to rest in the chair as long as she wanted.

As it got later into the evening she felt restless and decided to wander around the passenger lounge and tax-free shops. She felt incomplete, like an imposter travelling without any personal possessions, and this feeling seemed to mirror a numbing blankness in her mind. The usual vitality of her thoughts had been poleaxed. There was a lurking pain and anguish she was trying to hold back. And then as the shadowy awfulness simply contemplating her existence subsided, Abigail found herself floating in a light, even ecstatic mood, with a message flashing up in front of her as though in brilliant neon to the whole world: 'You have survived. Abigail Pangloss is alive and well. The Concorde had crashed into the hotel in which she was staying, killing all on board and others in the hotel, but you have lived to tell the tale.'

The elation was short-lived as her mood then sank again, this time consumed with a survivor's guilt. Why on earth was she not dead like all those poor souls who'd perished, as might naturally be predicted?

But again Abigail felt that vainglorious surge, a rush of adrenalin at the thought of her invincibility, her victory over death; she had survived. The rationale of this undeniable realisation of the infernal truth: she was a Pangloss.

This was the best outcome in the best of all possible worlds. Did she feel no shame for this selfish egocentricity? Now she was allowing herself to be drawn into that cranky family myth she had so polemically dismissed. But her survival gave her a sense of destiny, which, though not overtly arrogant, possessed a feeling of greatness of purpose, of some duty that would set her apart.

It is true that there are numerous historical case studies pointing to psychological factors, where surviving some deeply traumatic ordeal propels an individual to extraordinary self-affirmation. Because the survivor has not died they believe they therefore have some special destiny. It can cause obsessive focus that enables the subject to totally convince all around them of the object or message that they rationalise as the purpose for their continued existence. It is a messianic self-belief. It is the ultimate in self-fulfilling prophecies. And Abigail became possessed of this strange predisposition. She was going to save the Amazonian rainforest and then save the world from global warming. In the general scheme of things it was perhaps not a bad objective to be messianic and polemical about.

After settling into a settee in the corner of the passenger lounge Abigail slept soundly for six hours. She awoke thinking of her parents. She telephoned them: 'Hi, Mum. I'm safe. I'm OK. I'm on my way home.'

Edwina responded: 'Well, of course, dear, we shall look forward to seeing you. Terrible about the Concorde crash. How absolutely awful for all those poor dear casualties. But why shouldn't you be safe?'

Abigail felt relief that they could not know of her freak proximity to the disaster. 'Don't worry, Mum. I'll explain when I get home. Should be out of Heathrow by mid-day.'

On her return she spent a few months at the family home in Cheltenham. She had already anticipated other personal business while in the UK before resuming her work in Brazil. It was a tense time. She was on edge, and her physical and mental health was right now not that good.

Edwina: 'I think you should make an appointment with the GP, dear, just to get your chest checked, get the all-clear before setting off on your travels again.'

The recurring tension between Abigail and her father was, if anything, more intense, more with the feisty daughter baiting her dad.

Abigail: 'Why do you have to make that horrible slurping noise when you endlessly chew your food at the dinner table? It's disgusting.'

Or:

'Oh, if you knew how annoying it is when you whistle while doing the dishes.'

Or:

'God, I can't stand the way you always sit in the same chair, as though no one else has the right, stupid fuddy-duddy old man.'

Or:

'What's that bloody smell? Christ, Dad, what are you spraying on yourself?'

One morning at breakfast Abigail chose to swivel her chair around, balancing on one leg, while nonchalantly dribbling strawberry yogurt, so that she could look out into the garden, much to the controlled chagrin of David and, if the truth be told, Edwina.

David: 'Good morning, we are here as well, you know.'

Abigail: 'Oh, bugger off.'

Edwina gave David a stern look but said nothing. In a misplaced attempt to be reconciliatory David responded: 'Look, you've been through a terrible ordeal, you might have post-traumatic stress disorder, it's nothing to be ashamed of. Perhaps you should seek some counselling; talking things through can make a world of difference. It is something I do know a little bit about myself.'

Abigail: 'I'm fine, thank you. I don't need you to give me any psychobabble.'

Edwina: 'Oh, darling, do try and rest. It is like you have a "love/hate" relationship with him. It does none of us any good. He's not a bad man so please don't treat him like a verbal punch bag. He does get hurt by your comments.'

David's forbearance of his bright, clever daughter's garbled intellectual misapprehension about money was magnanimous, even if she dismissed as 'boring, humdrum, mundane' the means by which he had accumulated his modest wealth. And so it was correctly assumed, despite her verbal abuse, that David would shell out the requisite funds necessary to enable the purchase of a house with the aid of a mortgage. Abigail knew her father loved her and had no qualms in exploiting his affection with this subtle emotional blackmail. There must have been a residual guilt as well as connivance on Abigail's part as the question of purchase was addressed to Edwina, rather than David.

Abigail visited the doctor as suggested and, after referral for an X-ray, was advised that it showed some scarring of her lungs from the heat and fumes of the air accident and this could make her susceptible to bronchial infection.

Abigail and Sappho were together; they had become a firmly established item. Sappho had been offered a lectureship in ceramics and they were house-hunting in Gloucestershire.

Abigail: 'Mum, we've seen a cottage at Shepston-on-Churn, as the estate agent's particulars describe: beautiful honeycomb-coloured Cotswold stone, tastefully extended using locally sourced matching stone and suitable materials, including lime mortar, and bespoke joinery. And a good-sized garden that needs some attention, and at the bottom there is a delightful little tributary of the River Churn, with crystal-clear water teeming with lively freshwater trout. Isn't that amazing?'

They completed the purchase of the cottage. It was furnished with Sappho's ceramics and rugs and ornate chests from Goa. There was a statue of Shiva and, as a choice very much of Abigail's, a large framed print of Damien Hirst's shark in formaldehyde: *The Physical Impossibility of Death in the Mind of Someone Living.*

Within a month of the purchase Abigail flew to Brazil, but this was not to be a long absence as her new remit meant most of the year she would be based in London collating the fieldwork of others for presentation at conferences. She had realised that to influence policy, be heard and climb the ladder, she needed to be based at the headquarters. If anything, this increased her passion and combative drive.

It also gave her time to canvass and get voted onto Shepston-on-Churn Parish Council. She of course ran on an environmental ticket, which in such a rural idyll would always be favoured.

In parochial circles the council's reputation went before it. Its duly elected members, custodians of the values and traditions of English village life, had been in office, it seemed, since time immemorial. Little had changed over the years. Perhaps the biggest concession to modernity and political correctness had been acceptance by the chairman, Major Barrington Carruthers (retired), Master of the Hunt, OBE, JP, that it would no longer be de rigueur for him to attend meetings attired as Master of the Hunt. As will be noted from the wording, this did not expressly prohibit his attending so dressed, even though 'nouveau riche millennial townies' recently ensconced in the parish had signed a petition.

Differences did occur. The hitherto unrivalled autocracy of the council was frequently challenged by these new residents, who were viewed as interlopers and usurpers.

Planning matters had always been a bone of contention. Carruthers in the past had brow-beaten his cronies into following his views, but times had changed. The problem was the parish council could only ever proffer one countable view with local planning committees anyway and the consensus was changing.

Carruthers: 'Are we all in agreement in approving the state-of-the-art abattoir to be built at the western extremity of the parish boundary?'

Abigail: 'I've looked at the plans. Not happy with the drainage. One way or another, excess blood and gore will be hosed into the yard and make its way into the Churn and its tributary. Apart from anything else the organic allotments of the Vegan Society are located just down the slope. I doubt they will appreciate carnivorous sludge soaking into their broccoli and turnips. And stuff that does not get drained away and rots on the ground can become a serious health hazard, what with viruses and the like; there are even cases of anthrax in the literature. So no, I can't support the motion and I suspect neither will the majority.'

Carruthers: 'But it's been decided already.'

Abigail: 'No, it hasn't. And anyway, it's not as though the planning committee have to listen to us whatever we say?'

Carruthers: 'Ms Pangloss, *we* do not oppose decisions such

as these; it has been carefully thought out and discussed. I know this personally as I have friends in the planning inspectorate.'

Abigail: 'Good for you, but this committee speaks with one voice and that is unlikely to be yours.'

Three of the new parochial councillors were in the Vegan Society. She felt she had made new friends with her assertive representations, but she may have over-played her hand as she soon found herself on the back foot a few months later when she made an application to install in her cottage a natural recycling system for family effluence, which would then feed a watercress bed at the bottom of the garden. Some the enriched soil would also be used on the area of the garden where her vegetable patch was already well established.

The sacred waters of the Churn again came into the equation, as two hundred yards downstream from Abigail's garden the Churn garden flowed through the grounds of Carruthers estate. He, naturally, had a penchant for catching the fine rainbow trout in his waters and was deeply alarmed at the prospect of contamination by seepage of human manure.

Abigail presented the case herself and it was a good case. She objected on grounds of natural justice to old Carruthers sitting on the committee. '*Nemo dat quod non habet*' – no man shall be judge in his own case. Clearly, his very personal interest in the outcome of the proceedings in which he was actually the only objector would make his position as chair completely untenable.

Carruthers argued that of course he had a vested interest, just like everyone else on the committee, that was why they were on it in the first place, and anyway, the mere fact that he happened to have the casting vote was a trifling detail. He stated that his objection was one of principle based on the common good and environmental health. Abigail countered that she had been given the green light from the district council and had demonstrated that her scheme was in accord with the current green planning policy and legislation.

But the Vegan Society found themselves divided. How could they be sure that Abigail and Sappho would not, even inadvertently, compost waste meat products? It was easy enough to do. This would impact on garden crops and allotments in the vicinity.

Abigail: 'This is barmy. The countryside is awash with remains of animals that have perished in the normal cycle of nature, consequences of the food chain. Of course they are consumed by other creatures, by bacteria, their remnants leaching into the soil – that is the way it works. Are you trying to deny the natural ecology of the food chain?'

Carruthers promptly interjected: 'Hoisted by your own petard, dear madame. It was on this ground that you objected to the abattoir.'

Abigail: 'No, environmentally that was a completely different circumstance.'

On behalf of the vegans Marjorie Capsicum interjected: 'We perfectly well understand the food chain, but we would rather leave it to nature rather than risk possible consequences of human intervention in the process. I think we are with Major Carruthers on this one.'

Abigail's further protestations and mutterings of creepy salad-munching hypocrites did her cause no good. It was one of the rare battles that she lost; while never entirely forgotten, it did not detract from their enjoyment of living in the countryside. Besides she had bigger fish to fry. After all, she had yet to conquer the world and make it environmentally safe for future generations.

13

Tragic Infirmity, Misery, Mercy And The Wheels Of Justice

I

David: 'At first you ignore the occasional mishap or memory lapse, you laugh it off and jest that it was a "senior moment", and then you check yourself and think, *Hang on, we're still in our prime*, you don't get senior moments in your sixties, do you? That's the thing, it's only other people that notice that you are ageing – you don't, you are you and life is there to live. Even the fact that your interests change and for most people that means giving up playing football or rugby, but you still go the gym and jog or play tennis or have a round of golf, or whatever it is that floats your boat.

'Edwina and I loved our walks and we always walked at our own pace so we walked relative to each other and didn't notice if we were slowing down or not. And I was just as handy with the cars. Admittedly, I became less inclined to roll around under a chassis winched up with a trolley jack. Edwina still baked. That was one of the first things I noticed, when she would forget to put cherries in the fruit cake. We always had cherries. It was my favourite, that's why she baked it. And then her attention would wander more than occasionally when we were playing Monopoly, forget to collect two hundred pounds when she passed Go, or count the dice incorrectly, or even miss the chance to buy a hotel on Mayfair or Park Lane.

'But then we might also have been enjoying a glass of wine and relaxing while we played. I mean, board games came out at festivities and so distractions and conversation meant the minutiae of the game would not necessarily be the focus of attention. Scrabble, though we would regularly play each week, as brain food, like crosswords and sudoku, but those were more my cup of tea. But I noticed things changed over a matter of months, really. Edwina was always pretty good at Scrabble. I had to watch her as I was used to her testing me to see if she could get away with inventing a word. And then, as time went on, there was simply no contest in the games. She would manage a few three- or four-letter words and forget to pick up fresh pieces. I suppose I realised something was amiss but just brushed it off – what could I do? It would have been hurtful to confront her and tell her that she wasn't right. And I didn't mind. She was still my Edwina. The woman I loved and had been married to for all those years. As far as I was concerned she was the same person.

'And you know what? A strange thing she would do – hah, I don't like to talk about it actually, but I must admit it did hurt me; it just was not right, you know, what with her being a married woman. Some things are personal – it's a matter of dignity, isn't it? I mean, some things are private between a couple, aren't they? Anyway, she did it a few times. I saw her.

'There she was standing at the window, stark bloody naked, just waving her nightie and laughing at whoever walked past the window on their way down the street. Well, that's not my Edwina. I can't have that. "What are you doing?" I would ask. It was making me ill. I felt emotional – angry, actually. I can't have my Edwina being seen like that by any flipping man who walks past the window, can I?

'Then she forgot the dog's name. That was when I decided to tell her that I thought she should have a check-up. Actually, I tried to be diplomatic and say that I thought we should both go for a check-up, just to be on the safe side. She said, "What are you suggesting?" I said we might be becoming forgetful and she threw a cup at me which I dodged, but I got tea on my shirtsleeve. Ay should could be a feisty woman at times, my Edwina.

'In the end the doctor, who was an old friend, called round on the pretext of seeing me, but in so doing asked Edwina a set of questions, which were designed to provide a broad indication of whether there was an onset of dementia or some such forgetfulness.

'What year is it? What month is it? Without looking at a clock what time is it to the nearest hour? Count back from twenty to one. Say the months of the year in reverse order? Say back to me an address I gave you earlier.

'Well, it was not great; pretty bad actually. Any counting or reciting in reverse was a non-starter and witnessing her trying to guess the time of day and be so wide of the mark shocked me. It upset me. I was quite shaken. I realised this was something that could not just be shrugged off. I did not feel better when the doctor told me that he thought there may be an indication of dementia which, if his diagnosis was correct, would become progressively worse over time. He said the rate of loss of mental faculty can be slowed by medication, socialisation and mental stimulation. He recommended listening to favourite pieces of music.

'It was Edwina I felt bad for. I was not at all sorry for myself. Why should I be? She was mine whatever. I could look after her.

I would not be lonely; our relationship would continue, perhaps just a little differently.

'I still consulted her about everything, as we had always made most decisions together. It was weird, over time I could feel myself asking the question, *Shall we do this? What about visiting so-and-so? How about going out for dinner?*

'And then she would look at me with a puzzled smile, or sometimes just stare back blankly, and I would kid myself that she was really intimating her preference to me. I would then answer my own question for her as though there really had been communication and an exchange of opinions.

'It was like that for a couple of years, I guess. It was during that time that we decided to downsize and move to a bungalow. Funnily enough, Edwina understood that we were selling up and moving and it was her that was reluctant. She had forgotten that she had not been up the stairs for nearly a year. I had thought about a stair lift, but what was the point when I knew the solution was to move into a bungalow?

'It was when the reflex motor things started playing up that I found it difficult to cope, you know, waterworks and the like, especially at night, every hour or two. And those sporadic times when she couldn't move her body out of her chair? They checked that as well. She could be quite agile for weeks on end and then have days when she could not control her limbs. That was when they diagnosed multiple sclerosis on top of everything else.

'There were times when she could not move her legs and I then had to wake to turn her all the time, more than once an hour; to prevent bed sores – you know the way it is. Eventually I was going through the night and it felt as though I'd never been to sleep. The caring did not stop in the morning. It just carried on and I was becoming worn out. I was in a daze. I did not realise what a toll it was taking on me. I felt I had to remain strong for us both and I guess I became depressed.'

Police interviewing officer: 'Thank you for that, Mr Pangloss, I do not propose to ask you any further questions tonight. If there is nothing else you wish to add at this time I will conclude the interview until tomorrow morning. The duty inspector will review your detention and you can get some sleep in your cell until the morning. So, the time is 21.15hrs on 29th August 2007 and the interview is ended and I am switching off the tape-recording machine.'

Morning session, police interviewing officer: It is 10.30am on 30th August 2007 and we are in interview suite 3 at Cheltenham Police Station. This interview is being conducted pursuant to the Police and Criminal Evidence Act 1994 and the Codes of Practice made in accordance therewith. This is the second interview this morning as the first was terminated to clarify advice. Will you and your legal advisor please confirm your names.'

When David and his solicitor had done this the officer administered the caution: 'I must caution you that you do not have to say anything but if you fail to mention anything you later rely on in court it may result in an adverse inference being made against you, anything you do say may be used against you. Do you understand the caution?'

Solicitor: 'We have discussed the caution and I have explained it to David and I am satisfied he understands it.'

Interviewing officer: 'Right, David, have you had enough time to discuss the case further with your solicitor?'

David and his solicitor confirmed they had.

Interviewing officer: 'Now the doctor has visited and assessed you as fit for interview, is that correct?'

David confirmed he had.

Interviewing officer: 'Did you get some sleep last night? I gather the custody sergeant arranged for you to have the ready meal all-day breakfast, which is the station's signature dish. Actually, it isn't too bad, I occasionally have it myself. Sometimes the beans are a bit gooey, though. And you are sure you are ready to resume the interview?'

David confirmed he was.

'Right. David, you were arrested yesterday morning on suspicion of the attempted murder of your wife, Edwina Pangloss, and you were explaining background circumstances. I need now to deal with specific allegations.

'Yesterday we had a telephone call from a concerned neighbour who lives next door to you to say that she could see fumes emerging from under your closed garage door and they could hear an engine running for several minutes. The lady was so concerned that she went round and wrenched the door open, which thankfully you had not locked. When she saw you sitting in the passenger seat, not moving, apparently unconscious, she had the presence of mind to open the car door and turn off the ignition. If she had not done so, you may not have been sitting here and we would not be having this conversation. She thought you were dead. She immediately dialled 999 for ambulance and police emergency services. Your watch said that it was ten minutes to two in the afternoon, so your watch must have stopped because that is the time on the watch the custody sergeant obtained from you and placed with your other possessions for safekeeping while you remain in custody.

'A police patrol car was at your bungalow within ten minutes. When the police forced open the front door and entered the main bedroom to the left of the hallway they found an elderly lady in bed, unconscious with a large plastic bag loosely over her face. She had no vital signs; they thought that she was dead.

'Can you talk us through your recollection of the events that preceded the police and ambulance being called. What you were thinking and what was your state of mind at the time?'

Solicitor: 'I have advised my client to go no comment.'

David: 'No, I want to say how it was.'

Solicitor: 'We have had a discussion prior to interview and I feel as my client is vulnerable the interview should be terminated for further confirmatory instructions.'

Interviewing officer: 'Your client is deemed medically fit for interview and the interview has already been terminated once this morning for confirmatory instructions and since then no new circumstances have arisen.'

Solicitor: 'Then I strongly advise my client to remain no comment and not to speculate in any way about what he might or might not think may have been the state of his mind.'

Interviewing officer: 'As your client has clearly intimated he wishes to give an account I shall proceed with the interview.'

David: 'Yes, let's get on with it. It's the way I explained to you last night. We'd been at the bungalow for a couple of years. We liked our old house. We'd lived there a long time, you know.

'We had considered downsizing for some time, but I don't know, we were reluctant. We liked where we were, but as I say Edwina wasn't going to get any better after the diagnosis, what with the confirmation of multiple sclerosis and Alzheimer's disease.

'I'd only been retired a couple of years or so when the illness started. I mean, we'd both been looking forward to a long and active retirement. I have a good pension. We'd made all sorts of plans. We would travel, go on cruises around the world, sail into the cosmic colour of the Northern Lights, swim with the dolphins in the Gulf of Mexico, visit Machu Picchu and the Taj Mahal, look out across the Grand Canyon and feel the spray of the Niagara Falls on our faces. The world was our oyster and yet, in the end, we never did any of it, except, of course, visiting my cousin in Goa.

'Instead, the eventual priority was to look for a bungalow in the suburbs of Cheltenham. I eventually found a suitable place in Bishop's Cleeve. And so it was in June 2005 we finally moved from the house that had been our family home since 1976. It was about working out how much hallway space there was for wheelchairs, how near to the front door the car could be parked, safety handles on the front door and in the bathroom, ensuring suitably adapted baths, toilets and showers – you know, it was all those practical things.'

Interviewing officer: 'Thank you for that, David, but I need you to talk us through your recollection of the events that preceded the police and ambulance being called. What you were thinking and what was your state of mind at the time?'

David: 'Well, it's obvious, isn't it? It's the way it was, wasn't it? The way it was going to be, wasn't it? It was for the best, you know.'

Interviewing officer: 'Well, it may be obvious to you, but at this stage it is not clear to me. Let's park that one for a minute. Are you able to tell me what sort of medication your wife was on?'

David: 'All sorts. Pills for MS, pills to help her dementia. Tranquillisers, painkillers, you know?'

Interviewing officer: 'Were you responsible for administering the medication?'

David: 'I was her principal carer. So yes, of course. I mean, I needed medication myself as well.'

Interviewing officer: 'The prescription notes recovered from your bungalow list: donepezil, galantamine, paracetamol, tramadol, Ocrevus, Valium, doxepin, temazepam – quite an extensive list of medication, isn't it?'

David: 'Well, yes, I suppose it is, but whatever we tried our troubles didn't seem to go away, did they?'

Interviewing officer: 'Did you deliberately stockpile sleeping pills and painkillers?'

David: 'No, no, we had repeat prescriptions. If I was tired I might forget to give her medication and then more would arrive. Over time it just sort of accumulated, I was not stockpiling anything, heavens no.'

Interviewing officer: 'Did you place a plastic bag over your wife's face?'

David: 'Did I do what? No, well, yes, I thought she was going to be sick and it was the nearest thing to catch the vomit. It was me who would have to strip the bed down and wash all the sheets, and I have to do that often enough as it is.'

Interviewing officer: 'You have told us you have a good pension. You are an intelligent man – why didn't you buy in professional carers to help you? You had the resources to do so.'

David: 'Edwina didn't want that and neither did I. She's my wife, of course I should care for her myself.'

Interviewing officer: 'There were red marks on Edwina's face, not sufficient to cause a bruise or draw blood but probably caused by the exertion of pressure. Did you cause those marks?'

David: 'I would never wish to cause Edwina marks on her face.'

Interviewing officer: 'Let me be more precise. Did you give your wife an overdose of pills to put her into a deep sleep and then try to suffocate her with a plastic bag?'

David: 'She was sound asleep, but she was making a strange noise and I put a pillow over her head to reduce the noise, then I thought she was going to be sick. The polythene bag was to stop her being sick.

'Then she went still and quiet and I thought she had passed, so I then decided to finish off myself and I went into the garage and fixed a pipe to the exhaust on my Riley CME and sat in the driver's seat, started her up and had some swigs from a bottle of whiskey. That's when you guys turned up.'

Interviewing officer: 'You said you were angry when you saw your wife looking as though she was flaunting herself naked at the window to passers-by. Did that have any bearing on your feelings towards Edwina or your subsequent actions?'

David: 'Oh, no, no, Edwina's mine, don't you see? She's mine, I love her, she doesn't do that sort of thing for other people, she's mine. I care for her, always have, always will.'

Interviewing officer: 'Did you intend to kill your wife?'

David: 'Kill? As in you mean dead? No, as I've said, no, not at all, never. That's the whole point, I did not want my Edwina dead. I was setting her free. I was setting us both free, can't you see that? So that we could do all those things we had talked about, what we had planned to do, you know, dancing with the Northern Lights and all that. I kissed her, you know, and said Edwina, my darling, you and me, we are going to dance with the Northern Lights. She smiled, you know. There was a smile on her face. I could see her there. She understood. You don't kiss people you want dead, do you? As I say it was all for the best, in the best of possible worlds, given the circumstances, that is.'

Interviewing officer: 'Do you remember how you responded when your neighbour opened the garage door and then the driver's side of your car?'

David: 'Well, it's all pretty hazy. I mean, I'd had some pills and knocked back a fair few swigs of whiskey and I'd not slept what felt like for weeks.'

Interviewing officer: 'Do you have an interest in entomology, Mr Pangloss?'

David: 'Entomology?'

Interviewing officer: 'Are you someone with an interest in insects?'

David: 'No, not at all, why are you asking me that?'

Interviewing officer: 'Just interested. No particular reason. You had a large variety of flies, some pretty rare species in your garage and in your car. According to forensics some of them are not native to this country, other than at Kew Gardens. Anyway, most, but not all, had expired. As it was noted that the garage space was well maintained and kept neat and tidy, normally you wouldn't expect any kind of infestation.'

David: 'No, no. I didn't realise that. I mean, Edwina had her plant samples. She had a big collection over the years. You see she worked at Kew. She was a horticulturist interested in tropical plants, but not entomology, as you say.'

Interviewing officer: 'OK, no problem, maybe that explains it; moving on. The neighbour, Mrs Knowles, says that before your head slumped and you went silent, she noticed you had blue lips and a strange pink colouration, you were frothing at the mouth and muttering the word "slag" and also what sounded like bitch? What did you mean by that? Who was it about?'

David: 'No, no, I mean, I was out of it, I was feeling as though, I mean, I had drifted off, hadn't I?

'I may have said "slack" as loosening, relaxing, that sort of thing, and I really don't recall saying "bitch", but if I did it would be directed at that busybody Mrs Knowles who found me, because I really did not want anyone to find me, you know.'

Interviewing officer: 'The initial engineer's report tells us your Riley needs a new exhaust, it was leaking fumes into the garage that were then spewing under the garage door. In addition there is a gap in the canvas hood on the off-side, which let in air; it is his assumption that that somehow made a difference because the carbon monoxide levels inside your vehicle had reached, indeed had gone beyond a lethal level long before we reached you. You also had a high level of alcohol in your system. For the benefit of the tape and for your information according to the toxicology readings, scientifically you are supposed to be dead. How does that make you feel now, Mr Pangloss?'

David: 'What are you asking? How it feels to be dead? What sort of question is that to ask someone? I don't know. Well, I suppose that's science, isn't it?'

Interviewing officer: 'You were surprised last night that no one was able to confirm to you whether or not Edwina had died. Why was that such a shock? I put it to you that you planned to kill your wife by drugging her and smothering her with a pillow and then killing yourself by carbon monoxide poisoning?'

David: 'Well, what you are saying... you are trying to make it sound criminal, aren't you? What with everything you are saying, you make it sound criminal, but that's not the way it was, you know, Edwina and me. I did, I suppose, now I remember it, think she had gone, but the impression I got was they all thought she had gone, the doctors, the police officers and all, they said that she was in another place so that is what I thought. And yes, I had had enough, but I, as I've explained, did not want her to be dead as in "dead", as in the ordinary meaning of the word.

'We both had a lot of medication. I was so weary I can't remember what dosages were or were not given. But look, whatever you or anyone else might try and say, I love my wife dearly, with or without dementia. She is the most precious thing to me.'

Interviewing officer: 'I have already had a discussion with the custody sergeant. Apparently, Edwina is on cloud nine, no one can say how it will end for her, whether she will just float off. A medical and toxicology report will be available later this afternoon, so as we are still within the custody time limits the file will be faxed to a senior duty CPS prosecutor for a charging decision. You will have to go back to your cell now. If there is any change on that proposal you will then be bailed to return on an appointed day. If you are bailed and your wife's condition should by any miracle improve, there will be no question of you visiting or having any contact with her. There will be a strict bail condition preventing any contact while any proceedings are pending. Do you understand? Right, I am concluding this interview. The time is 11.10hrs and I am turning off the tape.'

Later that day David was charged with attempted murder and a section 18 assault with intent to commit grievous bodily harm. He was kept for a first remand hearing at Cheltenham Magistrates' Court the following day. The chairman of the bench explained that because of the seriousness of the case it could not be dealt with in the magistrates and would have to be committed to the Crown Court to progress. No plea was indicated, but David's solicitor made an application for bail.

David was a mere shadow of his former self. He was withdrawn and his talent for silky discretion, that ability to be present, to influence, to manage effectively without seemingly disrupting a meeting, once a managerial asset, now made him appear, quite frankly, ghoulish. His solicitor commented that at times you could be standing next to the man and not even know he was there. The custody sergeant had made the same observation when David was first brought into the police station. He had looked up from his desk paperwork and said to the arresting officer, 'Yes, well, where is he? What has come in today?'

And yet the quiet, unprepossessing, anonymous man was stood there in front of him.

After months of first a bail hostel and then a suitable residential placement while the matter was prepared for hearing the case finally reached a plea and directions hearing at Bristol Crown Court. There had been much discussion between the defence and the prosecution. David's advocate was never going to advise him to go guilty to an attempted murder, a charge that David did not accept, and for which on the basis of his interviews and the other evidence was speculative anyway.

Further toxicology reports had been prepared as well as two psychiatric assessments. The police national computer search confirmed that David had never been in trouble in his life. The statements of friends and witnesses also confirmed that David and Edwina shared a long and happy marriage.

The judge, Owen Griffiths QC, a benign, elderly, down-to-earth Welshman, managed to preserve a sense of humour even in the gravest of cases. His resistance to the trappings of grandeur and elitism that often accompanied judicial office was illustrated when during a bail application a contractor arrived to fit a chandelier that had, following delivery, been obtrusively sitting on the floor of the judge's chambers for over a fortnight. As its delicate glass snowdrops and wires were obtrusively spilling across the red carpet to the extent that lawyers had to carefully step around the extravagant adornment before commencing plaintiff appeals for the freedom of their clients. Anyway, the judge told the contractors he had no wish for the grandiose monstrosity in his chambers and requested they remove it at once.

His Honour was married to a judge, a matching set of his and her judges, which, though rare, is not unheard of but does prompt speculation as to the kind of sanguine judicious prudence that might be reciprocated to bless such an egalitarian union?

It can only be imagined. Sadly, the judge was not long of this world. In the robing room that year it was rumoured he had passed away. The judiciary do tend to be discrete, dispassionate, alarmingly utilitarian to the point of seeming not to care about such things. One judge goes and one judge arrives. The new appointment is always matter-of-fact, must never disrupt proceedings. No one actor is ever indispensable.

It was said the circumstances were sudden and dramatic. Perhaps His Honour had been working late in his study, perhaps he was weary from the stress of all the cases he had to sit through, perhaps there was an arrhythmia, perhaps he had imbibed a little too much port with his dinner, though there was never any suggestion of him having such a frailty. Perhaps it was just that he got his calling card; but whatever, he took a tumble down the staircase of his home, from top to bottom, crashing and thumping, rapid and rolling, no time to grip the banister; it was catastrophic. By the time he reached the hallway floor, first groaning and then silent, crumpled in a heap, he had died.

And no less a tragic event, sitting in the case of R v David Pangloss, the learned judge clearly displayed compassion for the defendant from the outset, a stance that a less experienced, less worldly member of the judiciary would have struggled with. At a directions hearing he said, peering over his half-rimmed spectacles, 'What are we doing with this case? Is it really an attempt murder or possibly, God forbid, if some further unfortunate eventuality should occur we may be faced with the prospect not of an inchoate offence, but rather the grim substantive version Mr Wilkie?'

The prosecuting counsel said that a case conference was scheduled for later in the week and that a decision would be made then as to any review of the charges.

Before giving directions the judge firstly alluded to the state of the defendant's mind and the question of intent and reminded counsel that while this might require expert psychiatric evidence, he noted that insanity or diminished responsibility had yet to be indicated as likely defences. In any event if on review the charges were to be substituted for lesser matters then those defences may not be appropriate anyway. There was no clear evidence of deliberate overdosing and while suffocation was an issue, an explanation had been given together with a denial of any intention to kill. As the judge understood it the defendant very much loved his wife.

And then the judge, a man not known for obfuscation and noted for usually being one jump ahead rather than prone to obtuse *non sequiturs* made a most curious observation.

'I also ask counsel in reviewing this case to consider what was to be understood by the meaning of the word "dead". Does it mean the same not being alive? If so by whose criteria? And to be human the law says we must be a 'reasonable creature in being'. This is after all the twenty-first century, these are strange times in which we live, what with cryogenics, avatars, AI, cyborgs, abortion, medically sustained life, decisions on whether dying is assisted or otherwise and then there are the many wonders of computer mind games and modern science.

We need to be clear in the legal definitions of these fundamental concepts. Is this a case where the literal rule should be followed, where dead means "as in dead", such as is determined by a medical practitioner based on various criteria? Or could it be that extraneous information should properly be brought to bear, such that some wider import might justly, as a legal concept, enable the word "dead" to include other meanings, situations or states of being?

'In this respect counsel will appreciate that without being clear about what we mean by 'dead' the more precise statutory references to the meaning of the word "kill" become superfluous, if in fact "dead" relates to those circumstances other than "as in dead". Of course, the law already recognises people as dead who actually may turn out to be alive and by the corollary, the law may be required during a statutory limitation period to deem someone as alive who may actually be dead. The question then is: can this principle of law accommodate the wider import that I have alluded to and thereby recognise as alive, people who would otherwise be treated as dead? I am sure you all follow my reasoning, do you not? I might add that it is something that has vexed me personally in recent times.'

The judge again peered intensely over his half-rimmed spectacles, surveying the row of lawyers, looking for an approving response for his novel legal enquiry. The defence barrister took the opportunity to endorse the judge's misgivings and then asked the court for a further direction for disclosure of unused material that should have been received a fortnight earlier following service of the defence statement.

It was a big step when the Crown finally decided that they would not proceed with the attempted murder. That in itself also automatically drew legal argument as to the withdrawal of the charge of grievous bodily harm with intent contrary to section 18 of the Offences Against the Persons Act 1861; as the defence counsel incisively pointed out, how could it then be appropriate to proceed when the issue in the case was about statement of mind and an intention to do serious physical harm to a person?

The proceedings were moving in David's favour. The case review team accepted that a count on the indictment contrary to section 20 of the Offences Against the Persons Act would also be inappropriate as this would require serious physical harm without necessarily having intent so to do. On the other hand on a true assessment of the extent of the actual provable injury presently disclosed, a section 47 assault occasioning actual bodily harm, might be more appropriate and proportionate to the reddening that had occurred on Edwina's face. Though the two offences potentially carry similar sentencing options following a conviction on indictment, a section 47 has altogether less sting in the tail.

Curiously, a contemporaneous note later endorsed on the prosecutor's file suggested the case might now be discontinued in its entirety. As it was, and not without just a little nudging from the judge, it was reported that David pleaded guilty to a section 47 actual bodily harm and, following a lengthy probation report, was given a twelve-month community sentence. As he was clearly already fully supporting Edwina, the judge saw no point in making a financial compensation order.

If the heavy cloud of legal proceedings was now lifted, the same could not be said about David's outlook on his life. The granting of his liberty did draw some surprise. The investigating police officer, upon seeing David coming out of a supermarket gave him a side glance and could not resist saying with some sarcasm, 'Got a good result then, given the strength of the evidence?'

'Thank you for your concern. I'm glad it's all over.' David quietly uttered as he side-stepped the incredulous-looking officer, who nevertheless continued, 'All that legal reasoning, all those erudite mental gymnastics, all those abstract concepts, what a word really means and the like, it becomes quite surreal, doesn't it? I'm a brass-tacks investigating officer. If it looks like a rat, smells like a rat, you know…? Obviously those highfalutin lawyers take a different view, don't they? Remind me, who was the judge?'

David: 'Judge Owen Griffiths, I think.'

Investigating officer: 'Not sure if that's right. He died a while back, fell down the stairs. His wife, the lady justice, found him at the bottom of the stairs in the morning when she got up to make the breakfast.'

David: 'Really? I'm sorry to hear. My probation officer did mention something.'

Investigating officer, scratching his head: 'Oh well, I can't say I'm not just a tad confused, must have got that one wrong. If it looks like a judge, talks like a judge… you know?'

Abigail had attended a hearing. She was late; breathless, she explained to the ushers that for some inexplicable reason she had mistakenly ended up at the general hospital of all places and found herself wandering the wards and corridors before eventually finding the crown court. While she did make her presence known to David's solicitor at the court building, she was flustered and presented as a cold, aloof fish who made her disdain of her father alarmingly clear.

Upon initial introduction the defence solicitor had welcomed Abigail's presence as a positive thing and assumed she would be a morale booster for his client. He was quick to tell Abigail how pleased David was that she had come to support him and how she must be so pleased about how the gravity of the case had now been diffused.

'He appears to be coping well, I am glad you are here. I expect you would like to speak to him to provide a little reassurance, these recent weeks have been stressful and painful for him, will he now be staying with you?'

Abigail's response soon disavowed the solicitor of any assumed conviviality. 'Stressful and painful for him. How do you think I feel? Do you know what he did to my poor mother? Do you not realise the absolute sense of betrayal I feel because of that man?

'Right now, as far as I am concerned he's a non-person, he does not exist; as far as I am concerned your client is no longer present on this planet, do you understand? He knew what he was doing. You can have him stay with you if you like, since you think he is such wonderful old man?'

To say the least, the defence solicitor was taken aback and disappointed at Abigail's brusque lack of compassion, so unequivocally dismissive of her beleaguered father.

Abigail had had to return from a project in the Amazon to make arrangements regarding her mother. She found it incomprehensible that her father could have done such a thing. After discussing the matter at length with the police investigating officer she had regrettably reached the conclusion that her father had acted with intent to end both his and his wife's lives. Her judgement was harsh. She wanted nothing more to do with him.

In his last plaintiff conversation with his daughter in the entrance lobby to the courthouse David desperately tried, to the point of exhaustion, to explain his actions to Abigail.

David: 'I was living in an impossible fog. I thought it was an act of mercy. In the calculus of painless oblivion compared to the pain of clinging to life and all the connected misery there was no contest. As I love her more than anything, it was my call, not dependent on some harsh doctrine of religion or the refinement of endless legal argument, not while the agony endured.

'And I was convinced that ending my own life would not be self-hate, self-murder, but rather the ultimate sacrifice of love to share in Edwina's fate.

'Maybe I was, underneath it all, really just testing the water and never did accept the finality of mine or Edwina's mortal existence. In the muddled haze of sleepless nights and prescription drugs, heaving her out of bed several times a night to use the toilet and then washing her to prevent infection and then turning her so that she did not get bed sores. And then morning, noon and night giving her the medication to take the edge off her condition and then trying to feed her so that she could be sustained in this purgatory. If only for a second you could imagine how it was. All that I did was because I love her.

'Maybe you think there is something redeemable in all the pain, somewhere, somehow something that still made life worth living. It's not like you to harbour garbled religious ideas about the grace and glory of suffering. It's just bloody masochistic, that's what it is. I'm not like Eamon and all that Eastern meditation, no one would accuse me of being a stoic or a Buddhist, and my Christian faith has long since faded.'

To be abruptly blanked in this way by his little girl, the apple of his eye, deeply hurt David. Was there an element of selfishness on her part? The whole debacle was an immense professional inconvenience to her, an unwelcome interruption in her busy, interesting life. She could have well done without it.

Her mum and dad were now disparate souls, forced apart by frailty, circumstance and flawed choices, alienated, drifting separately in the cosmic soup. Abigail realised that if her mother pulled through then there would have to be suitable alternative arrangements. It was out of the question for Abigail to put her life on hold to personally care for dear Mum. This would mean great expense, even the prospect of spending her own inheritance. All such a waste. At least her dad had a good pension and Abigail was going to make damn sure she would get every penny of it necessary to keep her mother in comfortable surroundings. She need not have feared on that account as that was precisely what David wanted for Edwina as well.

It mattered to Abigail that nothing would distract her from her own personal goals. This skewed her perspective.

She conveniently used the moral indignation at her father's inexplicable and outrageous conduct as a justification for abrogating her own personal engagement in the crisis. Rather, she would simply pay to delegate all the worry to others. She could not be waylaid by the minutiae of personal family matters; after all, she had been saved to undertake some great service on behalf of the human race. She needed a clear narrative to placate her own sense of duty. Well, in simple terms, her father could go and rot in hell and her mother would be properly cared for, and Abigail could feel sufficiently emotionally engaged by perusal of monthly reports faxed to her in Brazil or London or Shipston-upon-Churn or wherever. This remote monitoring would be topped up by fleeting visits whenever she could find the time.

Then Abigail found herself questioning the very notion of death, as though trapped in a flashback to her own impossible dice with oblivion, as though in her psyche there was now a denial of the inevitable, definite, unavoidable cessation of mortal existence. Even the most serious, intended contemplation of death was for her only really ever posturing, a mind game in which we convince ourselves we are ready, resigned to relinquish our atomised mortal presence.

14

Assisted Living and the Old Insurance Building

I

David was now a pariah; no longer merely a limping victim of childhood tragedy but an instigator of heartbreak and dissension, of a tragedy borne by a choice he had exercised, his agency. This was a catastrophe that could not simply be assigned to the visitation of disease and an evil alien, as had been indelibly etched in those early years in Liverpool. Yet he could not understand why in his daughter's eyes he no longer existed. To her he was eternally condemned. He was now a lone spirit, struggling in solitude, facing the prospect of being forever separated from his beloved Edwina.

This fact had been emphasised to him by the police, his lawyers, as well as the medical and social services involved in the case. It was delusional for him to imagine that the spousal threads could simply be picked up to carry on in that tortuous fog of disability and tranquillisers.

For him the greater agony was not knowing where Edwina was. What condition was she in now? Had there been some new treatment or medication that may have reversed her dementia or restored her mobility? No one would tell him. When he tried to ask either the words did not materialise or if they were uttered they fell on deaf ears.

He knew Edwina's faculties for communication or for remembering who people were had been so reduced even before the incident, so what mattered was that she was happy in herself, in a good place, cared for and felt no pain.

He knew money was not an issue and took some solace by being satisfied that whatever else, Edwina would be in swish upmarket comfortable surroundings. He had assigned to Abigail all his pensions, insurance policy benefits and funds to be applied at her discretion for the best interests of Edwina. Abigail would have insisted on nothing less. What else could be the situation?

Through his imaginings David would convince himself that Edwina was in Cheltenham; then on another day he might believe strongly that she was in London, perhaps near to Kew, then he would imagine that she was at the seaside. Wherever she was, the placement would be the best.

He had a recurring notion that had first floated in his mind when he sat in the Riley in his fume-filled garage. The notion became a voice of authority. As the fog of his trauma gradually lifted the tangibility of the message had increased, its recurrence and reaffirmation gave it the substance and quality of a fact. In his recollection it was as though he had been briefed by a medical or social work professional. The message was that Edwina was safe. She had her own garden that was regularly tended. She was in a good place; she was at peace.

For the next three years David returned to the bungalow and retreated from the world, lurking as a shadowy hermit in the stale space where he rewove a dusty web of the past, oblivious to the present and for whom the idea of a future was incomprehensible. He rarely ventured out during the day, other than to routinely purchase a few meagre weekly rations. Most of his days were spent mulling over what had been, carefully reading Edwina's favourite horticulture books, perusing birthday, Christmas and anniversary cards they had sent each other. He would inspect Edwina's collection of flattened plant cuttings. He opened the drawers of her dresser and let the familiar scent of her perfume imbue the still air of the bedroom, where the curtains always remained closed. He would neatly check her clothing, washing garments and then ensuring they were precisely placed back on coat hangers in her wardrobe. An instilled lifelong sense of propriety and discipline prompted him occasionally to bathe and shave as token amelioration of his slow, dishevelled descent.

David made a decision, the reasons for which probably related to destiny and his humble origins but also some more remote notions that he harboured, perhaps a wish for self-imposed penance, maybe a purgatorial banishment. He determined that in future the world he would inhabit would be of humbler fare, have no pretension or claim to aspirational attainment or material wellbeing.

His arrival at this point coincided with concerns raised by both medical practitioners and social services about the austere, hermitical old man who lived in the bungalow. And so it was David decided to hand his bungalow over to a homeless family and was accommodated in an unprepossessing care environment.

II

Derek's residential home was in a road full of residential homes. It was care in the community in a big way. The buildings tended to be grand old Edwardian or Victorian red-brick properties, whether semi or detached, they were now too big for the average modern nuclear family. These large houses had high ceilings, ornate fireplaces and extensive gardens. The original craftsmanship was of a high standard with features including wide hallways with intricate patterns on colourful floor tiles, sweeping staircases, sculpted mouldings, pronounced plaster coving and wall-to-wall picture rails. Original sash windows were still evident in many of the houses, though many had been ripped out after a hundred years of good service, replaced with UPVC double glazing, guaranteed to last for up to twenty-five years.

None of these buildings were listed, even though the road had been designated as being within a conservation area, so the local authority and private landlords could hack these glorious old houses about to their heart's content to provide accommodation for as many of society's multitude of walking wounded as possible. In so doing they would, of course, ensure compliance with building regulations for properties in multiple occupation. This inevitably meant partitioning grand old rooms into two or three smaller rooms, ripping out those glorious fireplaces and embarking on wholesale cladding of splendid old doors and encasement of the interior building in plasterboard, taped, jointed and then painted. This included enclosing hallways and staircases. It is true that insistence on rewiring and integrated fire alarm systems made these places safer, even if the net result was a charmless modern interior, in every direction a sparklingly bland washable magnolia, resplendent as a functionally adequate pastiche of building design.

Nevertheless, David's home provided shelter and warmth for its eight residents, who all had their own space. His room on the first floor overlooked the street. If he did not close his curtains fully at night the amber rays of the streetlamps would beam in and car lights occasionally flicker across the walls, disturbing the stillness of his solitude and light slumber. At least he was now sleeping better than he had done for years.

Personal artefacts from the bungalow were evident: one of the duvets, and of course a picture of himself with Edwina entwined on their wedding day and a family picture with Abigail, as well as her graduation photograph. He also had a framed picture of Eamon, who had at the time grown a rather silly-looking moustache in his RAF uniform, casually tilted, leaning forward in the picture as he posed with a pipe in his mouth looking uncharacteristically affected. He also had a model of his beloved Riley.

As a prudent insurance man, David had, by the time of his retirement, secured valuable private pension rights that should have placed Edwina and himself in an enviable position. But after what had happened a long period of remorse and self-loathing influenced the choices he had made.

There had been a power of attorney set up before Edwina's faculties had spiralled into steep decline. Abigail was the donee of the lasting power for both Edwina's finances and property and her health and welfare. There was a similar power in relation to her father that had yet to be required but which it was assumed she would seek to renounce. Beyond that there were the provisions of the will that, apart from a few charitable legacies, vested the residual estate in Abigail.

In the absence of any correspondence with David, with his blanket exclusion from the loop of communication, he relied on his dreams to imagine how things were for his beloved.

The meagre amount he retained for himself meant that his own living arrangements were more modest than they would have otherwise been. In this dotage he could have been fraternising with bank managers and businessmen and doctors in some rural upmarket retirement home, where the grounds might include a golf course, tennis courts and a swimming pool, where evening dining could be taken in one's private apartment or in the Michelin star restaurant attended by waiter service. Instead, David opted for urban basics in a home where most of the occupants were vulnerable adults placed there through social services.

David's appearance had changed since the court case. In a way he looked younger. His face had fewer bags under the eyes and the deep ridge between his brows had faded. He no longer had a full head of hair; it had become thin, the hairline noticeably receded, while the dark colour faded into grey. He was also noticeably more stooped, as his muscular skeletal framed receded with age and reduced activity. His voice had always been mild and remained so.

There was a communal lounge and a large dining room and adjoining kitchen area located in the basement. It felt more like a canteen than a homely retreat. The area had a lingering smell of a particular gravy powder that the cook chose to add to virtually everything he made, and then, at certain times of the day, when the place was cleaned and chairs stacked on the tables, there was a wafting disinfectant smell that would last through until the cooker went back and the odour would mix with the gravy powder in the preparation of evening meals.

For the first couple of years David was entirely absorbed in his own thoughts, in his memories and in reading and writing. Contact with other residents was minimal. He would wander around the building or stay in his room and no one really noticed him. This anonymity suited him. He was a monad immersed in his own world, a melancholy unextended entity. He would watch films on television and keep broadly up to date with current affairs. He was older than most of the other residents and probably healthier. His mind was active. He had no wish to be with other people.

He wrote long letters to Edwina, which he knew he could not send, in the hope that one day Abigail might give him her address. He knew Edwina would have been incapable of reading them or even comprehending who had sent them. It was unlikely that she would have even recognised David now.

They were love letters, long, romantic reminiscences documenting his life with his wife. What else, what more than finding an enduring love can there be to so fully validate someone's life?

David kept the letters in a locked drawer. He would dream of Edwina at night, stirring and believing he had by some transcendent energy connected with her, that beyond her mortal incoherence she was with him. On the days following those dreams David would choose letters that he was going to send. Sometimes he would get the train to Weston-Super-Mare and with a letter placed in a bottle, wait for a high tide and throw the bottle into the Bristol channel. Sometimes, he would go into a church and, though he would never pray, he would leave a letter folded in a hymn book. Sometimes, he would pin an envelope to a tree in the park. Sometimes he would simply lose a letter and watch it fly off in the wind. On one occasion he travelled to London and stood on Westminster Bridge so as to dispatch a letter into the Thames.

Because he was so preoccupied with reminiscing on the intimacy of the relationship, rather than specifying full names and places or more probably taking such trifling details for granted, the letters, though deeply personal, also remained almost entirely anonymous and discrete. While 'To my dearest darling Edwina' might have been deciphered on a few, they could have been the work of any befuddled old lovesick Romeo. In his more logical moments he would realise that it was ridiculous to seriously imagine that magically one his letters would somehow reach Edwina and even more ridiculous that she would somehow have a momentary reprieve from her cerebral decline to be able to read and comprehend the content.

Some nights he would suffer angst and beat himself up terribly about what would happen if someone actually found and read such a personal letter. Though it cannot be said with any certainty a letter so recovered was indeed one of David's missives, such a document was found by a journalist travelling on a train. The letter was tucked into the back of the seat. He wrote an article about it and was interviewed on the regional news. It was treated as one of those light, sentimental topics, a slightly whimsical mystery of who was 'my dearest love', providing relief for some of the more onerous news bulletins.

III

The first resident David became acquainted with was a slim, slightly hunched and bedraggled man of about fifty years of age called Jarvis Williams. He was polite and quietly spoken, rather on the timid side.

He was unkempt in the way of a man who lacks pride in himself, who has never been married, always lived alone, with no wife to remind him that he is a bit whiffy, to shave or bathe, change his clothes or get a haircut. It is a subtle thing and many men ageing in supported housing tend to a slow decline in their general appearance. Choice of diet may be an additional factor, as the convenience of takeaway food with saturated fats can give an odour that will blend with and permeate the inexpensive body wash that a man may buy for those infrequent ablutions.

To say that Jarvis had fallen on hard times would be to misunderstand his situation. While it is true that he fell from some greater height, to suggest that someone or some set of circumstances may have pushed him, would be erroneous.

Jarvis came from a good family, reasonably well-to-do; aspirational lower middle class would be a reasonable description.

He walked everywhere. His gait was a vaguely discernible one-sided shuffle and his pace was slow and cautious, as though he may have possessed an affliction for which he bravely struggled on. This was not actually the case; the laboured stance was purely the step-by-step process of overcoming his innate inertia, his overwhelming desire to do absolutely nothing. A harsher observer might just describe him as a very lazy man.

Jarvis had a pleasant disposition, inoffensive and peaceful, usually preferring to keep himself to himself. His daily routine tended to be walking to the local shop to buy the daily paper and to get some food. Sometimes he would make himself breakfast to go with his coffee. It was in the dining room that David first encountered him some months after moving in. They were both sat at a table that looked out into the back garden, which was quite a large expanse partially laid to a fairly well-kept lawn and beyond that a cultivated area, where the soil had been turned and various vegetable planted.

'Goes up at the back, doesn't it?' said Jarvis.

David replied, 'Pardon?'

Jarvis: 'The garden, goes up at the back, doesn't it?'

David: 'Yes, I suppose it does, and towards the left-hand corner, by the shed.'

Jarvis meekly smiled back at him and sipped his coffee.

His father had a clerical job at a building company and his mother had been a teacher who for many years was involved in the arrangements for the Cheltenham junior festival, which at that time was more concerned with youth drama and poetry and musical recitals. His mother's sister had money and paid for Jarvis to attend a private school as a day boy from the age of five until he was sixteen, when he left school with one O-level in English language.

Throughout school he was one of those anonymous, almost invisible boys, rarely contributing to class discussions; he kept his distance in the playground from the usual rough-and-tumble games and football. The most involved that he ever became would be as one of the less energetic boys who would pack a makeshift goal comprised of temporarily discarded blazers to make out where the posts should be. He did not have to do anything other than stand there so that the ball might hit him and be deflected from going in the goal. On one occasion it is recalled that the ball arrived at his feet and he kicked it away.

'Hey, Jarvis kicked the ball away,' the other boys chanted in celebratory amazement. That solitary moment was the totality of his sporting achievement.

A fellow schoolmate who was in his class remembered that on more than one occasion, even in the early years of his schooling, Jarvis had told him and other classmates that he had no wish to do anything with his life. He had no ambition whatsoever. He also said that he had no fear of failure because he had no desire to succeed, so what was there to worry about?

He said it was just the way he was and he was not depressed about it. As long as he was kept warm and safe in a hostel somewhere he would cause no trouble to anyone and that would be enough for him.

As he grew older Jarvis's life unfolded as he said it would. Like an inert gas he neither reacted nor bonded; he existed, protected from danger by his meekness and natural anonymity, surviving on housing benefit and welfare payments. Strangely he had a certain contentment. Unlike so many of life's walking wounded, casualties of the cruel world, Jarvis had no inner demons he had to do battle with each day. In a surreal sort of way you could say he was blessed. One could even speculate that if he lived in India, he might have attracted a following, the cult of inner peace through inactivity. He never did find work. Repeated efforts had been made to try and get him to train for some clerical position.

Jarvis used to obtain cigarettes from Nigel. He could not be accused of cadging, filching or mooching them, even though that was what he was doing, because there was an almost ritualistic routine between the two men. As Jarvis would walk out of digs, Nigel was always be standing there already, as though waiting with a fag in his mouth. Jarvis would skulk past and give him an insipid smile and Nigel would hold out his cigarette pack for Jarvis to take one. A curious one-sided affirmation of friendship.

Jarvis would then say, 'Another day another dollar,' which was one of his stock phrases, which was ridiculous because, as has been pointed out, he had never done a day's work in his entire life. But it meant that he did not have to think. Stock phrases are useful devices for lazy men. Jarvis really was not a bad type but underneath it all probably rather charmless. When he bought his newspaper each day, before he even looked at the headlines he would say, 'Bloody politicians.'

If you bought him a pint in the pub, which in truth was not all that often, he would invariably say, 'Down the hatch.' If he farted in public, or if one of the other residents farted in his presence, he would always say, 'Better out than in.' He was a master of cliché; he would utter things other people would not be bothered to utter simply because they were too obvious. But it saved Jarvis having to think of something else to say.

'Fine with sun until mid-afternoon, then cloudy, with some showers. It will turn colder tomorrow through until the weekend, you'll need your umbrella then,' Nigel said with a broadening grin on his face as the taken-aback passer-by would try and process this unsolicited weather forecast.

And if you were a familiar face, up and down the street, his mode would become religious: 'You been to mass? It's the Passion of Christ, or it's the feast of the Blessed Virgin, or the feast of St Peter in Chains, or today is the Assumption, or the Ascension, or the Maternity of the Blessed Virgin, or All Souls' Day?'

Nigel's three preoccupations were the liturgical calendar, the weather and how his vegetables were doing on a small plot in the back garden of the residential home, though he was fondly known as the weatherman.

He was in his sixties; outwardly you would say he was 'on the scale', although it was not clear when or whether autism had been a diagnosis. He was a local Gloucester man, podgy and balding, but with an endearing face, bright eyes and engaging manner. He spent much of the day standing outside of the residential home smoking and greeting people as they passed by. His speciality was to spark up a conversation and then provide a weather forecast for the coming days. He was usually right.

He was an obsessive. He was the youngest of four boys. His mother had been a devout Irish Catholic who had cleaned the church for the priests. She had lost her husband at an early age and brought the boys up on her own. Nigel had never left home. He stayed to look after his mother. He had been a taxi driver. When his mother died he had a complete nervous breakdown. It changed his personality. He had to go into therapy and take medication. When his condition stabilised he was placed at the residential home as care in the community. It was Nigel who made David privy to a certain matter that would present such a bizarre situation, something that a man of such advanced years could well have done without.

Then there was Ingrid: 'Bless this little chick, she has lost her mother. I was visiting her to bring food each day. She was pushed out of her home. I made her a safe haven in a box with leaves and straw on little roof at the end of some guttering, my little *süßes Mädchen* (cute maiden). I want to see her today.'

Nigel would characteristically give her a short-term weather synopsis and they would stand and share a fag. Ingrid always had her own rollies. She had boundless compassion for all the furry and feathery creatures that humans share the planet with.

Originally from Germany, Ingrid had been in the UK for over thirty years. She was an intelligent, engaging woman now in her late forties. When she was younger she was a tall, confident fräulein. But not now. The years of chronic mental illness had taken their toll. She was heavily medicated, morbidly obese, arthritic and required a frame to shuffle down the street. Her walking frame had a large square shopping bag attachment that she could store all manner of things in.

As a self-harmer, she constantly injured herself, in the jargon of mental health, 'cutting up', with the resulting myriad of old and new linear scars up and down the visible parts of her arms and legs and probably extensively covering her whole body. Her face was also marked and bloody with fresh scabs and gouges, possibly even self-inflicted cigarette burns that had blistered. Eventually, long after David got to know her, she was given a personal carer to accompany her on her walks. Her carer was supporting an application to get her a mobility scooter. She was always cheerful and sociable, seemingly in complete denial of whatever the internal crisis was that was prompting her self-harm.

In her twenties she had been diagnosed with borderline personality disorder and schizophrenia. She was prone to psychotic episodes. Since that time she had been on a cocktail of medication. In her younger days her favourite party trick was setting fire to things, which eventually included the accommodation where she was living, while other people were in the house. Arson with intent to endanger life, if the perpetrator is sane, carries a potential life sentence, otherwise indeterminate detention under a Mental Health Act hospital order. Matters were compounded when she was on bail awaiting sentence for such an egregious offence and then intimated and indeed then took steps to set fire to the trial judge's residence. Really, not a good career move. She did time. She could easily have ended up in Broadmoor, but somehow, in the opinion of the experts, she fell short of being hardcore criminally insane. More recently her condition was generally, in the broadest sense of the word, regarded as stable.

Yet she had a charming and sociable personality, with a flair for art and a deeply held concern for the welfare of animals. In particular, she now saw her mission in life to feed orphaned seagulls, and when she found gulls in distress she would rescue the limping birds and, much to the shock and horror of the other residents and management, take them back to her lodgings to help them recover.

There are many people in Gloucester who really hate seagulls. They constantly dive-bomb and blitz and shit everything and everybody. There are always so many of them. They follow the River Severn up from the Bristol Channel. The struggling independent traders in Westgate Street are of the view that dive-bombing seagulls actively deter custom and even the city council has on occasion taken steps to curb their numbers on account of the torrent of guano that gets splattered over tourists as they disembark from coaches. Some less intrepid travellers have been known to bypass an exploration of Gloucester's ancient history and travel on to Cheltenham, Bath or Oxford.

David was impressed with Ingrid. He well realised her inherent instability, which she wore on her bloodied sleeve, but her decency and creativity was also evident. When she was feeding some birds at a bird table in the garden she too pointed to the potting shed and then said of the garden, 'It goes up over there, doesn't it?'

David responded, 'Yes, Jarvis pointed that out. Is it really that interesting? It makes the shed look a bit strange, as though it disappears into the ground.'

Ingrid laughed as though there was something David did not know. David was not in the mood for secrets and riddles and had some shopping to do in town.

As one year moved into another David refused to be drawn into this rather puerile little riddle. His mind was focused on more pressing concerns.

IV

'Hi, bro. See you Wednesday.' The loud greeting filled the street even before an observer could take cognisance of the source, though it was at least as proportionately conspicuous to behold. A morbidly obese bald-headed man with a walking stick and round dark glasses shuffled into view. His limping gait made him old before his time. His baggy denims did not easily fit to the bulbous middle section, where the paunch required an over-hanging sweater. When he uttered these voluminous words he made a strange gesticulation, as though bonded by some shared knowledge to the intended recipient, some secret, so esoteric that it could not be betrayed even by bold, indiscrete public communication. What was this? Some new kind of freemasonry for down-and-outs?

The improvised sign language itself may fairly have been misinterpreted as a fat man trying to maintain his balance. As he passed the cut-price chicken and chips joint and then the florists next door, he kept looking straight ahead, not acknowledging the skinny, bearded beggar sitting cross-legged on the pavement outside the Tesco Express on the other side of the London Road as it heads out of Gloucester. The beggar shouted in the affirmative back across the road, 'Right, Dean, bring the Dipper,' before turning to someone entering the store and saying, 'You got any spare change, mate?' The response was a cursory nod to the negative, to which the beggar said, 'Have a nice day.'

The road ran from the Northgate Street side of Gloucester towards Cheltenham. Along the length of its suburban sprawl was a ribbon development of shops, garages, hostels, bus depots, a BBC radio building, residential flats and the derelict Trident life insurance building. There was also, rather incongruously, the blood transfusion service building. The further you travelled out of Gloucester the more sedate the area became and in the streets off the main road there were some fine old properties.

In recent times a stretch of the road had become a magnet for the homeless, for people with mental health issues, winos, weirdos and drug dealing. In this cloud of abandonment and hopelessness the vista was a curious blend of lounging, drunken, spaced-out idling. Bodies were sporadically humped on the pavement with trickles of spilt beer and urine running out to the street. Then wiry, hooded bodies suddenly whizzed past on pedal bikes. These cyclists would stop momentarily and some frenetic transaction would take place with a swift passing of a wrap into someone's hand or pocket. This transient activity might result in furious rows, where a cyclist might start swearing or even lashing out at some inebriated, loitering junkie. There might be a sudden array of mobile phones as others are telephoned or verbally abused in a public tirade with an irrational violent intensity indicative of cannabis psychosis. And then all would revert to the aimless semi-dispersed throng of life's casualties.

David's residence was in one of those sedate houses located on a road off the London Road. He had soon realised that he was residing near to the Trident insurance company, where he had spent over twenty years of his career and from where he'd retired as broker sales director.

One Monday afternoon, many years after becoming a resident at the supported lodgings, he was wandering out onto the street, passing Nigel, who had just finished planting some carrots. He wiped his hands on an old rag and took up his customary position next to the stone pillar adjoining the pavement. Nigel pointed his opened cigarette packet in David's direction and made a jabbing movement.

'No thanks,' said David, which was rather pointless as Nigel well knew that David did not smoke, so it was either a futile friendly prop to communication or assumed to be a persuasive gesture intended to bring him into the smokers' fold: meant with the best possible intentions, innocently doing the devil's work.

Then he said, 'My asparagus is looking promising this year, got some nice curly kale too.'

David replied, 'It must be so satisfying being a gardener.'

Nigel: 'Could say that. I've got my plot, might as well use the land. You seen my potting shed? Bit special down there, mind? The ground goes up at the back, don't it? I told Jarvis and Ingrid not to say anything, 'cos it would spoil it.'

David: 'Here we go again. It really does not interest me, it seems your need to tell me is much greater than my need to know... well, let me lighten your load... spoil what, Nigel?' David decided to exert some passive authority.

Nigel: 'Because it is the way in, isn't it?'

David: 'Way in where?'

Nigel: 'The old insurance building.'

David: 'The old insurance building, for heaven's sake... Is that what this shenanigan is all about? Why bother? Anyway, it's well secured and you know that it is strictly out of bounds. There is no way in there. I can see that some hooligans have thrown stones and smashed windows and the rough sleepers used to assemble around the perimeter, but no, not now with the additional measures they have put in place. There is no access to the building.'

Nigel manipulated his loose-fitting dental plate in his mouth, and as he wrinkled his face to smile a surge of frothy saliva emerged from between the large gaps in his dentition and he smiled a most unattractive smile.

'Ain't there? You sure about that? Here, you come down to my potting shed, but don't say nothing, mind, don't say nothing to nobody, right?'

'Right,' said David.

So Nigel led David up the garden path until they reached the door of the red-brick potting shed, which really was no more Nigel's than anyone else's.

When Nigel unlocked the door, the sunlight illuminated rows of shelves with old plant pots and garden tools, a pitchfork, a spade, shears, a rake and a wheelbarrow parked in the corner. The exterior brickwork was loose and needed repointing. The putty in the small window at the side of the door had cracked and was loose in the rotted wooden frame. At the back of the shed it looked as though part of the wall had collapsed with bricks and rubble littering the floor. Because of the elevation of the garden at that point, the rear wall was built into the ground and so behind much of the collapsed wall there was just earth and soil, but to the right a modern heavy-looking metal grill was evident. This grill was held on brackets to a concrete structure behind the soil. It had a latch that could be unlocked. On closer inspection it could be seen that between the old brickwork and the concrete, a flu vent ran overhead.

Nigel opened the grill with ease, and he and David stepped effortlessly into the dark concrete cavity with what looked like a narrow grill high up that let a modicum of light into what would otherwise be pitch dark on the other side. The subterranean structure was built as part of the foundation of the building.

'It's this way,' said Nigel as he moved towards a barely discernible door which opened into an office corridor, with a large window at the top of a staircase providing reasonable illumination.

David realised there was a vague familiarity about the location. He was in the basement of the Trident insurance building, the corporate hub of the business empire in which he had risen to such great heights so many years earlier.

V

The office building had been standing idle at least since the early millennium, many years before the financial crash of 2008. Window frames had rotted, glazing smashed, damp moss was growing on the front door and paint had been daubed at various places on brickwork.

New property agents were appointed in 2018 as a response to the increasing number of rough sleepers pitching up their paltry ramshackle stuff to doss down in the dry sheltered grassy dip on the London Road side of the building. This prompted a change in the method and numbers of vagrants visiting. This excavated depression was designed as a discrete siting for the insurance building, enabling it to nestle amidst the residential properties nearby. In recent summers anyone passing on a double-decker bus would think that it was a campsite strewn with tents, sleeping bags, lager cans, kit bags, papers, makeshift storage for foodstuffs. Some would stay for weeks or even months on end; others would move on much sooner.

Unbeknown to the authorities, all this was observed from the inside by the 'visitors', who could be there one moment and then make themselves scarce when the property agent's contractors checked around the property, bringing with them German shepherd dogs in the hope of flushing out any occasional vagrant ensconced within.

To those seeking improvised refuge in the building, they were now confronted first with a boarded barricade, a deterrent for the homeless. The fencing posts were securely rooted around the perimeter and then weather-resistant shuttering ply was firmly secured to the posts with razor wire nailed to the top, which for all intents and purposes should have made the building and its surroundings impregnable to any opportunistic homeless person looking for a place to get his head down.

The boarding provided virgin space for spontaneous street art and very soon graffiti ranged across the defences: 'Love Hurts', 'Man belongs to the earth', Media is the virus', 'RIP Sandra', 'To exist is to resist', 'Tories are Cunts', 'Save the Pangolin', 'Police the Police', 'Stop Badger Culling', 'No one rules if no one obeys', 'Leave Foxes alone, hunt the Hunt', 'Ban Battery Chicken Farming', 'Fuck Boris' and so on. These were occasionally neatly overpainted by the letting agents. There were also the official notices to be compliant with legislation – 'Danger Protected by Razor Wire' – and large billboards announcing 'All enquiries to Pall Mall Estates: 8,000–45,000 sq ft'.

For many austerity had kicked in long before 'official' austerity. 'Austerity' is not a term invented to reflect an early twenty-first century Tory economic policy, but rather a state of being that for many was all they had ever known or ever would know.

Within the boundary stood not one but two buildings, one very different from the other. Number 67 London Road was a disastrous early 1950s attempt at function over form, which would not have looked out of place as an administrative block in some far-flung corner of the Soviet Union (as it then was), such was its utilitarian lack of charm. It was a long rectangular building on three floors with a surfeit of windows, row after row that pre-dated double glazing, all with thin rusting metal frames interspersed with decaying matt panels and then a large expanse of paint and rendering over blockwork, all very dated. On the front corner a staircase enclosed in a four-storey glass canopy had been constructed, enabling direct access to the more modern and prestigious sister building, which at least, it was possible to imagine, had once been a busy, proud and affluent office hub.

That was number 69 London Road, purpose-built, intelligently designed, award-winning architecture, aesthetically pleasing in its own post-modern way, proportionate regions of neat red brickwork and an abundance of neatly recessed windows, sympathetic to the locality; yet with many windows now cracked and smashed and with bold large wild plants sprouting from the guttering and along the roof, this was sustainability by an organically enveloping return to nature. An observer would probably feel that this building deserved more and would wonder what mechanism in the nation's economy made for such a wasteful decline?

In contrast, number 67 was such an ugly slab that in a strange way it was in keeping with its wild, distressed and abandoned state. It could be imagined that in the mind of an observer, trained by over-exposure to dystopian movies, this was exactly the way the building should be, its destiny to become derelict, a necessary blight on the landscape, with its large outdated windows smashed, the paintwork peeling, and trees and shrubs growing out of the drainpipes.

David walked past these buildings most days. They were so familiar to him. They triggered recollections of his now-distant working life. He was disappointed that market forces should dictate such a decline, but there was also a personal sense of discomfort, as though the abandonment and dilapidation mirrored something about himself, as though he had been brought back here to witness his own decay.

From Toxteth to Cheltenham, from pre-welfare state housing and social neglect, then via the pinnacle of his own success, digital juggernauts and ethernet billionaires, to post-welfare state corporate waste, homelessness and deprivation.

David had, on occasion, more for amusement and to alleviate boredom, read the *Socialist Worker* religiously delivered each week to the residential home by a bespectacled young man in blue dungarees. To him the columns of rants about the collateral damage of an industrial revolution and intractable class system compounded by a morally vacant market system that monetised cultural worth and where the sole determinant of person's value was their price were so misguided. Why would they claim that social capital had been kicked into the gutter and that humankind had ceased even to pretend to be custodians of the planet for the betterment of their children?

He would smile and think of Abigail admonishing him for working hard to provide the family with a good standard of living. Then he would be maudlin and slump into melancholy.

He would ponder why a building where he had thrived and prospered, where his aspirations for himself and his family were realised was now abandoned? What had changed? Why had something in that wholesome model of prudence and hard work reached a dead end?

David remembered the bullish talk of the roaring eighties, the Big Bang of Thatcher's market deregulation of 1983 and then that computer program fault that caused the global markets to crash and then bounce back in October 1987. Maybe there was a lesson in those heady days that he and others should have heeded?

Instead there was always talk of equating volume of business to the size of commercial space. This made more sense with footfall in the retail sector, but why should lots of office floor space mean more business? More office workers, well, that was a good thing in bolstering employment. But was it not obvious as screens proliferated at desks and digital dealing became commonplace that computers were signposting a different story?

What about Moore's Law? They all knew about it. It remained true for a long time. Every two years the number of transistors that can be fitted on a microchip doubles as the price of the computer proportionately halves. Did we not realise that all that extra computer power would enable ever more sophisticated algorithms, ever more powerful search engines, ever more efficient digital management of databases? Did we not realise that labour would in many sectors become obsolete? That it would cease to be a vital factor in the means of production? So why on earth did we continue to invest in those grand, prestigious offices?

Of course the landlords needed to believe in the enduring value of these modern cathedrals to mammon. While no one disputes land is a scarce and a valuable resource in the UK, they needed us to believe, and many still do, that the raison d'être for the old legislation, in particular Part Two of the Landlord and Tenant Act of 1954, is still a relevant godsend, essential to modern business. It assumes that when businesses take over leases there is overriding concern to obtain security of tenure at whatever price and for as long as possible in order protect their goodwill. There is also an assumption that now belongs in cloud cuckoo land that this demand will keep forcing commercial rents upwards.

As an insurance man David also realised that many if not most of these buildings were assets in the property portfolios of pension funds managed for prudent ordinary middle-income folk. Book values of unoccupied office blocks are a sensitive issue. Revaluation, which must happen at some time, will have some impact on pension payments.

Add to this unimaginative local authorities who persist in demanding excruciating business rates and the conflicted government policy that rewards relocation to recently constructed commercial units with five years of tax concessions. All this is conducive to the emergence of a few highly successful, highly diversified internet juggernauts, transnational, fluid manifestations of the ethernet. They exist as a name on a wall plate and a number in a register in some island shelter; they pay no tax, read your mind, tell you what you want, bury themselves behind passwords and protocols that are in place supposedly to protect the consumer yet make it virtually impossible to cancel your direct debit.

A realistic hedge fund owner or commercial estates landlord would unambiguously recognise this as an unintended consequence of the vagaries of capitalism. Book values and numbers can sometimes militate against reality. A valuable office block, year on year, should, so the myth goes, not only retain its value but show marked appreciation in line with the buoyant property market. And there is a multitude of such property, deceptively prestigious assets in the digital columns of the corporate merry-go-round. It would be a disaster to simply write them off as redundant, derelict black holes in the books. Such a notion would be quite impossible.

As a life assurance company, Trident had sold and administered life assurance polices, offering certainty and financial security to the prudent, devising unit-linked products as a vehicle for investment, ensuring provision for the family. But the name 'life assurance policy' is really a euphemism for what are really death assurance policies; it is just that life is a lot easier to sell than death. So many of the great temples of wealth management adorning urban skylines with neon logos declare 'life' this and 'life' that.

Way back when the life company was born in Threadneedle Street as an adjunct to the shipping insurance, where the cargoes themselves were often a trade in death, as slaves succumbed to shackles and scurvy in crowded, dark, rat-infested holds on stormy trips across the Atlantic. But alas, are these not the 'perils of the sea'?

On 29 November 1781 the master of the *Zong*, a Liverpool slaver becalmed in the doldrums and running out of provisions, threw 132 living slaves overboard on the assumption that insurance would cover the loss. When the underwriters refused the claim the owners successfully sued, as it was found that throwing the slaves overboard because of reduced supplies of drinking water was a recoverable loss. The underwriters applied for a retrial. At the King's Bench in May 1783 Lord Mansfield and his fellow judges, on the basis of fault attributable to navigational errors by the crew, ruled in favour of the applicants, finding that there was no evidence that the loss had been occasioned by 'perils of the sea', as covered by the standard marine insurance policy.

Two years later Lord Mansfield adjudicated another case, where a Bristol ship had lost fifty-five slaves during a revolt off the coast of Africa. The dispute centred on which losses the underwriters were liable for under the slave insurrection clause in the policy. The court ruled that they were to compensate for slaves shot dead or who died from wounds incurred directly in the struggle but that they were not liable for deaths by other means, such as drowning, jumping overboard or 'abstinence' from despair at the failure of the uprising.

But hey, we all need insurance. The economy works on supply and demand, futures and derivatives, hedging beds, spreading the risk. It's what makes the world goes round. Cautious, temperate, pious men manage the fruits of our labour. That is all. It is not a matter for enquiry as to whether aspersions should be cast in their direction, where the moral compass of their clients or the means of acquisition of wealth might otherwise be called into question. Bankers bank, insurers insure and actuaries actuate, contracts uberrima fides, that is all. Do not question an accountant's integrity – the figures are correct, the books balance, pure, neat, honest numbers compiled and filed with utmost discretion; that, my friend, is next to godliness. That is professional. The only sin is a column that is arithmetically incorrect. So who can you fairly accuse? Who can you say is guilty?

And so today the urban landscape is fragmented with the tainted sheen of soaring glazed monoliths and once-sparkling diamond obelisks that, decades earlier, bragged a frenetic optimism teeming with a populace of bright people: ladies in fashionable business clothing, cloned by Topshop from Dior, Chanel, Louis Vuitton and Yves Saint Laurent, accessorised in the most tasteful and modern way; men in sharp suits and ties; a vista awash with pheromones floating on a heady mix of cologne, testosterone and filthy lucre. How else could it be? Could such a capitalist hive in all its boundless glitzy colour declare itself a purveyor of 'death assurance'? Of course not. It could diminish confidence, cause atrophy in the essential mix of adrenalin and endorphins that fuel the stock exchange.

But no one says that a building is dead. A building just persists, no matter that it has not been occupied for twenty-five years, uninhabited, dilapidated, incrementally handed back to the withering ferocity of nature that swallows the space with all manner of creatures and vegetation, reborn in the interstices of microbes and mycelium.

There was another thing that disturbed David. Whenever he wandered past number 67, which was more set back behind number 69 and more difficult to get a proper view of, there was, invariably, what he was sure was a light flickering in a back office on the first floor and the silhouette of what looked like a figure sitting at a desk. He had wondered if this was a play of light, of a streetlamp reflecting off some shiny object inside the window, but it did not matter from which position he viewed the office, the flickering light remained the same. In the end David decided it was one of those unexplained phenomena that sometimes happen and he got used to it on his nightly walks.

Well, if people predisposed to more exotic transcendent thought are to be believed, then why not assert that office buildings can at least be haunted?

But it is not claimed that this is a ghost story, nor is it intended to cast a resonant eerie shadow in the psyche of those with fragile sensibilities; although they might be forgiven for interpreting some of what is to be disclosed as suggestive of the supernatural.

15

Machinations

It is disconcerting that the motley, downtrodden, rain-soaked cohort gathered in the grim decay of a long, derelict office block should represent the trajectory of our modern world on a stage never designed to become just another dystopian wasteland. The 1980 construction of the Trident building had given a precocious, albeit tentative nod to sustainability.

The limping fat man and the beggar were there. The beggar addressed the fat man as 'the Big Bopper', which was a joke because the fat man could hardly walk, let alone bop. The reason for the title was more nuanced. The Big Bopper, whose real name was Eric, was a very retro sort of bloke. He was a fan of Buddy Holly. His mate drove around in a clapped-out 1950s jalopy, which had had a re-chrome job and respray. Unfortunately, both he and the Big Bopper, who had been in the passenger seat, had taken an excess of synthetic hallucinogen; the mate lost control of the vehicle – actually, the steering wheel came away in his hands while singing 'Peggy Sue'. He smashed the car up and exited this planet while the Big Bopper ended up with a mangled leg.

Jarvis would wander around looking to snitch rollies and then slope off. Occasionally, Ingrid would turn up, although it was rare on account of her mobility. Also, while dogs were always welcome, the producing of maimed seagulls from a shopping bag, even among the discordance of this dissolute assembly, was regarded as antisocial.

Another straggler with a bad attitude who found his way into the building was Grinner, the ageing former Hells Angel, one of those people who seemed to crop up from time to time as a charmless and unwelcome interloper. He was now in his sixties and for many years was a hard drinker. He still wore a grubby motorbike jacket and boots and always carried an antiquated helmet, which gave the impression he had just cruised in from somewhere, maybe after doing a ton down the motorway; but that was not the case, because Grinner had not owned a motorbike for twenty years. It was just the image that endured. That had been the way in his glory days when he walked into a pub as a younger man. It gave him a sense of purpose, identity, of being noticed, of having some interest in life, of being part of something. The carrying of the helmet did have more than a cosmetic purpose, as Grinner always carried his bacci, cannabis, rizla and matches in a polythene bag concealed within. Whenever the cops had wanted to search him, he would always say: 'OK, just let me put my helmet down.'

In recounting this it would be erroneous to suggest that Grinner had a clever side to him; even among the most forgiving beggars and inhabitants of night shelters, Grinner was one stupid son of a bitch.

A more curious interloper was a woman called Madelaine, who dressed like a hippy and liked to smoke weed, but there was an erudite air about her that made some of the others uneasy. She did not seem to be living on the edge; she was not desperate enough, not lethargic enough, not brow-beaten or disaffected enough. She had a resilience, could hold her own. She was an intellectual. But to her credit she did share her marijuana joints and would then laugh a lot when high.

Much of the time she had with her a magnifying glass, peeling back carpet tiles, scraping slime off the window frames, reaching outside to pull some plant samples out of the guttering, scooping dead insects into a plastic bag, flicking through rat droppings; habits not favourably embraced by fellow squatters. She had a notebook in which she would spend hours writing up observations.

She was passionate about ecology and uncompromising about the irresponsibility of government for failing to effectively tackle the short-termism that was causing climate change:

'Humanity is waging a "suicidal" war on the natural world, and you know nature always strikes back, and is doing so with gathering force and fury.'

Her specialist subject was the study of fungi, particularly the reproductive stage. When she was stoned she would tell those she was smoking with fascinating insights into mycelium.

'Magic mushrooms, you mean, if you eat enough of them and don't poison yourself in the meantime. Yeah, they are a pretty good high – lot easier just to pop a tab, though?'

She had recently been studying some flies, some still buzzing around and some scattered upturned and dead across a broken desk in a far corner of the office. She would sit for hours examining them closely with her head hovering inches above the desktop, using her magnifying glass as she examined samples with intense concentration.

'Hah, hah, well, well, this is interesting,' she would mutter to herself, oblivious to the noise and activities of the others.

'This is what my colleagues at the university were talking about – well, I never, this must be the Strongwellsea. Oh yes, you poor little flies, Coenosia testaccea, Coenosia sexmaculata, hmmm, yes, you're hosting those naughty old spores, aren't you, and you are still buzzing around, my goodness.'

Madelaine continued chattering away: 'They are doing it deliberately, aren't they, they are not only keeping you alive, they are doing something to your brains that makes you more sociable so that they can release millions of spores into your friends as well. It's an unusual tactic for keeping the host alive while releasing spores.'

Madelaine stopped mumbling to herself for a moment and wrote in her jotter 'active host transmission: an effective way of getting access to other healthy individuals'. Scientists think the fungi could be producing substances that 'dope' their hosts, who then become 'zombies', meaning they can stay fresh enough to live on after infection.

Nearby to Madelaine's desk was a rough sleeper who refused to tell anyone what his name was or where he was from other than that he was a rough sleeper. As he snored so much the others were content just to refer to him as 'rough sleeper'. Deficient in everything from vitamins and money to food and shelter, he nevertheless had a mobile telephone with internet access. He only became animated in his blogs. That was how he communicated; he had decided years earlier to give up verbal communication.

'The modern world skates on an ice rink of myth; a slippery unreliable terra firma, an all-encompassing monotonous substrate.'

He would amuse himself by sourcing from the web a smorgasbord of novelties, playful illusions, conjuring tricks, any counter-intuitive fantastical occurrence that could be shown to have been visited upon humanity. His Facebook pages were full of weird and beautiful phenomena, saved or salvaged from endless excursions across the internet.

For him the enchantment of illusions was that they possessed solvable uncertainty, uncertainty that had the potential to be cured without waiting for the future. In that way they surpassed time; for him their sublime quality was the elaborate trickery, that was what was transcendent. That was the essence of magic.

Madelaine read his blogs but was doubtful anyone else bothered.

'It's all a game of chance acting in reverse. The points of interconnectedness – let's call them "events" – are at the extremities of remotest probability. Anything run-of-the-mill, day-to-day routine, high probability, like, say, throwing a dice, even winning the lottery, is not the stuff an event, nah, none of that stuff, but talk of miracles, yeah, and magic, yeah, or any nature-defying phenomena and then you might be experiencing a meeting of parallel universes. And there is another way people can experience parallel universes interconnecting, but it requires the torment of psychosis, schizophrenia or dementia, doesn't it?

'I mean, human rights are great if you are included in the human race. There was a time, you know, when women were not, likewise if you were black or a slave, then human rights passed you by. Today, the child in the womb is excluded, unless and until validated by its mother, who sometimes might have to have her views validated by her husband or an expert. And then there are the twilight people, the people who talk to you at night and disappear in the morning, the voices and exotic visitors that both delight and torment a soul in crisis. For sure, they are validated by the people whose psychotic hallucinations configure them. Does that give them human rights?

'Then there are influencers on Facebook who are mere avatars or may have died years earlier. Are they not human to their followers and thereby have their human existence validated?'

But his default worldview was one of inevitable struggle, a fight against life's pre-ordained opposing current. This was the natural order. It validated the Freudian 'lack'; it was the energy created by deficit, the potential. Rough Sleeper was a modern-day secular holy man, parasitically dependent on modern electronics yet meditating on the carcass of a post-industrial dystopia.

Darren and Graham were the cuckoos in the squat, the culprits and agitators, the stirrers possessed of an anarchistic energy and natural street-fighting disposition. What is more, they brought with them organisation. And they both had form and history.

While usually spoken of in the same breath, they were very different characters, with different backgrounds and brought differing skillsets to the table. The only similarity, beyond their lawlessness, was their style choice in both habitually wearing sunglasses, night and day. It gave them a kind of mystique that added to the aura of power they held over their followers. They were leaders.

They had met in prison. Darren was doing two years for theft and fraud, Graham three years for wounding with intent. They could both be charming, display prosocial attitudes and were good communicators.

Darren had over a number of years been running a racket stealing and dismantling bikes, sometimes very expensive bikes. He would then mix all the parts up to reconstruct unrecognisable new bikes from the cannibalised parts, which were then sold on eBay. Even then, sometimes he would sell the same bike two or three times and disappear into the night with the money remitted to his account.

With the not-inconsiderable sum he had earned he bought a few acres of poor-quality woodland in the Forest of Dean and set up a zombie-themed paintball venue, ideal for festive occasions, stag parties, etc. He had no difficulty recruiting a couple of dozen of the long-term unemployed to be his living-dead army. This proved a great public-relations exercise and marketing ploy as it gained him a full-colour two-page spread in the *Gloucester Citizen*.

The job description predictably required getting dressed up in outrageous raggedy gear from charity shops and then wearing garish goth makeup, with synthetic wounds and an abundance of runny red dye. A certain level of fitness was expected as the zombies had to stagger around the woodland in anticipation of getting zapped by a variety of paintballs, that by all accounts did sting and had been known to cause bruises on impact. But it was better pay than dole and Darren provided cider and lager because he felt it all worked better when his employees were drunk.

All was going swimmingly well until the police caught up with Darren over the bike thefts and eBay scam. Eventually, he and about six others were arrested and charged and stood trial. Despite the evidence being overwhelming, the proceedings took an age to be dealt with due to the judge over-indulging the defence lawyers in the most spurious and idiotic submissions about the wording of the offence and objections regarding disclosure and the pagination of the exhibits. But at last Darren was found guilty and sentenced to two years' custody and with a confiscation order made under the Proceeds of Crime Act of 2002. This was on the basis of land and wealth derived from a criminal lifestyle.

When Darren came out of prison, he was an angry man slipping and sliding on skid row.

The police were effective in recovering the land and bank accounts and selling two jeeps and a minibus, all of which were seized before the gaudy livery stating 'Zombie Hunt' could be resprayed. Nevertheless, the paint guns were hidden in a garage together with a large supply of paint pellets, a high-pressure spray cannon and fifty ten-litre tubs of various colours of paint, all of which was ecologically friendly and sustainable. While for Darren this was for no reason other than price and availability and would not be otherwise worth a mention; in the precise circumstances of this story it proved to be a most favourable feature for David.

As the paint said on the bottle: 'Go Green with RAP4. Eco-Friendly Paintball is soybean-based, environmentally friendly paint… with bright fill at an unbeatable price! Comes in a clear plastic reusable bottle with a pop-up carry handle. Reuse the bottle to store your marker parts, tools, squeegees and everything else.

'Best of all for you is the price: £5.00 for a bottle of five hundred balls. Completely biodegradable, non-permanent, environmentally safe, the RAP4 Eco-Friendly Paintball is safe for back-country fields and full-time scenario fields alike. The splats fade in direct sunlight, and a good rain washes them away, where the organic material used in the shell and fill gets absorbed into the ground without hurting local plants, animals or water sources.

'The RAP4 Eco-Friendly Paintball shells are designed to shatter upon impacting your opponent, meaning more breaks on target. Part of this high-performance design is achieved through the use of soybean oil.'

It was this very supply that had been brought piecemeal into the insurance building. The original reason for doing so was not clear, but it was thought that the owner of the garage had got wise to the stock and Darren feared the police might raid it. There is no obvious suggestion that Darren, at that time, had any overtly sinister intent.

Even with convictions for violence, Graham was in most respects the more sophisticated of the two, more a man of passion and probably less calculating. He was someone who had a decent brain and thought outside the box, but the university of knocks had not been kind to him. Over time his use of drugs had convinced him of a grand conspiracy by the 'establishment'. The 'establishment' tended to be anyone he found himself in disagreement with. He was naturally drawn to an alternative lifestyle and was naturally athletic. He went everywhere with a skateboard.

And as if this disparate rabble of misfits and fellow travellers needed any more divergence, David's arrival amidst the decay and squalor must be noted. He might have continued to ignore Nigel's beckoning; he had, after all, done so for years. His preoccupations lay elsewhere, his sense of adventure had long since been dimmed by time, yet his curiosity about the play of light in the corner office of 67 London Road was enough to tempt him to play along, to be drawn in, even if he did not quite admit it to himself.

16

A Blast from the Past

I

In most stories the place of old age is a residual prop, at best located at a vantage point of wisdom so as to tell of what has already occurred in those raging, glorious, terrible, sad and happy days of youth and prime. It is a natural role for the elderly to tell the tales of those bygone times, of past valiant deeds, of fading memories, of romance and tragedy, of the vicissitudes, fates and fortunes of heady days of social flux, the days of energy and excess, the days of endless possibilities, where fearless youth invite risk and vulnerability.

In dotage are we not entitled to restful reflection? Remembering a life already lived? Ideally should they not be the years of gentle decline?

Based on those assumptions, there is a chord of alarm when those of senior years are swept up in a maelstrom of circumstance and drama, even in modern times of longevity. It is counter-intuitive; it disrupts the flow of nature and the narrative of poetic justice. And in contrast to David's persona, a man who would always choose peace, order and stability over conflict and revolution, a man who believed in compromise to find a solution; he found himself embroiled in battles and machinations he could well have done without.

II

Once inside 69 London Road, instead of following Nigel to join the throng nucleating in large open area on the second floor, he stood for a while looking around and getting his bearings from the ground-floor rear corridor. With purpose he made his way to the glass canopy that linked the two buildings and upon ascending the staircase made his way to the area of his old office located on the first floor of 67 London Road. The real focus of his investigation was the office area from where emanated that strange flickering light.

He realised it was in the area that had been occupied by the secretarial department. The company secretary, Stuart Baxendale, had his office in the corner of this area, at the end of an expanse of open-plan desk space. Back in the day that space was a hive of administrative activity: post-room clerks with delivery trolleys, typewriters tapping away, secretaries taking shorthand and answering telephone calls, investment managers scrolling across state-of-the-art screens full of share values and the usual hum of measured conversation.

And through that space, when their respective doors were open periodically during the day, David's eyes would meet those of Baxendale's in an involuntary, reciprocal way, while each was preoccupied with some issue within their own sphere of responsibility. David recalled those prolonged glares as anodyne, yet doubtless; a different agenda might have been imported by someone with a more suspicious mind.

The open office was now largely bereft of furniture and office equipment. Many of the carpet tiles, though discoloured, were still in place; many more were littered around, with large areas of stone flooring exposed. A large broken desk remained, as well as a stack of desk chairs with fabric-covered seats. Vermin obviously found the soft padding tasty because in most cases it had been nibbled and gnawed and the nylon stuffing messily distributed around the floor nearby. A few of the chairs had been taken off the pile to be used by the more recent clandestine visitors. Many of the panels in the false ceiling had also been dislodged, exposing a rusting metal grid and a dark cold void above. Wires hung loosely from the walls and ceilings, looking strangely organic and in keeping with the encroaching vegetation that was reclaiming the exterior space for nature.

Entropy and decline may be slow, but always a progressive, unremitting process. They do not follow some precisely engineered phase from one state to another. Closer observation would reveal that some light fittings were intact and even had light bulbs, likewise sockets on the walls. This, one must assume, was the case in Stuart Baxendale's office.

As David stood in the doorway there was a pervading darkness that was disorientating, as he tried precisely to locate from inside the building the source of the light he would see glowing at night from outside. While it was late afternoon in the season of winter and though the skies were overcast it was still officially daylight and the streetlights had yet to come on; but it was not light that next drew David's attention but a familiar voice.

Stuart Baxendale: 'Well, well, look who it is, if it is not David the doyen of broker sales. Welcome to my domain.'

The shadowy figure, with his desk lamp pointing more in the direction of David, began talking in a blunt, slightly taunting Yorkshire accent, which David recognised as familiar.

David: 'My God, this is bloody ridiculous… way too strange. Hey, what is this… Is that you? Really you? It can't be. Still as you were, dapper in your dowdy sort of way, countryfied chequered jackets and cravat complementing greased straight hair and mean-looking moustache. It's you, who else could it be? Stuart Baxendale.'

Stuart Baxendale: 'Well, us Northern folk who travel south to make good like to impress, don't we, David?'

David: 'Are you living... living locally, I mean? No... You can't still be living locally... you can't be bloody living anywhere. There was that business that blew up and you left and... I mean... you bloody died, for God's sake, I mean... I didn't get to your funeral, I know, but I read the obituary. That was over twenty-five years ago.'

Stuart Baxendale: 'I believe it was in the wise words of Heraclitus: "The way up and the way down are one and the same. Living and dead, waking and sleeping, young and old, are all the same." As you can see, I'm here, working late, David. Always a strong work ethic, me. I suppose if you turned your face to the wall right now, then you might question whether I am here, but turn back to face me and I assure you, it will be me.'

David: 'Working late? What do you mean, working late?'

Stuart Baxendale: 'Let's say late in a lyrical way. Unfinished business. If the toil of the day is not done well, as you know, we must carry on. I am still the bloody company secretary, you know. Oh yes, where the buck stops, hand on the tiller, belts and braces, salt-of-the-earth company man, that's me.'

David: 'What unfinished business? What do you think this place is? The buck stops with you? That is not quite how I remember it anyway, Stuart.'

Stuart Baxendale: 'Well, we had our differences, didn't we, David? But listen, we both wanted good outcomes for the shareholders, healthy dividends and a happy workforce, didn't we?'

David: 'You make it sound as though it was all sport and bonhomie for you. You know, for a long time I was taken in by your engaging, dare I say charming veneer, but underneath that convincing, plausible banter of yours, you were as calculating, conniving and manipulative as that reptile Janco Filch Du Preez.'

Stuart Baxendale: 'Janco? Oh, come, David. I was a company man and proud of it.'

David: 'I was hoping you were going to tell me that you've changed, but a leopard never changes its spots, does it? When I retired I felt I had done what I had to do. It seems the likes of you never retire, do you?

'You persist, endure, the undead, still in the middle of doing what it was you did, even after your time. Maybe going when you are doing what it is you do is the best time to go. Life is about becoming. Arriving is a kind of death, isn't it? Only made tolerable by the invention of a God. But what you've done is re-invent yourself, without, so it seems, all the many refinements available to a virtuous imagination. Oh, but then, why would you? For the narcissistic sociopath that you were… are, there could be no better version of you could there; the best of all the best possibilities?

'You sure are a company man, a company man who would tell lies to cover his tracks; a firm believer in divide and rule; I realise now how you gained ground in management tussles by deliberately setting people at odds with each other.'

Stuart Baxendale: 'Are you sure you are not confusing me with Filch Du Preez?'

David: 'Oh no, I never confused you with Filch Du Preez. That was one of my mistakes, wasn't it? What about Botswana?'

Stuart Baxendale: 'What about Botswana? What to do about Botswana? Hmm. What did we do about Botswana?

'Why do you bring that up anyway? It has all been filed, line drawn, today is a new day, new problems, new agenda. Besides, needs must, David, needs must. It was no time to be squeamish or emotional, you know. I had my hand on the tiller, that's what we did about Botswana. Let's face it, those bonds were perfectly legitimate, you know. Got a good price for the Botswana bonds. It's all in the microfiche.'

David: 'It damaged my broker's reputation. It damaged me.'

Stuart Baxendale. 'Why should you have worried? Legal got rid of the real dross and you know the old saying: selling insurance is like giving out umbrellas while the sun shines and then taking them back when it rains. Always liked that one.'

David: 'No, that's not how I ever saw it. We repudiated legitimate policies and sold others on, wrapped up as junk bonds. AIDS was not an act of God. Likewise all those mortgages – wrap them up, write them off, dump a junk bond, no accountability? The market does not forget; my team in the field got punished for that. It was like throwing the policy holders overboard and throwing our brokers under a bus, where many of them stayed.'

Stuart Baxendale: 'It's all in the microfiche. We had to sell those hairy little monsters on. Caveat emptor, David. Due diligence et al. The market is what it is. A lot of unforeseen death in Botswana. We just insure people, David. We don't want policy holders dying of mysterious diseases, but sometimes you have to be ruthless to cover your assets when this sort of stuff happens.'

David: 'All in the microfiche, that sounds convenient. What are you on about? You make it sound as though documenting legitimises an unconscionable act. I mean, Gaga Bevan wasn't so great either, was it?'

Stuart Baxendale: 'Gaga Bevan. Now that is not all in the microfiche. Don't you let his family hear you say that. All in a day's work. Client discretion, loyalty and service. It's all stuff you made your reputation on, isn't it, David?

'It was just a procedural shortcut to protect the market. How do you apply to the Court of Protection to appoint deputies to manage the affairs of the head of a merchant bank? Might cause a run, old pal, definite loss of confidence in that one, don't you reckon? No, we got that young solicitor to witness Gaga Bevan's power of attorney? OK, Gaga lacked capacity, he'd already lost his marbles, but let's face it, that drunken young lawyer was expendable, he wasn't going anywhere, he wasn't going to argue as long he could pay his mortgage and put food on the table for his family. Anyway, it worked out. As it was we didn't need to throw him under a bus. Business is business. No, we're not so different, you know.'

David: 'Do you remember the jumbo jets and the Australian forest fire in our general division?'

Stuart Baxendale: 'All in the frigging microfiche. Anyway, the chairman wrote the line, not me. Have to act within authority, articles of association and all that. I could never be accused of causing the company to act ultra vires.'

David: 'Ultra vires my arse. What sort of ultra and what kind of vires did you have in mind exactly?'

Stuart Baxendale: 'Corporate personality. You're the last person that needs lecturing on that subject. A thing of conceptual beauty; no body, just legal personality; it exists and it doesn't exist, depending on your perspective; physically you cannot grab it by the throat or punch it on the nose; and incorporeally, it has no soul and therefore cannot be accountable to God. I like that. The perfect trading vehicle. That suits me. Imagine if we could all exist like that? Wouldn't it be wonderful?'

David: 'I've heard this before somewhere. Was there ever a time when you could claim to have something remotely resembling a moral compass? A sense of social responsibility? Frankly, your attitude appals me. When I think how for a while I was actually taken in by you and your skulduggery, talk of being a company man, when it was always really about you and your self-aggrandisement.'

Stuart Baxendale: 'Ha, ha. You know what your problem was, David? You would hunt with the hounds and run with the fox. Some people call it hypocrisy. I remember the fuss you made about corporate waste. If it wasn't for corporate waste the economy would collapse. What are you saying? Would you have had all that hospitality cancelled?

'Come on, corporate waste was party time, man. Events, catering, music, all good for macroeconomics; got to see the bigger picture. You didn't argue when I got Anna Ford to present the sales awards. I mean, you never grumbled about the annual senior managers' bash at the Savoy, did you? As I recall one year we booked three days for a conference.'

David: 'No, not hypocrisy. I have no problem with hospitality. In cost-benefit analysis, hospitality builds loyalty, motivation. We both believe in reward, don't we? Besides, in a way you have to compare it with advertising; it might be extravagant and you can't know in advance what results it will yield, but by God, where would capitalism be without it?

'Corporate hospitality was always true to my roots and my values. Where I grew up people were nice to each other. You would not think of not talking to someone you passed in the street, whether you knew them well or they were just a familiar face or even often enough a stranger; families would help other families out. That was the way it was. That is what I understand by hospitality.'

Stuart Baxendale: 'Let me put this to you, David, since you wax so lyrically about the good old bad old days of your slum childhood in Liverpool: have you never asked yourself why you have never been back there? Never felt the need for some spiritual pilgrimage to the place of your roots? The reason is, David, you could not even if you wanted to. You are not the same person and Liverpool is not the same place.'

David: 'Well, of course I've moved on – worked hard, met my beautiful wife Edwina, moved south, started a family. What's not to like? I can't be criticised for that. It all feels like a dream now.'

(Pause in conversation.)

Stuart Baxendale: 'She showed me, you know.'

David: 'Who? What? What are you on about now? Who showed what?'

Stuart Baxendale: 'And Janco. It's all in the microfiche. Naughty snapper, our Janco.'

David: 'Does it amuse you to plague me with riddles, you infernal man? All in the microfiche, all in the microfiche, you keep going on about the microfiche, what bloody microfiche?'

Stuart Baxendale: 'You know, the microfiche. In the locked room in the basement.'

David: 'The famous locked room, that's still there as well, is it? The microfiche in the locked room. The stuff that when you looked for it the logging system would indicate the files weren't there or more often offer you a file that had not been requisitioned? What kind of organisation was that? Personally, I never got a look in there, even when I deputised for Phil. Only he as the chairman and the Americans had access, that vice-president guy who had his office next to Phil Herring.'

Stuart Baxendale: 'That was the idea. Built-in deficiencies can be useful, sometimes very profitable. They had the key alright; he used to take his secretary in there after work to give her a good shagging. She complained, said it was non-consensual. Never got her anywhere. But we're getting off the subject, aren't we? Let's keep it all closer to home. You know. I'll not spell it out for you.'

David: 'What are saying? Stop talking in these bloody riddles. What about Filch Du Preez? He was no more a friend of yours than he was of mine. Met a bad end, got too big for his boots, Herring drummed him out.'

Stuart Baxendale: 'Hmm. Your enemy's enemy is your friend. That's what they say, isn't it, David?'

David: 'He tried to high-jack the bloody Life Group; he tried to move direct sales and sales admin to a company he set up called Trident Du Preez; he then tried to tell all brokerages to ignore me and direct business through him. He thought he could go behind everyone's back and tell the City that clients should be buying his new products and somehow Herring would let him get on with it. The chair eviscerated him. Filch Du Preez let his ambition and the big green monster get the better of him. He had his desk cleared and his corporate pass and expense cards rescinded and his company limo reclaimed before he had time to put his hands in his pockets. If he was your friend you are as big a shyster as he was.'

Stuart Baxendale: 'It's water under the bridge, David. Petty foibles shouldn't trouble us in hindsight. All's fair in love and war.'

David: 'Talking in clichés and riddles again. I don't need it.'

Stuart Baxendale: 'No, come on, David, let's get back to basics, what drives a man, what gets him out of the bed in the morning, what makes him stay in bed in the morning, what drives a man to distraction. You were talking about advertising, that's all. We can get personal, I know it hurts, but it's there, the doubt, the imagining, the knowing and not knowing, the evidence, yes or no, good or bad. She showed me, that's all. I saw it, all of it mind. Very nice, lovely actually, it was all put on the microfiche.'

David: 'I'm not going to let a snake like you rile me with your falsehoods. I can see what you're up to, trying your best, you are, to get to me, unnerve me, hope that I will blink and you will trip me up. That was really the way it always was with you, Baxendale. But you will not succeed; the worst you can do is irritate me with your tedious discombobulation.'

Stuart Baxendale: 'Now, now, David, let's not get abusive. We're grown men, we talk about things in a calm, mature way.

'Let me tell you more about that room. They called it the room of risks; it was all in there. You film it, photograph it, document it, process it, trust your memories to that groaning old IBM computer, to its data storage bank. It needed a big room in those days.

'You know they secured that room because of the information the IBM was proliferating. What came out, what was extrapolated, what was generated, they couldn't let staff know about it. I mean, David, that's what I was saying. And all this was long before Tim Berners-Lee had his eureka moment – believe me, some of that stuff was a seriously long time before Berners-Lee.

'I heard it explained that the program devised by a geek for the new policy processing and administration software, the one they spent a million on and then shelved, well, let me tell you that mother did some seriously weird stuff. They called it re:REREA – reverse entropy retrograde extrapolation algorithm.

'Basically, what happened was, you can imagine giving a dog a bone and the dog chews the bone and then gives you back the bone with all the tissue, flesh and blood perfectly restored. And when it started doing that with company business, policy holders, brokers, employees, social lives, not to mention employees' wives social lives, not to put too fine a point on it, there was, by heck, some seriously deep shit. I think you might get the idea where all that might lead.

'They think it happened because when the program was written up and the geek handed his work to a colleague to input the program, and some whiz unwittingly included an extra "re:", re:REREA, which was only ever meant to be the usual mundane standard abbreviated correspondence reference, as in "re: Your policy holder Joe Bloggs".

'Stuff happens – remember MTB, the Millennium time bomb? Well, in the end that did not happen, but it might have, all because someone decided to write a two-bit year recognition rather than four-bit. Well, the unintended consequences of dropping this bollock might have been a thousand times worse and turned out to be what academics have called the time-scape of invisible hazards.'

David: 'Why don't we just keep the door locked?'

Stuart Baxendale: 'Ha, ha, ha. But that's not really what you want to hear, is it, David? I doubt there is anything I or anyone else could do to prevent your curiosity from venturing into that room. Ha, ha, ha. Just remember, 67691998.'

When David had found Baxendale sitting at his desk he'd questioned his grip on reality, pinched himself, quickly asked himself those simple questions to check he was compos mentis. Was this delusion or dementia, perhaps just a hallucinogenic episode?

Maybe one of the lodgers sneaked a tab into his coffee at breakfast for a puerile giggle. Such things did happen. If it was otherwise, then the person sitting behind the desk must surely be an imposter, yet David knew such a notion could not be possible; no imposter could so precisely have the demeanour, the smell, the accent and attitude of Stuart Baxendale. There could only ever be one Stuart Baxendale; nature would never tolerate a doppelganger for such an aberrant sociopath, and anyway, an imposter could not possibly know all the things about David that this man mentioned.

According to the record of history, as it was presented to David, Baxendale had died twenty-five years earlier following a brain tumour. Yet there he was sitting at his desk in the corner of the large open-plan second-floor office of number 67. Make no mistake, there was a full three-dimensional reality about him.

Even if the meeting had not been so nightmarishly surreal, even though David had bracketed the encounter as something provisional that may not be really happening, something he would need to deconstruct and ultimately force himself to consider his own sanity; beyond all this, even without these glaring defects in cognitive reality, he had reason to treat his dialogue with Stuart Baxendale with great circumspection.

David well remembered Baxendale as someone who had influenced his life, who by his actions and words had challenged his confidence and who now, it seemed, continued to do so to the extent of challenging his very sanity.

It is not good to be a senior manager and not know whether a colleague is a friend or foe, whether he was fighting for or against you. There is nothing more unsettling, except perhaps an unfaithful wife, than a nagging feeling and uncertainty about whether there could ever be any duplicity in the motives of a close colleague.

In a negative way it must be supposed that he helped form or reshape David's worldview. David had regretted the time he had spent confiding in and accepting words of wisdom from Baxendale. He probably compromised himself in the long conversations they'd had about people, business, insurance, politics, the economy and life in general. To what end?

At the time David felt it was a kind of talking therapy that somehow it would be possible to either disavow himself of these negative perceived machinations or otherwise know and then act decisively against the revealed enemy. It may also have been possible to patch things up, to clear the air, at least reach an understanding or compromise. That, it turned out, was never going to be the case.

In those former years, Baxendale had a self-appointed dual role as company secretary and as a maverick 'pop-up' investment manager. He claimed 'it went with the territory'. He delegated much of the procedural brief either to the assistant company secretary, who was an able and conscientious young woman, or otherwise to the in-house legal department. For specialist advice Baxendale would also outsource and instruct city legal firms.

He prided himself in taking a key role in strategic decision-making involving the board. This might include the sale or acquisition of office space for the company and its satellite brokerages, including prestige sites in Dean Street in London's West End.

All this freed up many hours of the day for Baxendale's favoured pastime of monitoring the data on the investment screens; as conveniently the investment under-managers had their desks close to the secretarial desks. The going bid/offer spread of one fund or another was his constant preoccupation as he shifted investments between funds. There were times when people in the company wondered whether or not he would prefer to be on the trading floor at the stock exchange.

But he did know his business and he had people around him to check the detail, whether it be the terms of a lease or a debenture or ensuring documents were presented for signature sealing and due execution, or the filing of the correct forms at Companies House.

The 1980s were a game-changer, first with the creation of the FTSE 100 indices and then the 'Big Bang' when all trading went 'on screen' rather than the hitherto open outcry of traders shouting and gesticulating at each other. This admirably suited Baxendale in his provincial domain, because the truth was he was not really a City type; he would have been out of place in a pin-striped suit lunching in an old boys' club.

But his maverick sojourns into investment activity brought Baxendale and David into direct conflict on a number of occasions. David did not suspect any deliberate manipulation of circumstances and viewed the situation as a structural blip in the hierarchical organisation. After all, company men are team players, on side for the betterment of the whole company.

It happened that they were both also co-opted to the board as ex-officio executive directors, and thereby both men singled out for greater things. And what both had to say as hands-on senior managers was listened to with close interest. As company secretary, it was Stuart Baxendale who drew up the business timetable as well as the agenda for meetings.

It was David's predisposition to take people at face value and he had built around him a close and loyal team. He relied on the results to do the talking. However, it became a pattern, certainly on more than a few occasions, when he was late for board meetings, on account of trying to revamp his own busy schedule at the last minute, when Baxendale would notify him of a meeting as though 'on the hoof', and on some occasions Baxendale would actually send a memo to David with completely the wrong commencement time, meaning that he would arrive fifteen minutes late and have to apologise to all present. It never occurred to David that Baxendale was engaging in Machiavellian intrigue, a devious subterfuge designed to undermine David's position.

Whatever else, the sales division's performance was the company's bottom line; ultimately it was their success that made the company successful. Furthermore, the chairman had such faith in David's integrity and acumen that he had placed his own trainee daughter, Priscilla, under his wing. Mostly, therefore, the malevolent posturing and manoeuvring had muted impact and remained under David's radar. This in itself had the appearance of great largesse on his part, as though brushing off irksome in-house corporate politicking, effectively signalling the perpetrator was inept by comparison.

Even then, Baxendale had a way that did hurt David, even if it did mean hurting the company as well. He embarked on a campaign that was reckless, disruptive and damaging.

David's carefully calibrated best advice was based on applying a lifetime's study of the markets to a long- and medium-term extrapolation of fund performance, whether equities, gilts or real estate.

By comparison and in tandem, through close monitoring of the investment screens and diverting funds based on daily short-term fluctuations, Baxendale could blow his own trumpet about short-term gains that might over-inflate the closing balances upon which the company's unit-linked products were based. Invariably the market would adjust and occasionally this inter-meddling would have disastrous results. When this did happen, much to David's deep despondency, it undermined the honest advice given to client investors, as well as disseminated via the direct sales force and brokerage arms. Baxendale was quick to point the finger elsewhere in the ensuing blame game.

David had later learnt that Baxendale, while he could not be accused of being an outright imposter – indeed, if he had been that would have been enough to secure his downfall – nevertheless, Baxendale had lied and exaggerated his CV. He had claimed to have been to Cambridge, the clear assumption being Cambridge University, when in fact he had at some stage attended a tutorial college in the city to do a crammer course for company secretarial exams. He also claimed that he had played cricket for Yorkshire, when what he really meant that he had played for Halifax District Schoolboys Under-15s and got a school's county trial at that age group. Nevertheless, he was a blunt, competent Yorkshire man, uncompromising and a bit of bully. And while he used to make much of the buck stopping with him, he made damned sure it never did. He would personally ensure the blame was targeted elsewhere, usually with one of his underlings.

If both men shared an ethic for hard work, were intelligent and knew their business, that was where the comparison ended. David was sensitive and empathic and led his workforce by example. He was a worrier, polite, always a diplomat and apologetic to his staff, and his management style meant that he got his way by reason, explanation and, if need be, negotiation on a level playing field. He avoided blank, incoherent commands.

In this way he brought his team in on the sales strategy. It felt as though they all shared the ownership and management of the business. He could be petulant, mainly when he was tired, and would rather beat himself up when something went wrong than find someone to blame. Socially, he always capable of an easy, unassuming Scouse wit and manner. He tended not to stand there and tell jokes; rather his style was to listen to other people recounting stories and then interject with often very amusing observations. He never tried to steal the limelight. This, it can be said, gave him a winning way.

None of us are without fault and there had been rumours of an enduring dalliance with his loyal secretary, whose position in the company was defined in the telephone book by reference to David's name. If it was true Edwina never found out, or if she did, she chose to turn a blind eye. Most of all, though, perhaps as a legacy of his noble, long-departed brother Cecil, David believed in fair play and always that things should be above-board. Integrity was his key word.

When David would concede some disadvantage in a product he was supposed to be selling to a client, his colleagues might at the time interpret this as a weakness. He would then explain the present state of the market. He would self-refer the matter to the board and try and rectify any deficiency in the product. This would result in a short-term loss of positioning in the market, but in the long-term strategic view, David was worth his weight in gold, and his association with the company became a benchmark for trust and integrity. And with this David moved up the line.

He was a company man, a rare and now-extinct species. As he quietly progressed he was, to most people, invisible, not making a noise, avoiding mistakes and also not obviously seen to be the man out front doing anything outstanding. But then it would have been against his nature to shout his successes from the rooftop.

17

The Locked Room

I

As a senior manager the journey to the new building from his office on the top floor of the old building was one he rarely had to make, except for board meetings in the chairman's suite. Junior clerks and runners from the post room were usually on hand to deliver internal memos, and besides, the internal telephone system was excellent.

David made his way to the stairwell and then through the glass canopy that linked the two buildings and arrived in the back corridor of number 69. The space was darker in the corridors. While they were wide and the carpet pile still surprisingly supple, the low ceilings made the space claustrophobic. He proceeded to the front of the building. He could hear voices from different rooms, loud voices, laughing, shouting, singing and swearing as though others in the building were getting drunk. The conversations were dispersed, one group would fade as another bellicose unseen throng would reverberate through the building. There was banging and clattering and smashing, then a loud thumping noise as though some large heavy item was being thrown down the stairs. Somewhere the distant sound of reggae music could be heard and then, David shifted his ear, the sound became intermingled with rap artists, as though he was adjusting a radio moving through overlapping bandwidths.

David sensed that the atmosphere was different: it was noisy, agitated; the clandestine occupants appeared belligerent and indiscrete, alarmingly divergent from what had been established as a workable status quo ante. The present mayhem was obviously unsustainable and went against the empathic street communication and good vibrations that had made the incursion a stable venue for this alternative society.

But David's mindset was elsewhere, tormented with the inner turmoil so mercilessly fuelled by Stuart Baxendale. It was as if the discordant pandemonium that had broken out dovetailed with his own personal demons. He was helpless, he had not chosen his mental crisis and as for what was happening around him, he neither knew for why nor was in any way complicit or active in the events that were to play out.

II

As he proceeded to the main reception area he could see the staircase to the basement. It was not an area of the building he was familiar with as any stored files would be requisitioned and enlarged photocopies rendered from the microfiche.

David looked at the solid door. He pushed it hard, then wrenched the handle. It was closed solid. He recalled Baxendale's mention of the number 67691998, which was memorable and uncomplicated as the numbers of the insurance buildings plus the year he retired. He again wrenched at and then twisted the handle, which this time came right off in his hands revealing a recessed key code. He promptly tried the sequence of digits and the door sprung open. He entered the room. The door closed firmly behind him.

The space within was bathed in a subdued light, brighter than the corridor. The below ground-level windows were lined with angled reflectors to optimise natural light. The air was cool and still and fusty. It was a large room with, amidst cobwebs, row upon row of desks piled high with dusty metal storage files that were linked by wires to a personal monitor and keyboard. In the scheme of computer technology, this was primitive kit, bulky units needed for data storage. One of the walls was lined with a large cinema screen. He leant his arm on the desk and in so doing was taken aback to discover the computer console had thereby been switched on. David had the weird sense that the assembled antiquated technical kit in the room was operating in an involuntary manner; was this a prototype Alexa that needed no prompting?

Barely had that idea emerged as a conscious thought when David was gripped by complete disassociation from his three-dimensional reality. He no longer felt the solidity of the chair he was sitting on or the desk he was leaning on; no longer was he aware of the room. He could not feel the floor beneath him; he could not be sure of whether or not he was upside down. Gravity itself had apparently abandoned him.

He was driving his car. Then it was not a car, but a soap-box cart. He was rushing with his mates to grab a load of conkers from Sefton Park. Then the room went dark as a rumbling sound grew louder and louder. Beams of light darted around as though surveying the sky as deafening explosions ripped through David's eardrums one after the other in rapid succession. The room became lit with a raging inferno. A football rolled out of the screen, hurtling towards him. It was spraying blood everywhere in its wake. It was not a ball. It was the head of a young girl, her silky hair matted and wrapped in the ghastly gore. David fell to the floor and Cecil walked over to him and picked him up, put him back into his soap-box cart. He felt a warm, ancient embrace which suddenly faded.

There was a screeching noise, and across the walls on all sides and then emerging as a three-dimensional fearsome image searing across the full space of the room there was a dogfight. A German Messerschmitt 109 came closer and closer. It was moving so fast yet David could see it so clearly, as though observing it in slow motion. Then a Spitfire came into view. The aircraft hovered in the middle of the room. Eamon was in the cockpit. David felt he too was in the cockpit. There was rapid fire from the cannons of the Spitfire. David watched as the tracer arrived at the German cockpit. The pilot could be seen inside. His eyes enlarged across the room with a look gripped in terror. His head then exploded and the cockpit became a cloud of blood and brain that splattered across the disintegrating canopy. David felt Eamon's elation and then his heart sank and he experienced unfathomable misery.

David watched the Spitfire flying through the air as it returned to base. Eamon was safe; he was going to land. He was flying back towards the cliffs of Dingli Bay, but the walls of the room were the cliff face. The aircraft was not going to make it. It collided with the cliffs and smashed into an exploding crumbled wreck to the rocks below, where it was then swept and overcome by the rough sea that swallowed it up.

David tried in vain to see if Eamon was floating amidst the wreckage. But then he found himself surveying a wild, wide-open ocean. There was a tempestuous squall immersing the whole space. It was reminiscent of JMW Turner's masterpiece *The Slave Ship*. The deep ocean was swollen and wild. Then he was on the deck of the *Zong*. The master was shouting at his crew to get a move on. The sailors all had whips and were bringing emaciated African slaves up from the hold. The stench from below deck was overpowering. The ship was packed with four hundred and seventy slaves. Supposedly, it had capacity for half that number. They were parched and had not had a drink for several days. Some were awake and screeching and wriggling, conscious of the fate that was about to befall them. They saw their husbands, wives, brothers and sisters and cousins systematically and mercilessly being tossed overboard. Some clung desperately to the side of the ship or anything they could grip, including the arms of the sailors manhandling them.

They were beaten, battered and bruised. He saw other bodies, over a hundred listless broken, emaciated rotting corpses floating in the choppy water.

Now David was back in his car. He was following someone, he did not know who, then he was searching; he was looking for someone. It became obvious to him that he was driving looking for Edwina. Edwina's face appeared on the walls of the room, zooming in on the arresting beauty of her eyes and then zooming out to the outline of her face. She was standing peering out from behind a curtain. David recognised the curtain. He was gripped with a paralysing stupefaction. Edwina stepped out from behind the curtain. She was coyly smiling, pursing her ruby-red lips. The smile and the gaze were so inviting. There was an intimacy, a reassuring cosiness, but as he kept driving, the road kept curving and his foot was stuck on the accelerator pedal.

Images of a man he did not know kept appearing. He was laughing, lustful and supercilious in a tuxedo. And then images of Baxendale and Filch Du Preez appeared. They were laughing too and were in tuxedos. They were in the luxuriant lobby of the Savoy Hotel. It is the insurance company's senior managers' ball.

Edwina appeared from behind a large blue velvet curtain. Her image was everywhere around him, multiplying with a holographic dimensionality. She emerged poised and curvaceous, confident and enjoying the moment, as though a burlesque performer in control of the voluptuous allure she exuded in a choreographed, controlled way. There was no exclusivity in this performance. David was not alone. This was not a private foreplay prescribed by him in the intimacy of their relationship in the seclusion of their home. This was Edwina teasing, emerging from behind a curtain in a lobby full of men at the Savoy. This ogling, lustful cohort were drooling, drinking, laughing and passing lewd comments. They were David's colleagues from work and others he had never met before. As she ceremoniously, in a teasing crescendo, presented all her charms to the assembly he was mortified even beyond the misery of what he imagined was the dark cloud of a psychotic episode that had cruelly swept him in.

He ran out of the hotel. It was daylight. The street was heaving with shoppers and sightseers. Amidst the heaving sidewalks lions and tigers were nonchalantly walking down a street crowded with shoppers. Surely, these wild beasts had escaped from the zoo. Volunteers tried to manhandle a bear onto an empty bus as the last of the passengers alighted. David decided to remove himself and, with a couple of ladies with their children, walked down into an underground station and then re-emerged. They walked past a private residence and three large muscular black dogs came rushing out. David was fearful and yet the dogs did not appear to be aggressive.

They walked on and found a coffee shop. The others sat down and ordered coffee and cakes. David was annoyed that it was assumed that the treat was on him. He was further irked when a well-dressed city gent came over and ingratiated himself to the ladies. He embarked on some cheery light-hearted conversation and then returned to his table together with the nice freshly baked muffin that David had purchased for himself. David walked over to the table to challenge the man, who was supercilious and condescending and vehemently denied that the muffin he was eating was the one purchased by David. It was the man in the tuxedo at the insurers' ball.

He was driving again. He had to detour to avoid a parade of exotic elephants dressed in embroidered rugs, upon which were seated their bare-footed mahouts. He was surrounded by Hells

seated their bare-footed mahouts. He was surrounded by Hells Angels revving their motorbikes and gesticulating in through his window. He looked through his windscreen; the visibility was misty. Suddenly, he saw a biker doing a ton driving down the middle of the road. Under the helmet the face could be seen. The face and body were split precisely down the middle. It was androgynous, one side fleshy with a benign, cheerful disposition and glistening teeth; the other side cadaverous, with an intense, glaring wicked eye and a grin comprised only of skull and gaping dentition. The bike collided with the car and then evaporated.

David felt the desk and his hands. They were damp and furry. He noticed encroaching fungi rapidly spreading from the top corners of the room. He felt his nose and mouth and wiped away a swathe of yellow green fungi. He saw that the floor was covered in large dead flies resting on their backs. Then the flies had human faces. He realised that they were not flies but humans and that some appeared not to be dead. They were moving and their eyes were staring at him. They had been infected by new strains of fungi. This was the Strongwellsea, ejecting their spores into the abdomen, denying their hosts the dignity of death but rather enabling the infected organism to live on in a zombie-like state, carrying out normal activities with apparent vitality, socialising while the fungus consumed their fat reserves, genitals and internal organs and finally muscle, all the while shooting out thousands of spores on to other individuals.

David remained detached from whatever shred of supposed meaning might be gleaned from this hideous kaleidoscopic spectacle. His face was no longer discernible. It couldn't be differentiated from the other apparitions; he was part of everything else; everything else was a body without organs; the locked room had become a convenient prop for a glib transient mocking. It was as though his neurons were programmed for sensory self-annihilation, orchestrated in some way by an externalised psychosis. David was helpless, socially and materially alienated; he did not know whether these fleeting, surging desires and fears he felt were his own or whether he was just a meek, pointless agency of this nomadology.

David buried his head in his hands and pressed his face into the desk. There issued forth a desperate, fearful, primal scream, as the old man wailed in torment, but no tear was shed.

18

Revolution

Exhausted by the sensory overload, his mind spinning in stupefied confusion, overwhelmed by the hallucinogenic roller-coaster, David walked out of the room and back up the stairs to the reception area. He looked at his watch, only to be further confused that the time remained precisely ten minutes to two.

He stood in the corner of the shaded hallway, his slim, hunched frame supported by his walking stick at first inconspicuous, a presence no more discernible than a run of darkened, damp paintwork on the stairwell. He could again hear the racket elsewhere in the building. Distant voices were shouting, a dog's bark, angry responses, tirades of foul language interspersed with screeching, banging and clattering reverberating around the building.

Almost falling into the lobby, police officers in high-visibility jackets over riot gear, some wearing protective headgear, manhandled a young, bedraggled man onto the floor. Fast on their heels a group of officers arrived in the process of arresting and overpowering another of the motley crew. He was a white man but with dreadlocks and he spoke with a pseudo-West Indian patois. There was a strong waft of cannabis as he rolled around on the floor trying to wriggle free of the police as they gripped his wrists to put the cuffs in place. One officer lost his balance and fell over the group of officers in front, who were still wrestling with the first man.

David shifted slightly in his shaded corner and a ray of light managed to reach his wily frame and flicker across his brow. A police dog barked in his direction and a police officer turned and called out to David, telling him to stand where he was, which was all he could do anyway.

'What are you doing here? You have no right to be on these premises.'

David felt intimidated by the officer clad in riot gear. ' Just killing time officer. I have no wish to cause offence.'

The officer got out his notebook and asked for details: 'Name and address. I am arresting you on suspicion of using force to gain entry, criminal damage, violent disorder and affray.' The officer then told him with lightning speed: ' You do not have to say anything but if you fail to mention when interviewed something you later rely on in court it may give rise to an adverse inference against you and anything you do say may be used in evidence.'

David obliged in giving his name and address but felt so befuddled he thought his mind was about to shut down all together.

The police officer then asked him, 'Who else is here that you know? Can you name anyone in the building?'

Despite his mind-numbing exhaustion, David did grasp that it was not for him to do the work of the police officer and nothing he had to say about anyone else in the building could impact on the allegations made against himself, which he knew were, in any event, false. And yet he responded to the officer by telling him that he had actually been in the other building having a discussion, a reminiscence of sorts, with an old work colleague.

'You are telling me that there are people in the other building?'

David: 'Only one person as far as I know. I was conversing with Stuart Baxendale until I was here... as I said.'

The officer got on his radio to tell his sergeant that he was making his way to check out number 67.

'Roger, over and out, V for Victor, proceed with caution, let me know if you need back-up, over.'

'Affirmative, Sarg. Over.' The officer then turned to David. 'Right, old man, lead the way.'

With that David, aided by his walking stick, ambled slowly down the corridor to the glass canopy linking the two buildings and then slowly up the flight of stairs to the first floor. Through the expanse of broken glass David glimpsed with surprise and alarm the frenetic activity outside. There were riot police strategically perched behind rows of police cars with livid blue lights furiously flashing, a media circus with white vans and satellite dishes were parked in a ramshackle way taking up any off-road space available. The main London Road out of Gloucester had been cordoned off. Journalists could be seen scurrying around, dividing their time between peering into the building with binoculars, poking microphones into the faces of locals, typing up notes on their laptops and bowing their heads into mobile telephones.

It had all the appearance of a stand-off between those who were inside and those who were on the outside. With laboured movement, David showed the officer into the office expanse. On the door an old sign remained which said 'Sales, Admin and Company Secretary'. On his left he pointed to a dark, derelict, abandoned space. He turned to the policeman. 'That's my office in there.'

The constable gave him a puzzled look and muttered into his radio, 'Is this a piss-take or a fruit cake, over?'

David walked across the large, desolate, open-plan office space and as he did so said to the officer, 'You'll forgive Baxendale's rather brusque manner – it's the way he's always been, typical Yorkshire. He's not an easy character. He may object to being disturbed. He tells me that he has a lot of work to finish off, hence the reason for him doing a lot of overtime.'

David arrived at the door, knocked and then opened it. It was dark inside with old blinds partially blocking the window. There was a broken desk, a smell of urine and moss growing up the damp wall, where rainwater had leaked in. As they both looked in, they could hear a squeal as two large rats scurried across the floor.

The police officer turned to David and sarcastically said, 'He must have nipped out to get some lunch.'

To this David replied: 'No, he always brings sandwiches.'

The constable grimaced with a frustrated expression. He was rapidly losing his patience. It was obvious that the room was abandoned: a filthy, damp, derelict corner of a rotten-smelling crumbling old office.

The constable got on his radio: 'Zulu, Zulu, come in, Zulu Puma Command Alpha 1, over.'

'Reading you, V for Victor.'

'Hi, Sarg, I think we have a fruit cake, over.'

'V for Victor, clarify information, over.'

'Zulu, Zulu Puma Command Alpha 1. No persons in 67. Old man either pulling my plonker or a fruit cake. Over. Suggest contact Tango Papa and arrange ambulance, over.'

'Thank you, V for Victor, over.'

'…Tango Papa, Tango Papa, come in, Tango Papa…' Then the constable turned to David and said: 'Do you see anyone in that room?'

David: 'Well, no, I accept there is no one there now, but there was at ten minutes to two. I had a long conversation with him. His desk was covered in paperwork. He had been checking through some investment files and had to make a couple of telephone calls.'

The officer looked at his watch and then looked carefully at David with a long, lingering, bemused glare. 'It's ten to two now?' The police officer levelled with David: 'It is obvious that this filthy room has not been occupied for years. Are you sure you wish to persist with your pointless, ridiculous story? Wasting police time is an offence, you know. As a matter of fact I am further arresting you for the offence of wasting police time.'

And then, in accordance with protocol, he again recited with the same rapidity the police caution.

With that the officer said, 'Right, sir, you are going to have to go back over to the main building and wait with the others for transit to the police station for processing, follow me.'

David, walking as promptly as his stiff old legs would allow, followed the constable back down the stairs, through the doors, along the corridor and up the main stairs, leading into a large open-plan area in the centre of the second floor of the 69 London Road.

As had been so clearly demonstrated, activity in the building was by no means a mere delusion. At some critical point this alternative, yet bizarrely functioning otherworldly motley assemblage had become visible to the outside world. What was largely delusional was the narrative conjured by the media to big up the story.

The radio bulletins and newspapers waxed lyrically at how the disaffected cabal coveted the rotting office space as a pure and beautiful mirage of freedom, in which they were the agents of nature reclaiming this mythical capitalist temple for the good of cosmic harmony. It was they who had become the legitimate authority by their occupation. At the same time many good citizens of Gloucester saw the occupation as an unholy spectacle, an abomination, ugly, discordant, disgraceful, antisocial, veritable threat to law and order.

The subject had attracted headlines in *This Is Gloucestershire* online and spawned a plethora of commentary in the readers blog section. By no means everyone was hostile, with socially minded contributors expressing concern about homelessness and the immorality of empty buildings, particularly in the winter months. But there were others, the mainstream, the comfortable majority who expressed great hostility in decrying these worthless drunkards, who are a blight on the landscape, lowering house prices by their presence and making no contribution. One blogger calling himself 'the captain' stated that he valued his old horses more and yet they were sent to the knackers' yard. He then propositioned that really such a tarnished and useless cargo of flotsam and jetsam, as were the miscreants laying siege to the Trident building, making no contribution to society, should be thrown overboard to ensure safe passage for the rest of us.

The revelation that beyond the seasonal sprawl of sleeping bags and tents, these grand office blocks were infested with drifters, tramps, people of mental instability, who did not work, who did not contribute but begged and took drugs and got drunk, spawned a feeling of outrage for many in the neighbourhood. How could these people breach the fortifications, evade property agents and security firms, take over a building, somehow wire up to electricity, sit and watch television and play video games? Yes, all that was said to be happening.

As the officer walked David into the central open-plan area of the second floor of 69, it was like walking into a war zone. He was immediately aware of confrontation, of more shouting and swearing, gesticulating and bare-knuckle unarmed combat. The officer, appreciating David's advanced years, shouted at another detainee to sit on the floor so that David had one of the few chairs in the corner to sit on. It was like being offered a ring-side seat, but in the midst of this volatile stand-off the retired insurance man sat there seemingly unnoticed.

At the other end of the room there was a barricade made of a dismantled office partition walling reconfigured as a ramshackle defence. At a rough guess there were a dozen people behind it, some of whom David recognised as street drinkers and dossers he regularly encountered on his walks into the city centre. Darren and Graham were centre stage surrounded by half a dozen followers still plastered in grotesque zombie makeup. There was an overpowering smell of cannabis wafting on a dense cloud across the wooden divide.

David: 'Well, where did they come from?'

Police officer (trying to maintain some ironic humour): 'Looks like we've been invaded by zombies?'

David: 'What… you mean people that come back from the dead? Ha, now I've heard everything; now't stranger than folk?'

The officer stared at him, bemused for a moment, before resuming his precarious duties of riot control.

The barricade seemed to offer protection on two fronts. One group was positioned along a section of window that faced out across the frontage of the building to the London Road, thereby providing a strategically prominent position overlooking a line of police in the road with their vehicles parked alongside. Where the windows had been smashed zombies with exaggerated 'Joker'-type mouths painted on their faces pointed paint guns through the open space and were taking pot shots at the police, who would dart behind body-length Perspex riot shields. Darren's salvaged paintball supplies had been brought to the second floor. His pals had taken up position in the chairman's suite of the new building. A police van was plastered in a mixture of lime green, pink and azure blue splats.

Darren then switched on a ghetto blaster playing 'How Does It Feel' by Bob Dylan.

On the outside the authorities were assembling a co-ordinated response. A police van with a radar scanner was parked near the fence. Police cars were parked on both adjoining streets. An ambulance arrived. A team of police discretely moved into place around the perimeter with access arranged through the fencing by the landlord's managing agents. The armed response unit was in place with orders not to fire until it could be determined whether or not there were firearms in the place rather than, as was believed, paintball guns.

As the spectacle unfolded Ingrid hobbled into view with her walking frame and shopping bag. It looked as though she had wandered inside a police cordon. She stopped and produced a seagull from her shopping bag which she started showing to an officer, who furiously gesticulated at her. This resulted in her carefully placing the bird back in her trolley bag. She then produced an information sheet on seagulls, probably similar to the one she had pinned to the security fence. She started distributing her leaflet. Police were taking the literature and briefly reading and then throwing it on the ground.

'Babies are born in April and May, and it takes six months before they are fully fledged.

'Gulls have a red spot on the underside of their beaks. Hungry chicks tap the parent's spot to encourage it to regurgitate their food.

'Gulls could live to thirty years, but most live no more than ten years because of accidents, etc.

'Plastic and Styrofoam pose big dangers to omnivorous gulls.

'There are forty-five species of gulls worldwide.

'The herring gull has grey wings and pink legs—'

A vexed and frustrated police officer eventually interrupted, 'Move along, miss, or I shall have to arrest you for an obstruction of an officer in the execution of his duty and/or section 5 Public Order.'

It might be wondered if this was an orchestrated distraction tactic, but no, just Ingrid doing her thing. And if there was any doubt she too took a pot-shot paint-gun splat to the side of her face, something perversely sympathetic to her masochistic tendencies and which she found most satisfying.

These disparate souls, blighted as they were by mental illness, addiction and social alienation, and for whom life was usually a grim, solitary endurance, found themselves united by a cause conjured for them by the media, but the only real commonality was knowing the way to get into the insurance building.

They would never grass each other up, each for differing reasons. Jarvis, for example, feared what some of the others might do to him if he dared to be indiscrete; although his lazy mode of articulation had the effect of keeping him safe. For Nigel, it was a simple matter of honest loyalty to his friends, to the people he knew and talked to on a daily basis. It never occurred to him that on some level trespassing was wrong, and in any event, as is well known in circles of alternative living, it does not amount to a criminal offence. And beyond that Nigel simply lacked the worldly guile to suspect for one minute that others might exploit the adventure for anarchistic motives.

As for Ingrid, the excitement of partaking in something clandestine and antisocial, something that might create conflict with the powers of law and order, primed her base instincts for masochism and anarchy. Here was a chance for her to play with fire, to press the self-destruct button.

There were others who had a hidden agenda as street-fighting men, some with aspirations to be political revolutionaries.

Perhaps at a more fundamental level there was a common agenda of sorts, as outcasts from mainstream society, people used to living off handouts and scrag ends, even those who had known better times. They all subscribed to or were the authors of the graffiti daubed on the perimeter fencing, which if read holistically amounted to a manifesto of disaffection and a plea for an alternative world order.

As events developed the more hardcore elements asserted themselves, provided the momentum, took control. So even though it was Nigel who first discovered the means of hidden entry and Jarvis and Ingrid were the first people he told, they increasingly became peripheral to the saga; actually, they remained peripheral to the building. None of them could be described as regular visitors and none of them became privy to the more ornate and outrageous machinations that evolved. In Ingrid's case, it was not through any lack of will or enthusiasm, but simply her increasing infirmity made physical participation difficult.

A message came through on the radio from the chief constable to the senior officer inside the building.

Chief constable: '...It's got political... Shelter, Greenpeace, Rewilding Britain, The Prince's Trust, The Tree Council... questions are being asked in Parliament, the local MP is sitting on the fence... the Bishop of Gloucester is praying for a peaceful outcome. They want us to provide a safe corridor for the Quakers to take in flasks of tea and jam doughnuts. We need the situation diffused without injury. Do you read me, Blue Command, over?'

Inspector: 'Reading you, sir. Confirming armed response unit to be stood down and the two police dogs inside building will not attack unless otherwise notified. If the situation worsens officers with headgear to be deployed to use pepper spray before releasing dogs.' He further stated that the paint guns were all second-hand stock that had not been reconditioned and were not likely to cause anything other than superficial injury from the impact of splattering paint everywhere.

Chief constable: 'No dogs or pepper spray unless express orders from me, over.'

Inspector: 'Understood, sir. But we don't need to tell these bastards that we've been stood down, do we?'

Chief constable: 'Not at this stage. I am going to tanoy the occupants now, over.'

Chief constable on public address: 'This is the chief constable speaking. We are arranging for drinks and refreshments to be brought into the building. We have no wish to harm any of you. We ask you to peacefully vacate the building and we will provide safe passage to the minibuses waiting outside for you. You will then all be offered warm, dry accommodation and a meal, but you must agree to peacefully and voluntarily vacate the premises.'

Darren replied by letting rip a salvo of multi-coloured paint pellets from the front open window, and as he did he shouted: 'This is the storming of the fucking Bastille, ain't it, mate? This is the fucking dog's bollocks – liberty, fraternity, égalité. Kiss my fucking arse.'

Graham: 'OK, don't get carried away, mate.'

A couple of ghoulishly painted zombies stopped for a sandwich and flask of coffee and felt prompted to contemplate the wider philosophical meaning of their predicament, to look for the underlying structures.

Zombie 1: 'It all went tits up when we stopped worshipping the sun, didn't it?'

Grinner: 'What you mean, like sunbathing?'

Zombie 1: 'Nah, don't be a daft. I mean, worshipping the fucking sun, as in like God, like the ancient savages did – they were right about that. That's why it all went tits up.'

Zombie 2: 'Well, what's tits up?'

Zombie 1: 'Tits up is fucking greenhouse gases and all that, ain't it? I mean, if you worship the fucking sun you don't mess around with nature, do you? I mean, all your ancestors is in the trees and the wind and stuff and you don't need no faith 'cos it's fucking well there in the sky, ain't it, that big fucking orange thing?'

Madelaine took a long draw on a reefer and then joined the conversation: 'Yes, well, he's right, you know. If we respected the land and didn't keep destroying the Amazon rainforest and spewing millions of tons of carbon dioxide into the atmosphere we could all slumber more soundly in our sleeping bags.'

Grinner: 'What, even when it's raining? I've never found a shop doorway that stops the rain and cold getting to me.'

Zombie 1: 'I told you, didn't I?'

Madelaine: 'I guess if we still worshipped the sun we might have a better chance of preserving the planet for our children.'

Zombie 1: 'I don't want children. Nah, they cost too much money. I have enough to worry about with getting my own shit together, man.'

Zombie 2, laughing out loud: 'Hey, I just got a copper in the bollocks, green paint all over his crotch, ha, ha, ha.'

Grinner started to feel unwell. Efforts at self-medicating on weed did not help him. There was nowhere for him to go. If he broke the line he would be a black leg, and apart from that he feared being devoured by one of the nasty-looking police dogs that looked like they were chomping at the bit. His breathing had become laboured; he had a hacking cough and a high temperature. Even so his doss in the insurance building was better than on the street. There was something comforting about his rancid sleeping bag. He asked to speak to Graham, who seemed less preoccupied than Darren with 'taking war to the pigs'.

Graham: 'What's up, mate?'

Grinner: 'I ain't right.'

Graham: 'Yeah we know, what's wrong with you?'

Grinner: 'I think I'm fucked. I can't breathe properly, never felt so shit in all my life.'

Graham suddenly twigged: 'Christ, you haven't got that fucking Covid-19 virus, have you?'

Grinner: 'All I know is I can't breathe properly and I feel like shit.'

Graham, realising they might have a serious casualty on their hands, called Darren over.

Darren (talking quietly so that Grinner could not hear what was being said): 'If we tell the pigs we need an ambulance to get one of our people to hospital that will be interpreted as relying on the establishment. I mean, that is like fucking surrender, mate, no way, mate. We didn't come all this way just to throw in the towel. I'm afraid old matey is going to have to grin and bear it.'

Grinner's lips started to turn blue and he was sweating, but suddenly he was talking furiously and sitting up.

Grinner: 'Oi, mate, matey, you bastards, listen. If this doesn't go well for me I want "I Did It My Way" played at my funeral.'

Darren and Graham looked at each other and said: 'Why? Done what your way?'

Grinner: 'Fucking Frank Sinatra, innit, "I Did It My Way", that's it. If it's my time, like.'

Graham: 'Bit fucking silly? Wanting classical music like that. I did it my way, fucking hell. Haven't you got people of your own to discuss all that stuff with?'

Grinner: 'Nah, don't know where they are. Haven't seen any kin for decades. Besides, I can't speak to them here, can I?'

Darren and Graham had to get back to the stand-off at the barricade. Apart from those who had been arrested earlier by the police, there was now a shouting match, but neither side was risking an all-out confrontation.

Ten minutes later Grinner groaned his final breath. No one noticed. He lay stiff in his sack until the siege was ended.

In the ensuing days the willpower of a number of the followers started to erode and their numbers dwindled. Apart from Madelaine, these were not crusaders committed to a great environmental cause. But that did not really matter. This was about perception, the interpretation of a set of facts that provided the ideal narrative to promote a just cause. How else can myth be validated?

At first one or two would slink off during a morning and then a couple more in the afternoon, and the others would watch and see what happened and realise that rather than the dogs being set on them or being wrestled to the ground and handcuffed, they were given blankets and cups of tea and then helped into an ambulance or minibus, as appropriate.

Graham and Darren would never be convinced that the authorities were doing anything other than trying to trick them. They had a few solid followers, a blinkered cohort of zombies, who did not budge. They probably totalled half a dozen and all were either on bail or on licence from prison. One was an absconder from the nearby Leyhill Open Prison.

The police played a waiting game but eventually re-entered the premises late at night, using bright lamps that they shone directly at the group huddled by the stack of old tables. As they were momentarily startled and blinded by the halogen beams the police grabbed them and attempted to lace the stragglers in handcuffs. Pepper spray was released, but it was not clear from where it emanated. While this was largely successful, the prison absconder ran to a rear window and climbed out onto a roof and hurtled down a drainpipe and made a dash for a neighbouring wheelie bin, which he climbed into with the hope of sitting out the commotion. His scent was soon picked up by the two police dogs, who dived at the bin causing it to topple over. They then proceeded to take some gruesome chunks out of the hapless fugitive's legs.

Graham and Darren took pre-emptive action as the police stormed in. Both let rip with state-of-the-art paintball cannons turning the SWAT team pink and lime green, the impact putting the two lead officers on the deck. The response was a barrage of taser fire zipping rapid barbs of fifty thousand volts incapacitating their central nervous systems, leaving the hard men writhing in agony on the floor as their muscles involuntarily contracted.

They were arrested and, along with a few other individuals, charged. Some were hospitalised. The absconder was quite badly injured. The police, wishing to avoid any risk of accusations of brutality associated with the siege, issued a press statement emphasising that the arrest was from a wheelie bin in an adjoining street. The absconder and some of those out on licence were returned to prison. Various public order charges were preferred. Both Darren and Graham faced a Crown Court indictment including actual bodily harm, assaulting police and aggravated burglary. Those who were already in breach of bail found themselves held for court.

Madelaine came out of it all smelling of roses. She wrote a most articulate article in *The Guardian* and was only too willing to perpetuate the myth that the siege cohort were motivated by environmental altruism.

Meanwhile, alarmingly, other people at David's residential home started to succumb to Covid-19. They would complain they had colds but then this turned into a wretched dry cough that seemed to persist day and night and was exhausting. There then followed a nauseating fever confining residents to bed. Their breathing became laboured. Even when they felt like eating a sudden loss of their sense of taste in the palate caused a loss of appetite.

It was at this time both Jarvis and Nigel started feeling unwell, which was not particularly significant because both had for many years been signed off from work for medical reasons. As smokers they often had sore throats and coughed up gunge. This time, however, they were disturbing the other residents during the night with loud, persistent, hacking coughs. Nigel came down for breakfast but was no better and, while not visible, Jarvis could be heard in his room. Nigel said that he was going to see his doctor. He then sat down at the table and just blankly stared ahead. He looked distressed. He was struggling. His breathing was difficult. He was gasping and saying, 'I can't breathe, I can't breathe.'

An ambulance was called, and both Jarvis and Nigel were taken to hospital. As events turned out David did not find out what had happened to his fellow residents.

II

In the end the charges against David never went to court. They were never proceeded with at all. The Crown Prosecution Service advised that even though the charging threshold had been met, there was insufficient evidence to provide a reasonable prospect of conviction. Strangely, there was no one who could say he was present and engaging in any criminal activities at the relevant time when specific offences occurred. Even the officers in the case found later that they were somewhat unclear about their dealings with David, beyond searching for the illusive Stuart Baxendale, which in itself was not an offence, unless they could prove that he was deliberately wasting police time, rather than merely mistaken.

Then the arresting officer could not find the relevant page in his notebook and even the custody record when reviewed was blank, other than the name 'David Pangloss' written at the top and a time of 'ten to two', which all must have been a computer error, or possibly the printer had run out of ink.

To add to the police frustration, when the footage from their helmet-mounted video cameras was checked David could not be seen in any of the frames, but of course at the time the focus was centred on the 'zombie' revolution and stand-off occurring on the first floor of the number 69 and so it was perhaps understandable.

To save face the senior case worker added a footnote that the reason it was not in the public interest to proceed because it was accepted David was a vulnerable old man of advanced years who presented as being in a confused state at the time he had somehow found his way into the building. It was also decided that he was not part of the actions of the riotous assembly, even though this did not rule out conspiracy or joint enterprise.

19

Reconciliation and Final Days 2020/21

I

Abigail: 'Dad, Dad, please listen? Dad, listen, will you?

'The stand-off at Trident gives me a revived affection for you. You know I'm here for both you and Mum. I'm proud of you, you did the right thing. I followed every detail of that cause célèbre in the press and the livestream.

'A symbolic demonstration of the subjugated underclass taking a stand against the inequitable waste in modern computer-driven capitalism, where the anonymous proprietors of search engines know the price of everything and the value of nothing and are oblivious in driving environmental destruction and forcing humanity towards Armageddon.

'My God, strong stuff. The idea that the insurance building was already succumbing to wilding and that "the people" had joined forces with nature was particularly appealing, such an irresistible argument.

'And you were ill, Dad. You were. I know a medic checked you over and delivered you to the accident and emergency department, and you were admitted to that geriatric ward for assessment. Is it possible you now have the onset of dementia, just like Mum? I know you put on a good act, Dad, but age is getting to you, you cannot deny it. Hah, do you know what they said? They said the patient appeared sometimes to be "with us" and then the rest of the time "absent". It appeared you liked to do your own thing. They concluded that your mobility was good for your years, provided you had a walking stick. You know they based that on unaided absences from your bed and the fact that no nurse ever had to help you use the toilet.

'Then they asked me if you wanted a mobility car and I said no. I declined. Why would you want one? If you don't use it you lose it, that's what they say, isn't it? So let's keep you getting around on your old pins, shall we? Anyway, the consultant told me that from clinical examination and MRI scans he was satisfied there was no generic dementia and that your mind was alert. Well, that is a matter of opinion, I thought. Then they discharged you and the paperwork specified delivery back to the residential home. Well, no, I thought. That is not going to happen. If you only knew how worried I was about you when I heard the news of that dreaded virus. Let's face it, what would your chances have been, what with being stuck in that hygienically challenged cohort at that residential home? My God, I dread to think.

'Oh yes, I knew you were there. It was just I needed time, a lot of time to get over the way it all happened, particularly with Mum. I hope you understand.

'What would have happened to you if you had caught that wretched virus? You'd have been a goner; vanished, just an idea in the memory of those who knew you, just another fading historical link in the Pangloss family tree. Can you imagine? Well, I couldn't have that, could I?

'No way would you survive the invasive trauma of a ventilator in an intensive care unit, with all those tubes and drugs, and given your age the authorities may not even have prioritised you, what with the pressure the staff were under. "DNR: do not resuscitate". That's what they would have written on your clipper board and then you would have been left in a corridor or languishing on a bed or trolley in an overcrowded ward where your viral load would have been boosted hour by hour.

'That's why I knew you had to stay with me. I needed you by my side, you and Mum. That was how to survive. At least if you were at the cottage in your own bedroom, you could be cared for.

'Mum always told me you were never much of a tough guy, you were always one of those risk-averse insurance types – never wanted to stress yourself too much, did you, Dad? Never wanted to test the limits of endurance, did you? Much rather operate from within a comfort zone, know the rules, play the game, doing your integrity thing within the conventions of the insurance industry, move up the line. Well, that's fine with me – well, no, it wasn't, really. I don't like it; well, I tolerate it because you're my dad. I forgive you. Anyway, I know what reconciliation means to you, because it means the same to me. You can take all the medication, blood transfusions, organ transplants, you name it, but nothing heals more than love and reconciliation.'

Abigail became restless and agitated, and her mood changed.

'Now stop… don't, don't embarrass me. Come on, it's just a convenient mind game you play. I can't stand it. You just play the same old game, the one you used to make money. Easy money. And you worked all those hours and told us how hard you toiled at the office. You and your bloody office types, peddling self-delusion to optimise profits. It was what you called the art of marketing?

'Sad thing is you bloody well believed it – convinced yourselves, didn't you?

'Oh, I am supposed to feel grateful for my education and for you buying my cottage. I know what you are thinking, yes: *It's OK for you with a silver spoon in your mouth, ladies' college and all, yes, young madam on your high horse, but can I just remind you of a couple of things, which you seem to have forgotten?*'

'That's always been your argument hasn't it? To remind me of how grateful I should be to you, that you did it all for me. Well, thank you, but shit happens. Do you realise what Paris was really like? No, I don't suppose you do.

'Oh, fuck, don't embarrass me, let it go. I am trying to help you. I have been very hurt by you and I am making a real effort to heal things, so please do not belittle me.

'I am so proud of the work I have done on the environment and anyway, of course I regard it as important. The trauma of surviving may have distorted my sense of self...'

II

Airflow, subdued sounds of clicks and blips and pulses, equipment sliding and shifting, subtle scents of perspiration and deodorant, multitudes of flickering eyes through reflective visors, amidst this intensity, concentration, professionalism, humanity and compassion abound, dispensed as though an interruption in the busy, smooth-flowing procedures, consultations, checks, calibrations, and documenting. Compassion, humanity, heartfelt personal touch, empathy not specified in the management audit, not part of the budget, a negative time input in administration cost-benefit analysis; how could pausing to convey messages of love to the fading, flat-lining patient ever be in the national income accounting? How could it ever be a recognised category in the gross national product? Yet it is the part of the job that the medics exude in spades. It emanates from vocation, the desire to do good, old-fashioned altruism, higher sentiments of human endeavour.

There is a silent desperation wrapped in the clinically tested, sanitised protective layers. It pervades the heaving efficiency of the intensive therapy unit. PPE, CPAP, ITU, CPR, DNR, abbreviations etched on the sterilised backdrop, flicker on screens, jotted on boards and roll off lips to punctuate the necessity of urgent truncated communication. Prone and face down, weirdly configured intubated patients hang on to life in rows of ventilators.

Consultant: 'She's out of the induced coma and intubation withdrawn. When did she come off CPAP? The patient is still so restless.'

Nurse: 'She has been agitated and chattering away for a few days now. She seems fine with it most of the time and then occasionally becomes anxious. Whatever else there must be a lot going on in there. And at least she now has the oxygen in her lungs to keep mumbling away. She keeps mentioning her mum and dad, particularly her Dad. She mutters "reconciliation" a lot and then becomes angry about her father.'

Consultant: 'The consultant neuropsychologist has been monitoring the dialogue closely. Has her partner been in touch?'

Nurse: 'Well, yes, on numerous occasions. We hold the mobile telephone near to Abigail's face and let her listen and see if her eyes focus sufficiently.'

Consultant: 'Good. She may still be semi-conscious in a dream state from which she is articulating. I think we need to try and stir her more and progress the rehabilitation. I want the occupational therapists to put a programme together.'

Abigail: 'Is Mum safe? She has her own garden. The trout won't be harmed by my watercress. I've forgiven Dad, I've been following him closely, so pleased he is with us, can't let him get ill after standing strong with our friends at that derelict insurance building.'

Sappho: 'Rest, darling. You've been away for a long time. I thought I might lose you.

Doctor: 'You need to understand that we have been monitoring the activity in her brain closely. It is evident that she has experienced a fluid alternative reality. This is likely to be deeply disconcerting for her, like existing in a parallel universe. To a certain extent these dream-like streams of thought are to be expected, although Abigail's case does appear extreme. Don't be too perturbed.'

If it helps, the neuropsychologist divided the various florid phases of her dream existence based on an interpretation of the recordings in the following way. Please note the headings are purely arbitrary:

Tragic infirmity, misery, mercy and the wheels of justice.

Assisted living and the old insurance building.

Machinations.

A blast from the past.

The locked room.

Revolution.

It was so impersonal to get no closer than a transparent screen around the bed and talk through an intercom. Sappho dug deep to be strong as welling up emotions tore at her as she negotiated these synthetic boundaries. It was only the realisation that these measures protected the fragile threads upon which Abigail's life hung. Even if the vocal excitement was palpable, Sappho later recalled feeling like an observer to this precious event as she remembered the visuals appearing as a confused moving collage. Through the screens and protective gear, through the contortions of the hospital bed with its high-tech monitors, tubes, dials and oxygen supply, the broad outline of Abigail could be seen. While her eyes were open and she was talking, her mind was somewhere else entirely. But over the ensuing days and weeks she progressed.

Nurse: 'She's all yours. She's sitting in the day room, ready for collection. Been a long old haul, hasn't it? It will take a little time, but you have her back. The OT will be in touch about follow-up sessions.'

Sappho (talking to Abigail) 'Hello, darling, I'm here to bring you home? Thank you so much Nurse, and all the staff who have cared for her these last couple of months.'

Nurse: 'Her things are in the holdall you provided. Did you get the letter from her locker?'

Sappho: 'No. Letter? What letter?'

Nurse: 'It was in an envelope that was addressed "To My Darling". At the bottom someone had written in bold ink letters "Pangloss". We thought it odd because, like most people, you had always communicated by mobile telephone. I made an enquiry. It arrived late one night about a month ago. The hospital receptionist had briefly gone to make a cup of tea and the envelope was on her desk when she returned. We put it in Abigail's locker, as obviously she was in no fit state to read it. In any event such material could not be brought into the ITU area. One of the ambulance drivers saw an old bright red vintage vehicle with a convertible top pulling away from the arrivals point. He recalled wondering what a private vehicle was doing there in the first place.'

Sappho: 'Well, how strange. Well, it is definitely not from me.'

Nurse: 'Oh.'

III

The months passed and slowly Abigail regained her health and vitality. It was summer. She was sitting with Sappho amidst the blossom of the early summer garden.

Abigail: 'While convalescing I have had a lot of time to think about my life, and while I feel very lucky in so many ways and proud of the little differences I might have made to the environment, I still can't help feeling a great void, a terrible anti-climax. It's quite depressing, really.'

Sappho: 'Oh, come on, Abigail, dear, you have absolutely no reason to feel like that.'

Abigail: 'But it's true – you know, I thought I was destined to save the planet from environmental destruction, that I – yes, little me – was somehow singled out to perform some momentous deed that I know now will never happen.'

Sappho: 'If I didn't know you better I would describe that as an narcissistic blip, an episode because of stress, but you are the last person in the world anyone could accuse of being vain and egotistical; headstrong, yes, but narcissistic, definitely not.

'Look, changing the subject, if you don't mind. You do remember our prolonged application to adopt? Well, it has been a few months since you came home. I mean, depending on how you feel, we can progress to the next stage.'

Abigail: 'I am trying to get my head round this. It is a wonderful prospect, my feelings have not changed. I am getting stronger by the day. It is going to take energy and commitment, you know. Now it is more than just an idea. We have to really want to do it in our hearts... And I think we both do. I know you've decided how you feel about it and yes, I'm ready to give it a go. I mean, they obviously thought I was fit enough at the interview last month.'

Sappho: 'Well, that's wonderful. The final forms have been awaiting signature for a couple of weeks now. The agency did telephone to ask how we were getting on. They said that they were trying to place two siblings from Afghanistan: orphan asylum seekers, boys aged seven and ten; parents killed in a bombing in Kabul.'

Abigail: 'Oh, what are their names?'

Sappho: 'Siyar and Dawood.'

And so it was, a further interview and home visit later, Abigail found themselves collecting two young Afghan brothers from the social services-sponsored adoption agency. Even though the two boys had only been in the UK for a year, they had both learned some basic English. Both Abigail and Sappho were stirred with delight at the challenge of teaching them English and the ways of what for the children would be a strange and alien new culture.

It is not part of this story to examine in detail the progress of these two charming young boys from the other side of the world, other than to say, despite their loss and suffering, their gratitude and sense of fun and joy for life lit up the world for Abigail and Sappho.

It is also worth mentioning that Abigail and Sappho combined their own surnames to form De Souza-Gloss, and in so doing felt sure that no mythical shadow would ever follow. And when the boys built a soap-box cart to collect conkers from the village horse chestnut trees, this was with an untainted and justifiable sense of freedom. There were no local factions, fights or intrigue. And furthermore, as has been shown, Abigail's well-grounded scientific mind never believed in poetic narratives anyway. History was never designed to repeat itself; to suggest such would be to claim a prescription for the future, predestination, which of course was ridiculous dare it be said even Panglossian.

As she sat on the wicker garden seat, Abigail sensed a calm presence smiling at the splendour of the well-maintained flower borders to the carpet-like lawn, as the boys ran and played. It was a fine garden, stretching down over two hundred feet to the little brook. It was slightly wider than her red-brick cottage, so while not narrow appeared like an elongated rectangle. On the rear wall there was honeysuckle. It had two apple trees, and near the brook a fine horse chestnut tree grew.

Abigail: 'You know, Sappho, this is it.'

Abigail exhorted with exuberance and urgency indicative of someone articulating a eureka moment, some dawning epiphany, the excitement of an existential catharsis.

'This is the purpose. There was never an anti-climax; this is what my life is meant to be about. I, we, have been working towards this all these years. This is our fulfilment. What greater purpose could there be? What greater challenge? What greater tribute to my mother and father?'

Abigail kept a collection of David's walking sticks by the front door. His birth date had been eighty-eight years earlier. His spirit lived on.

And despite her aversion to myth, tradition, religion or any other kind of declaratory truth springing from the mists of time, Abigail decided upon a service to celebrate her father's life, as she had done for her mother some years earlier.

It was held in a quaint Catholic chapel near to the cottage. Abigail, Sappho and the two boys were present. A small group from the parish turned up to sing. The priest arrived on the altar with his acolyte and greeted the small congregation, explaining that David had been baptised into the Roman church, and while his faith had flagged over the years, nevertheless, with prayer there is always hope and he was sure that it was God's will that David Pangloss should, as he would always have dearly wished, be reunited with his departed wife, Edwina. And so on that day together their lives were celebrated and remembered with a blessing.

Abigail read the mysterious letter that had materialised at the hospital reception:

Dearest love,

I write again in the hope that one of my missives might reach you, wherever you are. Believe me when I tell you that there is never a moment when you are not in my thoughts.

This world is not the best of all possible worlds, nor was ever designed to be. Human frailty is a guarantee of that. Imagine if we made the right choices all of the time so everything appeared perfect? Well, that is the problem. It is just an illusion. That the very endeavour is sure to end in failure and unhappiness is the tragicomedy of our existence.

And suppose we discovered perfection. How would we cope with it? It would be impossible. Our minds would be overwhelmed. It would give us so much to covet, so much more to lose, more to become anxious about. We would suffer all the more from jealousy and pride and feel falsely justified in venting anger at anyone who should challenge someone so blessed.

Dare I admit that my feelings for you were tainted by such neurotic ideas? It is me that is guilty. It was in my mind, not yours.

So it seems to live we must die; but that was always inscribed in nature. What would life be without the seasons? Imagine how mundane it would all be. What would the poets write about? And without poets where would love be?

Love, so often uttered with facile levity while embracing us all, often unseen and rejected, free for everyone, impossible to commodify, perfection that does not demand perfection, it blesses small gestures, little kindnesses, forgives mistakes, accepts frailty and lets us treasure what we salvage from the confusion and imperfection of the world. With such power we will find each other somewhere in this discordant, schizophrenic cosmos.

Eternally, your adoring husband

There was a request for no flowers just donations for the homeless and for Extinction Rebellion. No tears were shed.

20

Return to Nature:
The Walk Ends

I

Abigail eventually reached an opening in the woodland. There was a sweeping view across an expanse of English countryside, first Herefordshire, then Gloucestershire and beyond in the west through the restful haze was the distant shrouded outline of the Welsh Black Mountains.

She ran her fingers in the grooves of the carved wording: 'In loving memory of David Pangloss (1933–2007) and his adoring wife Edwina Pangloss (1928–2007)'.

So, on that sunny September afternoon 2021 Abigail lifted from her rucksack the two urns that had rested next to each other on her mantlepiece for the last fourteen years. She gently, quietly, discretely, in solitude, first poured the ashes from each urn into another larger container in her rucksack and then, with the top firmly on, shook the contents so that they were merged as one and squatting close to the ground, cautiously, in an effort to avoid any remnants that might otherwise remain in the jar, spread the powdery mortal remains of her parents across the lush green foliage of the hillside as it sloped away from the bench and down to a stream in the valley below. Now they would be together, their spirits imbued with this restful place, beings merged in eternal cosmic beauty. For a euphoric instant it was as though she was peeping behind a luxuriant, mystical curtain, privileged to experience this transcendent glimpse at nature's majesty.

She placed the two empty urns back in her rucksack and zipped it up. She sat on the bench and closed her eyes and felt the warm autumnal air bristling peacefully across her face. With her hands pressed against her pack feeling the edge of the urns within, she contemplated why it had taken so many years to scatter the ashes.

For an instant the tranquillity was broken by a strange, discordant thought, but it soon faded in the warm autumnal air and she felt so alive in this place, in this ephemeral spark in the flux of existence. Even Abigail might have conceded just for that moment that this was the best of all possible worlds.